Also by Anna Jacobs

THE BACKSHAW MOSS
SAGA
A Valley Dream
A Valley Secret
A Valley Wedding

THE BIRCH END SAGA
A Daughter's Journey
A Widow's Courage
A Woman's Promise

THE ELLINDALE SAGA
One Quiet Woman
One Kind Man
One Special Village
One Perfect Family

THE RIVENSHAW SAGA
A Time to Remember
A Time for Renewal
A Time to Rejoice
Gifts For Our Time

THE TRADERS
The Trader's Wife
The Trader's Sister
The Trader's Dream
The Trader's Gift
The Trader's Reward

THE SWAN RIVER SAGA
Farewell to Lancashire
Beyond the Sunset
Destiny's Path

THE GIBSON FAMILY
Salem Street
High Street
Ridge Hill
Hallam Square
Spinners Lake

THE IRISH SISTERS
A Pennyworth of Sunshine
Twopenny Rainbows
Threepenny Dreams

THE STALEYS
Down Weavers Lane
Calico Road

THE KERSHAW SISTERS
Our Lizzie
Our Polly
Our Eva
Our Mary Ann

THE SETTLERS
Lancashire Lass
Lancashire Legacy

THE PRESTON FAMILY
Pride of Lancashire
Star of the North
Bright Day Dawning
Heart of the Town

LADY BINGRAM'S
AIDES
Tomorrow's Promises
Yesterday's Girl

STANDALONE NOVELS
Jessie
Like No Other
Freedom's Land

JUBILEE LAKE SAGA
Silver Wishes

ANNA JACOBS

Golden Dreams

Jubilee Lake Saga Book Two

HODDER

First published in Great Britain in 2023 by Hodder & Stoughton
An Hachette UK company

This paperback edition published in 2023

1

A CIP catalogue record for this title is available
from the British Library

Paperback ISBN 978 1 529 35136 1
ebook ISBN 978 1 529 35138 5

Typeset in Plantin Light by Manipal Technologies Limited

Printed and bound in Great Britain by Clays Ltd, Elcograf S.p.A.

Hodder & Stoughton policy is to use papers that are natural, renewable
and recyclable products and made from wood grown in sustainable
forests. The logging and manufacturing processes are expected to
conform to the environmental regulations of the country of origin.

Hodder & Stoughton Ltd
Carmelite House
50 Victoria Embankment
London EC4Y 0DZ

www.hodder.co.uk

I

Autumn 1895

When Stanley Thursten died suddenly of a seizure, his wife felt nothing but relief. Her parents had forced her to marry him five years ago because they said she'd been left on the shelf at twenty-five. The marriage had brought her no joy. On the contrary. Thank goodness he'd spent as little time at home with her as he could, preferring the company of his friends and his parents to hers.

Their dislike had been mutual. She'd found out that he'd only married her because it was a condition of an inheritance from his grandmother that he should wed by the age of thirty, otherwise the money would be donated to charity.

Now that he was dead, she only hoped there would be some of that money left for her, otherwise she'd have endured his company for nothing. Even the house they lived in belonged to his parents and they'd had to pay rent on it.

The doctor cleared his throat to gain her attention and said quietly, 'I can write out a death certificate for you, Mrs Thursten, because I saw your husband at my surgery only a few days ago. I'd been warning him for months that he needed to moderate his lifestyle if he wanted to make old bones, but he only shrugged. Did he change anything at all? Drink less, perhaps?'

'No. He drank at least a bottle of wine every night.' She watched him shake his head in disgust and write the certificate. After he'd handed it to her, she escorted him to the door.

He said gently, 'You should change your life now. You need to get out more, make friends.'

She dredged up a faint smile and nodded. She intended to change things, she did indeed. And she'd start with her name. Why not? She'd never liked being 'Mary Janet'.

As she closed the door, she stared down at the death certificate and wondered yet again where Stanley had kept their marriage certificate. They were both such important documents for her now that she wanted to look after them herself, wanted to control her own life in every way from now on.

She knew his parents didn't have it because they'd suggested more than once to him that they look after all the family papers and mentioned that one specifically. Only he'd refused point blank to hand it over. That had been one of the few things where he hadn't done as they'd wished.

Where could she hide his death certificate? She wasn't handing it over to his parents.

In the end she put it between the pages of a magazine and put that in the middle of a pile of similar magazines that she'd been given to read by an elderly neighbour to whom she spoke occasionally when she was working in the garden. She doubted the Thurstens would even glance at them.

She went upstairs, took most of the money out of Stanley's wallet then put the wallet back in his jacket pocket. After some thought, she hid the money under the loose sultanas in their neatly labelled tin in the pantry, together with most of her housekeeping money.

Only then did she inform his parents of his demise by sending a passing lad with a note about what had happened.

As she'd expected they came at once, grim-faced and tearless, and immediately started telling her what to do with her life from then on. She didn't argue but she was determined to get away from them.

Lemuel Thursten took over the arrangements for the funeral, which was to be conducted from their house. She didn't care enough about that to argue because it meant the bills would also be sent to them. Anyway, they must know that she didn't have the money to pay for it.

As usual, Eunice Thursten said little beyond, 'Yes, dear,' or 'No, dear,' to whatever her husband ordered her to do or told her to think.

After the poorly attended funeral was over and the few guests had consumed the meagre refreshments and left, she was called into the Thurstens' sitting room.

Mr Thursten gestured to a chair and remained standing near the fireplace. 'I'm afraid I have some bad news for you.'

She looked across at him and waited. What now?

'As you know, Stanley was not good with money.'

She didn't say anything. He'd been hopeless at managing money, but could spend it faster than anyone she'd ever met.

'By a few months ago he had spent every penny of the inheritance that marriage to you brought him. Since then I've had to give him money to pay your household bills and he hasn't been paying us the rent he should have done. I don't intend to continue paying for you to live in that house on your own.'

She was so shocked by this she couldn't say a word. She'd hoped and indeed expected that there would be something left for her to live on because the money had come from her family.

'We intend to sell that house, which has too many sad memories for us now.' He took a letter from the mantelpiece and handed it to her. 'This is a formal notice to you to move out by the end of the week. We can offer you a home here with us. In fact, you shouldn't wait to join us.'

She didn't protest, just waited for him to finish.

'You only need stay in that house until you've sorted out your own clothes and small possessions ready for your move. We'll deal with the furniture and Stanley's possessions after you've left. The furniture you inherited from your godmother will pay our son's other debts.'

The way he was looking at her body made her shiver. She'd rather run away to Timbuctoo than spend one night under their roof and she didn't intend to hand over her furniture. But she knew better than to say that, and only inclined her head.

'We shall need to make sure you are not with child as well,' Mrs Thursten said.

'I'm not.'

'You can't possibly know that yet.'

'I can. I'm absolutely certain.'

'Well, we need to be certain too so you will move here with us as soon as you can, and I shall myself check that you are not with child. You can make yourself useful around the house to pay for your keep. We would have arranged for that to happen tomorrow but unfortunately your lawyer insists on seeing you alone before he completes the formalities, so that will take a few days.'

'I can't think about seeing Mr Baker yet. I'm too upset. I'll visit him in a couple of days.' She dabbed at her eyes, hoping she had hidden her anger and looked as if she were weeping. 'I'll walk home now, if you don't mind. It'll clear my head.'

'Oh, very well. A few extra days won't matter.'

They had never complained about her doing a lot of walking as it saved housekeeping money being spent on bus fares. But they had set someone to follow her from time to time when she was first married, saying when she challenged them that it was to check that she wasn't associating with undesirable people or taking anyone back with her into their house.

Given Stanley's threats about what he'd do to her if she invited anyone except her parents and his into their home, she'd never been able to make friends.

Her parents hadn't known how strange the Thurstens were and didn't care when she told them. They were only concerned with her being safe in a respectable marriage, as if she were a package to be handed over. They'd threatened to throw her out on the street if she didn't marry him. And they'd have done it too, which was why she'd given in. She'd thought marriage to him couldn't be worse than living with them. It wasn't but it was just as bad.

She breathed deeply as she walked along the street. That house always felt so stuffy. She didn't go straight home, however. Instead she went to see her own family's long-time lawyer since he had asked to see her. She was hoping Mr Baker would find a way to help her escape. She had only met him a couple of times but he'd seemed pleasant enough.

Before she went into his rooms, she walked past and made a detour into a nearby newsagent's shop, buying some sweets and checking the people outside through the shop window to make sure she hadn't been followed.

It had been two years since her last visit to Mr Baker. He'd sent her a message then, asking her to see him without informing her husband so she'd sneaked into his rooms while out shopping.

He'd told her she had a small inheritance from her godmother but it had conditions attached to it. The main one was that he must continue to manage the money and keep it out of her husband's hands. 'Your godmother was very concerned about your husband's drinking so wanted you to have something for yourself. There are also a few pieces of antique furniture for you to receive openly so that they don't suspect there's money as well.'

She felt sure he would keep her money safe so she agreed to leave it with him. She didn't need the quarterly payments until she found some way to escape from her husband and had let the Thurstens think the furniture was all she'd received.

They'd been pleased with it and she'd been afraid they'd take it for themselves, but Stanley had also taken a fancy to it and they'd let him keep it.

Her parents had died a few months later, both contracting pneumonia after a bout of severe influenza. There had been a lot of such deaths at the time. People had called it the Russian 'flu.

The Thurstens had been furious when they'd found that she'd inherited nothing from her parents, who had left everything to charity due to concerns about Stanley's handling, or, as they called it more accurately, wasting of money.

At the moment she had little money of her own except the small amount she'd saved from the housekeeping and what she'd taken from Stanley's wallet.

After checking one last time that she wasn't being followed she turned off the street into Mr Baker's rooms. When she gave her name the clerk showed her into his office immediately.

'My condolences on your husband's death, Mrs Thursten.'

She wasn't going to pretend. 'It wasn't a happy marriage. He might have been a stranger for all I cared.'

She ignored his look of surprise and explained her dilemma, showing him the official letter asking her to move out of the house within a week. 'Can they really throw me out of my home so quickly? It doesn't give me much time to make other arrangements.'

Mr Baker sighed, fiddled with his pen, then looked across at her. 'I'm afraid they can because it was a weekly tenancy. The letter you've received is an unusually harsh way to treat a daughter-in-law, however. You say they've offered you a home with them. Shall you take it?'

'No. Definitely not. I'd as soon live with a pair of hungry tigers. They'd make my life an utter misery.'

'I must admit that when they spoke to me they showed no sign of affection for you, and indeed, seemed to blame you for their son's death.'

'How could I have stopped him drinking? Or getting into those occasional fights? He'd been like that all his adult life. Everyone knew what he was like. He didn't even listen to the doctor's warnings about his health. Anyway, never mind him. I'm here because you wanted to see me before completing the final formalities.'

'That was an excuse to talk to you about your godmother's will.'

'Surely I can access that money now?'

'Not until you're safely away from them.'

'Oh dear. But I can get it soon afterwards, can't I? I shall need it to live on once I'm away from them. The problem is, I'm not sure where to go.'

'I can help you there. You'd be much safer moving away from Bolton, and doing it secretly.'

She looked at him in surprise. 'Secretly?'

'Yes. I've found out they intend to take action to gain control of you and your affairs by claiming that you are slow-witted and would not be able to look after yourself.'

A shiver ran through her. 'That's ridiculous.'

'I agree.'

'Are you sure? How did you find that out?'

'I happen to know their former lawyer rather well and he said he is no longer acting for them because they had no possible foundation for such an accusation and he refused to be involved in something unlawful and grossly unkind. Unfortunately, he suspects they are still intent on taking control of you with the help of a less scrupulous lawyer so he let me know.'

She stared at him in shock. 'I've never got on with them and they only arranged the marriage because of the money I'd bring and their hope that I'd provide them with a grandchild.'

'Yes. My friend said that he feels they're still hoping for a grandchild.'

'But I've told them I'm not expecting.'

He cleared his throat, flushed slightly and said, 'I fear they are plotting something to ensure that you do provide them with a baby.'

Horror filled her as the implications of this sank in, especially after the way Mr Thursten had stared at her today. Were there no limits to their nastiness? 'I need to get away from them quickly, then.'

'I think so too.'

'Can you let me have some of my godmother's money?'

'Yes, but only the money you didn't use from the quarterly payments. I'm not allowed to pass final control of the capital to you until you're safely established away from them.'

'Oh. Well, my savings should be more than enough to live off for a year or even longer if I'm careful. Will it be all right if I revert to my maiden name now?'

'It's probably an excellent idea to change your name. But don't use your maiden name, as they know that. You see,' he hesitated before saying, 'I'm rather concerned about your personal safety if you run away.'

'You think they'd try to hurt me?'

'Yes. And my friend does too, which is why he broke his clients' confidentiality to suggest I warn you. You could perhaps use your godmother's maiden name. They won't know that but you and I will.'

'And call myself by my middle name.' She tried them out. 'Janet Hesketh. Yes, that sounds nicer.'

He shook his head. 'It'd be better to make a complete change of name. Don't use either of your Christian names. They're too obvious. What's your favourite woman's name?'

'Lillian,' she said immediately. It had been the name of one of her favourite heroines in a library book she'd borrowed three times to read over the years because it had such a lovely ending.

'That name isn't connected with anything you said or did during your married life?'

'No. Stanley was usually drunk by eight o'clock in the evening so we didn't sit and chat.' Sometimes those evenings had seemed to go on for ever.

'Then how about calling yourself Lillian Hesketh?'

She mouthed the name, liking the sound of it. 'I would be able to live on my godmother's money if I'm careful, but how can I get away without them finding out what I'm doing? And where can I go? I must confess that I'm afraid of them, Mr Baker, and I'm sure they'd keep watch on me every minute if I ever moved into their house. Even Stanley was afraid of them.'

He stared into the distance for a moment or two then looked across at her. 'I have a nephew who has just set up a legal practice in the north of Lancashire, Greville Turnby he's called, my sister's son. He's moved to a rather small town called Ollerthwaite because his wife's family have a farm near there and she was desperately homesick, hated life in a town. May I take the liberty of writing to him and explaining your situation?'

She nodded without hesitation.

'Good. I'm sure he'll be happy to take over the management of your godmother's bequest as well as helping you find a small house to rent there. And once you're settled he can terminate the trust and hand everything over to you.'

'That's a good idea. I've never even been to that part of Lancashire. Do you think I'll be able to afford to rent a whole house there, just a small one?'

'I gather from my nephew that rents are much lower than here in the south of the county, so you should have enough money to rent a modest dwelling. And if you tell people you're a widow and behave accordingly, it'll be perfectly respectable.'

'Where exactly is this town?'

'In a small valley called Ollindale on the edge of the moors. Not many people know it exists even and I doubt the Thurstens will so they won't think to look for you there.'

'Perhaps I could find a house with a nice, large garden. I do enjoy gardening. Even the Thurstens approved of it as a hobby because they liked the fresh produce I gave them.'

'We can ask my nephew to look for a suitable house, then.' He gave her another doubtful look.

'What else is there? I can see by your expression that there's some other problem.'

'It might be wisest for you to slip away without telling them that you're leaving. That will have to be managed carefully.'

She was startled. 'Surely they'd not try to stop me by force?'

He was clearly embarrassed. 'Given our suspicions that they might have a – a disgusting reason for wanting control of you, I fear they might try that. The mother is grieving deeply for her only son, but Mr Thursten is apparently furiously angry that you haven't provided them with an heir to their family money and has started telling people he suspects that you are expecting.'

Mary – no, she had to think of herself as *Lillian* now – wasn't naïve enough to mistake what this might involve, not after her years of reading books of all sorts, covered by brown-paper wrappers, which she claimed were to prevent damage and fines by the library, but were actually to prevent *them* seeing what exactly she was reading and learning about. They had so little interest in books they'd not even bothered to ask, assuming the library would not buy anything except what they called decent books.

After one startled glance at Mr Baker for confirming her own suspicions at his earlier statements, and receiving only an embarrassed shrug in return, she turned and gazed blindly out of the window. 'How can I escape without them knowing? I'll need to take my personal possessions with me.'

'I can help you with that. I know a firm of very discreet removalists who have been used by other clients of mine.'

She turned back to him. 'Then would it be possible to take the furniture I inherited from my godmother with me as well? As you know, they're rather valuable antiques and besides, I'm fond of them. I remember them from my childhood visits to her.' She'd been happier there than anywhere else in her whole life.

When he frowned, drumming his fingers on his desk for a moment or two, she couldn't help asking, 'Must I lose everything from my own family?'

He looked at her sympathetically. 'You can't carry furniture with you, obviously. But if we can move your pieces out before you leave, I can have them stored safely till you find somewhere to live. It'll take me a day or two to make arrangements to get you away without leaving a trace. I'll find someone to accompany you and keep you safe till you're out of the district, but you should travel light, taking only one suitcase that you can carry easily.'

She couldn't speak for a moment. If a sensible man like Mr Baker thought this sort of precaution was necessary, she must be in even more danger than she'd thought possible. Would the Thurstens really go to those lengths?

She had another unpleasant thought. 'What if they claim I've stolen the furniture? Perhaps I'd better not try to take it.'

'When she made her will, your godmother suggested that I take careful note of what pieces of furniture she was leaving you, and get the list witnessed and signed by someone reputable. We are not living in the Dark Ages, you know. Married women are allowed to have their own possessions these days.'

She sighed in relief.

'Now, practicalities. I shall send some men to take the furniture out of the house secretly at night and deposit it in a warehouse I know of. In fact, why don't we do that tonight? Can you get everything ready by midnight?'

'Yes.' She wished she were leaving tonight as well.

'I'll tell the men to come to your back gate. Don't leave any
lights on for them, however, or the neighbours might wonder
what's going on. Could you pack most of your clothes and any
other possessions for them to take as well as the furniture?
Remember, only try to carry one suitcase when you leave then
you won't need help to move around.'

'I can get my other things ready but I don't have anything
to put them in.'

'I'll tell the movers to bring some empty tea chests. How
many do you think you'll need?'

'Three at most.' She wasn't rich in physical possessions.

'I'll find a reliable man to escort you to Ollerthwaite in a day
or two. When you've found a house to live in, let me know and
I'll send everything to you there.'

She left his office feeling both afraid and angry, but her only
chance of a better life seemed to be to escape from the Thurstens completely. And if a lawyer who was as well thought of
as Mr Baker suggested that such a desperate course of action
might be best, then they must be even more of a danger to her
than she'd realised, so she'd do whatever he said.

That night, two quiet, middle-aged men arrived at Lillian's house.
They brought their horse and a covered cart to the back gate at
midnight and carried three empty tea chests into the house.

One whispered, 'Please pack them quickly! We'll tidy the
contents and seal them up for you later.' So she piled in her
possessions any old how while the men carried the furniture
out. They used only the light of the moon to load things on
their cart and left as quietly as they'd arrived. Even the horse
hadn't made any unnecessary sounds.

The following morning she moved the remaining furniture
around as best she could without help in an attempt to hide
the gaps where two chests of drawers, a desk, a bookcase and
a few smaller items had once stood.

That left her with only the bare essentials of clothing.

The Thurstens had searched Stanley's things even before the funeral but hadn't found their son's marriage certificate. She'd told them the truth: she didn't know where he'd put it either and they must have believed her. His death certificate was still where she'd hidden it inside the magazine. Fortunately for her, the doctor who'd certified his death had gone away on holiday so she said she hadn't received it yet and was told sharply that she was to give it to them immediately it arrived.

She and her husband had never needed a suitcase because they'd never gone away on holiday but she knew there was one shabby suitcase stored in the roof space. This could be reached via a stepladder, but not wanting her in-laws to catch her getting it down, she waited till after dark to fetch the rickety old stepladder up from the cellar. She was panting by the time she'd carried it up two flights of stairs. It was a good thing there was a nearly full moon to see by.

Putting it in place under the hatch that led into the roof she climbed carefully up and opened the wooden panel. Only then did she light the candle she'd brought in her apron pocket. And yes, the suitcase was there to one side: a dusty, worn old thing.

'Oh, thank goodness!' she muttered. Once she'd wiped it down, no one would look twice at it as she carried it through the streets.

She glanced round the roof space, holding up the candle, but there didn't seem to be anything else up there so she blew her light out before climbing down the ladder. She was surprised Stanley had even kept the suitcase. It wasn't heavy but it would be awkward to carry it at the same time as climbing down the ladder in the semi-darkness, so she dropped it down on the landing to one side.

When she picked it up to put it on her bed, she shuddered at the spiders' webs that festooned the top but told herself not to be so weak-minded. She took the stepladder back to the cellar quickly, planning to get up as soon as it was light and check that it hadn't left any marks on the hatch.

She checked inside but the suitcase was empty. She'd put it on top of the wardrobe till she needed it. As she was doing that, standing on the bedroom chair, she noticed a flat cardboard folder, dark brown in colour, pushed to the very back. If you only gave the wardrobe top a quick glance, it didn't show.

To her surprise there were several papers inside it. They must belong to Stanley. And the marriage certificate was on top! Well, that was a big relief. Underneath it were letters from someone whose signature was hard to decipher and out of curiosity she read the first one.

'Oh, good heavens!' She stared at the letters in shock. She'd read about this sort of thing. And it explained so much about Stanley. No one must ever see these. She took them downstairs, not lighting any more lamps. There were enough embers still glowing in the old-fashioned kitchen range to burn the letters and she fed them in carefully one by one, making quite sure each was turned into meaningless ashes with no fragments left unburned.

By now, she'd recognised the sender and was shocked rigid at who he was, as well as at the few bits she'd read.

She retrieved the death certificate from among the magazines and put it in the folder with her marriage certificate. She was about to put them in the suitcase when she realised the bottom lining was torn and she could slide them inside it. They would be even safer there.

She suddenly changed her mind and decided to pack most of her clothes in the suitcase now and leave it on top of the bedside chair. She'd put her last few garments into it just before she left.

It was a long time before she could get to sleep. Her husband had been a strange man, his actions sometimes totally incomprehensible. And such letters from one man to another had been—shocking.

She couldn't wait to leave this house full of unhappy memories, a house where she'd wasted more than five long, weary years of her life.

As soon as Mr Baker sent word she'd slip out at night the back way, just as her furniture had done, and travel to the north with whoever was sent to escort her.

In the meantime she would stay at home most of the time. Because of the way his parents had insisted on keeping the family to themselves, she didn't have any friends or acquaintances left to say goodbye to, anyway.

She was hoping desperately that she would meet a few people in this new town, perhaps at church. She didn't want to spend the rest of her life as alone as she had been since her marriage.

2

A couple of weeks after the purchase of the Ollerton estate was finalised, Ezra Filmore was looking out of the upstairs window of his office in the legal rooms when he saw one of his clients walking towards him along the street, looking much happier than he ever had before.

Ezra felt rather pleased with himself, too. He'd done well by his new client. He hadn't been sure at first that he'd be able to push the sale of a large property through as quickly as had been insisted, but he'd succeeded.

Edward Seymour Ollerton was shown into the lawyer's office by the chief clerk and came forward with hand outstretched. 'My dear sir, I couldn't leave town without coming to tell you how deeply grateful I am to you for your efficiency.'

Ezra shook the hand. 'I'm glad we managed to do as you wished. Please take a seat.'

Mr Ollerton stood for a moment, staring once again at the modern Charing Cross gas fire, which surprised a lot of their customers. 'I can't believe how efficient that form of heating is. I must have gas fires like that installed in my new house when it's built.'

'I confess I'm still not used to it but like many modern inventions, it does save a lot of work and is far cleaner and easier to use than a coal fire.'

They'd had it installed a few months ago and it still made Ezra nervous but at least he'd learned how to switch it on and off now. Miss Simons, the lady employed in the practice to do the typing, had urged them to get a gas fire, because she said she wasn't hired to haul coal and stoke fires when the office boy wasn't there. She had hinted that she could easily find another job so the senior partner had decided to do as she asked. She was so efficient he wasn't going to risk losing her services.

Edward stopped staring at the gas fire and made himself comfortable in one of the armchairs.

Mr Filmore went to sit opposite him. 'Do you wish me to use your real name in public from now on?'

'Yes, please. I never felt like Mr Smith but the name served its purpose and concealed my identity during the negotiations.'

'Indeed it did, but you'll be Mr Ollerton from now on. May I ask what your plans are for the future?'

'I can't wait to visit the estate that was my family's home for nearly two centuries. I have such happy memories of living and playing there as a small child.' And unhappy memories of being forced to leave and live in a cramped house in a shabby area of London, where his mother wept when she thought no one was there to see her and where his father had died a few years later – in part out of heartbreak from losing his home, Edward had always thought.

He had never liked London nor had he been happy there, but he'd made the most of the business opportunities it presented. By hell, he had! And at least he'd had his cousin Della nearby. Well, when she was free, which wasn't often because she worked long hours. She'd trained as a doctor, to the horror of most of their relatives, but was finding it hard to set up a practice because though she had a small private income she said it wasn't enough to buy into a decent practice and anyway, she didn't intend to be used as a slave and given only the poorer patients to look after.

But she loved what she did and had never wanted to marry, so she insisted she'd find a way. He was going to miss her.

He realised Mr Filmore had said something. 'Sorry. My mind was wandering a little.'

'I asked if you are still intending to stay at the agent's house on the estate while you rebuild the main house, Mr Ollerton?'

'Oh, yes, definitely. It'll be very convenient to live nearby. You've never visited the estate, have you?'

'Well, Mr Kenyon told us the big house had been totally destroyed by fire twenty years ago and I didn't see the point of going to inspect the land, since you knew what it was like and you were getting it at an appropriately low price. Kenyon's parents had refused to spend a penny on clearing up the mess. As I told you they said the ruins were now overgrown, with some of the remaining walls unstable and dangerous.'

'Yes. But I shall have those remnants knocked down before I rebuild.' Edward felt sad as he thought of that. Ollindale had been such a lovely place in which to grow up. If truth be told, he remembered the grounds better than the house because he'd spent such a lot of time playing in them.

'I'm glad in one sense that Kenyon proved as bad as your grandfather and gambled the rest of his inheritance away. That allowed me to buy back my family estate more cheaply than I'd expected. And you can be very sure I'll never gamble. I despise the habit.'

When he didn't say anything else Mr Filmore waited then gave him a questioning look. 'Is there any further way I can help you?'

'Nothing today, but I hope to remain your client from now onwards, if that's acceptable?'

'It would be very acceptable, Mr Ollerton.' Mr Filmore offered his hand and they shook on the bargain.

'My most urgent need at present is to find an architect who will work *with* me instead of trying to dictate what *he* thinks the new house should look like. I want the most modern facilities inside it more than I want artistic and old-fashioned plasterwork in the ceilings.'

His eyes went to the gas fire again.

'And I want simple, elegant styling on the exterior, not fussy façades and variegated patterns of brickwork,' he continued.

'I share your taste, sir.'

'I spoke to one or two architects in London who had been highly recommended and I was not pleased with their attitude nor, to be frank, their arrogance. If you hear of anyone here in the north who might be more amenable to designing a house to my taste, please let me know.'

A nod and a genuinely happy smile were his answer from Mr Filmore. 'I'll make enquiries among my acquaintances.'

'Thank you. I think my next step will be to visit my new possession openly and look at how things stand in detail. I haven't lived there since I was about eight, so I shall need to renew my acquaintance with the whole district, not to mention seeing it with an adult's eye this time.'

He laughed gently then added, 'And no doubt the inhabitants of the valley will want to survey me too.'

He'd seen it secretly by night a couple of times before he bought it, thanks to a friend with a motor car, but you couldn't make out the details clearly by moonlight.

Mr Filmore made a small sound as if to attract his attention. 'One of the things I found out about Ollindale when making my inquiries was that a gentleman called Walter Crossley is a good man to get to know. He has apparently been doing his best to bring various types of employment into the valley, and to help people who are struggling to put bread on the table. He sounds to be a truly admirable man and a good businessman as well.'

'Thank you for that information. I'll introduce myself to him as soon as I can, Mr Filmore.'

'His farm is next to your estate so you're bound to meet him early on.'

'I'll remember the name.' He glanced at the clock ticking gently on the wall and stood up. 'I must be going now, sir. I'm planning to leave for Ollerthwaite tomorrow. The railway services that go there aren't very regular and are mainly geared to those people going outside the valley to shop, I'm told.'

Ezra walked to the front door with Mr Ollerton and stood in the autumn sunlight watching him stride off down the street. He genuinely liked this young man, who was a fine-looking fellow in his late thirties, tall and strong, with one of the sharpest brains the lawyer had ever encountered. He was quite sure Edward would make his mark on Ollindale.

The fact that this client was wealthy was due entirely to the young man's own efforts though he didn't flaunt his success or his money. He dressed neatly and modestly, and spoke courteously to everyone he dealt with, whatever their station in life. Ezra's chief clerk spoke very highly of him as did Miss Simons. Not everyone who came to the office treated their lady clerk as an intelligent human being and he'd heard her complain to the chief clerk more than once about some of his older male clients treating her as if she were a stupid child.

Ah, well, he'd better get on with his own business matters and leave Mr Ollerton to do the same.

Later the following morning, Edward disembarked from a mainline train and boarded a short, three-carriage train, which ran to and fro along the very minor single-track line to the small town of Ollerthwaite. He sat in solitary state in the only compartment provided for the better class of traveller and stared out of the window with great interest.

The train stopped at various points – you couldn't call them proper stations – en route to the only town in the valley. He knew his family had been among the wealthier inhabitants who had helped raise the money to create the rail service in the 1840s. These days few would have money to spare for such philanthropic investments.

He had brought enough bits and pieces with him to enable him to camp out in the agent's house, which was near the site of the main house. He intended to manage with what furniture had been left there until his own comfortable pieces arrived in a few days' time. However he couldn't face sleeping on a mattress used by a man who might or might not have had cleanly habits, so he'd brought a thin new mattress with him, rolled up and wrapped in an old sheet. It was sitting with a few other items in the luggage van.

The rest of his personal possessions and what furniture he wanted to keep would be brought to Ollerthwaite in a rather cumbersome wagon, the only one he'd found that would go there. He'd given his cousin Della the rest to either keep or dispose of as she chose.

Unfortunately the wagon's owner had said it would take him two or three days to get there by road, depending on the weather, because he had to take care of his dray horses with heavy loads and a hilly terrain, and he couldn't set off for a few days anyway because he'd agreed to do another job first.

When the train arrived, Edward got out and stood for a moment looking along the main street, which he could see far more clearly by daylight stretching beyond the station like a continuation of the railway. There was only a single platform and a three-sided shelter with a small enclosed cubicle at one end, presumably for the porter.

He remembered this small town fondly from his childhood and at first glance the main street didn't appear to have changed much, although perhaps when you looked closely the shops and houses looked shabbier than they had done.

His luggage was unloaded quickly and dumped on the platform anyhow by the elderly porter. Two women wearing wrap-around pinafores were tidying up the compartments at top speed. Once they'd finished he watched as a few passengers had their tickets checked and were allowed to board the train for the return journey.

A few minutes later the weary-looking porter gave a half-hearted toot on his whistle and waved a small, limp flag on a stick to signal to the train driver that they were ready to go. The engine moved away to retrace its journey, slowly gathering speed as it tugged the three carriages away from Ollerthwaite.

He was here now, Edward thought in rising excitement, cut off from the busy cities and grey streets. Back in the valley. His new life was starting.

3

On what would be her last day in her married home, Lillian went for a walk just before midday out of desperation to be among other people rather than pacing round an empty house. She'd had her books taken away, wanting to preserve her few loved possessions, but should have kept one to fill her time with. She intended to buy one today to keep her mind occupied and add to her collection.

She came home from her outing to find the Thurstens sitting in her living room, looking furious. She'd known they had a key to the house but hadn't expected them to be so ill-mannered as to come in uninvited.

'Sit down,' Mr Thursten ordered, making no attempt to greet her.

Mrs Thursten merely gave her the usual cold, disapproving stare.

Lillian stayed where she was near the door, not liking his tone of voice. She wondered why they were there and didn't want to go near Lemuel, who was a large and violent man, used to ill-treating women if the bruises she'd occasionally seen on his wife's limbs were anything to go by. Did he think no one noticed them?

Mrs Thursten spoke to her from across the room in a shrill, angry voice. 'What have you done with our furniture?'

'What furniture would that be?'

'There are quite a few pieces missing.'

'Only the things I brought to the marriage, not the ones that were here in the house already.'

'The things you brought became your husband's after you were married, as did all your possessions.'

Lillian forced herself to speak calmly. 'No, they didn't. The Married Women's Property Acts changed all that from 1870 onwards. What possessions I brought to the marriage therefore remained mine.'

'Not in our eyes and not morally,' Mr Thursten said. 'You will tell me where you're hiding them and we'll arrange to have them taken to our house. What's more, you've disobeyed my orders. I told you to close up this house quickly then come and stay with us. As you seem in no hurry to do that you'll leave here with us straight away.'

'No, I won't. You have no right to—'

'We have the moral right to insist you do that in case you're expecting a child.' He gave her body another of those horrible, assessing looks.

'I've already told you that I'm not. I'm *sure* of that.'

'*We* need to be sure of it, too,' Mrs Thursten said. 'And if you are expecting, we shall take the child and raise it in a proper manner.'

'But I'm not expecting!' she protested. 'Why do you keep saying I might be?'

Mr Thursten let out a little growl of anger. 'Because we know you're a liar and we'll be the ones to raise any child that belongs to our family.'

Even if she had been expecting a child she'd not have let it go and live with them.

'Now do as you're told or I'll teach you a lesson you won't forget.' He clenched his fist. 'You should be glad to have someone to look after you. Women are not capable of living on their own.'

As he started to stand up, she had a sudden fear that they might take her away forcibly, so turned and ran from the house as fast as she could, acting on sheer instinct. That took them by surprise. Luckily for her Mr Thursten had grown fatter as he grew older and was unable to keep up with her.

In the next street she managed to signal to a taxicab and asked the driver to take her to her lawyer's rooms as fast as his horse could go, thankful that it was only half a mile or so away.

The chief clerk took one look at her dishevelled clothing and showed her straight through to Mr Baker's office.

He too gaped at the sight of her. 'My dear lady! What on earth has happened to you? Do sit down.'

She told him about her two unwelcome visitors and her fear of Mr Thursten becoming violent in order to force her to do as he wished.

'I shall not allow that.' He summoned his clerk back and asked him to send for the local police at once and then to have his carriage brought round.

A sergeant and a constable turned up within minutes and from the deferential way the two policemen spoke to Mr Baker she could see the high regard in which he was held.

She had to explain again what had happened and the older policeman tutted sympathetically while the younger man stared at her in shock.

'We can go round to Mrs Thursten's house immediately in my carriage,' Mr Baker suggested. 'There is room for you two to ride with us, Sergeant. We shall be very relieved to have your support so that this poor lady can retrieve her possessions.'

'Thank you, sir. Always happy to be of assistance.'

When they arrived at her home, they found a taxicab waiting at the door. As they went inside, Mr Thursten called down, 'You can stop searching, Eunice. I've found her suitcase up here but it's locked.'

His wife called, 'Oh, good!' from the rear of the house.

Mr Thursten came hurrying down the stairs carrying the suitcase but stopped when he saw the two police officers.

Lillian gasped in shock. 'They're stealing my possessions. That's my suitcase and contains only my clothes!' Thank goodness she'd locked it or he might have found the marriage and death certificates that were hidden in the lining.

It took a loud argument and a threat by the police sergeant to arrest Mr Thursten and his wife for theft before they would allow the suitcase to be handed back to Lillian and her lawyer.

She had to produce the key and open it, showing its contents to the sergeant and Mr Baker. 'There you are. It contains only my clothes and a few personal possessions.'

The sergeant examined it, apologising for doing it as he lifted up the edge of the pile of folded garments to check that it contained only her clothes and personal possessions. He didn't seem to notice the torn lining, to her relief.

There was even more arguing before the Thurstens would leave the premises.

'I shall be back tomorrow with *my* lawyer,' Mr Thursten said loudly, acting as usual as if he believed people he considered inferior were deaf as well as stupid. 'This young woman has no right to claim independence when my family has been supporting her for years. As my son's widow, it's her duty to live quietly with the family and mourn his death, especially as I believe her to be expecting his child.'

When Lillian would have protested at this, Mr Baker gave a slight shake of his head and she closed her mouth, watching in silence as the policemen escorted the still-protesting Thurstens out to the taxicab.

The sergeant came back inside after the unwelcome visitors had been driven away. 'I don't think the lady should stay here on her own tonight, sir.'

Lillian agreed entirely. 'The trouble is, I have nowhere else to go.'

Mr Baker stared at her, looking rather irritated. 'You're right, Sergeant. I suppose she will have to move into my house for a night or two, after which she'll be leaving the district.'

She didn't like to accept an offer made with such obvious reluctance. 'I can't impose on you, Mr Baker. Perhaps you could help me find a hotel?'

The police sergeant shook his head. 'That too might be unsafe, I'm afraid, sir. These people seem very determined to get her into their clutches and they might bribe the hotel staff to help them. I can't protect her twenty-four hours a day.'

'Then we have no choice,' the lawyer said. 'Would you be able to accompany us to my house, though, Sergeant? Just in case they're lying in wait for her nearby.'

'Yes, sir. I'll be happy to do that.' He looked at Lillian. 'I have to ask: are you with child, madam?'

'No, I am not.'

'And how old are you?'

'Nearly thirty.'

'You look younger, but you're not of an age to need supervision, that's for sure. So there is not the slightest reason for you to go and live with them, legally or morally.'

'Can you get the rest of your possessions quickly, Mrs Thursten?' the lawyer asked. 'I don't want to linger here.'

'I only need to pack my towel and toiletries in the suitcase, and I'll be ready to leave.'

The sergeant inclined his head. 'We'll wait for you near the front door, then, madam.'

As he took the suitcase from her the lawyer murmured, 'We'll continue to call you Thursten if you don't mind. You shouldn't use your new name until after you've left this town.'

Mrs Baker couldn't hide her dismay at having an unexpected guest and said very little as she showed Lillian to a tiny bedroom on the second floor. 'You'll wish to unpack.'

Lillian didn't see the point of unpacking for one night but assumed her hostess wished to speak to her husband in private. She was looking forward to using her new name, couldn't wait to stop using Thursten. She hoped she'd never see her in-laws again.

Mrs Baker came back a few minutes later. 'My husband needs to discuss something with you in preparation for your departure. Could you please come down to his study?'

When the three of them were seated there he said, 'You're going to need some money, Mrs, um, we'll call you Hesketh now, so I intend to give you fifty pounds immediately from your funds to cover any expenses you may have during your journey and on arrival in Ollerthwaite.'

'Thank you.' She took it from him and put it into her side skirt pocket, tucking it right down into the curved bit at the bottom with a button to fasten it and keep its contents separate. She'd had to add that years ago for keeping things safe and secret when she came back from shopping.

'Good. That money should easily last until I can arrange for my nephew to take over the management of your affairs. It'll probably be better for you to find your own place to live. You should introduce yourself to him as soon as you've found one and apply to him thereafter when you need more money. You already know how much you will be entitled to per quarter and since you didn't use any of this inheritance while your husband was alive, you still have the money you saved in the separate savings account. Here is the Post Office savings bank book. It'll be up to you to let them know your new address.'

'I'll do that.'

She also had the money from her husband's wallet and her savings from the housekeeping, which she hadn't told anyone about. Stanley hadn't cared what she did with the housekeeping as it wasn't a generous allowance and because he couldn't be bothered to go through accounts. That money was still safely tucked into her bodice and special pocket. Thank goodness she'd kept it on her person.

Mr Baker took a cash box out of a small safe and counted out forty-five pounds in white five-pound banknotes and five pounds in smaller notes and coins. He counted the banknotes for a second time before he passed them to her. Then he asked her to sign a receipt for the money.

After that Lillian was treated to a solitary evening meal in the Bakers' morning room since they were going out to dine with friends. Clearly they found it inconvenient to have her there. She guessed they'd get rid of her as quickly as they could, and she would be very relieved to get further away from the Thurstens.

Once she'd finished her meal a maid came in to clear the table and build up the fire. She offered the visitor today's newspaper to read, or one of Mrs Baker's *Hearth and Home* magazines. Lillian chose the latter because she felt exhausted and unfit for doing more than flicking through the pages of the magazine and studying the pictures and advertisements. If possible, she'd go to bed early, but couldn't do that yet without her behaviour appearing strange.

The maid came back about an hour later to say a man was at the door asking for her and he'd brought a message from Mr Baker. 'He's been here before so I've shown him into the hall.'

Lillian went to speak to the man who said politely, 'I've been asked by Mr Baker to escort you to a safe boarding house close to the station, from which we can get on the earliest train in the morning to start our journey.'

Since the maid knew him Lillian felt he must be genuine but she didn't like his cold expression.

'If you'll fetch your suitcase we can leave straight away, Mrs Thursten.'

Why had Mr Baker not mentioned this possibility earlier? Perhaps his wife had persuaded him to arrange her departure more quickly. That lady had certainly been unhappy about Lillian's presence in the house.

She fetched her suitcase, scribbled a quick note thanking the Bakers for their hospitality and left the house with the man.

He didn't offer to carry her suitcase nor did he chat to her. She was starting to worry because she didn't like the way he kept looking at her. But she couldn't very well return to the Bakers' house because she hadn't felt at all welcome there.

When they turned into what turned out to be a nearly deserted and poorly lit side street, she saw a shabby carriage waiting at the other end of it and she stopped walking, feeling even more suspicious of him. As another man got out of it and looked towards them, her escort grabbed her arm.

'Hurry up, please, madam.'

The Bakers would never have hired a carriage for her when she could walk to the railway station from their house, she was sure.

As she tried to pull away, his grip tightened. Suddenly terrified, she gave in to her instincts and screamed for help at the top of her voice. A man walking down the other side of the street turned, saw her struggling and ran towards them.

'Help me! He's trying to force me to go with him,' she yelled even before he reached them.

Her escort tried to pull her along and when the tall stranger stepped in front of them, said quickly, 'She's been misbehaving and I've been paid to take her back to her parents.'

She kicked him hard in the shins and saw him raise his fist, as if he was about to thump her. He'd let go of her so she stepped to one side and said urgently to the stranger, 'That's not true. Look.' She held out her left hand. 'I'm a married woman not a girl. He's trying to kidnap me. Please, sir, help me get away from him.'

Her rescuer must have believed her side of things because he acted quickly, snatching the suitcase from her and saying, 'Run back to the main road with me as fast as you can.'

She didn't need telling twice because the man who'd been standing near the carriage had now begun running along the street towards them. Whatever happened, she would surely be safer on the main road.

Still carrying her suitcase her rescuer set a cracking pace, knocking her former captor to the ground when he reached out towards her.

As she'd hoped, there were other people in the main street and her companion called out, 'Help! Pickpockets are chasing us!' This made two young men hurry across to join them, looking excited.

As their pursuers reached the end of the street and saw the group of men now standing protectively round Lillian, they halted then fled back the way they'd come.

'Shows they're guilty,' one of the young men said. 'Pity they ran off. I was just in the mood for a bit of a scrap.'

'I can't thank you enough for your help.' She was unable to prevent her voice wobbling.

'You're welcome, madam,' one of the younger ones said. 'I don't know what the world is coming to when our streets aren't safe. Will you be all right now?'

Her first rescuer saw how upset she was and took over. 'I'll escort the lady somewhere safe and we'll keep to the busier streets from here onwards. We're much obliged for your help.'

The two men grinned and one said, 'I can't abide thieves and I'd have enjoyed giving them a good drubbing.' He tipped his hat to Lillian and they strolled away.

She looked doubtfully at the tall man standing beside her.

'My name is Riley Callan.'

'I'm Lillian Hesketh.' It was the first time she'd used her new name to introduce herself and it felt so much better than Thursten.

'Where can I take you? Is there someone you can go to?'

She shook her head slowly. 'There's no one. I shall need to get to the railway station.'

'I'm happy to escort you. Let's walk along the street as we talk, though. The further away we get from those men the better. I didn't like the looks of them.'

She could certainly agree with that.

4

Edward waited but there was still no sign of any vehicles plying for hire at the small station in Ollerthwaite. And anyway, a cab wouldn't have had room for all his boxes.

He had a fairly good idea of how to get to the estate but needed help with his luggage. He smiled wryly. He'd been persuaded by his friend to come last time in the new motor car, which Gavin had built after visiting Mr Benz and Mr Daimler in Germany and then consulting a Mr Parker in Wolverhampton. It would, Gavin said, be an excellent test of its reliability.

Since Edward had already ridden in and broken down in each of Gavin's two earlier attempts to construct a motor vehicle, he was reluctant, but his friend promised him that the latest one was far better, so in the end he'd given in. What was life if you couldn't have the occasional adventure?

On the first visit he'd had his fingers crossed mentally and to his relief the new vehicle had managed to get them there and back without any breakdowns. Maybe Gavin really would learn to build motor cars well enough for them to start up a business doing that.

His friend had studied detailed maps of the area before they'd set off and they'd not needed to go back into the town after stopping at the estate because there was another route across the moors. They'd left the valley by driving along the side of a small river then continuing upwards across 'the tops' as the locals sometimes called the moors, Edward remembered. The narrow road led westwards and stayed in Lancashire if you turned left but led east to Yorkshire if you turned right. For most of the way the track had only been wide enough for one vehicle, but as there were no other people out at that hour of the night, the drive had gone smoothly.

They'd come here the second time to check that the agent's house was still habitable. Once again they'd been saluted by a few watchdogs in houses they'd passed lower down the valley, but, to their relief, no humans came out to investigate the noise of the car engine.

He had no keys to the agent's house and the lodge, and some rather ragged curtains had been drawn in each, so they hadn't been able to see inside the two small houses on the property. He'd been reluctant to break into them since they were still owned by the last Kenyon. However, the exteriors had looked reasonable enough and he'd decided they'd do for temporary accommodation if he managed to buy the estate and come to live here while having a larger new house built for himself.

Someone yelled, 'Can I help you, sir?' and he realised the porter was staring at him. He went across the platform to ask how he could get his luggage and himself taken to the agent's house on the Ollerton estate.

The man looked at him and then at his pile of boxes in obvious dismay. 'Eh, I don't rightly know, sir. Frank Geeson, who has a wagon for hire, is out of town taking some furniture into Skipton. He won't be back for two days at least. And most of the other folk with wagons are using them for the harvest at this time of year. They're out on the farms and would be too mucky for you and your things, even if you did manage to walk out of town and find someone willing to carry you.'

'I can't walk anywhere because I need to keep an eye on my luggage,' he said in exasperation.

Another older man, better dressed than most people in the street, had been passing by just then and had stopped to listen.

When he heard what the problem was, he immediately took it upon himself to come over and join in the discussion.

The porter turned to him in obvious relief. 'Did you hear that, Mr Crossley? What do you think the gentleman should do?'

The name caught Edward's attention. Crossley! Mr Filmore had mentioned this person as someone worth knowing.

Crossley looked as if he was assessing the newcomer then gave a little nod as if Edward had passed some sort of test. 'Where do you need to go?'

'To the Ollerton estate. The agent's house.'

'Oh? Can I ask why?'

'I'm the new owner. Edward Ollerton.' He held out one hand.

The man shook it. 'Walter Crossley. Pleased to meet you. I knew some of your family years ago. How much luggage do you have?'

The porter pointed to the pile of boxes and cases at the end of the platform. 'All that belongs to the gentleman.'

Crossley studied it, head on one side. 'Good thing I've just delivered my load and my cart is nearly empty. I can fit your things on it then drive you out to your estate.'

'I'm sorry to give you such trouble but I'd be deeply grateful for your help.'

'It's quite close to my farm so not all that much trouble. I'll need you to help me with loading and unloading your boxes and cases, however.'

'Of course.'

'May I ask what you'll be doing there? The big house was burned down years ago so there's not much to see now.'

'I hope to rebuild as soon as I can. In the meantime I can live in the agent's house.'

'That'd be good. Welcome to Ollindale. So the original family's come back, eh? I knew Reginald Ollerton slightly.'

'He was my father.'

'He was a pleasant chap.'

'Yes, but too gentle for his own good and not very practical.'

'It was your grandfather who lost the estate. He was – well, let's be frank, a difficult man to deal with.'

'Yes. So my father always said. But I don't remember my grandfather very clearly. I was only a child when we left. I'm planning to live permanently in the valley while a new house is built.'

Crossley beamed at him. 'I'm delighted to hear that an Ollerton is back, and you'll be bringing employment too, which we desperately need here. I hope you'll be very happy in Ollindale.'

Then Mr Crossley's smile turned into a slight frown. 'It might be difficult to live in that house at the moment, though. The former agent didn't use it very often and didn't keep up with repairs at all. I fear the roof now leaks badly at one side.'

Edward was shocked. He hadn't been able to see that problem since his only visit had been after dark.

'And he sold all the furniture before he moved out, too.'

'Are you sure of that? It was listed as furnished in the inventory.'

'Yes, I'm quite sure there's no furniture left. I live nearby, so I've taken the liberty of visiting the house a couple of times to check that there's been no more deterioration.'

'That's very kind of you.'

'I care about my valley and its people, and I always hoped the estate would be sold one day and a new family move here. I covered one big corner leak with a tarpaulin till it could be repaired properly. I don't like to see buildings lost for lack of a little attention.'

Edward was annoyed with himself for not foreseeing some problem like this and at least checking that the inventory was accurate before he tried to move in. He'd normally have been better prepared for his first visit, as he'd tried to be for everything he'd undertaken over the past few years. Only, he hadn't dared risk coming here and poking around in the daytime, especially during the last couple of weeks before the sale had gone through because he'd been negotiating hard, determined to buy it as cheaply as possible.

And anyway, he'd been excited and absolutely dying to come back.

He gave Crossley a wry look. 'If the former agent is dead, I shan't be able to set the police on him for theft, then.'

There was dead silence for a few seconds then the porter who had been standing openly listening said suddenly, 'Hatton told everyone that the Ollertons had all died out, sir. Eh, that man were such a liar!'

'Not quite all of us are dead, though I think I'm the last male from the senior branch of the family. I have a female cousin but she's younger than me.' He turned to Mr Crossley. 'Perhaps you can advise me as to the best way to get around in the valley, sir? Is there no public transport of any sort here, not even an occasional omnibus going up and down the hill from Ollerthwaite?'

'Nothing apart from the local train that takes folk in and out of the valley to other towns. The better-off people usually have pony carts for getting around, some of the younger folk use bicycles and the rest walk, especially those who live in Eastby End.'

Edward considered this for a moment. He couldn't get a pony and cart yet because he'd have nowhere to keep one, not to mention no one to look after an animal for him. He'd not know how to drive a pony around, anyway, because he'd had a very urban upbringing and never dealt personally with horses of any kind. 'I think I shall have to buy a bicycle for the time being, then. I used to ride one when I was younger.'

'In that case, may I make a small suggestion? People who need to carry shopping or other goods back to homes outside town usually buy delivery bicycles, the ones that shopkeepers use with big metal baskets welded on above the front wheel. We have a man in Upperfold who sells them, both second-hand and new. Peter would probably be able to get hold of one for you quite easily.'

'That's an excellent idea. I might get hold of a motor car later for longer journeys. I've been thinking about doing that for a while but I'm waiting for them to become more reliable and less expensive. People are starting to copy the Americans and build cheaper motor cars for ordinary people here in England nowadays.'

Crossley looked unhappy. 'I hope you won't do that, sir. Motor vehicles are extremely dangerous and we're mostly free of them still in our valley. Drivers may stick to the speed limit of two miles per hour in towns but they often exceed the four-miles limit that is supposed to apply on country roads and—'

Edward was surprised at his grim tone and expression, becoming even more surprised when it was obvious that Crossley had to steel himself to continue his explanation.

'My eldest son and grandson were killed in a road accident late last year, not in our valley but just outside it, caused by a motor car going too fast on a narrow road and terrifying the horses pulling their vehicle so that they dragged it over the edge of a steep slope.'

'I'm sorry to hear that, Mr Crossley. The current speed limit is rather impractical, though, because it's far too low, so it'll have to change if the government wants people to stick to it. Friends in London tell me the powers that be are thinking of increasing it to ten or even twelve miles an hour.'

'Shame on them if they do. That's far too fast for older people and young children to get out of the way.'

'I don't think anyone can stop or even slow down the development of reliable motor vehicles. You see them quite often in the streets of the big southern towns these days. And passengers are protected from the weather in some of the newer types, which are not built in imitation of the styles of old-fashioned open carriages. Unlike horses, when they're not needed motor cars can simply be left standing under cover.'

He realised he'd been talking too much about one of his pet interests and Mr Crossley was still looking upset and sad. 'But that's for the future. I'm sorry to have stirred up such sad memories. For my present personal needs, and for pleasure too, I shall definitely purchase a bicycle.' He frowned. 'How badly does the roof leak on the agent's house? I shall have to find somewhere to live until it can be repaired. Is there a hotel in town?'

'No, but you have another house on the estate, which is fairly weatherproof. A day's work by a chap I know in the village would fix the problems in it. It used to be the lodge so it isn't nearly as big as the agent's house but no one is living there now, so you'd have it to yourself. We can stop on the way to look at it, if you like, and unload your things if you feel you could manage there for a while. Shall we load your boxes on my cart now and make a start?'

'You're being amazingly kind to a stranger.'

Walter shrugged. 'Apart from the fact that all decent human beings should offer help to others when it's needed, I'm encouraging more people to take up residence in our valley and you're not only about to do that but also to provide a few jobs if you build a house here. Indeed, the fact that you're planning to rebuild is some of the best news I've heard for a long time.'

They finished loading the cart and Crossley gestured to Edward to climb up on the driver's bench, and got up there himself with a nimbleness that said he was still successfully defying old age.

After he'd clicked his tongue to tell his neat little mare to start moving, he left her to it and said, 'If you need any items to make your temporary home more comfortable, I have a large stock of second-hand furniture and household oddments left behind by people who've moved away from the valley. I buy them cheaply and sell them again cheaply, but at a slight profit, more to encourage people to live here than to make money, though I do seem to make money.'

'It may be necessary to buy a few items so I'll bear that in mind, but I do have some furniture in storage that I'm having sent.'

'Good. Just another thought – did you bring any food with you?'

'Er – no. Can't I buy something to eat in the nearby village? I was told the house was within easy walking distance of it.'

'It is, but Upperfold is rather small and there's nothing like a café there. Besides, how will you carry your shopping home till you get your bicycle? It'll take you nearly an hour to walk into Ollerthwaite where you could buy a better selection of food. And if you do that it'll be getting dark before you can get home again.'

'Oh dear. I've planned this badly, haven't I?'

'We all make mistakes when going into new situations.'

'What do you suggest I do tonight?'

'There's a good baker in the village. It's on our way and they'll not be closed yet, so if we stop there they'll probably have something left that you can buy for your evening meal and breakfast. You can arrange to have fresh bread delivered daily from now on for a small extra payment. And I can let you have eggs from my farm.'

'That sounds a good arrangement. It surely can't be hard to learn to fry an egg or a piece of ham, though I confess I've never done that before.'

Walter chuckled. 'You don't cook and you're intending to fend for yourself?'

Edward smiled ruefully. 'No, I don't cook. I've run a business and I've usually had lodgings where food was provided.

I must seem very stupid, only I was so excited about coming back here.'

His companion patted his shoulder. 'It won't be hard to learn to make simple meals, Mr Ollerton. In fact, if you like, I can get my young cousin or my grandson's wife to teach you how to cook a few easy dishes. Once you settle into the agent's house, you can find a daily woman to do your cleaning and prepare simple meals.'

Edward looked at the kindly old man gratefully. 'Thank you for any advice you care to offer. I'd been thinking and planning for the big things about regaining my family home, but the small daily tasks are going to be important too, aren't they? One has to eat.'

How many other daily needs had he forgotten to provide for? Not too many, he hoped. 'Don't hesitate to tell me if you notice anything else I've missed doing, Mr Crossley.'

'I won't. But perhaps not tonight. And don't hesitate to ask for help if you need it, lad.'

No one had called him 'lad' since he was a child. It felt good, as if someone wiser than him cared about him.

5

As he continued to walk along the street next to her, Mr Callan asked, 'Where can I take you, Mrs Hesketh?'

It took Lillian a moment to realise he was talking to her using her new name. She tried to think of somewhere to go but couldn't. 'I don't know anywhere safe.'

He looked surprised at that. 'Then if it's all right with you, we'll carry on walking until we find somewhere we can stop without attracting attention, after which you can explain to me exactly what this is about. If you've broken the law, I shan't continue to help you.'

'I haven't. I wouldn't,' she stammered.

A couple of minutes later they stopped in the doorway of a shop that had closed for the night. The gas streetlamp next to it showed a steady stream of people strolling by so she felt safe enough and yet private enough to explain her situation quickly. Mr Callan was so much taller than her that she should have been afraid of him, but she wasn't.

Once she'd finished her tale, he shook his head as if disgusted. 'Shame on your in-laws. I think we'd better continue walking now and, if you like, I'll stay with you till I'm sure you'll be safe.'

'I'd greatly appreciate that. Thank you for believing me.'

He gave a wry smile. 'Mrs Hesketh, you've got an honest face and you are indeed wearing a wedding ring – and have been for a while, I'd guess, from the mark it's left on your finger. That gave the lie immediately to what that brute was claiming about you. I don't think you'll be safe going back to your lawyer's residence, though, if you've been taken from there once. Do you know where he was intending to send you when your real escort arrived?'

She told him about Ollerthwaite and he chuckled, which surprised her.

'A lot of people don't believe in coincidences, but I've had them happen to me more than once. As it happens, I'm on my way to the north of Lancashire myself after spending time in France and London. I'm looking for somewhere to settle down and start a business, you see. So I shall only have to change my planned journey slightly to take you to this Ollerthwaite place first. I can then leave you with the young lawyer who'll be handling your affairs from now on and resume my own journey.'

'Really? Oh, that's so kind. I can't thank you enough.'

He shrugged as if slightly embarrassed at being praised, then frowned. 'I've missed the train I intended to take but we can still catch the last train to Manchester and then spend the night in the waiting room there. It'll be both safe and respectable, though not comfortable.'

She nodded. She didn't feel at all threatened by him but would definitely feel safer in a public place with other people and officials nearby during the night in case the Thurstens sent someone after her again.

As they continued walking she frowned. 'What I don't understand is why the message I received was on Mr Baker's headed notepaper. Surely a respected lawyer wouldn't be involved in having me kidnapped?'

He paused for a moment, staring at her in surprise, then continued walking. 'Was that what happened?'

'Yes. I'm not stupid enough to have gone with the man otherwise.'

'I too doubt that a lawyer would betray you so I think you'll still be safe dealing with him or his nephew. In fact, I think you should write a quick note to Mr Baker when we're in the waiting room to explain what happened and suggest that he may perhaps have someone working in his household who could have been bribed to tell you the man who took you away regularly carried messages. And that same person could have filched a piece of headed notepaper from his study to make the story more credible.'

'Yes, you could be right. I think it could only be the maid who brought the message to me. I didn't see any other servant. I'll have to wait till I can buy a stamp to post a letter.'

'I think it's too urgent for that. I'll find a lad to deliver your note by hand. There are always some hanging around the bigger stations wanting to earn a few pennies here and there. One of the porters will tell me who to trust.'

'The Thurstens must have found out where I was, mustn't they?'

'Yes. They must have had someone watching Mr Baker's house.'

'Why are they doing this?'

'Sometimes grief can make people behave strangely, but it does seem beyond strange that they're going to such lengths to get hold of you.'

'Um . . .' She avoided looking at him, feeling her cheeks heating in embarrassment at discussing intimate matters with a stranger. 'They kept talking about me expecting their son's child, but I'm not. I know that for certain and so I told them several times. Why would they keep saying it might still be a possibility?'

'Ah.' He looked at her as if he could guess the reason.

'Surely even they wouldn't force me to . . . to . . .' She had doubted the lawyer's hints about the reason, thinking the idea that a man could do that sort of thing hard to believe, but if Mr Callan also wondered about that, it had to be likely. Even now she couldn't put her suspicions into blunt words, the idea was so shameful.

The man stared at her. 'I think we need to speak frankly. Some people will go to any lengths to get what they want and these two sound to be desperate for an heir. Your father-in-law has proved once that he can engender a child, so he may have decided to deal with this matter himself. And if you had been forced into that, I'd not have valued your life very highly after the child was born.'

'Dear heaven, that's so wicked.'

'Yes. All the more reason to act carefully and keep you safe.'

He looked up and down the street, which he had done a few times. 'I haven't seen any cabs pass by so let's continue walking. Can you manage to do that?'

'I do a lot of walking so I shall be fine.'

'Good. I'll keep my eyes open to make sure we're not being followed. Keep moving along steadily, even if I slow down and fall behind occasionally.'

He stopped chatting and paused now and then to stare in shop windows at the reflections of people who were behind them on the street. He also stole quick glances behind them sometimes as they turned a corner or crossed a road.

She walked briskly, not knowing why she trusted this man, but she did. He'd said she had an honest face. Well, he too had a face which looked honest and open. She wondered about his background. He had a slight northern accent and although he wasn't a gentleman, he was well dressed. Perhaps he was what people called a 'self-made man'. Oh, she had so little experience of the world beyond her home! She'd read a lot of books and newspapers, but that was a poor substitute for real life.

When they got to the station Mr Callan said, 'If you wait over there, I'll buy our tickets.'

'I have some money and I'd rather buy my own. I've imposed on you enough without costing you money.'

'Very well. I'll stand behind you in the queue. Don't walk away afterwards. In fact, try to stay next to me at all times. We can't be too careful.'

After they'd bought the tickets, he led the way to the left-luggage office and retrieved two large suitcases and a briefcase.

'Another useful coincidence,' he said. 'I've been out with friends for a farewell dinner tonight because I'm only passing through Bolton this time. I didn't want to struggle to and from a restaurant lugging these so I left my luggage here beforehand. I'd intended to spend what was left of the night in the waiting room in Manchester anyway, and catch the earliest train tomorrow morning, so I'll only be doing as I planned.'

'I'm glad. You're being amazingly kind.'

'I saw those thugs trying to kidnap you and it made me angry. I'll continue to protect you if necessary, but I doubt they'll guess that you're catching a train. We definitely weren't followed here.'

He couldn't carry all three of his cases and hers, and no porters were nearby so she took hers back from him and also the briefcase, and managed to smile. 'Even a gentleman only has two hands.'

'Yes. Thank you. This way.' At the waiting room he set one of his cases down and held the door open for her. Once inside, he put his cases in a corner so she did the same with hers, then he picked up the briefcase and gestured to the nearby chairs and sat down.

'I have some paper and envelopes here but you'll have to write your note to the lawyer in pencil. I don't want to risk spilling ink on everything. I have some important papers in it, you see, sketches of modern cars and their bodies. It's possible to buy a ready-made chassis and build a car on it, you see.'

After she'd written a quick note to Mr Baker, Mr Callan left her in the waiting room for a few moments. She watched through the window as he crossed the station and beckoned to a porter. After a short chat the man indicated a youth who was hanging about.

After a few words he passed over her letter and what looked like a couple of coins to the youth and another coin to the porter.

When he came back, he said, 'The lad has promised to push it through Mr Baker's front door.'

'Can we trust him to do that?'

'Oh, I think so. The porter vouched for him.'

After that they sat in a corner of the waiting room on two separate chairs as the clock on the wall ticked away the slow hours. He didn't attempt to chat to her and soon nodded off. She envied him the ability to do that but she simply couldn't sleep, tired as she was. She was too afraid, kept looking round, checking that she was safe, that they hadn't caught up with her.

The Thurstens had almost managed to kidnap her today. She prayed they would never find out where she'd gone. She'd changed her name and from now on she would live a quiet life in a small town few people in the south of the county would have even heard of.

Surely that would be enough to keep her safe?

6

Walter Crossley glanced sideways as he drove his new acquaintance away from the station, seeing the thoughtful expression on his companion's face and wondering how long this neatly dressed gentleman would last, camping out in a small house and cooking for himself. Would he really bother to learn how to cater for his own daily needs? If he was rich enough to buy the Ollerton estate, you'd have expected him to bring along a servant to look after that side of things right from the start.

He seemed a nice enough chap, though, so Walter hoped he would manage to muddle through. Best of all, Edward was an Ollerton, not a Kenyon, and thank goodness for that. Most of the Ollerton family members Walter had known in his younger days had been decent folk – all except for this one's grandfather, he added mentally. That man had been an arrogant fool who had proved conclusively that one person could fritter away a family's whole fortune.

He had a sudden thought. 'Shall we find out whether you can buy a bicycle today, Mr Ollerton? Our local chap's premises are on our way. As I told you, Peter repairs and sells second-hand bicycles and is just starting to stock new ones too. It's a small business that's thriving due to the fact that so many people want bicycles nowadays.' He cocked one eyebrow inquiringly at the younger man. 'After we've stopped to buy you some food, we could easily visit Peter's workshop and you could ask whether he has anything ready to sell. If not, he'll find you something suitable within a day or two, I'm sure.

It's always good to buy from local shopkeepers, especially if you're going to live here permanently.'

'I agree. As long as it's a modern safety bicycle. I used to enjoy riding an old-fashioned boneshaker in my youth but I'm too old for that sort of thing now.'

Walter chuckled. 'You don't seem exactly old to me.'

'I sometimes feel it. I've been working very hard indeed all my adult life, yes, and even before then I used to run errands and do little jobs to make a start on saving. I'm intending to enjoy a more peaceful way of living from now on.'

'I hope you manage it. Now, here we are.' Walter reined in the pony outside a small baker's shop, introduced his companion to the owner and when he saw Edward hesitating about what to buy, he exchanged amused glances with the baker and guided the younger man's purchases. Which showed how unused his companion was to catering for himself.

He then drove on to Peter's workshop, which wasn't far away, tied his mare loosely to a post and led the way inside through a pair of doors that were standing open.

He greeted the owner and gestured to his companion. 'This is Mr Ollerton who's coming to live in the valley and he needs a bicycle urgently to get around.'

The proprietor beamed at the customer. 'You're in luck then, Mr Ollerton. I have several bicycles available for sale at the moment. I'll show you one that I think would suit a gentleman of your height to ride on.' He went across to the side and wheeled one out.

'This is a brand new one, sir, so more expensive but it's a very good one. I'd not stock it else or ask such a high price. Why don't you try it?'

Edward wheeled it up and down. 'I'm rather out of practice so I'll take your word for it.'

He didn't quibble at how much he had to pay for it. Indeed, he had a hard job controlling his excitement about the purchase and Walter thought he looked suddenly more youthful. Peter would no doubt spread the word that the newcomer was a nice chap to deal with and was already spending money in the valley, which would be a good thing.

'I didn't want to make a fool of myself falling off it,' Edward confessed to Walter as they walked outside with him wheeling the bicycle. 'It seems like proof that I really have started my new life.' He stroked the gleaming handlebar with one hand then suddenly stopped to say, 'I didn't ask if it'd fit on your cart.'

'I'd have mentioned it if there wasn't room. I can wedge it in between your other pieces of luggage, if I move things round. But that's the last thing I'll take because I don't want to over-load my mare.'

As they continued on their journey, he saw Edward turn round a couple of times and beam at the bicycle but didn't comment. He didn't think his passenger had had much youth-ful joy in his life.

When they got to a crossroads a few hundred yards away from Upperfold, Walter reined in the mare and pointed to the right. 'That's my farm. If you ever need help, don't hesitate to come and ask for it, day or night. My door's always open to friends and neighbours.'

He pointed to the left. 'That's the lodge. The agent's house is a little further along, behind those trees.'

Edward knew that already from his night visits but didn't say so. 'Mmm-hmm.'

Walter continued, letting his mare move along slowly and choose her own path to avoid the potholes. 'This road desper-ately needs attention. It's never been allowed to get this bad before. Hatton didn't earn his money as the agent in any way.'

'If you can find me someone to do the job, I'll happily pay for that. I don't want to damage my new bicycle.'

'I can easily find someone to do it. I'll send a message tomorrow morning early with the lad who delivers our bread.'

He reined in his pony outside a cottage, which could have been pretty had it not looked so shabby. 'The lodge is a bit run down. It isn't furnished but it's been cleaned recently and is mostly waterproof. An old couple used to live here but the agent threw them out and they've moved to live further along the track that heads straight on from the crossroads. It runs along by the river, hence the little bridge near our farm.'

'Why did Hatton throw them out?'

'So that he could live here. He seemed to think their furniture belonged to the estate, which it didn't, and he was planning to move in after he'd sold the last of the stuff from the official agent's house.'

'Good heavens! He must have been a dreadful man.'

'He was. But he's dead now so he didn't benefit from his final few crimes. It's a relief to our poorer folk not to have him cheating and browbeating them about their rents. I hope you'll choose someone more honest to do that job of rent-collecting for you.'

'Yes, I shall. There are a few cottages in the valley that still belong to the estate so I shall need to find a new rent collector, shan't I?' He grinned at the older man. 'No doubt you can introduce me to someone suitable to do that, too?'

'Of course. Maybe a woman if it's only a matter of collecting rents. I know a widow who'd leap at the chance to earn a few more shillings a week. Now, let me show you round the house.'

He got down from the cart, this time leaving his mare free to crop the grass in a spot where it grew lushly, which she knew about already as she walked a few paces to get to it without needing his guidance. He waited patiently for Edward, who sat staring at the cottage for a moment or two longer from his elevated position then got down to join him.

'The Rainfords who used to live here always kept the front-door key under this stone, so I've left it in the same place. Yes, here you are. It's still here.' He bent to get it and held it out. 'You should open your own front door this first time, not me, on principle. But if I were you, I'd leave the key somewhere else from now on.'

He watched Edward turn the big, old-fashioned key in the lock and flapped his hand at the younger man to tell him to lead the way inside. 'We'd better check that everything is in order before you move any of your luggage inside.'

The house was certainly clean but sadly old-fashioned and in desperate need of better and more modern plumbing. There was a small new leak in one corner upstairs, luckily confined to the smaller of the two bedrooms.

Walter frowned up at it. 'I was wrong. It'll take two days' work to sort out the problems here not one. Not that it need stop you moving in. The front bedroom seems to be water-proof still.'

'Is there any way of improving the plumbing? I do prefer a modern indoor lavatory and bathroom, and I'm happy to pay for whatever changes are necessary to get them installed here.'

'That won't be as easy to sort out, I'm afraid. And of course it depends how long you're going to stay here whether it'll be worthwhile to do much to the lodge.'

'I shall want to rent it out after I move into the agent's house. Ah, I suppose that will also need its plumbing improving?'

'Oh, it definitely will. You'll also want to put some modern kitchen amenities into them both.'

'Why will it not be easy to arrange?'

'We only have one plumber in Ollerthwaite and he's usually rather busy so you won't get it done quickly, I'm afraid. He's getting on a bit, too, and rather old-fashioned. He's all right for simple jobs but not up to making major changes. I'll have to see if I can find someone more used to putting in modern bathrooms and persuade them to move to the valley because you're not the only one who wants to install better amenities. And indeed, I need one or two jobs like that doing at my own farm as well.'

'Well, if you can find me someone or persuade the chap from Ollerthwaite to fit me in quickly, I'd be grateful. I don't care how much it costs.'

Walter gave him another of those warm, friendly smiles. 'This will all make an excellent start to your living here, you know, buying the bicycle and providing work.'

After they'd finished looking round the lodge they decided it'd be best if Edward camped out in the kitchen and sitting room till his own furniture arrived. Then Walter helped carry everything inside and showed him where he'd left an old oil lamp for when anyone came to do jobs here. Fortunately it had some oil in it still.

Edward sighed. He hadn't even considered the need for oil lamps and all the cleaning and refilling that went with them. He was used to gas lighting.

Walter looked out at the sun, which was now getting low in the sky. 'Will you be all right now, lad? It's growing dark so I think you should leave it till tomorrow to walk round the ruins. They're full of potholes and piles of rubble that have been overgrown by weeds. Well, it's been nearly twenty years since the big fire. You don't want to fall and injure yourself. As for the agent's house, there's no lighting inside it, so that's better seen by daylight too.'

'I'm going to miss gas lighting very much indeed.'

'We could help each other there. I'm wanting gas brought into my house as well so we could share the costs of extending the underground pipes that deliver it, which will give people in nearby farms and houses the opportunity to get connected more cheaply too. Eh, we're behind the times in so many ways here in Upperfold, we are that.'

'I definitely want to get gas brought in if it's available and will pay whatever you think a fair share of the costs. And I'd be grateful if you could send word as quickly as possible to the various workmen I shall need to employ for the repairs.'

'Don't worry. I will. The lad who delivers our bread in the mornings will take messages round to all of them for us on his way back to the shop and I bet the chap filling in potholes will be at your door tomorrow as soon as he hears he's needed.'

Edward turned to look along the track. 'Is the agent's house really that bad?'

'I'm afraid so. It's not very clean inside, either. Hatton lived like a pig wallowing in his own dirt. I think you'll need a couple of women to come in and scrub that place from top to bottom once the repairs have been finished. You could get the walls distempered while you're at it. If they're white, it'll brighten the interior up a lot. I know several women who'd jump at the chance of the scrubbing jobs and a chap who'll distemper the interior walls for you.'

'I'd be hugely grateful if you could arrange that as well.'

'Happy to. And don't hesitate to ask me if you need any more work doing. I know my valley and its people.'

After he'd waved goodbye to Crossley, Edward walked round his new home again, more slowly this time, studying the details. Then he realised it was growing steadily darker and tried to be practical. First things first: he lit the old-fashioned oil lamp and decided to warm the place up so went out to look for coal and firewood. Walter had said there were pieces of old, dry wood and a few buckets worth of coal in a lean-to shelter at the rear and that there would be enough to last him a few days. He'd have to get some more delivered so that he could keep his house warm and do the cooking.

He was going to miss the landlady he'd had for the past several years and had offered her a job as his housekeeper. But Hester hadn't wanted to move, let alone live in a quiet little country town. Music halls weren't as popular as they had been, but she absolutely loved them still and went to a show every week, humming the latest popular songs she'd heard there as she went about her daily tasks.

He'd have to find a regular daily housekeeper once the agent's house had been repaired. His own furniture was too good to bring here till the work on that house was finished, and there was probably too much of it for a small place anyway, so he'd perhaps buy one or two items from Walter to tide him over.

He'd come here for a more relaxed life, but so far all he'd found were jobs that needed doing or supervising.

He grimaced as he lit the kitchen fire with some difficulty. Another job he wasn't used to doing or very skilful at.

Afterwards he ate some bread and jam standing in front of the fire, then began making a proper list in his little pocket notebook: firewood, coal, food, housekeeper, repairs.

Thank goodness his landlady had helped him pack. She'd insisted he brought the mattress, not to mention a couple of blankets 'just in case' his furniture took longer than expected to arrive. There was no bedframe so he'd be sleeping on the floor.

He yawned suddenly and admitted to himself that he was getting sleepy now. He went outside to use the amenities then spread out his bed, lying on the mattress, for which there was just room between the kitchen table and the fireplace.

He fell asleep quickly but slept badly and spent part of the night thinking that he was making a fool of himself because he hadn't dealt efficiently with the details of everyday life, details which would have seemed simple to most people.

It just went to show that successful businessmen didn't know everything. He now needed to learn quite a lot of the practical skills needed in daily life, and learn them from ordinary folk.

He'd do whatever it took, but as soon as the house was in a better state he'd get some sort of help to run it.

And this had to be the lumpiest mattress in Lancashire – or maybe the whole of England!

7

Edward woke from an uneasy doze to see the pale pre-dawn light delineating the window frames. He knew he'd not be able to sleep again; he might as well get up and start the day's work. He grimaced as he went outside to use the privy and suddenly realised he was only wearing his slippers. It was just light enough to see where he was putting his feet but the ground was rough and he stumbled a couple of times, stubbing his toes through the soft cloth.

Clogs, he thought, remembering seeing a maid use them to go in and out of one of the houses he'd lived in. He'd buy some and keep them near the back door.

When he came back, shivering, he lit the oil lamp, found some embers still glowing at the back of the fire and added twigs, moving them about carefully to get the bigger pieces of wood burning properly.

As the fire started to kindle, he slipped on his shoes and coat to go outside and fetch in more wood from the scattered pieces still lying around. He was gradually noticing more about his surroundings, watching the world being filled with colour by a glorious red-and-gold sky. He stood quietly watching the sun rise, forgetting for a few moments his lack of sleep and the many tasks facing him.

It was so beautiful to see the sun move gently up, transforming from being a mere glow on the horizon to a big globe that was now taking on itself the task of waking up this part of the world. How long had it been since he'd had the time to appreciate the beauty of a sunrise? Far too long.

Only when he shivered did he realise he'd been standing there in his nightshirt and coat, with his feet feeling the cold even when wearing shoes. What an idiot he must look! He went inside to dump the pieces of wood in the scuttle and poke small pieces of wood into the fire, which was starting to burn up a little in the middle of the grate. This seemed like a positive omen.

He'd have to see if coal was available or else get a pile of logs delivered. Out came the notebook again. He couldn't afford to forget anything. These items weren't luxuries but absolute necessities.

After taking a quick all-over wash in front of the fire he got dressed, grimacing at wearing the same shirt for a second day running. He was going to miss his modern bathroom and easily available hot water even more than he'd expected, not to mention his clean laundry that was put away tidily in his bedroom.

But he wouldn't miss the crowded town in other ways. You didn't see sunrises like that when you were hemmed in by rows of houses.

Lots to do today. But at his own pace, at least.

It was a bit early for breakfast but he was hungry so he made some toast on the fire, holding the slices of bread out to it at the end of a long-handled fork pulled from the box of miscellaneous kitchen equipment he'd brought with him. The items in the box had been put together for him by his landlady from oddments she'd bought for him. Hessie might not have wanted to move to a small country town with him but she had been determined to ensure that he had the items he'd need to cope.

He smiled down at the big fork as he finished browning the last piece of toast in front of the hottest part of the fire. He hadn't thought about how well these few pieces of wire were suited to their purpose until now, but three well-spaced tines at the end of a long handle held a piece of bread firmly so that you could dangle it in front of the flames without it dropping off and yet your hand remained far enough away not to get burned.

He kept the toast warm on a plate in the hearth and after making three pieces, he couldn't bear to wait a second longer to eat. He slathered them with butter and jam bought from the obliging baker yesterday and crunched them with great satisfaction before finishing the last drop of his big pot of tea.

Afterwards he washed the utensils as best he could in water warmed in the kettle and poured into a small enamel washing-up bowl, also provided by the landlady. *Thank you again, Hessie.*

Then he couldn't bear to delay any longer. He had to face the ruins of his old home and investigate them properly by daylight. All he'd seen so far were dark shapes hovering in the moonlight. He could see fragments of walls standing more or less upright farther up the slope from this cottage, some reaching higher than others, but there was little left of the top floor and attics except the occasional charred piece of rafter.

He remembered what Ollerton House had been like before, remembered surprisingly well considering he'd only been eight when his family had had to move away, but the fire had happened after they'd left so he'd never seen the burned-out shell by daylight until today.

He pulled on his old but still sturdy boots, not his shoes, and as an afterthought picked up his walking stick because he could see from here how rough the ground was, then set off for the ruins, stopping next to the first piece of wall. This part had been his mother's sitting room if he remembered correctly. The thought of her brought tears to his eyes.

His night-time visits had been mainly to look at the land and he hadn't been able to see the details of the big house clearly enough. In the early dawn, the ruins had looked like hands groping blindly for the sky and there was a threatening air to the whole place, even by full daylight. He hesitated briefly before going along the line of still-standing fragments of wall to explore, weaving to and fro where there was better footing among the rubble.

At the far corner there was a larger piece of wall that made it seem as if part of the house was still fairly intact—until he got closer and realised there was no glass in the window and the illusion of something taller still standing upright had been created by a huge tree trunk beyond it, now revealed clearly.

As far as Edward could tell, there had been no attempt whatsoever to clear the ground after the fire, so it was still littered with irregular mounds of tumbled debris that had gradually been taken over by weeds. As he threaded his way in and out of them, he stumbled and nearly fell into a hidden hollow. After that he slowed right down, picking his way carefully, poking uncertain areas with his stick before walking on them. He didn't want to risk spraining an ankle, or worse.

He stopped as he came to a place where it looked as though someone else had clambered over the ruins. It must have happened quite recently because the footprints in the soft earth would have been wiped out by any rain. Maybe it had been lads from the village exploring. Surely not scavengers after all this time because any worthwhile bits and pieces would have been taken years ago. He suspected quite a lot of fallen roof tiles had suffered that fate.

It must have been a huge blaze to cause such wholesale destruction. What had started it off?

He followed the occasional faint traces of footprints down a narrow path, which seemed to lead back to the lodge, then stopped, puzzled. He was away from the big house now and there was nothing but untidy vegetation, so what had an intruder been doing here?

Taking great care how he moved he continued to follow the intermittent trail. Then it stopped at a more open place where there were signs that whoever it was had been ferreting around. There was a mound of earth that was more loosely piled than the rest, with little channels in it made by runnels of rain. When he went closer his foot nudged some of the earth aside and he saw the gleam of metal underneath.

Strange! He kicked more of the earth aside and found it so loose it moved easily. Good heavens! It must have been dug up then spread deliberately to cover this hatch. He kicked more away.

This could only lead to cellars, surely? But these couldn't be the cellars of the big house. The hatch was too far away from it. Then he snapped his fingers as he remembered that there had been a previous smaller manor house before 'the new house' had been built. Was the hatch something remaining from that?

Feeling excited, he knelt and scraped more of the earth away with his hands, uncovering the rest of the hatch quite easily. He tried to lift it, expecting resistance, but it came up quite easily and as it swung it pulled him sideways. He let go hastily and it thumped down to the ground, leaving a gaping hole surrounded by a metal frame.

Instinctively he stepped back from the edge slightly before peering down. He was disappointed that he could make out little beyond the area directly below him. This definitely seemed to be a cellar opening, perhaps the type that was once used for deliveries of coal.

He squinted at a sort of chute to one side, presumably where they used to tip the chunks of coal or firewood down. Its surface was in a poor condition and the stones it was made from looked uneven with some missing. How had all this survived so long? The first house had been built in the mid-sixteenth century if he remembered correctly. There were no signs of a fire burning anything down here so perhaps they'd simply pulled down the old house and used bits of it to build the more modern one.

He'd need an oil lamp to see the cellar clearly. Only, how could he have known he'd need one in broad daylight? Nobody had ever hinted to him that any cellars might have been left more or less intact here.

He wasn't risking going down there on his own, though. If there was some sort of landslide or accident, he'd be trapped and no one would know where he was.

No, he had to find someone to come exploring with him, someone who could bring a ladder to get in and out, not to mention a lamp or two. Would Walter Crossley be too old to help him? Perhaps. But if he didn't want to go down, he would surely know someone of a more adventurous turn of mind who'd enjoy exploring. Best to consult his neighbour about how to do this.

He stood up, closed the hatch again and covered it roughly with soil, kicking it around over the metal cover, which didn't quite fit the frame properly at one side. He bent to examine it more closely. It looked as if a leak of some sort had washed away the harder earth round it and drained down into the cellar when it rained, so that the warped frame no longer let the hatch fit tightly.

He went back to the lodge, feeling sad at how little was left of his old home. There he cleaned himself up as best he could. He'd walk across to Walter's straight away and see what his neighbour suggested doing about the cellar. No, he'd have to go shopping before he did anything else. He needed to buy some tinned food and some fresh vegetables. Yes, and meat and perhaps bacon.

Oh hell, he really should have planned all this better and learned how to feed himself simply before he came to live here.

When he walked outside Edward was confronted by the end of a wheel of the shiny new bicycle jutting out from the side wall of the cottage. Fancy forgetting that! He could get around much more quickly on this but he'd need to practise riding it before he took it out in public. He was used to walking everywhere or taking taxicabs in central London, hadn't been on a bicycle in years.

He'd better have a quick practice before he went out on the road. He didn't want people's first impression of the new owner to be of a clumsy idiot wobbling along on or worse still, falling off a bicycle.

He stared down the hill towards Upperfold, well, as much of it as he could see from here. Apart from the farm, the nearest buildings were three cottages standing at this side of the village.

Walter had been right: the lodge was too far away from the village and town to walk there and back carrying shopping, especially when he had so many things to purchase if he was to make himself comfortable. He'd have to ask them to deliver some food. Surely there would be someone who did that?

The agent's house, to which he'd move once it was repaired, was even further away from the village. He hadn't even got round to looking at that yet.

He wobbled to and fro along a smoother part of the rough dirt track in front of the cottage, practising. He nearly fell off a couple of times, then suddenly seemed to get his balance and began riding along more easily. Yes, it was all coming back to him now. And thank goodness for that!

He locked up the house and hid the key under a different stone and too bad if anyone found it. He didn't want to carry the heavy iron lump around in his pocket.

It didn't take long to cycle to the farm. He knocked on the front door but no one answered. He knocked again, but there was still no response.

There had to be someone around surely? They got up early on farms, didn't they? He walked round to the back and when he heard a voice, he turned in that direction.

He found an unusually tall woman, who had to be around six feet, because she was slightly taller than he was. She was talking to some hens as she scattered grain for them, and the creatures were moving round her pecking busily. They kept looking up and crooning or clucking at her as if they understood exactly what she was telling them and were answering. He couldn't help smiling. What a delightful scene.

When he said, 'Excuse me,' she swung round, looking startled, then smiled as if she'd worked out who he was.

'Can I help you?'

'I was looking for Walter Crossley.'

'You must be Edward Ollerton. I was just about to make myself a pot of tea. I'm the only one up so far but I heard Walter moving about so he'll be down shortly. Would you like a cup?'

'I'd love one.' He followed the woman into the large farmhouse kitchen.

'I'm Maude Vernon, by the way, a distant cousin of Walter's.'

'Delighted to meet you.'

'You're an early riser, Mr Ollerton.'

He gave her a rueful glance. 'I hadn't provided myself with a proper bed and consequently slept badly. I shall be glad when some of my furniture arrives. I'm hoping that'll be within a few days.'

He turned at the sound of footsteps to see Walter come into the room, nodding at the sight of him.

'Good morning, young Ollerton. I shall be much more civilised after a cup of tea.' He sat down at the table and Maude picked up a cup, filled and sweetened it, then handed it to him.

He took a big mouthful, then another. 'Aah! That's better.'

A younger man joined them shortly afterwards and was introduced as, 'My grandson, Cameron.' The resemblance to

Walter was marked, another tall chap with dark hair and an intelligent expression on a lean, elegant face.

'Elinor is staying in bed a little longer. She's feeling nauseous again,' the newcomer announced.

Walter beamed so broadly at that news that Edward guessed that his grandson's wife must be expecting. His mother's friend had a daughter who had been sick in the mornings when she'd been in a delicate condition. He'd been quite young then and it had led to an explanation of the basic details of bearing a baby, which had sounded to be a terrible process to him as a child, and still seemed hard on women to him as a man grown. He was glad he didn't have to face that.

'Have you had breakfast yet, lad?' Walter asked him.

'I had some toast earlier.'

'Why don't you join us for a proper meal? You can't put in a hard day's work on a few pieces of toast.'

'If you're sure it's not too much trouble, I'd love to. Thank you.'

He found himself sharing some excellent ham and eggs with them and telling them about the cellar he'd found.

'We'll go and explore it with you after breakfast, if you like,' Walter immediately offered. 'You were right not to risk going down there on your own.'

'I'd really welcome some help exploring it.'

Cameron smiled across the table. 'I hope you don't intend to leave me out of the grand expedition. I'm as nosey as the next person and I can spare an hour or two this morning.'

'We can go back there in the cart and take a ladder and lamps, maybe a few tools too,' Walter said. 'No one from the village has dared explore the ruins openly because Hatton usually threatened anyone he saw with arrest for trespassing.' He frowned. 'Hatton must have known about the cellar further down the hill, though. I wonder if he'd been using it to store some of the things he'd stolen. I set the policeman from

Ollerthwaite on him once, but we found nothing in the agent's house. He'd hated me before but if looks could kill after that, I'd have dropped dead on the spot.'

'I heard at market that he took boxes out of the valley on Terry Catlow's cart a few times,' Maude said. 'And that they'd been seen carrying pieces of furniture out from the agent's house.'

'Catlow is one of our local villains,' Walter explained to Edward. 'Unfortunately he's clever enough not to have been caught or to come near my land, but we'll snabble him one day.'

After they'd finished their meal, Edward tried to be practical, much as he was longing to continue exploring. 'I'd better go and buy some food before we go down into that cellar.' He looked at his companions. 'I prepared very badly for coming here, I'm afraid. I was too excited at regaining our family home to think clearly, so if you have any hints about the sort of provisions to buy, I'd be grateful.'

Walter reached out to lay one hand on his. 'Quite understandable to be excited, lad.'

'I have to go into Upperfold and will be setting off shortly,' Maude said. 'It's market day, you see, Mr Ollerton. I sell our eggs and some of the garden produce every week and buy our main food supplies while I'm there. If you give me some money I can easily buy some food for you and have it sent out to the lodge. I hope you don't mind me saying so but I'll know far better than you what will come in useful. Sid Petby delivers things for sixpence or a shilling, depending how much there is.'

'You'll definitely do better than me. I can't thank you enough.'

'Tell me what you've got already.'

'I've only got part of a loaf and a couple of scones left, with a little butter and jam.'

'You could come and have your evening meals with us till you get settled, and pay the lasses what they think fair for the food,' Walter said. 'Then it won't matter as much what you eat the rest of the day.'

'That's incredibly kind, sir.' He couldn't help his voice coming out choked and wobbly. He had never met such warm, friendly people. It brought a lump to his throat after his years of struggling on his own.

Walter winked at him and said, 'You can arrange that with our Maude.'

He managed a smile in return, but only just.

Once Edward had given Maude some money to pay for what she would get him at the market, the three men set off to explore the cellar, taking a couple of Walter's old oil lamps and a ladder with them. They wound their way carefully across the rough ground and when Edward had kicked the soil away again, they all stood next to the hole, peering down it.

'I don't like the looks of that old coal chute to one side,' Walter said. 'There are stones missing. You were right not to clamber down there on your own, lad.' He shone his lamp further round. 'Look, you can see how the hatch has been leaking at this side. It's marked the nearby wall. And is it my imagination or is the ground more uneven below that? You've got younger eyes.'

'I think you're right,' Edward said. 'The leak must have eroded the stones that make up the floor underneath where the water dripped.'

Cameron was frowning. 'It'd have taken a long time for it to do that because it was soundly built.'

'Let's secure our ladder at the side away from the chute and the leak, then,' Walter said.

They did that then Edward tied an unlit oil lamp to his belt and swung himself round onto the upper rungs. He descended slowly and carefully and when he got to the cellar floor, he took out a box of matches and lit the lamp, setting it carefully on a big stone at one side to light up as much of the area as possible. By that time Cameron had joined him.

'You should stay up there till we've checked it all out, Grandad!' he called as he lit the other lamp, which he'd brought down.

'One of us should stay up here at all times, and it makes sense for me to do that while you two make an initial survey of the whole area. I'm not getting any younger.' Walter's sigh of regret about that was clearly audible.

Cameron flourished one hand at his companion. 'Your house, so you should go first. Here. Take this lamp and we'll leave the other one here.'

'Let's go round the perimeter of this cellar first,' Edward suggested. 'What would you say it is, about ten yards across?'

'Yes. And it's a rough oblong.'

They did a circuit slowly and carefully, shining the lamp on the ground ahead and studying each patch of wall and ceiling before they moved on. Someone had paved the whole area with big stone slabs, but it must have been a very long time ago from the way the paving was worn or cracked.

'These slabs look really old,' Edward said. 'The only ones I've ever seen that look like these have been in old churches or castles.'

'I'll have to take your word for that. We didn't have such old structures where I grew up in America,' Cameron said.

When they got to the rear of the space they found a heavy door and Edward opened it carefully, ready to duck back if the ceiling or walls near it looked unstable. But none of it moved. The door hinges creaked but it opened with a bit of a push, revealing how thick the old wall was.

Beyond the door was a passage about five yards long, which had another door at the far end and a door in the middle of the right-hand wall as well.

'These are certainly big cellars,' Cameron commented. 'Did you ever come down here as a child, Edward?'

'No, never. In fact, I didn't know this part even existed. I'd explored the whole house, of course, but not this part of the grounds. I had a tutor keeping my nose to the grindstone from six years old.'

When they opened the side door it led into a smaller cellar, which was empty except for a thick covering of dust. There were a few footprints near the entrance, covered by visibly less dust so they must have been made at a later date.

The door at the far end of the short corridor was jammed shut by something on the other side.

'Do you think the fire caused a cave-in of the area beyond this?' Cameron asked.

'If so, how did this part stay unscathed?' Edward wondered aloud.

Cameron gestured to the ceilings, which seemed to be made of solid slabs of wood. 'I'd guess this was part of the cellars of the earlier house that had been pulled down, so there weren't any connections to the fire.'

'You could be right. We clearly can't go any further so let's not waste any more time down here. Anyway, it gives me the shivers.'

They went back into the coal cellar and stood beneath the hatch, telling Walter what they'd found in case he thought of anything else to check.

He frowned down at them. 'People in the valley say there was a house in the same place, built in Tudor times according to the records in the parish church of Ollerthwaite, and they used materials from it to build parts of the new house. I didn't realise any of it was left.'

Edward looked round. 'I doubt this cellar is going to be much use to us. Unless my architect wants to build in the same place.'

'Well, that's up to you and him, but as we can't do much with it at this stage, perhaps we'd better close the top hatch to keep nosey folk out and get on with the rest of our day. We have to get you settled more comfortably in that house for a start, lad.'

'Yes, and a bed comes first. I spent a rather uncomfortable night.'

Walter looked down at them. 'You might as well leave one lamp and some matches down there in case you or your architect want to come down here again,' Walter said. 'Both lamps are old and we weren't using them. Keep the other for yourself.'

Cameron went up, then Edward walked round to the front of the ladder, stopping in surprise when one of the flagstones rocked about beneath his foot. He'd forgotten about the damage from the water leak. He bent to see what was wrong with it but he couldn't insert his fingers to lift the heavy stone.

'I'll bring some sand and a shovel next time to lever this out and then level it. We don't want anyone tripping over that sunken edge.' He followed Cameron back up the ladder. 'Do you want me to unpin the ladder for you, Walter?'

'No. It's an old one and I have better ones at home. It's sound enough, so let's leave it here for the time being. When you start work on your new home, the builder may want to use this place to keep some of his materials dry. And your architect may even want to use it as the basis of a new house. That'd save some work digging a cellar out.'

Edward's voice was soft. 'I'd like that. It would give a wonderful continuity to the original family home, wouldn't it?'

Walter studied him, eyes narrowed. 'You're looking exhausted now, lad. Maybe you should lie down and see if you can get a bit of a nap. I'm going into my shop, so I'll find you a bed base among the second-hand furniture and bring it over here after tea.'

'Thank you so much.' Edward couldn't help yawning again. 'I've got some furniture coming as soon as I give word but I can't do that till the agent's house is ready for me to move into. I just need to last until then.'

'We eat at six o'clock. Will you be able to wake up then or do you want someone to come and fetch you?'

'I brought an old alarm clock, so I won't be late.'

He slept soundly and would have continued sleeping if the alarm hadn't woken him. He had a quick wash and hoped he looked all right. He needed a mirror, had cut himself shaving, and added it to his mental list as he rode his bicycle across to Walter's house.

Maude was a good cook and he enjoyed a delicious meal but best of all, the company of four interesting and lively people. He told Walter, who helped him carry the bed outside while Cameron harnessed the mare, Jenny, to the cart, that he wished he'd had a family like this one.

'Make yourself a family from now on then, lad. If you haven't got blood kin, find some heart kin, people you like who're alone and need a family too.'

'Heart kin. What a lovely phrase.' And it was a lovely idea too.

They lifted the bicycle on top of the bed and Maude came out with a fluffy feather pillow to add to the pile. Then Walter drove his guest back to the lodge through the shadows thrown by the moonlight.

How had Walter become so wise? Edward wondered as he got ready for bed later on. The phrase 'heart kin' kept coming back to him, and the idea too. Only, he really wanted to start a new family of his own blood. Could he still do that? Who knew? But first he'd have to find a wife. He was thirty-seven, had left it rather late to start a family, but not too late, surely?

And why not welcome others into his life in the meantime, as Walter had suggested? Edward had been alone for most of his adult life because he'd concentrated on working hard to make money. He'd forced himself to ignore the lack of family in his life. His cousin Della had been in a similar position. She'd had to study for long hours to become a doctor so they could only get together occasionally.

He'd invite her to visit him here once he had the agent's house set up. He enjoyed her company.

But now he had to stop worrying and get a good night's sleep. There were men Walter had found coming to see him tomorrow about the various jobs needed on both his houses, and on the rough track that led to them.

He yawned and snuggled down. This bed of Walter's was not only more comfortable, even with a thin mattress, but kept him out of the draughts, too.

His eyes closed and his worries faded away.

8

Lillian felt safer when she and Mr Callan got on the train. He put their luggage up on the net racks and since they had the compartment to themselves, they sat opposite one another in window seats.

As they pulled out of the station, he said quietly, 'You should be all right now.'

'I hope so.' She couldn't help glancing towards the inner door of the compartment, though, and the corridor beyond. Anyone could reach them that way if they'd been followed.

'I'm still here, so you're not alone and I'm fairly sure no one followed us onto the train.'

She tried to smile but couldn't quite manage it. 'I can't thank you enough. I'm concerned that I'm taking up so much of your time, though I don't know what I'd have done without your help.'

'No need to feel bad about that. We'll be fairly close to my original destination when we get to Ollerthwaite, so you're not taking me all that far out of my way. Besides, I may be ready to settle down, but I haven't yet decided exactly where, so I might as well look round Ollerthwaite before I move on. Who knows? I may even decide to stay there.'

She was amazed. 'You don't have anywhere specific in mind to settle?'

'Not exactly. I don't have any close family left but I'd like to find somewhere in Lancashire, because that's where I was born and I do have some distant relatives and old friends here and there. All I'm really certain of is that I want to stop moving about all the time.'

That eased one of her worries at least.

His voice softened and he was almost speaking to himself as he added, 'My main dream at the moment is to make a real home for myself and it's going to be worth more than gold to me.'

'I've dreamed of the same thing for a long time, hadn't even dared hope it'd come true till my husband died so suddenly. A home of your own would indeed be more precious than gold.'

'I hope you achieve your golden dream.'

She smiled. 'Thank you. I hope the same for you.'

'I intend to *make* it come true. A few months ago, quite suddenly, I knew that I'd done enough travelling so I began to clear things up where I was working, which was interesting work but not in a place I could love. It's harder than you think to find somewhere to settle permanently when you don't have people you love to tug you back.'

'I can understand that because I feel the same.' She'd never wished her husband dead but, oh, she was so very glad to be rid of him. She hadn't liked him, on the contrary, so was in no way a grieving widow and wasn't going to pretend about that.

As the train rattled along, the rhythmic sound it made seemed to lull her to sleep she was so exhausted. She tried not to, but her eyes would keep closing.

'It'd be safe for you to have a nap now,' he said gently. 'I'm here to keep watch and this isn't a slow train so won't be stopping very often. You should be able to get over an hour or so of undisturbed sleep.'

She trusted him absolutely so gave in to temptation and let herself drift away, just for a few minutes.

She was woken by him shaking her shoulder gently.

'We're nearly there now, Mrs Hesketh. Perhaps you'd better use the facilities before we start moving from train to train?'

She nodded, feeling a little embarrassed at his frankness about a topic people usually avoided mentioning in public. But he was right. She did need to go.

He pointed to the left. 'It's that way.'

When she got back he followed her example and she was by herself for a few moments. She felt nervous but of course nothing bad happened and she was daring to hope that she really had got away from the Thurstens.

When he came back, Mr Callan stopped in the doorway of their compartment, studying her. 'I hate to see you look so on edge.'

'You must think me foolish and timid.'

'No. I think you've had years of being treated badly and it's made you nervous. I've seen other women in the same state and it always upsets me. Why do their families push them into these unsuitable marriages?'

'For financial security, I suppose. Women might be starting to go out to work nowadays, especially work in offices, but they don't get paid nearly as much as men, so it can be hard to earn enough to live on, even in the cheapest lodgings. They put articles about the unfairness of that in the newspapers, but nothing ever seems to change. Have you never wanted to get married?'

He shrugged. 'Yes. I nearly did. However I came to realise that the woman I was courting only wanted a home and children. She needed a husband to provide for them and bring in money to live off but any respectable husband would have done for her. I wanted a wife who cared about me as well as any children we might create and I wasn't sure about settling down yet anyway, because I was eager to see something of the world. Then—' He broke off as the train started to slow down before it entered a busy station. 'Ah, Preston. I'd better get our cases down. I'm afraid we'll have quite a wait for our next train, and then another wait for our final train.'

When they were off the train he said, 'Let's check the notice-board and see exactly when our train leaves.' He scanned it more quickly than she did. 'Over an hour to wait. We've time to get something to eat. I'm hungry even if you aren't.'

He took her agreement for granted and led the way into the refreshment room where he plonked the two big suitcases down near the entrance and gestured to a nearby table. 'I'll get the food. You keep an eye on our luggage. Tea and a bread roll all right for you? They'll be more filling than biscuits. There doesn't look to be much else on offer.'

'Anything will be fine, thank you.'

She watched the woman behind the counter fill a teapot with dark brown liquid from a big urn and get out two rolls from a glass-fronted display cabinet. These were already set out on small plates with pats of butter beside them and looked as if they'd been there for a while. The tea was stewed and she'd normally have avoided it but she was desperately thirsty so took a big mouthful, ate all her roll and even accepted a second cup of the stale tea when he offered to get her one.

'Very wise of you. Drink up quickly. It'll soon be time to board our next train.'

He swept her off immediately she'd swallowed the last mouthful and she did as he told her. He hadn't once barked orders at her, only suggested quietly and politely that they needed to do something. He seemed used to travelling, unlike her. What on earth would she do after he left her in this Ollerthwaite place? She had so little experience of the ways of the world.

He didn't seem interested in her as a woman and she didn't find him particularly attractive, for some reason. Well, she didn't want to marry again, so that was a good thing. But she'd like to keep him as a friend if he wasn't going to move on.

They'd timed their move well because passengers were now being allowed onto a side platform where a smaller train was waiting with a slender thread of steam trickling from its funnel, as if the engine was impatient to roar into action.

There were more people on this train, so they had to walk along to find a compartment with room for them and their luggage.

He stopped at an open door. 'Here we go.'

This time there were two women sharing the compartment with them but they had no suitcases, only a couple of shopping bags each so there was room for the luggage.

It was more than an hour's journey from Preston to their next change of train as this one stopped several times. The final train left from a much smaller station and was rather shabby, made up of only three old-fashioned carriages. They were the only ones in their compartment so again could take window seats.

'Final stretch of the journey,' he said. 'Then we'll see about finding you some lodgings till you can sort out a house to rent.'

She forced herself to say, 'And I can let you continue your journey.'

'I won't move on until I'm sure you've found somewhere to live. I don't like to leave a job half finished. Besides, I really would like to look round the town myself, as I've already said.'

'How will you know whether a place is right?'

'First it must feel right and have some pretty countryside nearby. After that it'll depend what other businesses are already operating in the area. I'd want to have the chance to earn a decent living. Don't you have any family at all left, Mrs Hesketh?'

'None that I've been able to keep in touch with. I've always envied people with big families and lots of friends. My husband wasn't at all sociable so we were without either.'

'How did he pass his time in the evenings, then?'

'When he wasn't at work, by reading newspapers, going out drinking with friends or visiting his parents. Sometimes he just sat at home drinking wine and scowling at me.'

'Well, I'm sure you'll make new friends once you settle down in Ollerthwaite. There's bound to be a church you can attend and that's a good way to meet people.'

Years of frustration spilled out. 'My husband didn't even like attending church and his parents didn't attend regularly either. On the few occasions when we did go, like Easter and Christmas, he kept a tight hold of my arm, so that I couldn't move away from him and pulled me on whenever other women in the congregation tried to chat to me.'

'That must have been difficult to live with.'

'Yes.' On the few occasions she'd tried to accept an invitation to join a ladies' sewing circle or some such group because she could do that secretly during the hours he was at work, he had found out and been furious. He'd forbidden her to go out tattling about their private affairs to everyone. It had felt wonderful even in the short time since his death not to have had the burden of keeping him from erupting into those dreadful fits of anger, which had got worse and worse. He'd even hit her a few times in the last month or two.

She saw how Mr Callan was looking at her, didn't want his pity and tried to speak calmly. 'Oh well, those days are gone now, I'm happy to say. I'm sure I'll manage perfectly well once I get used to my new freedom.'

She only hoped she sounded more hopeful than she felt. The thought of all that would be involved in finding even a small house to rent and setting herself up with furniture and other necessities was daunting. She'd have to do it, though, because she didn't want to spend her life in lodgings for single women, which was the most common respectable alternative if you didn't have family to live with.

So she'd do what she had to.

9

When they got off the train in Ollerthwaite, Lillian and Riley looked for a taxi but saw no signs of one. She was surprised at how comfortable she felt with her new friend now.

The station was tiny, consisting mainly of a long, narrow paved area on one side of the train. Near the exit was a three-sided shelter with benches for passengers to sit on, with a fully enclosed cubicle sticking out at the corner. The porter seemed to be both ticket collector and station master and was fully occupied with those duties at the moment. They could only stand on the platform next to their luggage and wait for him to finish his tasks so that they could ask his help in finding a taxi.

Lillian watched the other passengers stride away down the street and envied them having somewhere to go. There wasn't even a sign showing where to wait for a taxicab, so how did visitors to the town get anywhere?

A woman who'd been walking past the station slowed down to stare at them, seemed to realise that they weren't sure what to do and came across, simply stepping up from the street onto the unfenced platform and striding along towards them.

As she got closer Lillian realised she was about six feet tall, not quite as tall as Riley but far taller than most women. She appeared to be about the same age as Lillian, or maybe a little older, had a fresh complexion and looked full of vibrant life. Best of all she had a lovely smile.

'You two look a bit lost. Can I be of any help?'

Riley shot a glance at Lillian as if wanting her to respond first.

'We'd really appreciate some advice. We've just arrived and are each looking for somewhere to stay. Then I will be looking for a house to rent. Someone recommended Ollerthwaite to me after my husband died as a nice, quiet town to live in, you see.'

The stranger nodded and looked at Riley as if wondering how he fitted in.

'I'm Riley Callan. I met Mrs Hesketh by chance on a train going to Manchester and we got chatting as travellers sometimes do. It turned out that we were both coming here so we travelled on from there together. I've been working in France for a while and I too fancy settling down somewhere quiet.'

The woman studied them both, nodding as if they'd passed some sort of test. 'There's a widow who takes in respectable travellers needing a bed for a night or two. My cousin is in town with me and we arranged to meet here. If you wait with me for a minute or two, he'll be coming to pick me up in his cart. We don't have a taxi in Ollerthwaite any longer so I'm sure Walter will be happy to take you to Mrs Gleston's. That luggage looks far too heavy to lug round on foot.'

'Thank you,' Riley said. 'You're right. Are you sure your cousin won't mind?'

'He's always happy to help people. I'm Maude Vernon, by the way.'

Lillian noticed that the other two had both included their first names in their introductions, which probably made her 'Mrs Hesketh' sound stiff and old-fashioned. She must remember to do the same from now on. She so wanted to fit in with the locals here and make friends.

Maude gave them another of those lovely smiles. 'I'm biased but I think Ollindale is a good place to live and I hope you'll both be very happy here in the valley. You shouldn't have any difficulty finding a house to rent, Mrs Hesketh. And actually, my cousin Walter may have one or two available that you could look at to see if they suit. He owns several properties in town.'

Just then an older man drove a pony and cart along the street, waved to their companion and drew up nearby. He jumped down and tied up the pony to one of a series of posts along the edge of the open area outside the station before coming across to join them.

Maude gestured to him. 'This is my cousin, Walter Crossley.'

As they introduced themselves to him, Lillian could feel herself relaxing. He was older than the rest of them and had such a kind, fatherly expression that she didn't feel her usual nervousness with a stranger.

'What made you choose Ollerthwaite, Mrs Hesketh?' he asked.

'My lawyer has a nephew, a Mr Turnby, who has just started up a legal practice here. He suggested, from what his nephew had said, that this might be a nice, quiet town for me to settle in. I'm a widow, you see.'

She didn't intend to tell anyone how recent that status was, if she could help it, so must ask Mr Callan to keep quiet about it, yes, and mention that to Mr Turnby too when she met him. She didn't want to spend a year in mourning, didn't intend to wear black for Stanley at all.

'Ah, yes. I've met the young gentleman in question. He's fitted in well here. His wife was born and bred in a village just outside the valley and her parents still have a farm there, so they live nearby in the southern part of Ollerthwaite. Someone told my grandson's wife Mrs Turnby had been unhappy living in a big town. I must admit, I would be too.'

When he found out that they needed to find lodgings for a few nights, he immediately offered to drive them 'up the hill' to see Mrs Gleston and it didn't take long to load their cases on the back of his cart. After that Lillian was invited to squash onto the driving seat between him and Maude, while Riley clambered up on the back and sat beside the luggage, holding a loop of rope attached to the back of the driving seat.

Once they got there Maude jumped nimbly down and went to the front door with Lillian to ask Mrs Gleston about rooms.

The woman looked at them in dismay. 'Oh dear! I'm that sorry, Miss Vernon, but both my rooms are taken, and for several days too.'

'Do you know of anywhere else we could try?' Lillian asked.

'There's nowhere suitable for a lady like you, I'm afraid, only a couple of rough lodging houses where they all sleep in a big room in bunk beds. We don't get a lot of visitors to this town, you see, and they mostly come here to see relatives or friends.'

'I'm afraid she's right,' Maude said.

Panic filled Lillian as that sank in. What was she going to do?

Walter called across from the driving seat, 'In that case, you two had better come and stay with us for a few nights.'

Both Lillian and Riley stared at him in amazement.

'We can't impose,' she said automatically.

'Nonsense! We're happy to help you,' he replied at once. 'Isn't it in the Bible somewhere: I was a stranger and you welcomed me?'

'Then we're extremely grateful for your kind offer.' Riley could see that Lillian was lost for words.

Maude gestured to her to get back up on the cart. 'It won't be the first time we've put up travellers. We have several spare bedrooms.'

Walter was looking thoughtful. 'We really do need a small hotel in Ollerthwaite and there are a couple of houses standing empty that would do the job. I must set my mind to finding someone suitable to run one.' He realised they were all waiting to set off again. 'Sorry. I was thinking aloud. But we really are happy to put you two up for a few days. And if you're looking for a house to rent, Mrs Hesketh, I have one or two available and I can show them to you tomorrow. No obligation if they don't suit.'

'Oh. Well, thank you very much. That'd be extremely helpful.' These people were so wonderfully different from Stanley and his family.

As they set off again, Walter shot a glance towards his other passenger. 'Did I hear you say that you're thinking of starting up a business, Mr Callan? What sort of work do you do?'

'I'm a plumber. If I can find somewhere suitable and there aren't too many other plumbers working and living nearby, this is the sort of place where I'd like to settle. I do have other skills and interests I want to use commercially in the long term as well, but they can wait.'

'We'll have to have a chat about that and see if I can help you, or rather we can help one another. We're actually desperate for another skilled plumber in the valley so you'd have plenty of business. We have a chap in Upperfold who can fix simple problems, and does a good, honest job, but sometimes there's a need for more skilled help and he can't cope with that.'

'What sort of work is needed so desperately?'

Walter gave one of his gentle laughs. 'We're no different from other folk here in the valley. A few people have had proper inside bathrooms put in over the past few years, and others are envying them and talking about doing it as well. I'm one of them.'

'Proper bathrooms make a big difference to people's lives,' Riley said. 'Especially women with large families.'

'We're rather behind the times here in some ways, I'm afraid, but thanks to the Ollerton family's generosity a few decades ago, the town at least has its own reservoir on land up near the moors that they donated. It provides good, clean water that doesn't need a lot of treatment to make it safe to drink.' He smiled and cocked one eyebrow questioningly at Riley as he waited for any questions.

'Is there no one else suitable to do that sort of plumbing?'

'There's a chap in the southern part of the town and he's good at it, but he's booked for weeks if not months ahead. I'd be happy to help you set up a plumbing business here, very happy, and I'd advise you to do that in Upperfold, because you can cover the northern part of Ollerthwaite from there as well. I even have an unused workshop where you could make a start, though you'd probably grow out of it within the year, if you're good.'

Maude saw the surprise on Riley's face and explained cheerfully, 'My cousin has taken it upon himself to encourage people to move here to Ollindale so that we can bring the town more fully back to life. It was apparently quite a thriving place in the old days when they used water power for spinning, but as steam engines took over and people moved away to work in the big new mills, houses here were left empty. Some are still without occupants all these years afterwards.'

Riley watched Maude's expressive face, trying not to betray how attractive he found her. She wasn't exactly pretty but she had a wonderful smile and her eyes absolutely sparkled with life. And she was nice and tall. He always felt too big and clumsy with small women. He tore his gaze away from her and turned back to Walter. 'That sounds a potentially worthwhile situation for me to look into, Mr Crossley.'

'I'm sure you'll find we can provide you with a lot of work,' Walter said. 'People always need plumbing.'

'Perhaps you could show me your workshop.'

'Happy to do that, Mr Callan.'

'Do call me Riley. I feel as if you're talking to my grand-father if you say Mr Callan.'

'Riley it is, then, lad.' After a pause, he added, 'Another thing I'm working on is our lake. I'm trying to get it finished properly, so that it'll give people who live in nearby towns somewhere to go at weekends and if we allow a shop or café to stay open then, they'll buy refreshments and bring money into the valley. It could be pretty to walk round or picnic near if the improvements that were started were to be completed. Besides, our local people need something to be proud of.'

'We saw the lake from the train,' Lillian said. 'I love looking at fresh water. There was only a canal where I used to live and its water always looked opaque and dirty. My grandma used to say that clear water sparkles like silver in the moonlight and gold in the sun.'

'What a lovely way to describe it! Our lake used to be called Randall's Pond but no one knows nowadays who this Randall was, so we renamed it Jubilee Lake in honour of the Queen's Jubilee. It used to be much smaller with swampy edges and it didn't do much sparkling until the townsfolk got together to improve it. We cleared out most of the reeds and dug it out to make the lake bigger.'

He shook his head sadly. 'Unfortunately we didn't get it finished for the dear Queen's Golden Jubilee because of the outbreaks of Russian influenza. Perhaps we'll manage it for her Diamond Jubilee if she lives that long. I've still not given up on that.'

Maude turned to Lillian. 'There are paths all the way round the lake now except at the top end, though some parts are a bit rough so you need sturdy shoes to walk there. Elinor and I sometimes go round it on a fine day. You'd be welcome to join us if you like walking.'

'I'd love to do that. I really enjoy going for walks.' It had kept her sane for the past few years and she'd always been able to prove that she'd been to the library by changing her books or going shopping for food. The Thurstens hadn't guessed that she'd sometimes walked much further than necessary, just to stay away from her husband.

'Then we'll arrange to do it,' Maude said.

At the far side of the village Walter reined the mare to a halt on a gentle slope and pointed to the left, where three cottages were standing quite close together. 'The one standing alone at the higher end belongs to me, Mrs Hesketh, and it's not only vacant but partly furnished still. The other two belong to the Ollerton estate.'

She studied the top one, liking what she saw. It could have been pretty if its garden had been better cared for, as the others were.

'It was occupied by a young family,' he went on, 'but when the mother died suddenly, the father took his children back to live with his parents in Manchester because they were still very young and he couldn't care for them himself as well as earn a living. He took most of his furniture and household goods but left a few oddments because he didn't need everything.'

'That must have been sad for him.' She cocked her head to one side and studied the house again. 'The outside could be made nice quite easily and I enjoy gardening, but I'd have to see inside as well.' She needed to find a place where she felt safe on her own but didn't like to admit that to strangers. 'Does it have an inside bathroom?'

'Er, no. Well, not yet anyway.'

'Oh dear. Living on my own, I'd not like to have to walk outside to a privy after dark with such an open back garden, I must admit. And I'd not find it easy to lug a tin bath in and out on my own, either.' Was she being too picky? Well, she didn't care. She wanted to find somewhere she could live peacefully and happily for years.

'I could have a bathroom installed for you if you were going to rent it. I'm gradually modernising the houses I own as I rent them out, but I don't do it while they're standing empty.

I could bring you down to look inside tomorrow if you like the looks of it. You can even see the lake in the distance from the far end of the back garden because it's set on rising ground.'

'I do like the looks of it,' she admitted.

Walter turned his head to grin at Riley. 'What are you like at installing bathrooms from scratch, Mr Callan?'

'I've done quite a lot of that sort of work. I enjoy it because it makes people so happy.'

'Well, there you are, then. Your first job is already waiting for you if you fancy moving here.'

Walter didn't wait for an answer but clicked to the pony to continue. 'I showed you that house, Mrs Hesketh, because you said you wanted a bigger garden and I thought a woman on her own might feel safer in a cottage with neighbours close by than in one standing on its own.'

'You're right, Mr Crossley.' Oh, she did hope the house would be nice inside.

It didn't take long to drive up the gentle slope to a crossroads. Walter stopped again there, pointing to the right. 'That's my farm.'

'What a pretty building!' Lillian exclaimed involuntarily.

'I think so. It's been in my family for nearly two hundred years, though my great-grandfather added a new wing to house his big family. Mostly girls, so unfortunately they moved away once they married.'

He pointed to the left. 'That track used to lead to the local manor house but sadly, it burned down about twenty years ago. There's a new owner just turned up, one of the original Ollerton family. He arrived in the valley a few days ago and is living temporarily in that cottage, which used to be the gate-keeper's lodge. He says he's going to rebuild the big house. I sincerely hope he does. It would be a real boost for our valley and provide employment for a few years building it, then need servants and gardeners afterwards. He seems a nice chap. I'll introduce you at teatime. He's been having his evening meal with us each day while the agent's house is repaired for him to move into.'

'You seem to be taking all the new arrivals under your wing,' Lillian commented. 'That's very kind of you.'

Walter shrugged, looking slightly embarrassed. 'I try to do my bit for my fellow human beings.' He shook the reins and his pony obligingly turned to the right and moved towards the farm. Without needing any further guidance she trotted round to the back and stopped.

Walter got down and offered her a rather battered carrot, which he'd pulled out of his pocket. 'Lovely girl, this one. Been with me for five years. I could go to sleep on the cart and she'd still get me home safely. A motor car couldn't do that, could it?'

Another young woman came out to help them unload the shopping and was introduced as Walter's grandson's wife.

Elinor greeted with a serene smile the news that they'd have two guests staying for a few nights, as if having visitors suddenly imposed on her was an everyday occurrence.

The kitchen was huge and the minute she walked into it, Lillian felt more at home than she ever had in the house she'd shared with her husband for those long, dreary years. Families had enjoyed living here, you could tell. It was as if their happiness had been embedded in the walls of the big, comfortable room, which had a window at each end, one showing views up towards the moors and one looking down towards the town.

Riley was staring round, half smiling as if he too liked the farmhouse.

As they were taking their coats off, she seized the opportunity to whisper, 'I'd rather not tell them how recently my husband died.'

'I can understand that. He sounds to me to be best forgotten.'

Riley hadn't looked at all disapproving so she relaxed still further.

10

When Edward woke he couldn't work out where he was and jerked instinctively into a sitting position to scan his surroundings. After a few seconds it all came rushing back to him. He was still at the lodge but some of his furniture had arrived yesterday so he'd had his own comfortable bed put upstairs in a proper bedroom.

He smiled at that thought. Well, this bedroom was 'proper' if you didn't mind a small room with no curtains at the window and bare though well-scrubbed boards on the floor. But who was there to see him from out there in the grounds? No one, that's who. The nearest dwelling to this small cottage was Crossley's farm, which was about five hundred yards away and after that there were a few cottages further down the hill fronting on the only road up the valley, a road that wasn't even covered in tarmac at this upper end, or 'made up' as the locals called it.

He didn't have to rush to get up because the repairs to this cottage were finished for the time being and the two men from the village had started the bigger job of sorting out the far more serious problems in the larger agent's house, which was another few hundred yards away along the track. That house had four bedrooms, a proper sitting room and would, he was determined, have a proper inside bathroom as soon as this man Walter had told him about, who'd just arrived in the valley, could set up his plumbing business and fit him into the work schedule. In fact, he'd get interior bathrooms put into both dwellings.

He snuggled down again, enjoying the utter comfort after several nights of sleeping on a thin mattress on a borrowed iron bedframe pushed against the wall at one side of the kitchen. That bed was now temporarily gracing the second bedroom, though he didn't expect to have any guests staying with him for a long time.

He'd spent the evening sitting in comfort in his own armchair, reading by the light of a good oil lamp, and for the first time since coming to the valley he'd slept right through the night.

He listened to the dawn chorus of birds singing in his grounds. It was beautifully peaceful here away from crowded towns.

Then he had to get up and use the outside privy, which always annoyed him. That side of life had been a lot more civilised in the towns. One of the few things he'd decided about the new manor house was that there would be more than just a couple of bathrooms put in. At least four! Sheer extravagance but hang the expense. He'd need one or two for the family, one for guests and one for the servants.

There were some wonderful modern inventions these days for people's homes. They'd even had electric light installed over a decade ago at a big house in Northumberland called Cragside. He'd read about it and since then he'd heard about electric lighting being put in elsewhere in the north. It wasn't common yet but it would be, he was sure. He'd seen for himself that it provided a far better light than gas did and was much cleaner, too, and yet, even gas was better than oil lamps, with the tedious work of cleaning them and checking the gas mantles every day.

He had such big dreams for the new Ollerton House, wanted to leave his descendants with a home to be proud of – if he ever had any descendants.

After he'd boiled a kettle and had an all-over wash at the kitchen sink, he made some toast on the fire, something he was an expert at by now, then ate a slice of excellent Lancashire cheese and crunched a rosy apple to finish off with. Maude had suggested he boil a couple of eggs in the mornings or fry a piece of ham but he couldn't be bothered fiddling about. At least toast didn't leave you with a lot of messy pans and splattered fat to clear up.

He wondered what to do with his day. It still felt strange having nothing urgent to attend to. He'd wanted to live more quietly when he came here but not as quietly as this. He couldn't sit around for the rest of his life and there was a limit to how many cycle rides you wanted to undertake, plus he didn't even attempt to do that on rainy days.

He really must find an architect to design and supervise the building of a new house. He felt as impatient to find someone as he had once felt about moving here after he'd bought the estate back. He laughed at himself for that.

While the building work was going on he'd get some of the grounds looking more civilised. But he'd need help for that too because he'd never had time to muck about in gardens and didn't understand the practical details.

He wanted to create some interesting walks leading up towards the moors which bordered the upper end of his estate. And before winter struck, with its rain and snow, he'd indulge in some long tramps up there purely for his own pleasure and let the wind blow away years of working in stuffy offices. Even outside his front door the air was so clean you could taste the difference from that in towns.

As he strolled around outside he suddenly remembered the two little girls he'd seen playing with whips and tops in Ollerthwaite a couple of days ago. He'd stopped to watch them, thinking how innocently happy they looked.

People said women longed for children. Well, men did too, he was sure. He desperately wanted some of his own now that he had the estate back, was more than ready to marry and, he hoped, produce them. But first he had to find a wife and that wasn't going to be easy.

His parents had been mismatched and had rarely had a day without a quarrel. Even now he remembered that with a grimace. He didn't intend to marry a woman who would make his life a misery or one who couldn't give him children. Thank goodness he'd lived with his maternal grandparents for part of his youth and seen what a happy marriage could be like.

Twice over the years he'd met a woman he thought might suit him, but then found that one woman was modifying her behaviour and restraining her temper in order to get herself a wealthy husband, and that any husband with money would have done. The second woman had been gentle and sweet-faced but not very clever, and had soon bored him to tears. He wanted a wife he could converse with intelligently.

He'd have to set about finding a wife now, though, before it was too late to have children. He'd seek compatibility of temperament and enjoyment of one another's company, and never mind how she looked. If there were such a person.

And of course, he was assuming he would be able to attract someone suitable. He wasn't good looking; none of the Oller-tons were with their lean faces and hawklike noses. His hair was getting a little thinner on top, too, and was speckled with grey. But he didn't think he was ugly either. How did you know? He had so little experience with women.

He continued to walk to and fro in the area nearest to the ruins of the old house as he considered the situation, because he always thought better when he was moving about.

Then he stopped abruptly as he saw the remains of foot-prints, which looked quite recent. Those under a group of trees must have been protected from the weather but the trail vanished in the open patches of land except for an occa-sional partial footprint. They all seemed to have been made by the same person. Who had been poking about round here recently? And why?

At midday Edward made himself a few sandwiches and ate a big chunk of cake from the baker's shop, after which he sat down at the kitchen table and began to draft another letter to his lawyer asking him to find an architect as soon as possible as he was now ready to make a proper start. He'd already mentioned the desire to find one but wanted Mr Filmore to know he was now eager to begin in earnest.

Once he was satisfied with his letter, he wrote his final version out neatly and stored the rough draft in the box he would have to use until he had a bigger room to put his desk in.

He'd had lodgings furnished by his own pieces and he missed them very much. His former landlady had sent on the first few pieces, like his bed, but there were others he cared for and wanted to have round him.

He cycled into Ollerthwaite to buy some stamps and post the letter, enjoying the ride down the hill because it was sunny today. When he introduced himself to the man behind the counter at the post office so that his incoming mail could be delivered to his temporary home, people nearby stared at him openly.

Then he suddenly noticed that one man was scowling at him from near the door and when their eyes met across the room the fellow actually spat in the way people did when they saw something that upset them. That puzzled him. He'd never met this man, he was sure of that, so why this reaction to his presence?

He knew from his studies of history that sometimes when someone came into an inheritance they might also inherit long-term problems and differing loyalties, but it had been over twenty years since his family had lived here. The Kenyons had taken over but surely no one would blame him for something one of them had done? Since his own parents were dead and his cousin

Della, although related to the Ollertons, was not one herself, she would know less than he did about his family background.

He was tempted to go across and ask the man what was wrong, but before he could do it the fellow suddenly strode out, rudely pushing one customer aside.

He asked the man serving behind the counter who the chap who'd been scowling at him was but neither he nor any of the nearby customers would admit to having noticed him. Which had to be a lie because the fellow had been quite distinctive, with a bald head encircled by a narrow fringe of grey hair, and a small scar drawing up one corner of his mouth slightly.

Was he someone they were afraid of?

Edward didn't like to accuse them of lying nor did he wish to make a public fuss about finding out who the man was. He would keep his eyes open from now on, though. He was bound to see the fellow again in such a small town.

Since he needed to deal with the sheet of stamps he'd bought, he went to the shelf-like surface placed along one side of the area for customers' convenience. He tore off one of the stamps, licked it, grimaced at the taste, and stuck it on the envelope then went outside to post his letter.

He'd asked his lawyer to find an architect quickly if he could and if he didn't know of a suitable person, could he please put an advert in relevant newspapers or journals. And if he got any answers, would Mr Filmore please conduct preliminary checks on anyone who replied, looking into their reputations and willingness to do work in the north.

This was one of the snags of living in an isolated Pennine valley, which didn't have its own local newspaper and didn't even get the day's newspaper until the early afternoon.

Since the sun was shining, Edward then gave in to temptation to do something for pure pleasure and cycled to Jubilee Lake instead of going straight home via the town centre and the main road up the hill.

He had intended to ride all the way round the lake but unfortunately the top end was too rough to cycle along. He turned back and went home via the well-used path that passed a couple of what looked like small farms and then Walter's house.

In the late afternoon Edward smartened himself up and strolled across to enjoy his evening meal at the farm, looking forward most of all to chatting to Walter and his family.

He found two newcomers to the valley newly installed there as guests, more people in need of help, it turned out. The woman seemed at first to be a mousy type with very little to say for herself, but Walter concentrated on the man for a while, getting Riley to talk about his search for somewhere to set up a plumbing business and offering to help in any way he could.

Next Edward watched Walter, backed up by his grandson's wife, Elinor, draw Mrs Hesketh out skilfully to talk about why she'd chosen to come here. He saw her gradually relax with the two of them. Though she didn't say a lot, she did mention wanting to get away from her late husband's family, shuddering visibly as she mentioned them. Walter didn't press her for details of why exactly she'd had to get away.

That was probably why she had been so monosyllabic at first and had watched so intently as their host talked to Riley. She wouldn't have been sure whether she could trust any of them. Edward smiled at that thought. He would guess that most people trusted Walter Crossley instinctively – well, they did if they were normal, decent people.

His host drew him back into the conversation next by saying, 'You and Mrs Hesketh seem to have a lot in common, Edward, even if on a different scale. You're both looking to make a home and excuse me if I'm wrong or being offensive, but a happy home is something neither of you has had for quite a while.'

Edward nodded involuntarily at this and saw her do the same and that sad expression come back to her face, which seemed to give it a lovely, Madonna-like quality.

Walter added, with a pointed look in Riley's direction, 'And both of you are in need of the sort of jobs doing, which our other visitor is expert at. Having an indoor bathroom is becoming everyone's dream these days, it seems. I certainly hope he'll eventually decide that this is a good place to set up his new business.'

Riley said suddenly, 'I'm already of thinking seriously about it, Mr Crossley, especially after your kind offer of help.'

'You've decided it already? Really?' Maude couldn't hide her surprise.

'Yes. I tend to make decisions rapidly. I can usually sense quite quickly when something's wrong but it's harder to be sure something is right. And yet, this time, I feel fairly certain settling here would be the right thing to do.'

Edward was surprised to see Callan's eyes linger on Maude as he spoke. Was he taken by her so quickly? Though he wasn't attracted himself, Edward did consider her a fine woman. And a clever one, too.

'You can never be sure of things going perfectly in this world,' Walter said. 'You just have to do your best with what you choose and with what life dishes out to you as you progress through it.'

Edward couldn't disagree with that. A short time afterwards he watched Maude steal a glance at Riley and turn away quickly when she saw him watching her, as if she didn't want to betray her interest in their guest. It was early days but he envied them finding someone they might want to get to know better, he really did, and hoped things would go well for them.

Then he saw that the quiet lady had noticed the others' unspoken interchange as well and now had a rather envious expression on her face. Even as he watched, she seemed to realise that she was revealing her feelings and schooled her features into their previous calmness. He wondered how calm she really was behind that mask. How long ago had her husband died? Was she still grieving for him?

He heard Walter arrange to take Mrs Hesketh to look at a cottage just downhill from the nearby crossroads the following morning because she was apparently looking for somewhere to live.

She frowned slightly. 'And the inside bathroom?'

'I would have one installed if I had a tenant and could find a plumber with the necessary skills. Do you want that job as your first work in the valley, Mr Callan?'

'Yes, please. In fact, why don't I come with you tomorrow and check the cottage's suitability for modernisation?'

Walter beamed at him. 'Excellent idea.'

Mrs Hesketh brightened visibly and nodded as if approving this.

Edward seized the opportunity. He didn't want to be last in the queue if Riley did set up a business here. 'Perhaps you could come and look at the lodge and the agent's house while you're at it. Both of them need to have modern plumbing installed.'

'Yes. We can come and visit you afterwards,' Walter offered at once. 'In any case, I want to see how the chaps I recommended have done the work on the lodge.'

'I'm pleased with it. They worked hard and quickly.'

'They're both good men.' Walter turned to Lillian. 'You won't mind coming with us afterwards, will you?'

'Of course not. I shall enjoy seeing more of the valley.'

She had a low, musical voice. Edward liked that.

'Good. We'll see you later in the morning then, lad.'

He had to swallow his emotions as he remembered that later. How long was it since anyone except Walter had called him 'lad'? It still touched him greatly, felt so warm and caring.

11

When she got up the following morning Lillian found she was the first person to come down for breakfast so asked Maude what she could do to help get things ready. 'And – and could you please call me Lillian?' she faltered, afraid of a rebuff.

'Happy to. We didn't like to presume.'

Lillian let out her breath in relief, then confessed, 'I'm not used to friendly people and their ways. My husband wasn't very, um, sociable so we lived quietly. He didn't like me to invite anyone into our home except his family, or to go out and visit other women from church, even.'

Maude shot her a quick glance. 'It must have been terribly lonely to live without friends.'

'It was.' Twisting her hands, Lillian gathered her courage together and risked saying, 'It may sound heartless but I felt only relief when he died and I could move away from his family. I hadn't wanted to marry him in the first place, you see.'

'How dreadful for you.' Maude went across and gave her a big hug.

At first Lillian jerked in shock then she clutched the other woman convulsively and hugged her back, resting her head for a moment against the strong shoulder being offered to her.

'I hope you'll be happy here in the valley.' Maude smoothed Lillian's hair back and flicked away one teardrop with her fingertip. Which brought another tear rolling out and led to a second hug.

At the foot of the stairs, Walter had been eavesdropping involuntarily, not liking to interrupt such a delicate exchange and the emotions it had roused. He shook his head, feeling sad for the poor young woman's wasted years. How long ago had her husband died? Not long ago, he guessed. She hadn't recovered from her unhappiness with him yet, that was clear.

He'd always thought there was some sort of magic here in Ollindale. He'd seen the atmosphere in the valley and the friendliness of most people win over Cameron and Elinor earlier this year and lead them quickly into a happy marriage.

He was hoping his cousin Maude would find someone too. She'd make such a good wife and mother if it wasn't too late for her to have a child. He'd noticed how Riley looked at her yesterday evening. It was too soon to know if this attraction would lead anywhere but he could hope, couldn't he?

Perhaps the atmosphere in the valley and the friendliness of most of its inhabitants would help heal Lillian as well. If he could do anything to help her towards a happier life, he would.

As he tried to judge whether it was safe to join the two women in the kitchen he hoped that one day their visitor would tell him the whole story. He was a firm believer in talking about things that had upset you. He'd learned that the hard way after his son and grandson had been killed in an accident the previous year. He'd kept his misery to himself and it had weighed him down. He'd almost turned into a hermit when it came to meeting people, though he'd still tried to help those he could.

Then Maude and Elinor had taken refuge with him, needing his help, and Cam – the grandson he hadn't even known he had – had arrived on their doorstep. Their presence had made a wonderful difference to his life.

He smiled wryly at the thought that one of the delights of being old was that you could interfere more easily and if you had a little spare money, people rarely dared tell you to mind your own business when you offered them advice or practical help.

Ah! The sounds of crockery being set out and the faint sizzling of something cooking told him that confidences were over, at least for the time being, so he went into the kitchen to join the two women.

Riley came down soon afterwards, his eyes going to Maude before anyone else. When he saw that, Walter crossed his fingers under the table.

After breakfast he said to his visitors, 'Shall we leave to look at the house now? We could leave in about ten minutes? If that's all right with you, I'll go and harness Jenny.'

They both nodded and went to collect their outdoor things.

When Lillian came downstairs again, Maude took one look at her dowdy old-fashioned hat and had to control a desperate urge to grab it and throw it on the fire.

'I can't find my hatpin and I wondered if you had a spare one I could borrow, Maude? This hat blows off easily but I left in a hurry and it's the only one I brought with me.'

'I always wear a beret when I'm out and about. That stays on much more easily. Why don't I lend you one of mine?'

'I can't impose.'

'You keep saying that. It's not an imposition to borrow something more suitable when it's offered. One day I may need help from you and then you'll pay me back.'

Lillian took a deep breath and said, 'I'd be very grateful for the loan, then.'

'And would you mind if I dispose of this horrible thing?'

'What?'

Maude gave in to temptation, grabbed the ghastly hat and tossed it into the heart of the fire in the kitchen range. 'That's all it deserves. Whoever helped you choose it wasn't doing you a favour.'

Lillian was still gaping at the fire. She wrinkled her nose at the smell of felt burning. 'It was my mother-in-law who chose it. She said it was respectable.'

'Well, it may be, but it's one of the ugliest, most unflattering hats I've ever seen in my life. I'll just get a beret for you and you can keep it. I have several.'

When Maude came down she watched Lillian put the beret on, then stepped forward and moved it to a more rakish tilt before inserting the hatpin. 'There. That's how you should wear it. You look much younger and prettier now.'

Lillian stole a quick glance in the mirror, her mouth curving into an involuntary smile at the sight of her improved appearance. Then she looked at the remains of the hat, still burning slowly, and chuckled. That made her companion follow suit and they both had a hearty laugh.

'Well worth the horrible smell.' Maude opened the door to let in some fresh air and get rid of the acrid odour.

Walter watched Lillian come outside, delighted that she wasn't wearing yesterday's sad lump of dark grey felt on her head. He saw Riley study her too and nod as if in approval of her improved appearance. He didn't look at her like he looked at Maude, though. Good.

They all three squashed together on the driver's bench and Walter signalled to the pony to set off. 'It's not far down the hill to the cottage, if you remember. We could easily have walked there from the farm but we'll be calling in at the lodge afterwards and then going along to the agent's house, and who knows where else we may need to go to find you a new home, Mrs Hesketh, so I thought it better to take the cart.'

A few minutes later they stopped in front of the nearest of the three cottages, which had a shoulder-high wall separating it from the next pair and continuing around all sides of the garden.

He gestured towards the houses. 'The other two estate cottages are rented out to some very nice older people who work in Upperfold. I'm sure you'll get on well with them if you come to live here, Mrs Hesketh. All three houses have bigger than usual areas of land at the back but as you can see, this one's gardens are in a sad state after months of neglect.'

He got down and the other two followed suit. 'We can leave Jenny here. She won't move away with that nice patch of grass to nibble at.'

He led the way along the path and unlocked the front door. 'I'll show you round quickly, then, if you're interested, leave you to study the interior more carefully on your own, Mrs Hesketh. I'm not in a hurry.'

Her voice was almost a whisper and it shook a little as she asked, 'Could you – would you mind calling me Lillian? I notice you all use each other's first names.'

'Of course. I was only waiting for you to ask me. It's a pretty name. And you'll call me Walter, naturally.'

From the way she'd asked, he guessed it had taken a lot of courage. Eh, the poor woman must have been badly bullied for years to be so afraid of offending anyone. Still, she had said it, hadn't she? That was a step forward, rather like a butterfly starting to break out of its chrysalis and then gradually crawling out fully and spreading its wings. What would she be like when she spread her wings? He was looking forward to finding out.

The interior of the cottage was slightly dusty but when he pulled the frayed old curtains back, the windows let in plenty of light. The sitting room was quite large for a cottage and their footsteps echoed on the bare boards. At the moment it only contained a couple of armchairs, which looked as if they'd been left behind because they were tired and shabby, nearing the end of their useful life.

He watched her turn slowly round on the spot, then nod approvingly. Riley winked at him when he saw that.

They went back through the narrow hall into a large kitchen with an old-fashioned scrubbed wooden table still in place at one end. It looked as if it was waiting for at least ten people to come and enjoy a meal on it again, Walter thought every time he saw it.

There was an adjoining scullery and off the hall at the far end, entered under a sloping ceiling caused by the stairs, there was another much smaller room, which jutted out into the garden at the rear corner. A small structure that was obviously the lavatory stood so close to the window it blocked out half the light. The person who'd built it there must have been an idiot, he always thought, because its visible presence made this a much less pleasant room.

He gestured round them. 'I thought this might make a good bathroom. Would that be practical, do you think, Riley?'

He looked round, then nodded. 'It's an excellent idea. The water and sewage pipes can't be too far away if that's the lavatory. I'll go outside and check that in a minute.'

'It certainly wouldn't be a pleasant room to sit in as it is,' Lillian said and the two men murmured agreement.

The stairs led up to two bedrooms with dormer windows, smaller than the rooms below. One looked out to the front and the other to the back. The rear one contained a single bed with a sagging mattress and a battered chest of drawers. The latter had a couple of the drawer handles missing and a circular burn mark on the top.

When they went back downstairs Riley went outside and left the others to discuss what they'd seen.

Walter asked gently, 'Do you want to look round again on your own, Lillian? Or is it not your sort of house? I shan't be upset if it isn't. I have a few others I could show you, though none with such a large garden.'

'It's a lovely house, but I need to get the feel of it on my own, if you don't mind.'

'You go ahead and do that, lass. I'll see how Riley's investigation into the possible plumbing linkages is coming along. You are on mains water and the valley's sewage system here, at least, but I don't know where exactly the pipes lie. The town council had a reservoir built up beyond my farm by damming the river some decades ago.'

Lillian watched him leave. She felt quite sure he'd keep his word about installing a bathroom.

Seeing that both men were busy outside now, gesturing and pointing, she took a deep breath and closed her eyes, not moving but simply finding out how she felt by standing in the kitchen on her own. She did that in each room because her secret worry had been whether she would feel safe living alone.

To her relief she felt quite comfortable here. In fact the house felt cosy and 'right' in every way, or it would once the bathroom was in. There were strong locks on both outer doors, which was important, though she'd ask for bolts to be put on them as well because she didn't think she'd ever feel completely safe again without such precautions, as she couldn't help worrying that her in-laws would still try to hunt her down.

She realised her mind was wandering and forced herself to concentrate on the house again. She liked the way the windows had criss-cross leading. There was even a little stained glass panel in the front door at head height through which you could make out who was knocking. It sent a stream of rich ruby, gold and blue light flooding across one wall of the hall at this time of day. She went closer and held out one hand, letting the colours play on her skin then clicked her tongue in annoyance at herself. She shouldn't waste time on such childish play.

She went upstairs and stood in each of the bedrooms in turn. The odd pieces of furniture that had been left were old and shabby but they would save her money till she could afford better things, so she wasn't too proud to accept them.

When she brought the furniture she'd inherited to Ollindale, the house would look a lot better downstairs especially.

She went outside at the rear and was glad to hear the men's voices coming from round the front now because she wanted to explore the garden on her own as well as the house. She liked the way it sloped upwards in several well-defined shallow steps, each level held in place by a single row of large stones. She could arrange a vegetable garden very nicely out here.

How would it feel to stand right at the top? She set off to find out.

When Walter went back inside through the front door to look for Lillian, Riley went round to the back again and saw her moving slowly upwards, nearly at the top of the long, narrow garden. He watched her stop suddenly and reached up to push a branch aside and pluck what looked like an apple from among the leaves of the tree. After smiling down at it she began polishing it slowly and absent-mindedly against her coat.

As she let go of the branch it knocked her beret to one side and some of her hair came loose from its tight bun. The sun was shining brightly now and he could see that her hair was a lovely chestnut brown, falling in a mass of shining waves across one shoulder till she fumbled for it and pinned it up again. Pity. That had made her look younger.

If she'd been his sister he'd have told her not to wear it scraped back so tightly. None of the women of her age that he knew would be seen dead with such an unflattering and old-fashioned style of bun.

She continued up the last few yards to the very top of the garden and stood at the wall there, staring across what must be the grounds of the Ollerton estate.

Riley was about to go up and join her when Walter came out of the house again, looking round the garden.

He saw Lillian and smiled. 'She looks relaxed and happy out here, doesn't she?'

'Yes.'

'Everything all right with the plumbing, lad?'

'Yes. It'll be easy to put in a bathroom quickly if you don't mind giving up that small room at the back. It'd be a bit big for a bathroom, so we could maybe make a big cupboard out of what's left of the space, a full-length one with a door opening into the corridor. That'd be easy enough to do.'

Walter nodded.

'And we can connect the present lavatory to the bathroom by building a small hall between them and putting a doorway in the wall of the new bathroom. That shouldn't be expensive to build if you know a good bricklayer. We shan't need any extra windows because there's a small high one in the lavatory and one in the room. A flat roof on the corridor will do. No one will even see it from the main road.'

Walter slapped one hand against the other. 'We'll do it that way, then. I know chaps who can do small jobs like the bricklaying if you can tell them exactly what's needed and then keep an eye on them.'

'You'll need council permission to do it.'

'I'll have a word with a friend on the council to make sure it'll be all right to make the alterations and put in an application. They want to encourage newcomers to move to the valley so they won't try to block anything if it's done according to the rules. But don't put in anything fancy. I'm not made of money.'

'And a bathroom suite? Where do people buy them round here? How much do you want to spend on one?'

'I bought several of them a couple of years ago at a bargain price from the widow of a plumber who'd died suddenly so I've already got a few. The suites and taps are nothing fancy but they'll do the job. Ironically enough, I don't have an inside bathroom on my farm yet. I must look into that now you're here.'

'You having the bathroom suite makes it even easier to do the work quickly. Can I borrow your cart to bring it here?'

'Yes, of course.'

Lillian came down the garden towards the house, looking genuinely calm now. 'I like this cottage and the garden very much, Mr – I mean, Walter. Can I really keep all the odds and ends of furniture left behind?'

'Yes, of course. Saves me the trouble of carting them away.'

'And the bathroom?'

Riley explained how he could fit one quite easily and that brought a happy smile to her face.

'Any idea how long it'll take you?' Walter asked him.

'A few days once you've checked with the local authorities. Getting permission to make changes usually takes longer than a day or two, though.'

Walter grinned. 'Not in Ollerthwaite, it doesn't, especially as I'm on the council. That's one of the benefits of living in a small town.'

He turned to Lillian. 'You can move in as soon as the bathroom is finished, my dear, and you're welcome to stay with us till then.'

She hesitated then said in a rush, 'I'd rather move in straight away and manage without the bathroom for a few days. That is, if I wouldn't be in your way, Riley? I have some other furniture, a few pieces my godmother left me that my husband's family didn't find out about. My lawyer said he'd arrange to have them sent to me once I was settled. So I shall only need to buy a new mattress and some sheets and blankets for that old bedframe, oh, and a few kitchen chairs to use with that table you're leaving me.'

'I can probably sell you some chairs more cheaply than you'd find them in the shops if you don't mind second-hand ones.

I have an old sofa too, if you'd like it. It's just taking up space in the unoccupied house I use for storing things at the moment.'

'I shan't mind second-hand things at all, especially if they're cheaper.'

'Good. It'd be no trouble for you to stay with us till the alterations are done, though.'

She hesitated then told him the truth. 'I'm eager to make a home of my own, Walter. It's been my secret dream for such a long time that I shan't believe it's really happened till I'm living here. You've made me very welcome and I'm grateful but, well, I'd like my own home now.'

He took hold of her hand and patted it. 'Let's make your dreams come true then, lass. I'll help you move in tomorrow and I'll give you some of my collection of worn sheets and blankets as a present. They've still got some wear in them and I had them washed when the owners died or moved away, but they may need a bit of mending. And we'll see how we can help with whatever else you need, oddments of crockery and so on. I sell miscellaneous household oddments in my little shop for a pound each box, which include oddments of crockery and napery. You might find one or two of those useful.'

'Thank you so much. That all sounds a wonderful help. I'll be grateful for anything you can give me.' Her voice came out as a choke on the last words.

'I shan't need my pony and cart this afternoon so I'll let my lasses use it to take you to the house where I store things that are too worn to sell but too good to throw away. They'll enjoy sorting stuff out with you. Then you can go on to my little store in Upperfold and choose some boxes of cheap oddments if they seem useful. It's not far away from the farm and your new home.'

She took another deep happy breath at the last word. *Home!* It was a minute or two before she could continue speaking.

'That all sounds wonderful. And . . . there's one other thing. Do you think . . . Is it hard to learn to ride a bicycle?'

She suddenly sounded breathless and anxious again, he thought. The poor lass had so little confidence in herself. 'It's not hard at all, just takes a little practice. Were you thinking of buying one?'

'I was wondering if I could find a cheap, second-hand one. I can't afford to be extravagant, but I do have a little money saved and a bicycle would be such a big help for shopping and getting around.' She'd stood at her bedroom window watching other women ride them for years, feeling so envious as they sailed past her house in the street. Having one had been a very small dream but she hoped she would be able to make it come true.

'We'll get Maude to teach you how to ride a bike and I can speak to Peter who sells them. I'm sure he'll be able to find you a cheap one. We've bought all our family's bicycles from him. Anything he sells you would be sound, even if not new, I promise.'

She beamed at him. 'That'll be wonderful. Thank you so much, Walter. I'm really grateful for all your help. Oh – what about rent? I was so excited I forgot to ask how much it is.'

He told her, watching her reaction carefully. 'Is that all right with you?'

'Yes, that'll be fine. In fact, are you sure it's enough?'

He hoped he sounded convincing. 'Oh, yes. I just need to pay myself back gradually for what I'll be spending on the cottage. It'll be good not to have it standing empty, especially in winter, and you being there will save me coming round regularly to check it.'

'Oh, good. I'll take great care of it, I promise you. It feels as if it's been a happy home for years.'

'Yes. I thought that too when I bought it. Even though the lady who lived there died suddenly, they'd been a happy family until then. It always seems to me that houses are similar to people; they don't like to feel lonely and unwanted.'

She gave him one of her solemn nods.

He gestured to the apple she was still clutching. 'They're a bit tart but they're good for eating or cooking. Try it.'

So she crunched her way through the apple as they all squashed onto the driving bench again and went back up the slope, turning left at the crossroads towards Edward's house this time.

As they arrived she looked at the core and said, 'I think that was the nicest apple I've ever eaten.'

'You can toss the core in the pig bin at the farm. We don't waste any food if we can help it. The pigs at the next farm love our leftovers.'

Walter exchanged quick smiles with Riley. Was it his imagination or was she looking almost pretty today? Eh, she was like a plant that hadn't been watered for a while and now someone was giving it a little care, it was starting to grow properly again.

Give her a bit of attention and who knew what she'd do with her life? She wasn't stupid, on the contrary, but she was still afraid to be herself.

12

Riley studied the lodge as they turned left towards it at the crossroads. There was a space in front of it he assumed had been for callers to stop at before they went to the big house. Where they were directed to go next by the lodge keeper would have depended on whether they were guests of the family or tradespeople delivering goods. The track leading to it from the crossroads looked as if it had just been levelled and wasn't used very often.

His mind was now on the possibility of the other, bigger plumbing job, which would give him a good start at setting up on his own, and then Walter wanted work doing at his farmhouse. If he got busy, he'd need somewhere to work and keep his tools, so as long as Walter's workshop was suitable for his initial needs he'd rent it. Walter had already offered to lend him a few of the common tools Riley would need for Lillian's job till his own could be sent on.

He'd have to get his specialist tools back as soon as possible, though, not to mention his other possessions. A friend in Oldham had been looking after them while he was out of the country and they were packed in boxes ready to be sent as soon as he knew where he'd be living. A quick telegram would hopefully bring them here within two or three days.

He'd go into town this afternoon and send the telegram. He wanted to settle here and not just because of the work available. He liked the little town but more importantly, he'd like to get to know Maude better. She was a fine-looking woman and so cheerful with it, she'd lifted his spirits every time she'd chatted to him. Not that he was downhearted, but she seemed to make the world a happier place. That would be nice to live with.

Walter pointed towards the lodge as they drew to a halt. 'This is where Edward wants a bathroom installing as soon as possible. It's the smaller of the two houses, just a cottage really. It needed only a few repairs to make it habitable so he's had them done and moved in for the time being, but it hasn't got an inside bathroom.'

He smiled conspiratorially. 'I doubt he's lived without one for a good many years.'

Riley chuckled. Once people had enjoyed that sort of amenity they didn't want to go back to the old ways.

'The other house hasn't got inside facilities either. It's a few hundred yards further along this track behind those trees so you can't see all of it yet. It's much bigger but it needed several repairs to make it fully weatherproof and further repairs doing to the interior where it's had serious leaks in the roof. That useless agent did nothing about them, was too busy stealing things and cheating his employers.'

Riley winced at the mere thought of anyone being so careless about looking after a house. One day he intended to own a place of his own, not just rent it. He'd make it modern and bright, and then care for it and his family properly. He'd seen enough of the world now and all he needed to settle down was to find the right woman.

His thoughts paused there. He hoped he wasn't mistaken but he might have found her already. Amazing how quickly he'd been attracted to Maude.

'We need to speak to Edward first, Walter, and confirm exactly what he wants, then I'll have to check both houses and find out whether the necessary services are available nearby.'

'I should think they are since they're there at Lillian's house. I'm hoping it'll be quite easy to fit a bathroom into the smaller house and to add a geyser to provide a better hot water supply to it and one for the kitchen too while you're at it. He may not have thought of that, but his servants will expect one.'

Walter shook his head. 'I should have had all the services extended to the farm while I was at it, but I was a bit short of money just then because I was helping a few people stay in the valley. I'm going to have gas taken up to the farm now that I've got my finances in order and I shan't over-extend myself ever again.'

'It seems to me you've been a force for progress in the valley.'

Walter shrugged away the compliment. 'I do my best. Anyway, we were discussing Edward's needs. He isn't happy going back to what sanitation and plumbing were like in his childhood. We're lagging behind in some of the modern ways of living here in the valley, but it's worse for Edward after he's lived in town with all the comforts of running water, gas lighting and servants, not to mention shops and cafés nearby. He was excited to come back to his childhood home, but the reality of how much he needs to do here to live comfortably while he builds the new house is beginning to sink in.'

Riley nodded. 'I'm not skimping on the work needed for Lillian or anyone else, so if he wants me to do his jobs he'll have to wait till I've finished putting in the bathroom for her. I can make a start on the digging needed at the back of her house this afternoon, but I shall go into town first to send a telegram. I need to get my own tools back before I can do some of the more skilled inside work.'

'Well, borrow any of my tools that you can use till yours arrive.'

'Thanks. And you'll find a bricklayer to put up the connecting walls for the lavatory?'

'Yes, of course. I know exactly who I'll ask.'

Riley frowned. 'Which reminds me: you said you had a workshop in Upperfold that I could rent. That's good but I shall need somewhere to live as well.'

'The workshop has a room at the back where the previous owner lived. It's not up to much but it's clean, with a fireplace and a sink, plus an outside convenience in the back yard. And I know a woman who lives nearby and will do your cooking and wash your clothes. You could manage there for the time being until you make up your mind where you want to live permanently, perhaps?'

'Is there any problem you can't solve, Walter Crossley?'

The older man looked sad for a moment or two. 'Oh, yes,' he said softly. 'Some things are immutable.' He fell silent briefly then shook his head to banish what looked to be sad memories and continued the discussion. 'Don't rush things when you start work on Edward's bathrooms. It's important to get them done perfectly, if that's possible, because people will ask him if he's been satisfied with your work. Once it's known that you've done two jobs for the new owner of the Ollerton estate, and that he's extremely happy with your work, other folk will come knocking on your door, trust me. But put my house next after his, if you please.'

Riley smiled confidently. 'I'll do that. I promise you that I'm a good plumber and I never skimp on any job. The work will help me get my business up and running properly, but I have other ideas I want to follow up as well, long term.'

'Can I ask what?'

'Not yet, if you don't mind. I'm still working them out and negotiating with someone who's thinking of joining me.'

'The more people who come to the valley the better. And going back to Edward, you should charge him slightly more for his two jobs than you charge me for Lillian's house and my own. Not badly overcharge but he can well afford to pay a bit more and you'll be rushing your start-up to suit him, after all. If I sell you the bathroom fittings for his places, I shall charge you more for those than I would if it were a job for a poorer man.'

He held up one hand to prevent Riley speaking. 'That's not because I'm greedy but because it'll add to the money I'll have available for helping others in need. I don't have unlimited funds so I need to stretch what I've got as far as I can. We're not a rich community here but at least we've stopped losing our population to other towns, except for the normal coming and going.'

Riley nodded. He'd bet Walter was partly responsible for that. He'd heard what Lillian would be charged in rent and wondered if she realised how low that was. He looked sideways at her. She was deep in thought, but with a happy expression on her face now, not a worried one. If he'd ever had a sister, he'd have wanted someone like her.

Helping her escape had brought the two of them close together more quickly than usual for strangers. She was such a nice, gentle person, but not the sort of woman he was attracted to because she was too small and quiet. He preferred women like Maude: taller, lively, outgoing. He was going to be busy on those bathrooms, but he was going to make time to get to know her better, by hell he was.

Regretfully he pushed the thought of her aside as Edward came out of the lodge to greet them. It was Lillian to whom Edward spoke first, however, which surprised Riley.

'How did it go? Have you found a home?'

She beamed at him. 'Yes. It's a dear little cottage and it's going to have a lovely garden when I'm done with it. It goes right up to your boundary wall.'

'So we'll be neighbours and I'll be able to wave to you as I walk past.'

'Or come in for a cup of tea.'

Walter saw Edward look at her in surprise. No wonder. He was surprised too. Had they only arrived here a few days ago? She seemed to be changing already from the self-effacing mouse of a woman Riley had rescued and brought to the valley. Today's woman was definitely pretty. It was as if finding a home had made her open up like a flower.

Eh, he was getting fanciful today. Only, it felt so good to make people happy. Even helping make the tiniest improvement to someone's life gave his own spirits a lift too. Besides, he'd fallen lucky with these two in other ways, because not only had he found a tenant for another of his empty houses but also a plumber had turned up just when they needed one round here.

As Edward waited for them to get off the cart, his attention turned to Riley. 'I'll show you round the two buildings and then perhaps you'd tell me how quickly you can do the jobs and what you'll charge.' His voice was more decisive than it had been when speaking to Lillian. In fact, he sounded like a capable man dealing with business matters, rather than a gentle friend.

'I know very little about plumbing so I shall take Lillian for a stroll while you two are conferring,' Walter said quickly.

After a surprised glance at him Riley turned back to Edward.

'I can sit here quite happily if you'd rather go with the other men, Walter,' Lillian whispered. 'Look, there's a bench over there.'

She'd got some of that anxious look back, as if she was afraid of upsetting him. He didn't like to see that.

'I'd far rather go for a walk with you, my dear. Talking about plumbing isn't my favourite way of passing the time and I was telling the truth when I said that I have no practical expertise to contribute to the details.'

He offered her his arm and she took it. As they set off, he saw that the other two men were already speaking earnestly and gesticulating as they moved towards the front door of the lodge.

Walter didn't hurry, stopping to look round every now and then because he was usually in too much of a hurry to do that when he came to the Ollerton estate. Lillian seemed content to stroll at whatever pace suited him, though she did slow down once of her own accord and touch a bush with gentle fingertips.

'What a shame that this bush has been neglected when all it needs is a careful pruning.'

She sounded as if she really did know about gardening and she had touched the bush with loving fingertips, as he thought of them when he saw the way some people behaved in their gardens.

After a while she stopped and turned slowly in a circle on the spot, as if studying that particular part of the garden. 'Why did someone look after the bushes near the house and not the ones further away? It wouldn't have taken much more effort.'

'The Rainfords lived here and did what they could, but they're both quite old and don't have as much energy as you young folk, and they find it harder to bend down.'

'Where are they now? Did they die?'

'No. The agent was being unkind to them so we found them a nice cottage further up the river, near the old water mill. They're enjoying setting a much smaller garden in order. They can manage that quite easily and enjoy their produce. Their nephew takes them food and other people chip in too.'

She gave him a sideways glance as if guessing he'd been instrumental in looking after them and was still helping feed them.

As he looked round he could only agree with her about the grounds, though. Most parts not close to the house had been shamefully neglected for many years. 'This garden used to be so pretty when the Ollertons lived here. The Kenyons dismissed all but one gardener and let things he couldn't manage go wild. They allowed the Rainfords to continue to live in the lodge at a reduced wage on condition that they kept the area near it tidy, but the poor things struggled to keep themselves fed on so little money. After the Kenyons left, Hatton never did a thing in the gardens and no one from the family came to check whether as their agent he was reporting truthfully to them.'

'The shrubberies could be brought back in order again quite easily.'

'Yes, I can see that but I think Edward is a bit of a townie where plants are concerned, unlike you, so who's to do it all? It's surprising how many of the bushes have managed to survive. Perhaps it's because we get plenty of rain in Lancashire.'

A short time later he said, 'I'm enjoying our walk. I haven't had a real look round the estate for ages.'

'How exactly did Edward's family lose the estate in the first place? I'm not asking to be nosey, Walter, but so that I won't say the wrong thing to him.'

'His fool of a grandfather lost almost all their money in poor business deals and gambling, so in the end they had to sell up. The Kenyons bought the place but I think they'd expected to lord it over the locals.' He chuckled. 'Lancashire folk don't take kindly to that sort of treatment, so the new owners were never happy here and folk avoided working for them if they could. Then, a few years later the big house burned down completely one night while they were away visiting friends in Halifax.' He stared blindly into the distance for a minute or two, looking unhappy at the memories that brought up. 'Eh, I didn't see it from my farm till it was well alight and of course I went to see if I could help, but it was too late by then.'

He frowned then added, 'I've never seen a fire take hold so rapidly. Folk told me afterwards that they could see the blaze from miles away. It had spread so quickly through the building that those of us who rushed to help didn't even attempt to put it out. Well, where were we going to get enough water? It was summer and our little river doesn't flow close enough to where the big house stood.'

Another sigh, then, 'A few months later we heard that the Kenyons had bought a new home at the seaside with the fire insurance money. I wasn't the only one to wonder if they'd had the place burned down on purpose. I had a look round and the fire must have started in several places at the same time, and how could it have done that unless it had been set on purpose? I've never seen a building destroyed so completely.'

'That would be a terrible thing to do.'

'Some people do dreadful things, lass.'

'Yes.'

He could tell from her expression that she was thinking of her own past. He suspected she'd run away partly to stay safe. What from he had no idea, though he'd probably find out as he got to know her.

'Well, it didn't do the Kenyons much good. They died quite young and ironically their son turned out to be a gambler and a womaniser as well. They hadn't managed to sell the estate after the fire and I think he lost so much money that in the end he had to accept whatever he was offered for it in order to pay his debts. That's how Edward got his family estate back, and I don't think he's the sort to gamble it away again. He has a steady look to him and I'd trust him.'

She nodded. 'I agree. I'd trust him too.'

They stopped walking for a few moments to study the ruins.

'It was a lovely old house,' he said quietly. 'Everyone was sad about it being destroyed.'

'Is Mr Ollerton going to build the new house on the same site as the old one?' she asked suddenly.

'I don't know, lass, and I don't think he does yet, either. He'll have to find an architect to design his new home before he can make any decisions. Why do you ask?'

'If it were me, I'd not build a house in the same place but a little lower down the slope. You can imagine a house nestling happily into the slight dip in the hillside there, just in front of that clump of trees.' She pointed.

He was surprised by how sure she sounded and looked towards the place she was indicating, studying it carefully to see if he could picture a big house there. To his further surprise, he could. 'I agree with you. I think an earlier house must have once stood there because only the other day Edward found the remains of some cellars under the ground right there. Even I hadn't known they existed. You should share your thoughts about where to build it with him.'

'Oh, I couldn't do that. It would sound so impertinent.'

'I don't agree. He seems a man of sense and will be wanting to consider various ideas and information before he takes any final decision. Building a big house is a huge undertaking and it'll be years before it's finished. I doubt he's the kind of man who'd let himself be pushed into doing something he didn't agree with, and I'm sure he'll listen to a lot of suggestions before he comes to any decisions.'

He pulled out his pocket watch and clicked it open. 'Eh, I was enjoying talking to you so much I forgot to keep an eye on the time. I should think they'll have finished looking at the plumbing possibilities now, so we'd better turn back.'

Edward and Riley were standing chatting as they waited for them so when they got back Walter shared Lillian's opinion of the site with them, causing her to flush in embarrassment.

The two men considered it, each frowning in thought, then Edward said, 'Let's go and look at that spot where the cellar is again.'

Walter led the way up the hill and took over, pointing out the exact place Lillian had thought suitable.

Edward walked to and fro in silence, considering it from various angles, then he turned to her. 'I think you're right. This is a much better spot for a house. What made you think of it?'

'It's a level space partway up a slope. It just – looks right.'

'And the old cellars are underneath it so there was probably a house here before,' Walter said.

Edward walked round the level patch, then turned to smile at her. 'You have a good eye for landscape and design, Lillian. There's a lovely view from here and unless my architect has a better idea, I'll definitely consider putting it here.'

'Have you been down into the cellars again?' Walter asked.

Edward shook his head. 'No. I'll wait till I can take a builder or architect with me to make sure they won't collapse on anyone. I'd never go down there on my own. It'd be too risky. And there's not much to see anyway because there's nothing stored there now.'

'Don't they lead anywhere at all?'

'Only into a dead end where the ceiling must have come down to block the passages that I'd guess led from the old cellars to the new ones. I should think the fire at the big house caused some of the underground spaces to subside.'

'You're wise not to risk anything, lad.' Walter pulled out his watch again. 'Let's go back now and have a quick something to eat. Riley here needs to go into Ollerthwaite to look at a workshop of mine and buy a few bits and pieces, and the lasses need to help Lillian make arrangements to move into that house tomorrow.'

She looked at him and asked, 'Do you think I ought to see Mr Baker's nephew first and let him know I'm here?'

'Do you need more money?'

'No. Mr Baker gave me plenty. I had some saved, you see, and he kept an eye on that as well as my inheritance. Even if I have to rough it, I want to move into a home of my own more than anything else in the world.'

He patted her shoulder. 'Then Elinor and Maude will help you gather together a few necessities.'

He turned back to Edward. 'We'll see you for a meal tonight as usual, lad.'

'I shall look forward to it.'

Edward watched them walk away, wishing he were staying with the group. He couldn't help noticing how gracefully Lillian walked.

She talked about gardening as if she was knowledgeable about plants. Once she was settled in, he might ask her help about what needed doing urgently in the grounds of his estate, especially the part near where the new house would stand.

He looked down the gentle slope. That was the roof of her new home so he'd be able to cut across and chat to her over her back wall. It would make a pleasant stroll.

Would she mind him visiting her in that casual manner? He hoped not. He needed to make a few friends here. And . . . who knew what else might come of their getting acquainted?

He stopped moving in shock, then admitted to himself that he was attracted to her – to the woman who was coming out of her shell, anyway.

When they got back to the farm Lillian wasted no time in telling Maude and Elinor about the cottage, and they were thrilled that she'd found herself a home. When she confessed that she was dying to move in, they immediately started discussing how they could help her gather enough furnishings and cookware to do that.

Walter listened for a while then, after telling them they could take things from his stores, left them to it.

Lillian tried to protest that she couldn't expect them to do all that and they both chuckled.

'It'll be fun,' Maude said. 'We can find you all sorts of small, everyday items from Walter's stores at no cost and there are also his one-pound baskets of oddments. If you like reading he has a few old books as well. We'll let you pay for any of the baskets you feel contain items useful to you.'

'But—'

Elinor clasped her hand. 'You need help now and we're only giving you stuff that no one else wants. From what you said, you've got some furniture coming from your old home so this will be mainly oddments. One day you can pay us back for it by helping us provide for someone else in need.'

Lillian stopped protesting and soon realised that they really were enjoying helping her. Their friendliness made her feel better than she had for years. How wonderful to have found such good people!

But most wonderful of all was the thought of a home of her own. Her impossible dream really was about to come true.

The three women took the pony and cart and spent the afternoon looking for items in Walter's stores and stuffing them into old pillowcases or sacks. Maude especially was very sure which items would be necessary. And Lillian could easily afford the four baskets of oddments that seemed best suited to her needs at a pound each. The baskets themselves, worn as they were, would come in useful as well as their contents.

At one stage Lillian couldn't help shedding a few happy tears as she looked at the pile of things that now belonged to her. Her husband and his family had chosen everything for the house she'd shared with him.

'May I ask how you have money now, but they forced you to marry this man you hated?' Maude asked suddenly.

She shook her head sadly. 'I came into a little inheritance later on, but not in time to avoid marrying him. My godmother understood my situation and arranged for her lawyer to keep the money in trust until I could have it for myself. She was a very astute woman and must have noticed what sort of man Stanley was. It's that inheritance I shall be living on from now on. I'll have enough to manage but not a generous fortune.'

They both hugged her then carried on sorting out bits and pieces. Even rags would be needed for cleaning the house, after all.

They put everything near the door of the shop for Walter to pick up first thing in the morning and went back to the farm to get the evening meal ready.

Edward joined them and Lillian found herself sitting next to him at the table. She enjoyed telling him about her afternoon and he seemed genuinely interested.

As she got ready for bed that night she sighed happily. It felt as if she were part of a normal family now, as if her companions truly cared about what she wanted and needed. How wonderful that was!

When he got back to the lodge, Edward felt lonely in the little cottage as he tried to get the fire blazing up to take the chill off the room. It was too soon to go to bed, so he got out a book Walter had lent him and sat near an oil lamp. He couldn't settle to reading it, however. He kept remembering Walter surrounded by his family and with many friends in the town.

Could he one day achieve something like that? He could try, couldn't he? In fact, seeing Walter only made him more eager for a family and friends of his own, and he definitely wasn't going to wait for the new house to be built to look for a wife.

After he went to bed, his last thoughts were of Lillian, for some strange reason. He'd watched Walter continue to coax her out of her shell and somehow bring out her good points. She was not only intelligent but pretty, not beautiful but nice to look at and interesting to chat to.

A very nice woman, in fact.

How had Walter worked this magic on them all so quickly? Not only on Lillian, but on Riley and, yes, on himself too. Edward had to admit that he'd been rather stiff with people at first but somehow you couldn't help relaxing and feeling welcome when you were with that very special family.

He wished he had such a gift for friendship but he'd spent too much time alone during the past decade. He'd have to watch these people and learn from them, and he was hoping desperately that they'd all continue to be good friends.

It wasn't too much to ask for, was it?

13

In a large but tumbledown house at the eastern edge of Oll-erthwaite, Terry Catlow clouted his second eldest son for being cheeky and scowled at his wife. 'When's that tea going to be ready, you lazy bitch?'

Nora drew herself up to her full five feet two inches tall and signalled to their children to go outside and leave them alone. After one quick glance at her expression they hurried out to the back yard. When Ma got that expression on her face you did as she told you, quick smart.

Kicking the door shut behind them, she turned to confront her husband, hands on hips. 'What's got into you, shouting and complaining over nothing? And in front of the children, too. I'm not having it.'

He breathed deeply but the anger stayed on his face.

'If you ever call me a bitch like that again, Terry Catlow, I'll throw the nearest heavy object at you or go after you with the poker. I won't put up with being treated badly. What's more, in case you've forgotten how to read the figures on the clock, it's not time for tea yet.'

She waited, foot tapping impatiently. 'Well? What's wrong with you?'

He almost spat the words at her. 'There's an Ollerton come back to live on the estate. That's what's wrong.'

'How do you know?'

He thumped his clenched fist down on the table. 'I've seen him walking round it, heard folk talk about him.'

'You ought to stop going there, Terry. It only upsets you.'

'I'll go where I damned well please.'

Her heart sank. 'Is it the old man come back?'

'No. This one's a bit younger than you and me from the looks of him.'

'Apart from the fact that it's got nothing to do with us who lives there, if this one is younger than us, he can't have been the one who did it.'

'He's an Ollerton, isn't he? Probably the grandson of the one who got my father put in jail and made sure he never came out of it alive. I swore after Dad died that I wouldn't have any member of that sodding family settling in the valley again and making trouble for ordinary folk who're just trying to put bread on the table.'

'Your family were never short of food. Your father was jailed because he'd stolen the Ollertons' family silver, and a lot of it, too.'

'He always denied that.'

'I'm not stupid. There was no doubt he'd done it because the police found some of the pieces buried in the back garden here.'

'Someone else could have done that to put the blame on my dad.'

'And pigs might fly. He'd been thieving things all his life. Some of the pieces were never found and he refused to say where they were. That's why he got an extra-long sentence.'

'One of my friends heard the Ollerton chap asking the judge not to be lenient. He had no business doing that. My poor dad got the longest sentence possible. He pined away and died in jail because of that bloody family.'

'What's that got to do with this younger man? He may be different, kinder even. You shouldn't judge him till you've met him.'

'Don't you dare take their side! He's an Ollerton and that's enough for me.' He took her by surprise, clouting her hard across the side of the head and making her stumble sideways. She screeched and ducked behind the table, throwing two plates at him, and hitting him on the forehead with one. Then she picked up her rolling pin and waved it threateningly as she yelled at him that if he dared try that again, he'd never sleep soundly in her bed again for as long as he lived.

He stood still for a few moments, then said, 'Aw, shut up. I'm not going to hit you again. The news took me by surprise, that's all, and I was so angry I lashed out.'

'I've told you before – I won't put up with you hitting me. Not – ever. Next time you feel like lashing out, go out and punch a hole in the wall. I thought we'd settled that years ago. Do I have to prove it all over again?'

Years ago, the first time he'd hit her, she'd tipped a bucket of icy water over him when he'd lain on the rug sleeping off a booze-up, then pounded him with her poss stick as if he'd been a piece of dirty washing in the tub, so he believed her. He'd never forgotten the utter shock of it and how long it had taken him to feel warm again, even huddling in front of the fire, because she'd hidden his dry clothes. And his bruises hadn't faded for days so folk who'd seen them jeered at him because she'd made sure they'd known where he'd got them.

He'd worried about sleeping next to her for a while as well, because she'd kept her rolling pin on the floor at her side of the bed and when he'd asked why, she'd said she might need to grab it quickly. She'd never used it, but he'd slept on the edge of the bed for weeks, leaving her plenty of space.

He scowled and muttered an apology, ending, 'But don't you ever badmouth my family again, Nora, or I *will* thump you. What do you know about why they did anything? My brother was ill and dying for lack of decent food and medicine, and he did die after my dad went to jail.'

She glared at him, then put down the rolling pin, because he was right about that. But it hadn't been her fault, had it? So she kept her favourite weapon within reach. 'I still don't think you should take it out on this younger Ollerton chap. And you'd definitely better not touch me again.'

He shot her a dirty look. 'I'll do as I choose with that family, but I'm sorry I hit you.'

She could tell that he'd started calming down because his voice was quieter, so she let the subject drop and got on with making his tea. She knew that although Terry had idolised his father, his mother had been glad to be rid of her husband, who had been growing so rash in his thieving that he'd put them all at risk of getting into serious trouble with the law more than once.

At least what had happened to the old man had made her Terry very careful indeed about how he stole things and disposed of them, and he'd never been caught. Suspected, yes, but nothing had ever been proven against him. So they'd managed to hang on to this house, which one of his ancestors had bought outright during better times.

She only wished their oldest son would follow his father's example and be more careful how he did his thieving, but Jezzy was as reckless in his ways as the grandfather he didn't remember. Even Terry had got fed up and sent Jezzy to live with Terry's younger brother Ken in Manchester for a while after he'd got into trouble for stealing kids' pocket money earlier in the year.

She was dreading their son coming back because life was a lot easier without him stirring up trouble in the family or upsetting the neighbours. And he was as tall as her now. She reckoned he'd be taller even than his father before he'd finished growing.

He was supposed to be learning a bit of sense from Ken, who was the cleverest one in the Catlow family, but she doubted any of it would sink in. Jezzy had always been bull-headed when he wanted something, even as a small child. And though he wanted money, he didn't want to work for it, the lazy sod. When Terry had found him a job last year delivering goods for a shopkeeper after school, he'd stolen some of the items. So he'd been sacked and threatened with the police if he ever so much as set foot inside that shop again.

Her brother-in-law Ken, unlike any of his brothers or sisters, had gone into business on the outskirts of Manchester and had worked hard. He now owned a couple of shops, one a pawn shop, the other selling second-hand clothes, and his eldest son was working with him. Ken was making an honest living out of them and a good one too. Even Jezzy didn't dare cross him, because he was a big man. Eh, she wished her husband were more like him.

Ken had told them recently that his nephew was a clever lad, and he'd do his best to persuade him to settle down into some honest occupation. But he didn't get on well with his cousins so Ken would look for some other job for him. He wasn't giving up easily, knew how Nora worried about her son. But she didn't feel optimistic about Jezzy's future.

She envied her sister-in-law their family's more settled way of life, not to mention the scrubbing woman who came in to do the heavy housework twice a week, she did indeed. She had to take in lodgers to make ends meet and she scrubbed her own floor even now when she was getting older and rheumatism was setting in.

It worried her when Terry got into one of his dark moods like today and got 'that look' on his face, but what could she do about it? Nothing, that's what, except make sure he didn't dare touch her again. Other women might be stupid enough to put up with that sort of thing but she wasn't. She'd never been a doormat wife and she wasn't going to change now. That at least she could make sure of.

She banged the pots and pans as she prepared tea, which let Terry know she was still angry. She worked quietly for a minute or two then banged something down suddenly, pleased to see him jump in shock.

But underneath it all she was seriously worried. She knew he was planning something and it was to do with the Ollertons. And there was a limit to what she could do when he got in one of these dark moods.

14

Lillian woke up very early on the day of her move. The gap at the side of the curtain showed her that dawn was barely gilding the horizon so she didn't get up, not wanting to disturb the others.

She lay in bed feeling excited and thinking about how she'd set things out in her new home. Thanks to Maude and Elinor she even had a couple of ornaments and a mirror that was only slightly speckled with age. She'd hang it over the mantelpiece and stand the taller ornament in front of it at one side to hide the worst of the marks.

When she heard Elinor get up and go downstairs, she got up too and packed all her night things in her final bag. After that she took the sheets off the bed and carried them downstairs, in time to see Elinor run into the scullery. She heard her friend being sick so didn't go in with the sheets yet because you could do nothing to prevent morning sickness. Some women suffered badly from it; others were lucky.

She wished desperately that she'd been given the chance to find out which sort she was.

It was a few minutes before the other woman returned, looking white and shivery, by which time Lillian had poured the boiling water into the teapot.

'Sit down for a minute or two and when the tea is brewed I'll make you a weak cup with plenty of sugar to settle your stomach. I can set the table while you're drinking it.'

Elinor gave her a wan smile just as Cameron came into the kitchen. He nodded to Lillian but his attention was mainly for his wife. 'I told you to lie in bed a little longer today, love. I was going to put the kettle on and bring you a cup of tea but I dozed off. Sorry about that.'

'I might as well get it over with.' Elinor sighed. 'It doesn't go away till I've actually thrown up.'

'It's time you went to see the doctor. There can't be any doubt now that you're expecting and I'd rather he kept an eye on things.'

'I'm not going. I don't like Dr Twilling and he's no use anyway. He talks to women as if they're all stupid; he's so prejudiced against females.'

'If I hear him speaking to you like that, I'll tell him to mind his language, doctor or not.'

'He doesn't speak as scornfully when the husbands are with them. All the women know that. But he doesn't pay half as much attention to his female patients and he's really old-fashioned in his ways, so I will not trust him with something as precious as our child.'

'Why didn't you tell me sooner what Twilling was like, Elinor, love?' Walter asked from near the hall door. 'I've never liked him but I didn't know he treated women that badly.'

'I didn't tell you because there's nothing you or anyone else can do about it. Doctors are usually men and a lot of them think they're superior to women, even if they're not as bad as him.' Elinor scowled and added, 'Which they're not!'

Maude came in and joined the conversation. 'I can't stand Dr Twilling either. I went with a friend to consult him and decided I'd have to be desperate to go and see him because I'd not believe a word he said. Lie down and think sensible, calming thoughts is not a treatment for anything.'

'If there was a female doctor here, I'd go to her.' Elinor's voice was bitter. 'At least she'd know what it feels like to have a woman's body. But there isn't one in the area.'

There was a moment's silence then Walter said slowly, 'Perhaps it's time we looked into getting one to come here, then. I'll have to see what I can do. Yes, and I'll get some of the other people on the town council to join me in helping a woman doctor to set up a surgery in Ollerthwaite.'

'Dr Twilling will throw a fit if you even try. And he will get the men on the council who think his way on his side to vote against it.'

'They won't succeed in stopping us now that I know.'

'Anyway, it'll take time to find a female doctor so that's no use to Elinor now,' Maude said thoughtfully. 'There aren't enough of them trained yet. You might get a nurse much more quickly, though. Twenty years ago they set up a training school for nurses at the Liverpool Royal Infirmary, including finding district nurses who visit poor people at home.'

'How do you know that?' Walter asked.

'I wondered about becoming a nurse for a time when I was a lass, but my mam needed my wages and she had no money to spare to help me do it. Then Elinor's mother died and I was needed to look after her. I couldn't have left her because, young as I was, I could manage her better than anyone else.' She was quiet for a moment or two then said, 'Why don't we contact one of the training schools for nurses as well as trying to get a woman doctor? I'll help you write the letters, Walter.'

He looked at her in surprise. 'How did you get to be so well informed?'

'I still like to read the newspapers and find out what's going on for nurses, yes, and for female doctors. Our Queen intervened a few years ago, God bless her. People collected money for her Golden Jubilee of being on the throne and there was some left over, so she said it was to be used to set up a national institute for training nurses. Not every part of the country joined in. This valley didn't and you can guess why, but most places did. There are still a few independent institutes left doing the same thing, as well, though we in the valley don't have any official contact with any of them. I bet it's because Dr Twilling has made sure of that.'

'Now I come to think of it, he did speak to the council a year or two ago and say an institute was unnecessary here and would only cost a lot and cause too much paperwork when people needed to hire a nurse,' Walter admitted.

'He would say that! He acts like he's king of the valley. We need another doctor or two. That'd put the old fool in his place.'

'Eh, he has upset you, hasn't he?'

She smiled wryly. 'Yes. I'm not the only one he's upset either.'

Walter was almost talking to himself when he next spoke. 'There are so many things I wish I could do to improve the world when I look round and see how some folk struggle. But if my family is going to start having babies maybe it's time to see if we can improve things in that area at least. I shall look into it.' He paused to frown in thought. 'Yes, and I'll see if I can get Edward Ollerton interested as well as one or two people from the town council. At least we've got a couple of women on it these days.'

Lillian had listened to this in surprise at first, but she soon realised why Walter would try to take action now. It was obvious how deeply he loved his family.

She spoke without considering her words. 'I've never found any male doctor who didn't talk down to me. Not one. I hope we can get a woman.'

Walter sighed. 'I should have done something sooner.'

Maude went and put an arm through his. 'You can't take on all the problems in the valley single-handed, Cousin Walter.'

He shrugged. 'I can't do it all, that's true. But I can write to this organisation in London and see if they can help me find a nurse for our valley folk. And I can get some other people from round here to help me find money to pay her wages and find her somewhere to live.'

'I don't have any money to spare but if there's anything I can do – copy letters or keep an eye on children, or whatever – I'd be very happy to help,' Lillian said quietly.

Walter looked at her approvingly. 'I'll bear that in mind, lass. We'll have to take one step at a time.'

Maude let out a sudden spurt of laughter. 'Dr Twilling will throw a fit about you taking even half a step. I wish I could see his face when he finds out what you're doing, Walter. But we'd better stop talking and get breakfast ready now or poor Lillian will never get into her new home. That's our first priority today.'

Walter was rather quiet, looking thoughtful as the two women bustled round and put breakfast on the table, a hurried meal for once. Afterwards Elinor insisted on coming with them to the new house.

'I can feel sick there as easily as here,' she declared.

Cameron had arranged to meet a man who was selling some sheep, so he was the first to leave.

When they were ready Walter suggested Riley ride to the cottage on one of the family's two bicycles in case they needed anything else fetching quickly from the little shop in Upperfold.

'Will it be all right if I go into town on it later to buy a few things so that I can make a start on putting in a bathroom at Lillian's?' Riley asked.

'Of course it will.'

Lillian didn't say much on the way there but sat watching eagerly as they drew closer to her new home. Elinor had ridden on the cart, leaving Maude to ride the second bicycle. Lillian could hardly breathe for excitement as they stopped near the front gate, could only squeeze her companion's hand. Home! She was about to move into her own home.

Walter got down and held out his hand to help Elinor, by which time Lillian was on the road at the other side. When Maude passed her one of the pillowcases full of bedding oddments and towels to carry inside, she hugged it against herself and waited near the front door for the others, feeling that it'd be rude to go inside till they were all with her.

When they joined her, carrying various other bundles and baskets, they waited in a semicircle, smiling and gesturing for her to unlock the door and go in first. So she took a deep breath and did that, thinking, *I'm home now. I really do have a home.*

Riley helped Walter fetch the rest of the bundles and dump them at one side of the kitchen, then got back on the cart to drive to the storage house and fetch the furniture and other things Lillian had chosen the previous day.

'I'll come back here with you to help unload Lillian's things before I go to the hardware store Walter's told me about in Ollerthwaite,' Riley said.

Maude said firmly, 'No need to do that. There isn't a lot of furniture to unload and it's all fairly small stuff. I'll be all right helping Walter carry it into the cottage.'

'You're sure?'

She rolled her eyes. 'Sure that I'm capable of helping carry a few small pieces of furniture into the house? Of course I can. I'm not a weakling.'

He lowered his voice. 'You being tall and strong is one of the many things I like about you. Weak little women always make me feel clumsy. I'd hesitate to kiss one, let alone give her a hug.'

For a moment she looked at him in surprise, then gave him a slow smile. 'Well, just so you know, I do like being kissed and hugged now and then, especially by a tall, strong man.'

Riley grinned. 'I'll remember that.'

As he went off with Walter, Riley was still smiling at her response to him. She was such a fine-looking woman. He let out a happy little sound. He'd not be able to stop thinking of her now that she'd given him such clear encouragement. Did he even want to stop thinking about her? No, definitely not. Sometimes the way people looked at you said a lot more than mere words ever could.

'She's a fine lass, is our Maude,' Walter said unexpectedly.

'Yes.'

'And she likes you.'

'Do you think so?'

'I'm sure of it.'

'Good. Because I like her a lot.' He stole a quick glance sideways. 'Is that all right with you?'

'It's more than merely all right. I think it's excellent.'

Riley relaxed and after a brief pause he changed the subject. 'Do you think Lillian will be safe living there, Walter? Her husband's family sent two nasty brutes to kidnap her. If I hadn't been there she'd have been in trouble.'

'It was kind of you to help her. I gather she was a complete stranger at the time.'

'She was, but I can't bear to see anyone ill-treated or bullied. We can only hope they'll never find out where she is.'

Walter frowned. 'Hmm. I'll ask the people in the other cottages to keep an eye on her and to go running to her aid if she ever shouts for help. But really, unless those in-laws of hers are sick in the head, there shouldn't be any trouble with them now she's left the area. And they can hardly keep pretending she's expecting, can they?'

'I think they were intending to make sure she was expecting, in any way necessary.'

'Let's hope they remain ignorant about where she is now.'

Both men shook their heads in bafflement at such behaviour then Walter said quietly, 'It's very quiet up at this end of the valley. She should be safe here. It's not a long way from Eastby End, not much over a mile, but it feels like a different world, what with the fights and yelling at one another that go on over there.'

'Why does everyone sound disapproving when they talk about Eastby End? Maude pulled a face when she mentioned it last night. And you seemed to say the word as if the place were distasteful.'

'It's our only local slum area, lad, and most of our dubious characters seem to have either come from there or have ended up living there. You'd better ask for payment in advance for any jobs you do for people in those parts.'

'I'll remember that.'

'We shall need to sort out some furniture for you as well before you move into the workshop. You won't need much but you'll need some.'

'Yes, but we've already agreed that I won't move out of the farm for a few days so that I can work on Lillian's and Edward's bathrooms more easily. My personal needs aren't urgent and I'm not fussy. As long as I've got a bed and a table to prepare food and eat at, I shall be all right. If you'd rather I move out of the farm sooner you have only to say.'

'I'm more likely to suggest you stay on for longer, since your first jobs are both nearby and then you'll be working on my house. We're enjoying your company too, especially Maude. She deserves some happiness.' He nudged the younger man and winked at him.

'She's – a very special person.'

'She is that. She'll make some man a fine wife. Now, let's get back to the business side of things. We're glad to have you and your skills in the valley.'

'I can't believe how quickly I felt at home here.'

Walter was looking thoughtful. 'Actually, I think Lillian and our two lasses would appreciate being left to sort out arrangements inside her new home for an hour or two, so why don't I take you to see the workshop later on? No use making plans till you've seen it in case you can't stand the place.'

'Thanks. That'd be good.'

When the door closed behind the last of her visitors just over an hour and a half later, Lillian peeped out of the window to watch them leave then let out a huge sigh of happiness. Riley and another man had finished work on her new bathroom for the day, too, so the whole place was quiet.

She was truly grateful to them all, but she needed to be alone to get a proper feel for her new home. Since no one could see her, she gave in to her urge to twirl round a couple of times in the front room out of sheer joy.

She then moved the best of the armchairs into the kitchen, because that was where she would be spending most of her time. No use heating another room as the weather grew colder.

She tugged the table round slightly, setting the four scuffed wooden chairs into what she felt were better positions at one end. She'd give them all a good polish and make matching cushions for the seats when she had time. There would be lots of jobs like that to keep her busy. She'd do her chopping and food preparation at one end of the table and eat at the other end. Such a lovely, large table.

Another couple of joyful twirls then she realised she hadn't checked that the back door was locked and ran to do that before sitting down and pouring out the last lukewarm cup of tea. One teaspoon of sugar, a little milk, then she stirred it gently before taking a mouthful. It didn't matter that it wasn't a perfect cup of tea. It was hers, made with her own hands in her new teapot, which had a tiny chip in the edge of the lid but was otherwise intact and of a very pretty design. The cup was pretty too, and if it didn't match the saucer or teapot she didn't care.

She lifted the top off the biscuit barrel that Elinor had filled with some homemade shortbread, but she wasn't really hungry and put the lid back on again without taking out a piece.

After that she went up to her bedroom and bounced on the bed. It'd be easy to mend the frayed corner of the bedspread, and there were two blankets and a faded quilt to keep her warm, as well as an earthenware hot-water piggy sitting in the kitchen ready to fill if she needed to warm her bed.

She didn't have a wardrobe to hang her clothes in yet though Walter had said he'd see if he could find her one cheaply. In the meantime she folded her underclothing and blouses neatly and put them in the scuffed chest of drawers, then hung the few pieces of outer clothing over the back of her one upstairs chair to prevent them getting crumpled. She put her night-dress under her pillow, ready for later.

She'd need some more clothes. She hadn't been able to bring much with her when she'd run away, but all in good time. When her furniture and other clothes were delivered, she'd check what exactly she had before she spent another penny.

Still smiling, she went downstairs and simply sat there getting the feel of the house, the way it creaked and how the sunlight touched lightly on one side of the kitchen window at this time of day. Thank goodness there were curtains there that covered it completely. She'd not dare to sit with a light on in the evenings if there weren't.

'My home,' she said aloud.

After a while she went outside into the front garden and did a little weeding along the sides of the path, just on principle of setting her mark on it.

When an older woman came walking up the hill carrying a heavy shopping bag, Lillian straightened up and waited, wondering if this was one of her neighbours and if the woman would bother to do more than nod a greeting.

To her delight the neighbour stopped at the gate next door. 'Moved in, have you?'

'Yes.'

'We live next door. I'm Gladys Hicks. My husband's Bill but he won't be home till later.'

'Lillian Hesketh. I'm a widow, so I'll be living here on my own.'

'Eh, you're young to lose your husband. Welcome to Upperfold, love. I hope you'll be happy in this cottage. We'll be glad to have someone living here again and keeping the garden nice. Don't hesitate to ask if you need help lifting heavy stuff. My Bill's a strong man.'

'Thank you. You're very kind.'

'Ned and Pearl Cornish live in the other house, but they won't be home till later. They were going to have tea with their daughter and family in the village tonight.' She turned to go into her house, then turned back. 'We all keep an eye on each other's houses, by the way, so you've only to call out if you need help.'

'That's good. I'll keep my eyes open too.'

'That's what neighbours are for. What are they doing at the back?'

'Putting in a bathroom.'

'He's a good landlord, Walter Crossley. I'm hoping the new owner of the estate will look after our house better. I'd love an indoor bathroom. Well, I'd better get on. I need to put my Bill's tea on to cook.'

After another smile and nod, Gladys vanished into the house.

Even the neighbours seemed friendly, Lillian thought as she went inside again.

She didn't go to bed until she was exhausted, was a bit nervous of being on her own here at night.

But she reminded herself that Bill Hicks was just next door and would hear if she called out, so snuggled down in the bed – and the next thing she knew it was morning.

15

In the middle of the following morning Walter came up the road from Upperfold with a bicycle lying on the back of his cart.

Lillian was washing the outside of the two neat little front-room windows because she wanted her house to look lived in and inviting to visitors and passers-by, but she turned round at the sound of a cart.

When Walter waved to her and slowed down, she dropped her wet cloth into the bucket of warm water and hurried towards the gate, wiping her hands on her pinafore and watching as he stopped. Was this – could this be her bicycle?

He went round to the back of his cart and lifted it off, wheeling it across to her and looking at her with his head tilted slightly to one side as if to ask whether she liked it.

Excitement rose in her as she realised Peter had found her a bicycle, and before she knew what she was doing she'd given Walter an awkward hug, which had included one of the bicycle handlebars. The paintwork was rather scratched but the wheels moved easily. Oh, it would make such a difference to her life to have a way of getting around. You could walk to most places in towns but distances were greater here in the country and destinations could be much further apart, not to mention there being no buses at all.

'Good morning, Lillian. Peter found you this bicycle. If it's too battered-looking he can easily sell it to someone else, but he assures me that it's in perfect working order and he says you aren't likely to find another good one which is as cheap.'

She moved to stroke the handlebars, feeling excited but also nervous.

'Do you know how to ride a bike?'

Sometimes it seemed as if he could read her thoughts. 'No. I've always wanted to learn but never even been allowed to sit on one.' Her parents and her husband's parents had all disapproved of women riding round 'showing their legs to any man passing by like brazen hussies'. Her husband hadn't cared what she did as long as it didn't upset his parents.

Walter turned to look up and down the road. 'Hmm. It's not hard to learn but I don't think you should make your first attempts here. The slope would make it more difficult to get your balance.' He frowned for a moment, then looked up the hill. 'Aha! I'll ask Edward if we can try it out in front of his house. It's nice and flat there, better than in front of my farm.'

She was disappointed but in one sense she agreed. She definitely didn't want to make a fool of herself by falling off the bike in public. There wasn't a lot of traffic going up the hill, but she felt sure if she tried it for the first time here someone would pass by just in time to see her fall.

'Nothing ventured! Let's go up there now and ask Edward if he minds, though I'm sure he won't.' Walter studied her appearance. 'Your shoes are nice and sturdy, but do you have a shorter skirt than that?'

'No, but I can roll up the waistband to make it shorter. And I'll shorten it properly tonight.' She'd shorten all her skirts. They'd be more fashionable that way as well as easier to move around in.

'Right then. Lock up your house and get on the cart.' He picked up the bicycle and put it on the back of the cart again.

She took off her pinafore and tossed it into the hall, locked the front door and got up beside him. As they bumped up the road and turned off towards Edward's cottage, however, she suddenly had the urge to jump off and run back home. What if she couldn't manage to ride it safely? He'd think her such a fool.

Walter seemed to be reading her thoughts. 'Stop worrying. Trust me. It's not all that hard and it'll be fun.'

She managed to nod her head, hoping he was right. Anyway, they were here now.

Edward must have heard them coming because he came striding out of the house. 'How lovely to see you.'

'We need somewhere flat for Lillian to learn how to ride her new bike.'

'I, um, never had a chance to try one before,' she put in quickly. 'I'll probably fall off a few times.'

He gave her one of his lovely smiles. 'A few days ago I got on a bike again after years of never going near one, and I had to practise a bit too. This bit of flat ground was a very good place for me to do that and I'm happy for you to practise here too any time you like, Lillian.'

That made her feel better. It was uncanny how he always seemed to say things that did that.

Walter got down off the cart so she did too.

He lifted the bike off the cart and the two men studied it. 'Peter says it's in good working order, even if the paint is somewhat scratched.'

He turned to Lillian. 'Tuck your skirt up and then we'll go over the details, like how to use the brakes and so on, before you have your first go.'

So she did that and listened carefully to his instructions.

Part way through this, Edward seemed to realise that she hadn't quite understood some of what Walter was saying and took over. To her relief he proved to be much better at explaining how things worked and she began to understand not only what to do but why and when.

Then Edward held out his hand. 'Come on. I'll hold the back of the seat at first till you get a feel for the balance. I won't allow you to fall off, I promise.'

Feeling better about doing it she let him help her onto the bike, feeling safe because he was still holding the seat with one hand, such a strong, firm hand it looked.

He walked slowly up and down the level space at one side of her, but a little way behind. They crossed it several times and he continued to be a comforting presence. And she didn't fall off once.

Then he said quietly, 'You've been riding on your own for the whole of this time across.'

She panicked then and he grabbed the back of the bicycle seat again, laughing in such a kind way that she suddenly saw the humour of it too.

'It's not half as hard as I thought.'

'No. But you'd be best riding slowly for a while. It's a pity the road is sloping outside your house. I think you should practise here again before you try going out on the roads in town.'

Edward took charge of the bicycle, wheeling it across and leaning it against the side of his house. 'Now, let me offer you both a cup of tea before you leave.'

Walter shook his head. 'Thank you, but I'd better go now because someone's coming to see me later. But if you'll walk home with Lillian afterwards, I'll leave her to enjoy a cup of tea with you.'

'I'll be happy to see her home.' He looked at her. 'You will stay for a while, won't you, Lillian? I'd welcome some company and intelligent conversation. I'm fed up of the sight of my own four walls.'

Walter went to take the nosebag off his pony. He'd got up on the driving seat and set off before she could think what to say.

She looked at Edward, a bit worried about this. 'I'm sorry to impose on you. If you want me to go straight home so that you can get on with your day, I'll do that. I can wheel the bicycle. I don't need an escort.'

'I don't want you to leave. I don't know many people round here yet and it'll be really nice to have some company. It's quite sunny today, so I can bring two chairs outside and we can enjoy our tea here, looking out over the valley. And if you like, I can store your bicycle till tomorrow or whenever you've got time to come for another practice, to save you pushing it to and fro.'

She was finding it a bit lonely too, in spite of her happiness about the house, so could understand how he was feeling and she said yes before she could stop herself.

They enjoyed a pleasant half hour's chat as well as a really good cup of tea, then they strolled down the hill to her home, chatting about his neglected estate as they passed through the near part of his grounds.

She pulled up a couple of big weeds automatically as they passed them and when she commented on a bush and said it needed pruning, she saw him look blank. Realising he didn't know much about gardening, she offered to come and give him a lesson about caring for the shrubs and other plants that had survived the years of neglect.

'Are you sure you can spare the time?'

'Yes. I'm not going to rush to set my own house and garden to rights. And I've done a lot of gardening so I do understand what's needed. Besides, like you I get a bit lonely.'

She immediately wished she hadn't revealed that but he only nodded and tactfully changed the subject, saying he'd appreciate her help with the garden then talking about something he'd seen in the town.

When they got to her cottage, he reminded her that the top part of her garden was bordered by his wall. 'I'll come and go home that way in future and gradually get to know all the little paths. I might own the estate but I don't know my own grounds very well at the moment.'

As he started walking back up the hill, Edward wondered whether Walter had been matchmaking by leaving them alone together.

That was followed by another thought that surprised him. If that's what the older man was doing, he didn't mind at all. He'd never had a chance to get to know a woman in this slow and comfortable way before, and he enjoyed Lillian's company.

Did she enjoy his company? He was surprised at how much he hoped so.

The postboy startled him by riding past on his bicycle and ringing his bell. That brought Edward out of his reverie.

'I was just coming to deliver this letter to you, Mr Ollerton, but I can give it you now, if you don't mind,' the postboy said cheerfully, getting off his bicycle and holding out an envelope.

Edward took it from him automatically

'Bit of good luck me bumping into you like this, sir. I don't have any letters for Mr Crossley today or for Mr Fordham up at the old water mill, either, so I can get back to the post office straight away. Delivering to the water mill when I have to come this way as well adds nearly twenty minutes to my working day.'

He tipped his cap to Edward, got back on his bike and rode off down the hill, whistling tunefully.

Edward studied the envelope and saw that it was from Mr Filmore. He didn't open it but walked on more quickly, eager to get home and see what it was about.

He got the fire burning higher in the range first and filled the old kettle, standing it on the hot part of the heavy iron top. He intended to get a gas cooker put in if at all feasible, both here and in the agent's house, yes, and gas lighting too. Walter had said he'd need to share payment for the gas-supply pipes to be brought to the various houses on his estate but he didn't care how much it cost, and the sooner it was done, the better. He didn't intend to live in the old-fashioned way his parents had done, or to ask his tenants and the servants he'd be hiring later to do so, either.

He sat down to wait for the kettle to boil and slit open the letter from his lawyer.

My dear Mr Ollerton

Re: Your search for an architect to design your new home.

I have a suggestion for your consideration. A friend of mine has a nephew (Lewis Brody) who has trained as an architect and has had several years of experience working with reputable architects in London.

I thought of him when you said you were looking for someone to design your new house, but I wanted to talk to him before mentioning you to him because though I knew his uncle, I'd never met him.

I have now had a luncheon meeting with the younger Mr Brody and I thought he seemed intelligent and pleasant. He shared some interesting ideas about modern house designs once I got him talking.

Mr Brody is thirty-two and feels ready to set up in business on his own but doesn't wish to live in London. I spoke briefly about your needs and he said if you were willing to consider employing him, it might be worth him visiting you in Ollindale.

I explained that you had some ideas of your own about what sort of house you wanted, and he said he'd be the same if he was going to build a new family home.

I believe it will be worth the two of you meeting and discussing your needs and wishes in more detail. After *that you can decide whether you'd like to use his services or not.*

I have attached some more detailed information about his training and experience.

Please let me know if you're interested in meeting him and I'll suggest he comes to see you.

Yours sincerely
E. Filmore

Edward got up to check the kettle but it wasn't boiling yet so he re-read the letter and stood staring at it. Would he want someone who was relatively inexperienced to manage the whole of this important task? He wasn't sure. But he'd spoken to a highly experienced and well-regarded architect and not found him at all willing to consider his client's ideas. In fact, the fellow had put Edward's back up with his arrogant attitude. And preliminary discussions with another man had suggested he would have a similar attitude.

After some thought he decided it would definitely be worth meeting this Mr Brody. He had a great deal of respect for Mr Filmore and didn't think his lawyer would recommend someone unless he had been genuinely impressed by him.

It seemed a long time until the kettle boiled. He made a pot of tea and absent-mindedly poured a cup before the tea in the pot had had time to brew properly. Sighing at his own ineptitude he sat sipping the weak tea slowly as he read the letter a third time.

It couldn't hurt to meet the man, could it? He'd ask Mr Filmore to suggest that Lewis Brody come and visit him, all expenses paid. Then it suddenly occurred to him that there were no hotels in Ollerthwaite and he added that information, offering to give Mr Brody (or anyone else who came to see him) a bed in the lodge for a night or two. Mr Filmore should warn his client that the amenities would only be very simple.

He smiled at the sudden realisation that this would probably weed out any snobs like the first architect he'd spoken to.

He rode his bicycle into town and posted the letter immediately to catch the last post of the day before going to look for the furniture shop Walter had mentioned. He wanted a more comfortable bed to offer a guest than the creaking old-fashioned metal bedframe and thin mattress presently gracing his second bedroom.

The man running the furniture shop fussed over him and showed him a suitable bedframe and mattress, which he tried out. 'I'll take it. Can you deliver it first thing tomorrow morning?'

'Happy to do that, sir.'

Edward was about to ask if they could remove the old bed at the same time, then remembered that Walter collected oddments of discarded furniture for people in need so decided to offer it to him for such people first.

Edward was glad when the time came to go across to the farm for his evening meal because after years of an extremely busy life he was finding the day passing rather slowly and would welcome some intelligent conversation. You couldn't go for walks all the time and he'd made all the lists he needed for the moment.

He walked across to the farm, where he found two new people joining them for the evening meal. Bryn Fordham seemed very much at home with Walter and his family, and it turned out he'd travelled to the valley from America with Cameron and set up making furniture in an old water mill.

He'd brought his apprentice with him for a meal, a lively lad called Tam, who ate more than any of the adults and wasn't afraid to join in their conversations.

It turned out that Bryn was not only an experienced cabinet maker but a skilled carver. He'd been visiting a friend in Rochdale, leaving Tam and the lad's next brother to look after the premises and do some simple jobs while he was away. It was good to see the lad's beaming pride when he and his brother were praised for how well they had coped.

It was amazing how many friends and protégés Walter seemed to have collected. The more Edward got to know him, the more admirable a person he showed himself to be and the less his age seemed to matter, since he had a lively, inquiring mind as well as an innate kindness that won people's hearts quickly.

Edward and Bryn left at the same time and walked to the crossroads together with the lad following quietly behind them.

'I'd like to see your carvings sometime, Bryn, if you don't mind.' It'd be nice to have something to decorate the agent's house when he moved in.

Bryn pointed to the fourth road leading away from the crossroads. 'Feel free to visit us any time. Follow that path, go past the old water wheel and mill, which you can't mistake. It's now my factory and home but if you approach from here, you have to go past it before turning right off the river path and go round to the main door at the rear that way.'

Edward nodded. 'I'd like to do that.' Bryn was another person he'd enjoy getting to know better, he was sure.

He said goodbye to them and continued towards the lodge, not hurrying because he was enjoying strolling home in the moonlight.

Then he suddenly heard something moving in the bushes to one side of the path. As he stopped to stare in that direction the noise stopped abruptly. After all the years in big cities, he had learned to be cautious about going out on foot at night, and he didn't intend to let himself be waylaid and robbed here in the country, either.

Walter might be sure this part of the valley was safe, but Edward didn't think anywhere in the world was totally safe, not as long as there were people with twisted minds and morals ready to steal from others. He'd not have walked around so carelessly on his own like this in London and perhaps he shouldn't have done it here, either. He should at least have brought a walking stick.

He took out his pocketknife and flicked the blade open, then started moving again, setting his feet down as quietly as he could this time. Once more he heard faint sounds to one side.

He stopped, turned round and yelled, 'If you're intending to rob me, I should warn you that I have a knife and know how to use it to defend myself.' Which was true. He waved his hand about to make his blade flash in the moonlight.

Keeping the pocketknife at the ready he continued to move forward as quietly as he could so that he'd hear anyone rushing forward to attack him. However he heard no further suspicious sounds, none at all, which suggested to him that whoever it was had taken heed of his warning and was standing still.

When he reached the cottage he wondered if he'd been over-anxious and had mistaken the sounds of an animal for a human, but he still took care not to turn his back to the world completely as he unlocked his front door. The second he got inside he shut the door and slid the bolts.

He stood in the darkness peering out of the kitchen window. Had he been imagining that he was being followed? He thought about that then shook his head. No, he had excellent hearing and there had definitely been something moving in the bushes – and from the types of sounds, not to mention the way they stopped and started as he did, this had been a person not an animal.

He would bring along some better implement of self-defence the next time he went out at night. He had an old walking stick with a sword blade concealed in it, which he'd brought with him in the first load of possessions simply because it had been his great-uncle's and he was fond of it. He'd never thought he might need to use it to protect himself here but it would be good to carry it.

Then he remembered that Lillian's bicycle was parked at the side of his house and reluctantly decided that he'd better bring it inside in case it got stolen—if it hadn't been taken already.

He fetched the old walking stick and removed the sword blade from it. It was attached to the handle and if you gave the wooden part a quick twist while holding it in a certain way it came apart easily. Holding the handle of the now naked blade, he slipped out the back way, locking the door behind him, then moved quietly and carefully round to the side of the house.

The bicycle was still there and the ground was clear of shrubs nearby, so it'd be hard for someone to sneak up on him.

After standing perfectly still for a few moments listening, he decided there was no one close enough to attack without him hearing them approach and took hold of the bicycle, wheeling it quickly round to the back door. After listening he again unlocked it and wheeled the bicycle quickly inside.

He stood it against the wall and locked the door again, leaving the bicycle where it was. This cottage needed a much bigger shed at the rear and the tiny and rather dilapidated one now standing there should be pulled down or repaired. He'd put it on his list.

It felt ridiculous to act in this way, as if he were a character in one of the mystery novels by Mr Freeman or Mr Hume, which he very much enjoyed reading, but so be it. He had definitely heard someone nearby and wouldn't be taking any chances from now on. He'd rather be thought foolish and over cautious than be taken by surprise and injured, or worse.

But he hadn't expected this here and would definitely tell Walter and his other friends about it.

When Terry Catlow heard what Ollerton called out, he stood absolutely still, shocked that he'd been noticed by a townie. He stayed there motionless until he was sure the newcomer was staying indoors then detoured round the cottage and made his way quietly down towards Upperfold through the grounds of the estate.

Used to protecting himself, that one was. Who'd have thought a townie would be so aware of his surroundings in the country? He'd thought they were all soft.

Well, let's see how Ollerton liked having his house damaged every now and then. It'd be easy to find a time when the man was out. There were other ways to make life unpleasant for someone as well and he knew most of them. This man was a member of that damned family so deserved to be driven from the valley – or worse.

When he got to the edge of the village a dog came rushing out of one garden to attack him, but Terry's kick sent it back where it came from, yelping loudly.

Unfortunately the owner came out then so he had to run away in order not to be recognised. He'd have to go round another way to get back from his little outings in future.

He took his time walking the rest of the way home. He enjoyed going out at night when there were hardly any other people around, always had done. You could learn a lot from watching others and some people were stupid enough to sit in lighted rooms without closing their curtains.

His own family were all in bed when he got back. They were used to his little moonlight strolls and knew better than to talk about them to anyone else. He had a bottle of beer standing waiting in a corner of the pantry, so got it out and enjoyed a drink.

He had a lot to think about.

All he'd decided so far was that he wasn't letting that sod stay in this valley. Whatever it took. Now he had to decide how to make sure the man left.

16

As soon as it was light the following morning Edward went outside and took a careful look round, taking care not to put his feet down anywhere till he'd checked the ground ahead. He carried the walking stick for protection but with the sword blade sheathed. He didn't really think he'd be attacked in the daytime, however.

He was reminded of his younger years working in London, was glad now that he'd had to learn to protect himself in the meaner areas of the capital when he'd first moved there. He hadn't forgotten how to do that, and never would.

He sucked in his breath in sudden surprise when he found some footprints that weren't his near the rear door of the house and more to one side of the front door. It was obvious that someone had stood by the windows in each of those places, presumably trying to look inside. Thank goodness there were curtains fully covering the windows, however ragged, and he'd drawn them each time he went out, day or night.

He studied the footprints carefully. They belonged to someone with bigger feet than his and the intruder's boots were down-at-heel and needed repairing. He couldn't find any other footprints apart from his own so he didn't think there could have been more than one person following him home last night.

Why? Simple robbery or something else? He shook his head, unable even to guess.

He could probably deal with one person if he was attacked but would rather not have to put that to the test. He didn't enjoy being forced to resort to violence, which had always seemed to him to be a poor way of dealing with any situation.

He found more of the same large footprints among the bushes then followed a trail of them here and there in the damp earth. The person must have been walking around quite a lot. Thank goodness the ground had been damp or he'd not have realised.

Part of the time the intruder had been moving along a narrow path that Edward hadn't noticed before. Well, he thought it was a path. It wound in and out among some trees and overgrown shrubs and when he followed it downwards, it led him to the shoulder-high wall surrounding his grounds on the village side, meeting it just beyond the top end of Lillian's garden.

The footprints stopped after the three houses with a couple of deeper prints on the other side of the wall where the trespasser had presumably climbed over it. From there the prints led directly towards the road that led down into the village.

Did this person live in Upperfold? If so, it might be possible to trace him. If he lived in Ollerthwaite that might be more difficult. Edward knew that neither Walter nor any of the others wore boots like that. They were poor men's boots, made to be tough not elegant, worn for hard physical work.

Who had been looking round the outside of his house? And why? They must have been doing it for a while to leave all these traces. There were so many questions and possibilities to think about.

Had the person been intending to rob him last night? Or worse? No way of knowing at this stage.

Should he say something about it to Walter? Maybe, but he didn't want to go running for help every few minutes.

He'd definitely mention it if it happened again, though. He'd smooth out all the footprints he could find today and then make daily checks for new ones appearing along that rough path or near his house.

He'd found out as a lad that it was hard to move around in absolute silence, let alone without leaving tiny traces or being noticed by someone, far harder than most people realised. So he'd slip outside the back door a few times in the evenings and move around here and there near his cottage, simply listening, as well as checking for new footprints every morning and afternoon.

Perhaps it had been someone curious to see the new owner. But why do that after dark? No, that couldn't be the reason because he'd been out and about in the village and town already.

He'd keep a careful watch on his surroundings from now on. Very careful indeed.

Later that morning, with her few chores finished, Lillian left an older man putting a roof on the one yard of passage connecting the lavatory to her new bathroom and walked up the hill road to see whether it was convenient to practise her cycling near the cottage. She had to leave her house open at the rear but the man said he'd be there for most of the day.

It would have been quicker and more direct to clamber over the wall at the top of her garden, but she didn't like to do that without Edward's permission.

To her relief he looked genuinely happy to see her when he answered the door. She was happy to see him too. He was, after all, one of her closest neighbours, though not close in the normal sense of being next door.

She explained what she wanted and he immediately offered to come out and help her again. She turned to fetch her bicycle but he grabbed her arm.

'It's not there.' He let go and gestured to the house. 'I put it in my hall because there was someone skulking around outside my house last night and I was afraid they might steal it.'

He immediately regretted telling her that because she lost her smile abruptly and it was replaced by an apprehensive look. 'It was someone trying to find out about me,' he explained quickly. 'There were footprints in various places all round my cottage. I'm sure it was nothing to do with you.'

She still looked doubtful, so he added, 'To hell with possible gossip about you and me. Come inside and tell me about what brought you here to Ollindale and why you're so afraid. How can your friends help you if you keep the details of all your worries to yourself?'

'You count yourself a friend?'

'If you'll allow me to.'

'Oh, yes, please. That makes me feel good.'

They smiled at one another then went inside and she sat next to him in the kitchen.

'Now tell me,' he said gently.

At first she was hesitant to explain, then it all poured out and she told him about her unhappy marriage and her in-laws, how they'd sent men after her and Riley had saved her.

He'd heard parts of the story before but not the complete story. 'You still haven't said why they were so determined to get hold of you.'

She closed her eyes, swallowed hard and pushed her embarrassment aside to explain what she thought they wanted, then looked him in the eyes and said firmly, 'I am definitely not expecting Stanley's child or indeed, any child.'

He thought for a moment then nodded, feeling sickened by the thought of such worries haunting her like this. Thank goodness Riley had found her. 'Grief can make people do strange things.'

'It wasn't grief. They'd behaved strangely before, especially Mr Thursten. Their son hated them but was too afraid of what his father might do if he disobeyed their orders, so he hardly ever resisted. Well, they held the purse strings, didn't they? He had a clerical job and it didn't pay much.'

After another short silence he said, 'I do wish you weren't living alone, Lillian. Even hiring a young maid would make your life there much safer.'

'I can't afford one.' She hesitated, then added, 'I'm saving up to buy a house of my own one day, you see. It's not that I think Walter would throw me out; it's that I need to feel permanently at home, to have a place that's truly my own.'

'I can understand your feelings. It's why I've put so much effort into providing a new family home for the Ollertons. I'm sure you'll get your home one day.' He reached out to take her hand and pat it, and she let hers lie in the warmth of his grasp for a few moments.

Friends, he'd said. And now he was holding her hand, not in any nasty, suggestive way but for comfort. Oh, she'd longed so much for friends and now it was happening. Another of her dreams was coming true. She had gone for years without even touching anyone, had hungered for human contact, only not contact with *them*.

She had to force herself to pull away and get her emotions under control again, but she smiled at him as she did it. 'This conversation has reminded me that I need to go and see the lawyer in Ollerthwaite about my money so that I can get my inheritance in order and control my own savings.'

'Would you like me to come with you?'

She looked at him in slight puzzlement.

'I've very good with accounts and figures. I can probably learn enough about this lawyer from your initial conversation with him to work out whether he seems like an honest fellow and also whether he's any good with money. I don't want to boast but I'm better than most people at dealing with finances and making the best of assets.'

'His uncle is a well-respected lawyer,' she said doubtfully.

'And yet it was in his uncle's house that you were found and persuaded to go out into danger after dark. He might be a good lawyer and he might mean well, but he's careless about details and security. How do we know his nephew will be any better?'

She let out an involuntary, 'Oh!' of shock at this blunt criticism. 'Surely Mr Baker wouldn't have been colluding with my in-laws to kidnap me?'

'Oh, no. I doubt that. But I've found over the past decades that people can surprise you, not only in good or bad ways, but in carelessness too, which can also lead to problems. So you should take care how you deal with this nephew.'

That made sense. 'Then I'd better learn to ride that bicycle properly so that I can get around more easily – or get away quickly if necessary. I wonder . . . since you offered, could you spare the time to come with me this afternoon to the lawyer's? I know it's imposing on your kindness but – well, I am rather ignorant of legal and financial matters.'

'I'd be happy to.' For her he'd make the time. 'Let's go outside and practise. I think you'll find it easier to get your balance today.'

And so it proved. Her natural grace of movement, something he'd noticed about her before, translated quickly into an ability to ride a bicycle steadily. Well, mostly steadily.

After she'd gone home, this time riding the bicycle with a very tense look of concentration on her face, he followed her for a short distance on his own trusty steed. When they reached her house, she stopped and he waved goodbye then rode on into Ollerthwaite.

In the town he found out from the chatty lady at the post office that the lawyer she needed to see had an office just behind the main street, but that he lived outside the town on the southern side. And the woman he talked to also volunteered the information that Mr Turnby was a 'nice young chap'.

He found the lawyer's office easily and went inside to make an appointment with the young clerk for Lillian to see his employer that afternoon. Afterwards he did some necessary shopping for food, rather surprised at how often you had to do that if you wanted fresh food, and went home.

He might as well use the time until he found an architect and his life got busier to help her, he decided as he ate some bread, ham and celery just after midday. He was finding her circumstances quite interesting but he didn't know the local situation well enough, so he went across to Walter's farm.

He was lucky to find that his neighbour had just returned home so they sat and shared a pot of tea and a piece of delicious sponge cake in the privacy of the sitting room and Edward confided his worries about both his own intruder and Lillian's situation to the older man.

'I'm glad you told me. We'll all keep our eyes open from now on. I've seen footprints in the grounds of the estate near the two small houses occasionally over the past few years but I thought it was just lads poking their noses in.'

'I doubt a lad on his own would be out after dark following me home, stopping when I did, moving only after I moved.'

'Definitely not. Who could have been doing it, though? That baffles me.'

'Me too. How could I have any enemies here when I've only just arrived in the valley? It doesn't make sense.'

Walter frowned then spread his hands in a helpless gesture. 'Must be enemies of your family.'

'After all this time?'

'Who knows with some people? You're right to take care. That walking stick sounds a useful item to carry when you go into town. I'd like to see it next time I'm at your house.'

'I'll bring it along this evening to show you, but you're welcome to visit me any time. And I've had enough practice in the kitchen to make you a decent cup of tea now.'

'I'll look forward to that. In the meantime I think you should take Maude with you and Lillian when you go to see her lawyer. It'll not only look more respectable but she can drive the three of you there and back in our cart. Apart from anything else we don't want Lillian to get known for flirting with you. A woman's reputation is precious but fragile.'

Flirting with him! Edward smiled at the thought of that. But they were getting more friendly. And he not only enjoyed her company but found her attractive. He didn't rule out the idea of pursuing matters further with her but at the moment he had other things to attend to, especially someone stalking him.

He rode his bicycle back via Lillian's house where Riley and another man he didn't recognise were working hard at the rear on the new bathroom and making more rapid progress than he'd expected.

When he told her what he'd done, Lillian nodded. 'Walter's right. It will look better to have Maude with us. I continue to be surprised at how kind people are here.'

'Most people, anyway. You will be careful, won't you? Particularly after dark. Don't let Riley leave any way for intruders to get into the house.'

She smiled wryly. 'Walter has already made that very clear to him and to me.'

'Good. Maude and I will come for you at about half past one, then.'

'I'll be ready.'

When the cart drew to a halt at the front of Lillian's house, Edward got down and waited for her to join them. He was looking more smartly dressed than usual and so was Maude. Lillian was wearing the best clothes she had, but she was shabby compared to them and wished her other possessions would arrive.

It took her only a minute to go across to the cart and get up on the driving bench next to Maude, who was holding the reins. When Edward got up on the other side of her she felt safe and happy, not to mention excited at the prospect of getting complete possession of her money. She could afford to have a few new clothes made, more attractive ones.

Mr Turnby looked nothing like his uncle and behaved in a much more friendly manner.

'I'm delighted to meet you, Mrs Hesketh. I presume you've come to make arrangements about your savings and quarterly payments?'

'Your uncle said he'd get the bank to send the money from my inheritance into your charge here.'

'Yes, that's been done.' Mr Turnby didn't continue but glanced towards Edward and Maude as if asking what they were doing there, and she realised she'd forgotten to introduce them.

'I'm so sorry. I should have introduced my friends. This is Miss Vernon. And Mr Ollerton.'

'Pleased to meet you both. I've seen you around town of course, Miss Vernon, but we've never spoken.'

Maude held out her hand just as men did and he looked surprised for a moment, then shook it before shaking Edward's hand.

'You must be the new owner of the Ollerton estate.'

'Yes, I've brought it back into my family's hands again.'

After that, in some way she couldn't quite work out, Edward gently took over the conversation.

'I'm Mrs Hesketh's financial adviser as well as a family friend, so I shall be helping her and you with the management of her finances.'

Mr Turnby couldn't hide his surprise at this. 'My uncle didn't mention that. Did he ask you to intervene?'

'No. This is nothing to do with him. I've dealt with finances for years so naturally I help my friends too. From what she tells me your uncle simply let the money accrue standard bank interest instead of putting it to longer-term use and making a little more money from it.'

'Er – yes.'

The lawyer looked back at her. 'Are you happy with this intervention, Mrs Hesketh?'

'Very happy. I have absolute confidence in Mr Ollerton's financial skills. But first I need to get a new bank account in my name only. I gather the money will be available to me immediately. Am I right?'

'Er, yes. Well, it will be as soon as I inform the bank and you go in to sign the various papers.'

'And after that I'll leave its management in Mr Ollerton's capable hands from now on.' She didn't know why she had such absolute trust in Edward but she did. 'But I hope you will continue as my lawyer, Mr Turnby.'

He brightened slightly. 'I'm happy to do that.'

She glanced sideways at Maude, seeing her friend watching them with bright-eyed interest. It was the way the other woman always seemed to deal with the world and Lillian suddenly wondered if she kept her feelings too hidden. Maybe, given how her life was improving now, she should try greeting the world more cheerfully.

'Once we've finished our business here, we can all go to the bank and sort out the transfer of the money to Mrs Hesketh's care, if that's all right with you,' Edward said. 'It isn't far away.'

'Um, yes. Certainly.'

After they'd completed their business, the lawyer walked with them to the bank, where the manager was very happy to welcome a new customer in person and fussed gently over Lillian.

The manager also seemed impressed to find that Edward was an Ollerton and was helping her with her finances, and even happier when Edward said he too would like to open an account here.

By the time they came out, Lillian was the owner and the sole controller of a bank account containing over two hundred pounds, thanks to her frugality, with a further fifty put into Edward's charge for investment. He had insisted he would feel better showing her what he could do before he dealt with more of her money than that.

Another of her secret dreams was likely to become a reality within a few years, if she continued to be careful: buying a home of her own, not just renting one like most people did.

She had enough saved already to purchase a very small house, what they called a terraced dwelling, but it would leave her without much money in the bank to cover emergencies, so she intended to wait a few years longer till her finances were more secure – and till her personal life felt secure, too. She didn't want or need a large house but she did want one with a big garden in a respectable area, not to mention with a modern interior.

'It's shameful that your previous lawyer just left the money to sit doing nothing,' Edward muttered as the three of them stood in the bank doorway watching Mr Turnby cross the street and go back into his rooms. He turned to smile at Lillian. 'I promise you I'll make you more money than that man would. We'll start with this first fifty pounds to give you confidence in my skills. My own money has been hard-earned, I assure you, which has left me always erring on the cautious side.'

'I trust you absolutely.' And she did. She also saw Maude nod agreement to that.

'You'll be surprised how steadily the extra will mount up over a year or two. I'm still maintaining relations with an associate in London about my own investments, so he and I can help you place yours with mine wherever we see a different opportunity.'

'I'm grateful for your help, Edward.'

'I'll always help my friends.' He turned to Maude. 'We've taken up a lot of your time today, I'm afraid.'

'It's been very interesting,' she said. 'My savings are tiny compared to Lillian's but I'd still like to make the most of them.'

'Are you saving for something special or just to have money behind you?'

'Like many others it's to have money for my old age. I've never aspired to owning my own house. At the moment my cousin Walter has given me a home, but since he's older than me I have to prepare for the future when I'll be on my own.'

He couldn't help thinking of how Riley looked at her and went as far as to say, 'You might still meet someone and get married.'

'I can hope that it'll happen but even if I do, I'll feel better if I always have something of my own to fall back on in case things go wrong.'

'I'm happy to offer you advice about financial opportunities. We should talk about your savings at some quiet time.'

'Good. I'd appreciate that.'

He didn't know what made him say it but the words were out before he knew it because he felt so comfortable with both these women. 'As for marriage, I'm past the usual age, too, but I haven't given up hope of finding someone. I'd dearly like to have children to continue my family's direct line, otherwise it'll die out after me.'

'I don't have a family line that I care about but I do wish I'd had children,' Maude said.

Lillian's voice was very quiet. 'So do I.'

They all three fell silent for a few moments, then Maude said briskly, 'Now, I suggest we stop at the baker's in Upperfold on the way back and buy some cake to celebrate Lillian getting her money through. My treat. They have a table where you can sit and buy a cup of tea or a glass of lemonade to go with their food.'

No one objected to that suggestion and every crumb of the delicious Bakewell tarts was consumed.

As they drove back home afterwards Lillian thought how lucky it was that she'd chosen to come here. Mr Baker had been right about that, at least.

Could the lawyer have been complicit in the attempt to kidnap her? No. She didn't think so. She'd had years of knowing that her in-laws were spying on her. They must have set someone to spy on her lawyer too, especially after he'd asked to speak to her alone. They'd hated him doing that, from the sour expressions on their faces.

In fact, they seemed to be suspicious of the whole world, and Mr Thursten in particular could get very vicious when he spoke about other people he didn't approve of.

When she got down from the cart, she thanked her friends then went to see what progress Riley had made on the new bathroom.

To her delight there was a new wall almost finished, connecting the outdoor lavatory to the house and bathroom, but there wasn't a hole in the house wall yet and wouldn't be till the last minute, so no one could break in.

'Will you be all right using your home like this overnight?' Riley asked.

'I'll be fine.' She could feel herself flushing in embarrassment, wasn't going to go into details about the chamber pot now residing under her bed, something she would empty in the early morning before they started work.

When they left, the house was securely closed to the outside world. She'd gone round it again once she was alone just to be utterly sure.

She was looking forward to a quiet meal, then she'd sit and read a book Maude had lent her. She hadn't dared keep a diary during her marriage, but she might buy a brand new one and start writing in it now. There were so many interesting things happening to her. She didn't ever want to forget how her life had unfolded like a beautiful flower lately because it was a wonderful thing to experience.

She might not have children to love, and talking about that had made her feel sad, but at least now she was making friends with people who did care about her, as she was starting to care about them.

She didn't get much reading done. She kept listening carefully to the noises from the other houses, and peeping out of the windows to check her own garden. She'd feel more comfortable here when she was used to what were the normal sounds outside, surely? At the moment, every sound she couldn't identify was something to worry about.

Mr Baker's clerk opened the first delivery of letters and put the ones his employer needed to deal with personally into a little pile. As the lawyer was out that morning and wouldn't be coming in till the afternoon, the pile sat there undisturbed.

During the midday meal break the junior member of staff left in charge of the office moved quietly along the corridor and into the lawyer's room. The letter from his employer's nephew, which he'd slit open for the head clerk, was at the top of the pile and it was the work of a few moments to pull it out and read it, then put it back.

It brought a smile to the man's face. She'd turned up at last, had she? That news would bring him a nice little reward from certain people.

He was back at his desk when the others came in and then took his own lunch break. Only he didn't go out to eat his sandwiches in the park but hurried through the streets to a small office on the first floor of a short terrace of buildings occupied mostly by minor businesses.

The occupant of the office looked at him eagerly. 'Ah! He's waiting impatiently for news. Did you hear something already?'

'Yes. But I want paying the agreed amount before I tell you.'

'I've always paid before, haven't I?'

'Yes. But I'm not risking this being the first time you don't. I never take risks where money is concerned.'

When the man had handed over a sovereign, the information was given in exchange and then the junior clerk walked back to the lawyer's office. It was worth going hungry to earn that extra money. And he'd continue to keep watch. He didn't care about the rights and wrongs of the situation. All he knew was that his children were forever wearing out their shoes or needing new clothes, and his wife got worried about money regularly.

The letter was still there waiting for Mr Baker to get back. He blew it a mental kiss as he passed it and went back to his own cramped desk in a small room down the corridor.

17

Lewis Brody sent a telegram to Edward to say that he was currently visiting family in Yorkshire and could come across to Lancashire to meet with him in two days' time rather than going back to London first, if that was all right. And he wasn't fussy, would be grateful for whatever sleeping arrangements could be organised.

If it seemed possible that they could come to some agreement about designing and building a house, he would like to spend a few days there to check the terrain and discuss in more detail exactly what sort of spaces were wanted inside the house.

Lewis was both surprised and pleased to receive an immediate reply suggesting he come to visit but saying he should let Mr Ollerton know exactly when he'd be arriving so that he could pick him up at the station since there wasn't a taxi service in the valley, either.

Well, that settled one thing he'd been wondering about: his beloved tricycle. These weren't nearly as common as bicycles, and some drivers of carts and carriages complained about them, saying they went too slowly and took up far too much room on narrow country roads. One or two people had even tried to edge him off into the ditch.

But he found it far more useful as a means of transport than a bicycle would have been. The Leicester Safety Tricycle Company produced very reliable and efficient vehicles these days and Lewis sometimes needed to carry his tools and equipment around. Their rear carriers held more than a two-wheeled bicycle's front basket did and the three wheels kept both rider and the heavier load steady.

Their main fault as far as he was concerned was that they attracted attention. Nosey people wanted him to stop and tell them about his tricycle. And cheeky lads called out insults, which they thought funny and he thought rude.

He sent a telegram asking for directions to the lodge and explaining that he'd bring his tricycle so that he could travel around on it once he got to Ollerthwaite.

Edward responded with another telegram saying he was looking forward to seeing how this type of vehicle performed and giving Lewis the necessary directions to the lodge. He didn't mind the extra expense of another telegram because he was dying to get started on planning the new house.

A minor point was that he was intrigued by the prospect of getting to know how a tricycle performed. He hadn't had a lot to do with them as they weren't nearly as common as bicycles, especially in city centres.

What he really wanted for his own future transport was for motor cars to become more reliable and cheaper, as they seemed to be doing in America. He was sure they were the vehicle of the future and he'd already invested in his friend's embryonic business, which sounded to be at a promising stage.

Sadly, at the moment, cars were mainly used by richer folk in England and there didn't seem to be anyone in the valley who owned one. He was rich enough to buy a car now but he wasn't an engineer and didn't want the annoyance of regular breakdowns and repairs. Give them a few years and he was sure they would become more common and more reliable, and then he'd be at the head of the queue to buy one.

The arrival of the architect wouldn't stop him trying to help Lillian, he decided, as he prepared the second bedroom at the lodge for his visitor. And since she seemed to have an eye for the positioning of houses and had made some good sugges-tions for arranging garden plants and flowerbeds to best effect, he'd ask her to join them for at least some of the discussions.

She'd surprised him by her ability to visualise how things would look. He could spot talent when he found it, which was how he'd made some of his money, and he now wanted her opinion on where the house should be built and what sort of rooms would be needed inside a modern dwelling, as well as how to organise his garden. In return he'd manage her money to better effect.

Apart from any other consideration in designing the house, women made up half the population of the world, and they too lived and worked in houses. He would consider it ineffi-cient to leave them out of the planning.

He smiled, remembering how he'd listened to his mother complain about the various houses they'd rented. If he'd heard her say once that 'men should have to work in the kitchens and sculleries they design so badly', he'd heard her say it twenty times.

Riley finished a hard day's work and pedalled tiredly but happily up to the farm, looking forward to spending the evening with his friends. It was Maude he especially enjoyed chatting to, he admitted to himself.

To his delight she was the only person in the kitchen when he got back. She told him that Cameron and Elinor had gone out for a stroll by the river and Walter was still busy in his little office at the other side of the farmyard.

Riley hurried up to his bedroom, washed and changed out of his working clothes as rapidly as he could, then hurried down to rejoin Maude. He let out his breath in a happy sigh when he found her still alone in the kitchen.

She came to join him at the table. 'The food's ready and I'm only waiting for everyone to gather before I get the casserole out of the oven. If you're ravenously hungry I can give you a piece of bread and butter to tide you over.'

'I'd rather sit and enjoy a chat with you.'

When he picked up her hand and held it as he asked how her day had gone, she gave him a quick glance and a shy, uncertain smile. She didn't pull away, though.

After they'd talked about his day's work, they inevitably got round to discussing modern bathrooms and kitchens, about which she had some very firm opinions. She let go of his hand to gesticulate as she talked and he listened carefully and in some surprise. Not only did her ideas and practical solutions catch his attention but they made him ask if she had any more thoughts on what she'd consider more practical ways of finishing off bathrooms.

When she stopped talking it took him a minute to marshal his thoughts and she began to look worried.

'I shouldn't interfere, Riley. You're the expert, after all.'

'Yes, you should tell me what you think. I asked because Edward said Lillian had some good ideas about the practicalities of designing and choosing sites for buildings and I think you have some good ideas as well. Please continue.'

At one stage he held up one hand to stop her and said, 'That sounds like a particularly sound idea. Can we discuss it in more detail when we're not likely to be interrupted? I think it would suit a modern kitchen much better than the way I'd been planning to arrange things in the next kitchen I deal with.'

She looked at him in surprise then chuckled.

'What's so amusing?'

'When you fell silent, I thought I'd annoyed you and I was just about to apologise and start minding my own business.'

'On the contrary, Maude. But let's continue the discussion another time. Don't hold back if you have other ideas. Things are changing rapidly these days as to how houses are built and what is installed in them, and I think plumbers should also change some of their ways of doing things too.'

She beamed at him. 'I'd love to talk about that sort of thing. I often look at kitchens and wish I could reorganise parts of them. After all, we have to wash the dishes and cook several times a day.'

'How about coming down to study what we're doing in Lillian's bathroom tomorrow and seeing what you think? If you can spare the time, I mean.' He hesitated then added, 'And how about coming for a walk with me at the weekend as well? I really enjoy your company.' He waited and wasn't disappointed in her reply. She was proving to be one of the most straightforwardly honest women he'd ever met and he loved that because he was no good whatsoever at guessing what other people, particularly females, were thinking, and was pitifully bad at making meaningless conversation.

After she'd stared at him in surprise for a moment or two she said, 'I like spending time with you, too, Riley.'

'Good. So you'll come out with me for a walk on Sunday? I usually find walking with women rather difficult because I'm so tall. I have to bend sideways even to hear what the softer-voiced ones say. You and I are close to the same height and that will make walking together far more pleasant.'

'I'd love that. I have problems with my height too. Shorter men usually try to avoid walking beside me at all, even when we're in groups.'

He nodded. 'I've noticed it happening to other tall women. How about a morning walk? Or were you intending to go to church?'

'Definitely not. The new preacher's sermons are boring and very trite so I've been avoiding it lately.'

'What about the Sunday dinner? Don't you have to cook that?'

'I can start off a leg of lamb roasting and leave Elinor to keep an eye on it and prepare the vegetables. She'll be past the early morning sickness by that time. Could we walk right round Jubilee Lake, do you think? I love it there. And we'll see more if we go on foot than we would whizzing along on bicycles.'

'I agree. You can chat better on foot, too. I love walking near water. Silver to salute the moon and gold to greet the sun, Lillian called it – I liked that saying.'

'What a nice picture it paints!'

Walter came in from the yard just then and the others soon followed, so their private chatting stopped, but Riley glanced at Maude more than once as the meal progressed, admiring her liveliness.

He was pleased to catch her staring across at him a few times, too.

When people discussed what they were planning for the weekend, Riley told them that he and Maude were going for a long walk on the Sunday. He had a moment's fear that someone would volunteer to come with them. But when Edward opened his mouth, presumably to do that, Walter jabbed him in the ribs and shook his head.

'Let's hope the weather stays fine for the weekend,' Riley whispered to Maude as they snatched another few private words when everyone started getting ready for bed.

He smiled about her frankness as he lay in the darkness in a nearby bedroom. Why couldn't everyone be like that and say what they really felt or wanted? It'd make life so much easier.

Riley got his wish and Sunday turned out to be a beautiful autumn day with the sun shining but no real warmth in it, which was perfect for a brisk walk.

Shortly after they set off, Maude beamed at him. 'Our strides match perfectly.'

He risked adding something else. 'I think a lot of things about us fit rather well.'

She surprised him by stopping dead at that, giving him a searching look, then taking a deep breath. 'Can we speak openly about how well we're getting on?'

'Yes, let's. I'm no good at pretending about things that are important to me, and as for wrapping my thoughts up in fancy words, I can't do it. So I'll ask you straight out: can we walk out together regularly?'

'Yes. And . . ,' She hesitated.

'Go on.'

'I'm terrified of making a fool of myself, especially at my age, Riley, so can we be even more clear about exactly where you intend the walking out to lead?'

'You're terrified? Of me?'

'Not of you, of course not. What I'm afraid of is mistaking your intentions and making a fool of myself. It's happened so quickly – you and me meeting and getting on well, I mean – that I'm still finding my way.'

'I'm surprised at the speed of it too, I must admit, but I'm not terrified.'

'It's easier for men. Women so often have to guess. You do mean – well, that we'll be courting? That's what people usually mean by calling it walking out.' Her cheeks were scarlet now.

'Of course I do. I thought that was obvious.' Now he was the one feeling anxious. 'Is that all right with you?'

She let out her breath in a big whoosh of relief. 'Very much all right.'

'Let me say it loud and clear then – I'd like to walk out with you officially with a view to spending our lives together if we continue to get on so well. Is that all right with you?'

'Oh, yes. I love being with you. You've never bored me, not in the slightest, whether we're with other people or chatting together. It'd be no fun courting someone who bored you, would it?'

It was his turn to give her a beaming smile. 'No fun at all.'

As they continued walking, holding hands openly now, he asked suddenly, 'How old are you? I don't even know that.'

Her expression turned apprehensive again. 'Thirty-nine, almost forty.'

'Really? You don't look it. I can't understand why no one has ever come courting you before. You're a handsome woman.'

'It's partly because I'm too tall for most men and partly because I was looking after Elinor for years. Once I'd grown to love her I couldn't have left anyone else to raise her. I knew how to look after children even though I wasn't much older than her, you see, because there were a lot of them around when I was growing up.'

'Didn't her family look after her?'

'Not really. What about you, Riley? How old are you? And why are you not married? '

'I'm thirty-seven and I've nearly got married a time or two, I must admit. Only somehow I always lost interest in the woman after a while, however pretty she was, so I moved on.'

'Do you mind our age differences?'

He gave her a puzzled look. 'What's to mind about them?'

'You're younger than I am.'

He let out a sudden snort of laughter. 'Of course I don't mind that. Anyway, it's only a couple of years.'

'That's good. But there's another thing we need to discuss. At forty I might be past having children.'

'I'm not far behind you. I might not manage to create any children. We'll have to wait and find out. Stop worrying and let's just enjoy being together from now on, eh?'

They started walking and he smiled warmly sideways at her from time to time but didn't fill every minute with words. Well, what was the point of mindless chatter?

At one point, since no one else was in sight, he pulled her closer and kissed her. She was the perfect height for kissing as well as for walking with.

Then there were suddenly loud whistles and cries nearby and they jerked apart to see a group of children standing a short distance away, jeering at them. The biggest boy was making loud kissing sounds and kissing the palm of his right hand, than laughing mockingly.

When Riley took a step towards them they ran off, shrieking with laughter, and he was smiling too when he turned back to Maude. He felt as if the whole world had changed for him today, as if his feet had been firmly set on a new and better path to follow through life in both work and family life.

The weather echoed his happy thoughts because the sun kept shining down on them, a cooler autumn sun but it still made the water ahead of them sparkle enticingly.

When they got to the narrower top end, the path vanished and some of the ground was uncleared and rough underfoot.

As they stopped to study the terrain, he said, 'You know what? It wouldn't take much to improve this part of the path so that everyone, young or old, was able to walk all the way round the lake, including people pushing prams or in wheelchairs. Even in winter it'd make a lovely outing on a fine day. I wonder why it's unfinished?'

'Cousin Walter said that years ago he'd organised a group of people from Ollerthwaite to make the lake bigger and it's now twice as big as it used to be. They wanted to finish it in time for the Queen's Golden Jubilee in '87, which is how the new lake got its name, but they didn't manage to put in a proper path all the way round it in time for the celebrations as they'd originally planned.'

'Why not?'

'Because the Russian 'flu stopped work. And then it came back more than once in the following years.'

He didn't move on, kept studying the nearby area. 'I wonder if Walter could get enough people interested again so that we could finish the job in time for Her Majesty's coming Diamond Jubilee? I'd be happy to help with that.'

'What a good idea! That jubilee isn't for another two years, so we'd have time, surely – and as long as the Queen stays in good health, of course. I'd be happy to help too.' She considered this, head on one side, and he couldn't resist planting a quick kiss on her nearest cheek.

That brought him another of her wonderful smiles, though she pretended to scold him. 'Concentrate! We were discussing the lake. If enough people helped we'd surely have time to finish the job. Let's suggest it to Walter when we get back.'

'Good idea. But we'd better start moving again or we'll be late for Sunday dinner. I love roast lamb.'

They were back in plenty of time. Outside the house she tried to take her hand away from his, but he held on to it.

'I'm not ready to face their knowing looks yet.' She whispered the words even though there was no one close enough to hear what she was saying.

'I'm ready. And people have seen us walking together, so your family will find out anyway and be upset that we didn't tell them ourselves first.'

'Oh dear. So they will.'

He pulled her forward. 'Come on, love. Be brave.'

And heaven help her, Maude let him lead her inside and they stopped in the doorway as everyone turned round to stare at them.

Riley held up his free hand for silence, then said quietly before any of the others could speak, 'Maude and I have decided that we get on rather well, so we've started courting.' He held up their joined hands and everyone clapped or made approving noises.

Walter spoke for them all. 'That's excellent news. Best thing I've heard for a while.'

There was a further chorus of approval, then he took over again. 'Now, everyone, let's give these two time to get used to one another in peace. Elinor, is that food nearly ready? I'm famished.'

When Maude slipped across to help with the final preparations for dinner, Walter winked at Riley and gestured to the chair next to his. 'Welcome to the family, lad.'

'Thank you. I'm very happy about that.'

'You should be. She's a grand lass.'

18

Lillian had been invited to Sunday dinner at the farm, but had asked if they could please excuse her this time because she was still sorting out her new home and couldn't settle till she'd done that.

The truth was, she needed time, peace and quiet to find herself again, and to try to cast off the meekness imposed by her former life. Her husband and his parents had squeezed all the joy out of her during the past few years. Somehow, pottering about in her house and garden seemed to be helping her regain her old self and feel happier generally.

Pottering about inside her mind too, she thought with a wry smile. She was doing a lot of thinking.

She worked indoors for a while, then went outside, walking up the side path to the wall at the top. When she looked over it she saw a rock that would just fit into the top low wall where one was missing. The rock was lying nearby and before she could think twice, she'd clambered over the wall, picked it up and brought it back. She'd been right. It did fit nicely into the top retaining wall.

After that she started to repair the other low walls separating the different levels in her upward sloping garden because they too had occasional gaps. She seemed to have an eye for rocks that would fit into them.

Doing that gave her an instant reward because it made the whole area look better to have tidy boundaries to each level. She didn't think Edward would mind her taking a few chunks of stone and it was easy enough to climb over the wall, using the cracks between stones for toeholds. She only took rocks that were hidden among vegetation or lying near the perimeter, not ones that looked to belong where they were as part of a border.

As she bent down behind a bush to pick up a piece of exactly the right size and shape to fill the end corner of one of her walls, she suddenly heard stones and twigs crunching. Someone must be moving up the slope towards her. She froze. She knew Edward wasn't at home so who could this be?

She was wary of strangers, still afraid of the Thurstens, so she stayed where she was, crouching out of sight and listening carefully. When the person had moved past her, she risked raising her head a little to peep through the upper branches of the group of bushes and find out who it was.

She didn't recognise the man but could guess from his slow movements and sideways glances that he didn't want to be seen, so she stayed hidden. He must know Edward was out or he'd not be prowling around here, but there was something rather furtive about him.

It puzzled her that he was carrying a spade, puzzled her even more when he used it to start digging a shallow trench among some low shrubs. She moved into a more comfortable position kneeling down but stayed where she was, watching him, ready to jump to her feet and run away at a second's notice if he caught sight of her.

The ground was soft in this part of the estate, some areas of which must once have formed an ornamental shrubbery, and the intruder dug quickly. He was a big, strong man and she didn't like the way he scowled whenever he glanced towards the lodge, which was another reason for her to stay hidden. After a while he lay down full length on his stomach in the trench, head slightly raised at the cottage end, staring across at the building. When he got out, he dug the trench a little deeper all the way along, scattering the earth carefully here and there to hide what he'd been doing.

It looked as if he intended to keep watch on the cottage from the trench. Why on earth would he want to do that? Was he planning to burgle it? No, that couldn't be the reason or he'd have broken in today while Edward was away. Why, then?

When he put down the spade and lay in the hole again, he was completely hidden and even knowing he was there, she could hardly see him, not even when he lifted his head slightly and peered out, because he was wearing a dark cap. He must have a good view of the front door from there.

After a while he got up and brushed the dirt off his clothes, smiling. It was a nasty smile, not a happy one, which made her even more thankful she'd stayed out of sight. She wouldn't like to get on the wrong side of this man.

She watched him pick up his spade and set off back the way he'd come. Relieved that he hadn't noticed her, she remained where she was till he'd clumped noisily past her hiding place and gone further down the slope.

When she next risked a glance he was moving along the boundary wall at the back of the three cottages in a crouching position. Once he was a few yards past them he stopped again and glanced round before standing up. A few paces further along he clambered quickly over the wall, dislodging one of the topping stones but not bothering to pick it up.

He hurried across the rough ground towards the road, tall enough that she could see him for a while. He walked openly along the road that led down the hill to Upperfold, but he held the spade close to his body so as not to draw attention to it.

Something about him made her feel deeply uneasy so in case he turned round to scan the hillside, she stayed where she was until he'd completely vanished from sight where the road met the next group of cottages. Only then did she go to examine the trench more closely. You could hardly see it till you got right next to it, because it was surrounded by bushes on this side. On a sudden impulse she edged through them and lay down in it, facing the same way he had.

That confirmed what she'd suspected: the spot was very cleverly chosen to look directly at the front door and living-room window of the cottage. She could see it all clearly without being seen herself as long as she didn't wear any bright colours that might show through the foliage. He must have removed a few branches of the bushes at the side nearer to the cottage to get such a clear line of sight.

She stood up and brushed the dirt off her clothes, then walked slowly back towards her own garden. She'd tell Edward about the intruder as soon as he came back, but that wouldn't be for a while so she might as well carry on with her gardening in the meantime.

There had been voices and occasional laughter coming from the other cottages when she'd started work out here, but now there were no sounds at all. Maybe they'd had their Sunday dinner, usually people's best meal of the week, and were indulging in the luxury of an afternoon nap. A lot of people did that. Her husband always had done, thank goodness.

After she'd filled in most of the gaps in her walls, she washed her hands and decided to bake an apple pie, which she'd been promising herself since she'd first seen the apple tree. The lower fruits were easy to reach and she'd picked a big bowl of ripe ones earlier. She'd see if she could borrow a ladder to pick the higher ones. Maybe she could get up into the roof and store them carefully spaced out on sheets of newspaper, then most of them would survive longer.

She got all the ingredients out. It'd have to be a plate pie because she didn't have any suitable shallow dishes, but she did have a few old plates of the right sort from Walter's baskets of household oddments. And why not make two while she was at it? She'd bought a big packet of lard and had plenty of flour, was sure Edward would welcome one.

There might be some bottling jars going cheap among Walter's stocks too. She should have thought of that. She could cook and preserve some of the apples. It was easy enough to peel them, cook them with a little sugar then bottle them in scalded jars.

She wondered whether there was an orchard on the estate. If so, that might yield more fruits. She'd have to find out. If they couldn't be used they could be given away to people from the village so as not to be wasted.

Making the two pies filled the time till she guessed Edward would have returned from the farm. She took them out of the oven and left them on a rack to cool because she couldn't bear to wait a minute longer to go and tell him.

She risked taking the shortcut over the wall and when she got to the cottage she was pleased to find that she'd guessed correctly about Edward being back because his bicycle was standing in front of the house. He opened the door to her knock almost immediately, smiling at her.

Before he could speak, she said baldly, 'Someone came onto your land while you were out. I don't know who he is, but he dug a trench among the bushes in a place where he could lie and watch your front door without being seen.'

Edward gaped at her for a few seconds then said simply, 'Show me.'

She took him along to the trench and they stood side by side looking down into it.

'Lie in it on your stomach with your head facing the house and you'll see what I mean.'

He followed her instructions and lay down in it, muttering, 'Hell fire!'

When he got out he said, 'You're right. It's perfectly placed to see my comings and goings. Why would anyone want to spy on me?'

She couldn't answer that.

He frowned and was silent for a minute or two, then shook his head slowly. 'I can't think what there is going on at the cottage for anyone to be interested in. I'm out much of the day and we're nowhere near to actually starting building yet. And there's nothing valuable kept inside. On the contrary.'

'I've been trying to work that out too.'

'Thank you for letting me know. Why don't you come in and have a cup of tea and I'll tell you the good news.'

'Tell me now. I'd love to hear some good news.'

'Riley and Maude went for a walk to the lake this morning then came back hand in hand and announced that they're courting.'

'That is lovely news. It's happened quickly, hasn't it? Did they look happy?'

'Very happy indeed. Soppy smiles, to say the least.'

They both chuckled then she said, 'Well, if anyone deserves to be happy, it's Riley. He saved me from my in-laws even though I was a complete stranger. I wish I'd had a brother just like him.'

'I took to him at once as well, and he's a hard worker. He's nearly finished your bathroom already. I'm dying for him to start work on mine. Now, how about that cup of tea?'

She decided to be frank. She'd had to face enough lies in recent years. 'Better not go inside. If anyone saw us, they might talk. Now, is it all right for me to pick up a few stones from the edge of your land near my house? I confess that I've taken a few already.'

'What on earth for?'

'To repair gaps in my little retaining walls so that they won't give way when I plant my vegetable gardens on each level.'

'I doubt I'll even notice that any have been taken. Help yourself.'

'Thank you. And I made you an apple pie today while I was making one for myself. It wasn't cool enough to bring and anyway, I haven't got a big enough flat basket to put the plate it's on into safely. But if you come to my cottage now, it'll have cooled a lot and you can take it home. Do you have a largish basket? If not you'll need a cloth to hold it with.'

'I do have a basket actually. My kind landlady packed all sorts of oddments in an old one of hers.'

'Then bring that.'

'I won't be a minute.' He ran back to his cottage and returned with a battered but perfectly usable basket. 'That's very kind of you, Lillian.'

'There are plenty of apples on that tree. I'm not going to waste a single one if I can help it.'

'I bet there's the remains of an orchard near where the big house used to be. I never thought to look for fruit.'

'I wondered about that too.'

They climbed the wall easily, laughing at themselves for acting like children as they sat on the top to stare down at the view of the valley and point things out to one another.

When they continued down towards the house, she showed him how she had mended the little walls in a few places.

'You're doing a good job.'

'I'm enjoying setting things to rights. I've longed for a home of my own.'

She made him a cup of tea but took care to serve it outside, sitting on the lowest wall so that the neighbours wouldn't think badly of her for entertaining a man.

'I'll buy a bench to put out here,' she said.

'Or I can make the wall a little wider, which won't cost anything.'

'I'll help you carry the stones to do that.'

'Good.'

They were quiet for a while and the silence was as comfortable as the chatting had been.

As he walked back to the cottage carrying the apple pie, Edward felt happier than he had for years. It had been a day full of friends and conversation, new friends admittedly whom he didn't know very well yet, but he felt sure they would stay friends. Best of all, however, had been his time with Lillian. She was . . . special.

He glanced down into the basket, licked his lips and broke off a piece of crust. The pie smelled wonderful and the crust was delicious.

But when he came near the shallow trench, he moved off the path to look at it again. His happy mood faded and he stopped to frown down at it, still unsure how to deal with this intrusion on his land.

He'd have to ask Walter's advice again, whether to fill it in or keep watch to see who had done this and try to work out what exactly the person was after before he pounced on the one who'd done it. And he would pounce eventually, he was sure of that. He hadn't made his fortune by letting people trample on him.

Nothing was ever straightforward, was it? Life usually dealt you a mixture of good and bad, whoever you were, and having plenty of money didn't prevent that.

He counted meeting Lillian and the others as some of the best things that had happened to him for years, though. The very best.

19

In Bolton, Eunice Thursten was visiting the people she thought of as *those dratted female paupers* at the hospital. These visits were a recent development and she didn't enjoy spending time with the women, but her husband wanted her to keep an eye open for a young woman about to have a baby or who had just produced one.

Today there was a new patient, a youngish woman expecting a child within a few days. Eunice studied her as she helped her get washed and into one of the hospital gowns the paupers had to wear, noting that she had the right colour of hair and was quite tall. Even her nose was a close match in shape to that of Eunice's son.

As always, tears came into her eyes at the thought of Stanley. How could he have died so suddenly and so young? She blamed his wife and one day she was going to make Mary pay for the poor care she'd taken of him. Only, Lemuel said Mary was calling herself Lillian now. She'd run away soon after the funeral.

Lemuel had been cunning as usual and had bribed Mr Baker's junior clerk to keep an eye open for a letter from her. He'd already found out where her furniture was being stored. Even so, Eunice didn't see how they could force her to come back here.

Her husband said to leave that to him and he usually managed to get what he wanted – well, except for making a lot of money. He hadn't managed that.

The thought of having a baby to raise brought her hope and she didn't care what they had to do to get one. She loved babies.

When the time was ripe Lemuel had vowed to bring the young widow back and make her do her duty to the Thursten family by helping signal to people that there was a new heir to raise. And he'd said Mary must have some money or she'd never have escaped. He would be able to look after that much better than she could.

Eunice looked down at the patient, who was now lying quietly in bed, looking exhausted. 'Can I get you anything, dear?'

The young woman shook her head. 'No, thank you, missus.' She turned over, looking uncomfortable. Eunice had seen it before. This woman was nearing the time to bring the infant into the world.

After that they could take it over.

Sure enough, the people at the mother-and-baby home looked after Clara and fed her properly, and she did produce a healthy baby a few days later. It was a little boy, not as pretty as Stanley had been but still rather nice to cuddle.

Lemuel came to the hospital with his wife and had a good look at it while the mother was asleep.

When she woke up, they sat with her for a while and offered her a live-in job with them when she left the hospital.

The nurse in charge overheard them and stopped them on the way out. 'Are you sure you're doing the right thing, Mr Thursten? What will you do about the baby?'

'Look after it, of course,' he said. 'We lost our own son recently and have vowed to devote our life to looking after the children of the poor, making sure they have a better start in life than their parents can usually provide.'

The nurse hesitated, then said, 'I still think you could find a better subject for your charitable works than this one, frankly. Clara was working on the streets, selling her body to men before she sought our help for the lying in.'

'We know,' Lemuel said. 'But we have vowed to save her body as well as her soul. We've managed it before, though not without a struggle, I admit. But the Lord is with us and we shall overcome.'

He bowed his head as if praying, but Eunice knew he wasn't. He never really did, just used those quiet moments to study people and work out his little schemes.

By the time they took Clara and her son home a few days later, Lemuel had found a wet nurse and bought the furniture and clothing they'd need to start raising their 'grandson'.

'We'll speak to Clara tomorrow,' he said. 'Then I'll take her to wherever she wants to go.'

'You're sure she'll agree?' Eunice worried.

'Oh, yes. She's not at all interested in her baby. I could tell that very quickly. We've fallen lucky with this one.'

The next day he offered Clara twenty pounds to hand the child over to them, then go away and never come near this part of Lancashire again.

She stared at them in amazement. 'You mean that, don't you?'

'Yes.'

'I want to see the money first.'

Lemuel pulled out three five-pound notes and five sovereigns and put them down on the table, keeping his hand splayed across them.

Clara licked her lips. 'I'll do it.'

'If you ever come back for the child, I'll pay someone to hit you over the head and drop your body in the nearest mill race,' Lemuel said in a calm but firm voice.

She gaped at him for a moment or two then let out a burst of harsh laughter. 'I shan't come back, believe me, Mr Thursten. I don't want saddling with that damned kid. I'll not only stay away from it, I'll *move* right away from this town this very day.'

'Even better.'

'It'd be easier to do that if I had a few more respectable clothes.'

She glanced down at herself and Eunice held her breath. Would that annoy him? Would he fly into one of his rages?

But no. He looked at her thoughtfully then nodded. 'I'll take you to a second-hand shop I know and buy you a few clothes, then I'll take you to the station and see you get on a train. I don't care where you go to.'

'Don't worry. I really do intend to leave Lancashire. You won't see me again.'

He studied her, nodding. 'Good. We're in agreement about our little bargain.'

He turned to his wife. 'Take the baby upstairs as soon as we've left, Eunice, and tell the wet nurse to feed it, then give it a bath and put its new clothes on. I'll burn those rags it's wearing later.'

Then he turned to the young woman. 'We'll leave straight away.'

Clara stood up and walked to the door, not even looking across at the baby. 'Can't be too soon for me, Mr Thursten. And I'm grateful for this. Believe me I'll never come back.'

'And you're never to speak of this to anyone, either. That would make me very angry if I heard about it.'

She winked at him. 'It'll suit me even more than it suits you not to talk about it. I'm going to turn into a widow and my cousin has found an older man looking for a second wife. I was going to leave that baby at the foundling home once I was fit to travel.'

When he came home after watching Clara get on a train to Manchester, he went up to the nursery and found his wife watching the wet nurse change the baby's nappy with a smile on her face.

He smiled too as he went back downstairs. Women were made to serve men and rear their children, his wife included. You just had to be firm with them.

The next thing he intended to do was to fetch his daughter-in-law back. If she ever chose to reveal their deception it'd upset all his plans. He'd thought to make her live with them, but he was now wondering whether the best thing to do would be to wipe her from the face of the earth, then no one would ever be able to find out that the infant wasn't their grandson.

He frowned. Would it be best to let sleeping dogs lie and leave that bitch where she was?

No. As long as she was still alive there would always be the worry that she'd come back.

Besides, he'd not feel right till he'd paid her back for defying him. Of that he was determined. And he fancied having her in his bed before he killed her, only not here at the house. He knew a place where he could hire a room and no one would care what he did in it.

He was looking forward to the night he'd spend with her greatly, dreaming about what he'd do to her when she was in his power. So now he had to wait for the clerk to get him the information about exactly where she'd gone. The fellow was very eager to earn money any way he could so he doubted it'd take long.

20

Lewis Brody arrived in Ollerthwaite around midday on the Monday, having set off early. He was both excited and a bit anxious because this meeting was so important. If things went well, it could be the start of a new stage of life for him. If he didn't get the commission he'd have to dig into his savings and take on a few small jobs to tide him over till he could find another job to apply for.

However, when he got off the train with his briefcase, he had to contain his desire to get on with finding Mr Ollerton for a little longer and wait for the elderly porter to collect the tickets from the passengers who had already disembarked.

He caught the porter's eye and jabbed one finger in the direction of the luggage van at the rear end of the train.

'Sorry, sir,' the porter called. 'I'll start unloading the luggage as soon as I've dealt with these tickets.'

There was nothing Lewis could do to hurry matters and to be fair, since this was the terminus there were more jobs for the porter to do than there would be at a quick stop somewhere in the middle of a train journey. The poor fellow seemed to be the only one here to do them.

As no one else was inconvenienced by this delay, Lewis didn't even have anyone to chat to, so he strolled around, full of repressed energy after sitting on the train during a final journey that had stopped and started its way through several tiny local stations.

The minute the porter unlocked the luggage van and started piling its contents on the platform, Lewis went to help with the unloading because his tricycle was hemmed in by boxes and bundles, and he was impatient to set off.

As they got the tricycle clear and lowered it carefully onto the platform, he stowed the luggage carefully in the rear carrier so that it didn't get jolted out on bumpy roads.

'We don't get many of these tricycles here, sir,' the porter said.

'No. I don't suppose you do. Here, let me help you with that. It's heavy.'

He was thanked so warmly for his help with a particularly awkward box which belonged to someone else that a protest at the delay died unvoiced. The man was doing his best. No one could do more than that.

After a quick check that the tricycle hadn't been damaged, he put his briefcase into the smaller basket attached to the front handlebars.

The porter, pressing chores finished now, watched with interest as Lewis made sure the small tarpaulin that covered the top of the rear carrier was firmly attached. He used it on rainy days or to hold in place items that were in danger of being shaken out. This was such a small town that he was already guessing there would be uneven surfaces to the roads once he got out into the countryside.

Since the instructions in the telegram were rather brief, he asked the porter's advice about how best to get across town from the station to the village of Upperfold, then through it to the lodge on the Ollerton estate.

The directions the porter gave were very clear so he tipped the man generously and set off, bracing himself for what usually happened when he went out and about in places where tricycles were rarely seen.

It was easy to ignore the stares of pedestrians but he found the jeering questions as embarrassing as ever. They were usually yelled at him as he rode past by younger chaps who considered themselves wits. He'd heard the one about which iron mare bred iron horses a thousand times and it hadn't been funny when first shouted at him. Well, maybe not quite a thousand times, but sometimes it felt like it.

The porter's directions led him straight through Ollerthwaite and up a gentle hill to Upperfold, where the houses had clearly been built over a variety of different eras and in many styles. They were scattered about untidily except for the small group forming what had to be the main street, since it contained two or three shops and a few slightly larger detached houses, with a tiny chapel at one end.

From the village he rode up an unmade road to the crossroads he'd been told to turn off at, stopping there to catch his breath and stare round.

There mustn't be enough people living round here to make it worthwhile for the local authorities to tarmac the road. The phrase 'ends of the earth' floated into his mind, only you usually thought of that as referring to a foreign country and this rather remote place was nestled in the northern end of the Pennine spine of England.

Mind you, in some ways this probably did seem like a foreign country to most people from further south and vice versa. The way they spoke here was markedly different. He'd heard talk from people who'd never even been there about the north being backward, partly because people spoke more slowly, which was utterly ridiculous. It was just . . . a different dialect. He had relatives on his mother's side in the north with whom he'd just spent a few pleasant days. He always felt at home here and they were just as clever as anyone else, for heaven's sake.

He studied the surrounding terrain. He loved this stark northern countryside with the moors hovering protectively over the small valley and no doubt rolling away into the distance in the opposite direction once you got up on the tops. He'd go for a walk up there if he had time – at least he would if it was fine during his stay and he won the job of designing a new house for the estate's owner.

The weather didn't always co-operate in a county whose rainy climate was the reason the cotton industry had been established there so successfully in the first place. For much of the earlier part of this century the north had actually been industrially ahead of most of England, not lagging behind.

To the right of the crossroads was what looked to be a substantial farmhouse. It was set at the top of a small slope as if keeping guard over the roads that met nearby. He liked the look of the building, the larger part of which must have been built in the early eighteenth century, at a guess. Later extensions had followed a similar design, which meant their exterior style didn't clash with that of the main house. He nodded professional approval of how it had been done.

The farm looked well loved and cared for, the gardens neat, the windows sparkling and the paintwork fresh. He only hoped he'd be able to design houses that fitted as cosily into their surroundings and pleased their occupants so much that they would love and care for them as someone surely did this one.

Having caught his breath he turned left and headed towards the rather tumbledown cottage a few hundred yards away because he'd been told the lodge was the first dwelling you came to on the property. This little house didn't look at all loved or cared for, yet it could have been pretty, poor thing.

As he drew up outside it, the door opened and a man came out to greet him, staring at the tricycle with obvious interest. 'Mr Brody?'

'Yes. And you must be Mr Ollerton.'

'I am but we'll be sharing a small house and most people round here use first names, so do call me Edward.'

'Thank you. I'm Lewis.' He got off the tricycle, activating a special extra brake he'd devised to ensure heavier loads didn't make it roll back down slopes, then he undid the tarpaulin and rolled it up neatly.

Edward stepped forward to join him. 'Let me help you bring your things in.'

They each picked up some of the packages and bundles, then his host led the way upstairs.

'There are only two bedrooms and I'm afraid yours isn't fully furnished yet, but at least your bed is brand new.' He led the way towards the rear bedroom and gestured. 'There you are. Have a quick bounce on it.'

Lewis did that. 'It's fine. And I shall enjoy the view as well as the bed.' As they went downstairs again, he said, 'I can manage to take up the rest of my things. I didn't bring a lot.'

'I'll put the kettle on, then.'

When Lewis rejoined the man who might become the first major client of his embryonic business, they sat together at the table and waited for the water to boil. The friendly welcome was a good omen, he hoped.

'This place used to be the gatehouse or lodge, whichever name you prefer,' Edward said. 'I'm afraid it was allowed to run down but at least it's waterproof again now. The agent's house is a few hundred yards further along this track but it's partly hidden from here by those trees and it's still being repaired.'

'I think I caught a glimpse of part of it.' Lewis gestured to the sweeping vista across the valley. 'What wonderful views to look out on. I hope the location you've chosen for your new house has similar ones.'

'It's just a little way up the slope, so it does. The views are one of the reasons I bought the estate, but the main reason was that it had been my family's home for nearly two centuries and I lived here when I was a child. I'll move into the agent's house and bring my furniture from storage once the repairs and repainting are finished. In the meantime, at least the lodge is easy to heat and it only needed minor work to make it water-proof.'

'And the big house burned to the ground, I gather? Was it close by?'

'Just up the hill a few hundred yards. There are only black-ened ruins left now. The house was gutted completely and collapsed in on itself. We can go and look at the ruins after we've had our cups of tea, if you like. I know one thing already: I want a stone-built house, not a brick one. The local stone is very attractive. And I want the place to be as fire-proof as possible.'

'I think modern building methods will give you more secu-rity, but no building is totally fireproof, I'm afraid.'

The tea was quickly made and they added a dash of cold water so that they could drink it straight away, after which the two of them set off up the hill.

21

When the ruins came into view Lewis stopped dead for a moment, horrified by the sight of such massive destruction. A soft murmur of shock escaped him as they drew closer. Nothing of the upper storey or roof had survived in a recognisable form, except for a few blackened beams jutting out here and there. The walls on the ground floor were so badly damaged they looked like giant black teeth planted in the ground. Mounds that must be rubble from the fire lay around, overgrown by grass, weeds and even small shrubs after all these years.

There were a few smaller gaps in some of the remaining lower walls, which looked like more recent damage, as if someone had taken a hammer to them years after the main fire. Why would anyone do that? Just for the pleasure of destroying something or for a reason?

Edward seemed to read his mind and said grimly, 'I don't know why or when that last damage happened but it's recent, isn't it?'

'I'm afraid so.'

As they walked along what had been the front of Ollerton House, both men continued to frown and eventually Lewis said slowly, 'I doubt this was a normal house fire, Edward. It looks to me as if it started in several places at the same time, which isn't likely to have happened by chance.'

'I've been wondering about that too. The house was apparently heavily insured and the owners used the money they were paid to live out their lives in luxury on the Fylde Coast. They put the estate up for sale, but didn't manage to find a buyer for years, not until I came along, because of the lack of a grand house and its distance from any large town. That enabled me to purchase it at a very low price. I didn't scruple to push them down still further after what I believed their family had done to my old home.'

Once they'd finished their circuit of the ruins, Lewis said quietly, 'I don't think I've ever seen such complete destruction of a large house by fire. I'd guess that no attempt whatsoever was made to extinguish the blaze.'

'The owner of the nearby farm, who is a wise old chap, said it happened during the night and by the time he realised what was going on it was too late for him to do anything.'

Lewis shook his head, saddened by what he'd seen.

'The only parts left intact are the cellars from an earlier dwelling, which once stood just down the slope from this site. There's little left above ground now.' After a brief silence Edward continued, 'We found an outer entrance to some cellars a few days ago, a metal hatch, and got in through it to have a look round. We're guessing these belonged to the original house, but we think that at one time they must have been connected to the cellars of the new house. Sadly there had been a cave-in between them so we couldn't check for certain.'

'Interesting. I'd like to look at the cellars you did find, if only to get an idea of how the land is structured below ground.'

'We can go down there another time but I'm not doing it without someone else to keep watch above ground in case there's another collapse.' He was also afraid his trespasser might cause damage that trapped them below, but he didn't say so because it might seem too fanciful.

'Very sensible of you. Now, at this stage in our discussions I'd find it useful to walk round the ruins again, if you don't mind making another circuit. Or I can do it on my own and come back to join you at the lodge afterwards.'

'I'll come too in case you have any questions, but don't think you have to hold a conversation if you have things to think about and examine in more detail. I enjoy being out of doors and watching the wildlife.'

Lewis took him at his word and they walked round mostly in silence. This time the architect went slowly, stopping here and there to jot down a few notes. He made a few rough sketches of the terrain too, including one showing the entrance to the old cellar, which Edward showed him afterwards.

As they went, he kept adding to an overall rough plan he was making of the whole area, which included a tentative outline of the old house's foundations, all measured by the number of paces he'd taken.

'You have a talent for drawing,' Edward said after a while.

'I enjoy sketching and it's a useful tool for an architect. I also take photos of the site but one has to wait to get those developed.' He smiled. 'You won't realise it but I trained myself to move in paces about a yard long, so I can be fairly accurate about distances.'

'Clever.'

Just before they got back to the lodge, Lewis stopped and turned to look first up then down the slope. 'Would you want to build the new house in the same place as the one that burned down or where the older house stood? It'd be difficult to build any further up the hill because I can see from here that the ground there contains rocky outcrops as well as being steeper and uneven.' He turned slightly and added, 'You could build further down than the old house, near the lower edge of your land, but then you could only get narrow gardens to look out across and stroll about in.'

Edward had been listening and studying the land as his companion spoke. 'Hmm. I don't think I would want to build again at the spot where the house burned down. It might sound foolish but I feel it'd be unlucky to site it there again. A friend has suggested the place where the older building once stood, however, and I quite like that idea. It would put it directly above the remaining cellars, too, which might be helpful and save some effort.'

They both studied that area, then Lewis nodded. 'Your friend was right. The ground is relatively flat there, which is probably why it was chosen in the first place, and it'd give you a good view of the valley and room for nice, wide formal gardens at the front. There is more than enough level ground to put kitchen gardens behind, though you'd perhaps have to lay that out in steps, with some of the higher parts held in place by low retaining walls.'

'I'd like the continuity of following my earlier ancestors' example and using that part of the land for another house,' Edward said softly.

'Then let's walk round the lower site with that in mind.'

As they reached the metal hatch, Edward was about to point it out to his companion when he stopped and looked at it in puzzlement and stretched out one arm to prevent Lewis moving forward. 'This is the hatch but I stopped you because there are fresh footprints just a short distance away from it. Look!'

He studied them. 'I wonder if they were made by the same intruder. He can't have gone down into the cellar, or the earth would have been far more disturbed, but it seems to me that he knows of its existence.'

'Can we look down it?'

'Yes, but not go down.' He raised the hatch and they stared into the darkness.

'The part I can see looks dry, except for a small leak over there,' Lewis said.

'I noticed a loose stone underneath it.'

'Caused by the rainwater dripping in over the years, I expect.'

'Let's close up now.' He did that and kicked the loose soil over the ground, removing the traces they'd left not only from the hatch but from further away. 'We'll notice now if whoever it is comes back. I don't think there are obvious traces of our visit now. Can you see any?'

Lewis shook his head.

As they walked back towards the lodge, Edward gave his companion a very firm look. 'I'll say it again: don't ever go down into the old cellar on your own in case there are further collapses or the intruder has done more damage.' He didn't add, 'on purpose' but he thought it and he could see from Lewis's expression that he understood that.

'I'd not do it anyway. Do you have any idea why someone would be messing about in the ruins or damaging them further?'

Edward hesitated then told him the rest. 'Someone has been seen preparing to spy on what I'm doing at the lodge as well.'

'Spy on what? There's nothing there of any real value, surely, except the land itself. I'll certainly keep my eyes open for further signs of intruders as I check out the ground, though. Perhaps it's the same person or people who've deliberately added to the damage at the ruins.'

'Perhaps it is.'

On the way back, Edward went down the slope to just past the lodge and showed Lewis the shallow trench. 'My unknown watcher dug this out. You can't see anyone lying in it from the house. A neighbour saw him doing it and told me what she'd seen, but he was a big, rough-looking chap so she stayed out of sight till he left, which was very wise. She's new to the valley so didn't recognise him.'

'Hmm. You seem to have a few puzzles to solve.'

'Yes. I'm undecided as to whether to fill the trench in and challenge him if he turns up again when I'm around or pretend I've not seen it and try to catch him doing it and charge him with trespassing.'

'I'd go for filling it in and putting up a big *Keep Out* sign.'

'I'll have to think about that. I've only just found it. In the meantime please keep your eyes open as you walk round the estate. I don't want you getting hurt. There should be no one around except you and me, and my two neighbours, Mrs Hesketh and Walter Crossley. He's the one who lives in the farm with several members of his family, whom you'll meet shortly.'

Lewis risked asking, 'You want me to stay for a while, then?'

'Yes. I like what you've said today so we'll continue to pursue the possibilities if you're still interested.'

'I definitely am. I'd enjoy designing a house for this lovely setting. As to your intruder, I'll keep my eyes open for signs, but I'm not a weakling and can usually defend myself if I meet any trouble.'

Edward nodded. His visitor wasn't as tall as he was but Lewis had an air of physical confidence about him that said he could indeed look after himself. In fact, this young architect had made a good first impression on him in several ways and in a very short time, too.

When they got back inside the lodge, Lewis produced a portfolio with a series of small sketches of possible house styles for Edward to look through.

'I can adapt the inside of your dwelling to any of these styles.'

For some reason these had more life to them than anything Edward had seen in books, with clouds in the sky, realistic trees and bushes, and even a cheeky-looking little dog in the corner of one sketch. It took him a few minutes to realise something else. 'The houses are set in a landscape like the one outside, as if they had been built in Lancashire.'

'It seemed more suited to your needs to do it that way. It wasn't hard. I know Lancashire quite well because I have relatives here in the north.'

Edward was impressed. He tapped the folder. 'It was a good idea to bring those. Could you leave them on the end of the table so that I can study them and come back to them as I think about what I want?'

'Happy to do that. Don't hesitate to ask questions about them and please bear in mind that details are usually quite easy to change. We're only looking at basic styles and outlines of exteriors here. You'll have to work out what you'll want inside your house by way of rooms and amenities before the outline details can be finalised.'

'I'll give it my consideration. Now, you must be getting hungry and I'm being a very poor host. How about a cup of tea and a piece of cake? I've arranged for us to have our evening meals at Walter Crossley's farm while you're here because even if I had a proper kitchen, I'm no cook.'

'I noticed the farm and admired it. It looks like a warm, friendly home. What sort of farming does he deal in? I think I saw some sheep on the slopes beyond the farm.'

'He's not the one supervising the farming there these days and it's mixed farming. You can't grow lush crops on hilly land. His grandson joined him from America a few months ago and Cam now sees to that side of things. He's still getting used to the farming methods and possibilities round here, as well as introducing a few ideas of his own, but has made a name for himself already as a hard worker.'

'That doesn't hurt in any area of life.'

'I agree. Walter is very hospitable. He's rather an important man in the valley. He's on the town council, he runs a few small businesses and he's trying to revive the valley generally and bring in a few businesses. I quickly found out that he's helped a lot of people to get through hard times or to set up in small businesses. I really admire that.'

'Um, revive the valley after what?'

'It started losing its population when two or three water mills closed down a few decades ago. One mill is still in use, but it's adapted to a different purpose these days. The others were left to fall into ruin. Steam engines could provide the power for much larger mills, you see, which made their owners a lot more money. Only, they needed a big area of level ground to build on and also space around them for outhouses, stables and so on. They usually had to provide housing for their workers too, which created new villages.'

'That would be sad for the people employed in the old mills and living in smaller places.'

'Yes. There wasn't a suitable area to build a large mill in a small valley like this and gradually the younger people started to move away, slowly at first, I'm told, then more followed. Even after the exodus slowed down again, there was still need for a bigger population here if the town and its people were to create enjoyable modern lives.' Edward glanced round fondly before continuing. 'In one sense I'm glad it's stayed rural here. I'm enjoying living in the quiet countryside much more than the bustle and noise of cities.'

Lewis nodded agreement. He was already hoping he'd be able to produce a design that would win him the further commission to supervise the building of the house, because he too had quickly taken to Ollindale and would love to spend time in the starkly beautiful valley.

He couldn't afford to stay here even for a few months unless he was being paid, because he wasn't a rich man and had a living to earn. He'd have to find somewhere permanent to live if he stayed here, a place that didn't cost a fortune to rent and yet wasn't lodgings for a group of men, which might be noisy.

To take the next step in his career he had to establish a good reputation and felt sure he could do justice to this commission. He'd also prefer to make his start here because he liked Edward personally and felt sure they'd work well together. Some clients of the firm he'd left recently had been devils to please and had insisted on what he thought of as *wrong* designs for their buildings.

Sadly for him, as he'd already discovered, potential clients were usually more interested in older, experienced architects than younger ones just starting off their careers. And to some people, thirty-two was young, though it didn't always feel young to him.

In the late afternoon the two men strolled across to the farm and Lewis followed Edward into the house he'd admired from the crossroads. He was delighted at the chance to look at its interior more closely. The main room was huge, a real farm kitchen, and the table matched that. It was surrounded now by a group of people chatting happily, though they broke off what they were saying when the newcomers came in to smile across at them.

Lewis was introduced to their host and received a warm, welcoming smile. From the way the older man had been beaming as they'd come in, it was clear that Walter enjoyed having visitors.

Two other people arrived shortly afterwards and he watched Walter grab the lad and give him a big hug.

'Nice to see you, Bryn. Find yourself a place to sit, but you are to come and sit here by me, young Tam, and tell me what you've been learning to do this week.' He smiled across at Lewis while keeping one hand on the lad's shoulder. 'This one's an apprentice carpenter and doing really well.'

The lad looked at him adoringly, as if he were his grandfather, and the woman on his other side gave the boy another hug and asked him something that made him nod vigorously.

Walter turned back to Edward. 'If you need any furniture made, Bryn's your man. He has a real feel for using wood, not just for making furniture but for appropriate carvings to enhance it or just to decorate a room. That's one of his.' He gestured to a small panel on the wall at one side, an exquisite carving of a mother rabbit standing motionless beneath a tree, her young by her side. It made you feel peaceful to look at it.

Elinor and Maude were introduced as the cooks, and they'd produced a hearty and delicious meal of lamb stew with crusty bread and homegrown cabbage lightly cooked in some way with onions that Lewis didn't recognise but was delicious in its own right, not the usual soggy mess of plain boiled cabbage. That was followed by chunks of apple pie with fresh cream.

Everyone said at some point how nice it was to have a newcomer join them and add interest to the conversation, and Lewis continued to feel extremely comfortable with these people. He watched in admiration the way Walter managed to listen to Tam, move in and out of various other conversations and yet still study him occasionally with a very sharp, assessing gaze, making no attempt to hide his interest.

It was surprising how tall most of them were. All the men seemed to be six feet or more, which made him feel unusually short at a mere five feet ten. Maude must have been nearly six feet, too, though Elinor wasn't quite as tall as Lewis.

He stayed mainly quiet, as was wise till you knew people better. When Walter asked him about his work, however, he didn't try to hide how much he loved designing homes, rather than other sorts of buildings.

'You call them homes, not houses?' the older man asked.

'Sometimes I'm obliged to work on *houses* that are being created to show off the owner's wealth, but I like to design *homes* where people will be happy and comfortable.'

He was interested to hear Edward invite the two ladies to join them the following morning and share any ideas they had about what might be useful in a house. Elinor declined the invitation with a slight blush, as she was expecting and tended to feel unwell in the mornings, but Maude accepted with alacrity.

Lewis said, 'I'll be interested to hear your views. I don't know why more women aren't consulted about houses being designed. After all they're the main ones who have to run the daily life and chores there when it's finished.'

Maude joined in. 'That's because most men have been brought up to believe that women don't have as good brains as them.'

'We don't believe that in this house,' Walter said firmly. 'We Crossleys aren't stupid, whether men or women. You share your ideas with Edward and Lewis, Maude, lass. They make sense to me.'

'I'll be happy to do that. But just so that you know, Lewis, I'm more interested in the practical details inside a house, especially in the kitchens, than the exterior style.'

'I've also invited Lillian to join us,' Edward said thoughtfully. 'She isn't here tonight but when she walked round the grounds with me, she seemed able to see the overall picture very quickly, including where the house should be sited.'

When the conversation changed, it turned to the tricycle. 'I must admit,' Walter told him, 'that I'd like to have a good look at this tricycle of yours and maybe take a little ride on it if you don't mind. It might be worth getting one for the farm because there are times when we need to take bigger items somewhere, things than won't fit in the basket of a bicycle. And I don't always feel like catching and harnessing the pony, especially in rainy weather, let alone looking after her needs when I return.'

'I think moving around will be a lot easier when motor cars become cheaper and more common,' Lewis said. 'They're mostly a toy of the rich at the moment unless you're an engineer and can build your own.'

He was surprised when this casual remark seemed to upset his host and one or two people shot worried glances at the older man. 'Did I say something wrong?'

Walter took a deep breath and held up one hand to stop his grandson when he would have intervened.

'It's all right, Cam, lad. I'll answer our friend. You're bound to hear about it, Lewis. My elder son and grandson were killed a year or so ago in an accident caused by the careless driver of a motor vehicle which drove too close and terrified their horses, causing them to upset the cart. They tumbled down a steep bank to the side of the road, horses and men all killed there and then except for one poor animal, which needed to be put down because it had two broken legs.'

Lewis looked at him in horror. 'Oh, no! I'm so sorry.'

'Nay, I have to get used to hearing about motor cars because you're not the only one to mention them these days. There aren't any of them based permanently in the valley yet, though we've had one or two driven here by people visiting or just passing through on their way to enjoy the Pennine scenery of the upper road across the moors. Noisy and smelly things, they are, to my mind. You must have seen a good few in London.'

'Yes. They're quite common, not only motor cars but vans and lorries, especially in the parts where wealthier folk live or work.'

Maude changed the topic of conversation then and people gradually relaxed again. No one stayed late because they all had work to do the following day.

As they walked back to Edward's house, Lewis said, 'I was sorry to have upset Walter.'

'You weren't to know. I should have warned you but I was selfishly thinking about my house. Actually, I don't agree with Walter about motor vehicles. One or two people in the valley are thinking of buying or building them. I'd have to buy one not build it myself because I'm no engineer, but Riley is planning to build his own once he's settled in here and don't tell Walter but he's maybe going to set up a small manufactory in conjunction with a friend. I should think that by the end of next year there will be several motor cars based in the valley.'

'Poor Walter.'

'You can't hold back progress, however much it might hurt.'

Inside the house he yawned. 'I'm ready for bed. If you want to stay up you're welcome to but don't forget to turn the oil lamp out. I was up early and I can't keep my eyes open much longer.'

'I've had a busy day and I'm ready for my bed as well.'

Lewis was thoughtful as he got ready for sleep, still thinking about their discussion. He'd had a go at driving motor cars a few times as well as riding in them, and wished he could afford to buy one.

He smiled as he slid towards sleep. What would the valley lads shout after motor cars if they considered a tricycle fair game for silly comments?

Or would they be begging for a ride in one as he'd seen lads do sometimes in towns? He'd seen cheeky lads jump on the backs of vehicles when the cars slowed down in streets full of traffic, holding on to the luggage rack for a while, looking gleeful.

22

The next day Riley started work on a bathroom in the lodge, again to be installed in a small side room at the rear. He'd more or less finished the work at Lillian's house but sometimes you had to wait for things to dry or settle before you could complete a job.

He had been surprised when Edward had insisted that he wanted bathrooms in both the lodge and the agent's house, and had added that he intended to put several into the new manor house, not just a couple. But Riley wasn't complaining about the work that job would bring him.

And since he'd already had an inquiry from a householder in Ollerthwaite about putting in a bathroom, gas stove and gas geyser for hot water, he'd soon have to find a labourer to work with him and train the chap to do it right. Later he'd take on an apprentice officially too, well, he would if things continued to go well.

He wanted to be able to offer Maude a decent life when they married and set up home together. He felt quite sure their courtship would lead to marriage and sometimes found himself standing motionless, smiling like an idiot at the mere thought of her. No other woman had ever affected him like this.

In fact he wished they could get married straight away. It wasn't like him to rush into new situations but, then, she was a very special person.

As Maude cleared up the kitchen, her mind was on what would be needed in the kitchen of a big house to make it as modern and practical as possible. She was looking forward to the coming discussion, especially as a lot of it would involve being with Riley.

They would need a big modern gas cooker in the scullery or kitchen. That was an absolute necessity – or even a cooker in both rooms, since it sounded as if it was going to be a large manor house, not just a single family residence.

She'd seen pictures in newspapers and magazines of modern tall kitchen cabinets that stood back against the walls. She particularly liked the ones that had glass-fronted shelves in the upper cupboards and an enamelled or tiled surface that you could slide out from under the top cupboard at the right height for preparing food on, then drawers or cupboards in the bottom half for storage.

Putting together various remarks Edward had made, she thought it sounded as if he was thinking of installing several bathrooms in his house. Just imagine that! He'd need water geysers in them all, as well as in the scullery. He wasn't always practical about details – well, look at the way he'd come here without checking out that there was furniture in the lodge, even – but if Riley was doing that work, she'd be able to help them and keep an eye on the practicalities. It would make such a difference for servants to be instantly able to get hot water.

And like many tradesmen's wives, she hoped to help out in the business, keeping accounts, ordering materials, talking to people (especially women) about what was possible. She wasn't going to spend all her days shut up in a house on her own.

Edward would need two or three servants to run a big house properly and one or two of them at least would have to live in, though she'd read in magazines that rich people didn't seem to have as many servants even in big houses nowadays. She agreed with Edward that the servants would need a bathroom as well.

Walter said he was going to bring the mains gas pipes right up to the farm and wanted modern amenities installing here too. She'd tell him to have two bathrooms put in as well because it was a large house and he often had guests to stay.

What a difference all that would make to the daily tasks involved in running a house and even the type of food they prepared! Before she'd gone into service, she'd grown up living in two rooms, sharing the two outside lavvies with everyone in their end of the terrace, and thinking themselves lucky to have a cold water tap of their own in the back yard at the shared house. Her mother would have thought herself in heaven to have a whole house of their own, however small, let alone an inside bathroom and hot water geyser.

Riley had told her he'd be finishing things off at the lodge this morning before going to join Edward's group of advisers, so they weren't starting their discussions till the middle of the morning. That would give her time to make some scones to take with her, because Edward was bound to offer them a cup of tea. She must suggest to him buying a pound or two of biscuits and an airtight tin to keep them in. They sold some nice gingernut biscuits loose at the village shop.

She always found that discussions went better if you had refreshments on hand and her Riley had a healthy appetite. She smiled at the mere thought of him, still bemused to have started courting at her age.

Riley arrived at the lodge just before Maude got there, and he greeted her with a beaming smile and a big hug. Since they were both a bit early and Edward wasn't there yet, he took the opportunity to give her a lingering kiss as well.

'Someone might see us!' Maude pulled away, trying not to let the basket spill its contents. 'And mind the scones.'

'Hang the scones.' She looked so adorably confused that his next words jumped out before he could stop them. 'How soon can we get married, do you think? I can't think of any reason to wait.'

She looked startled and nearly dropped the basket, so he had to steady it till she was calm again. Only she wasn't exactly calm; she was staring at him as if she'd never seen him before.

'You're that sure of us being suited already?'

'I am, Maude. I feel so right with you. Aren't you sure too? If not, why are you kissing me so often?'

She couldn't help smiling at his teasing. 'Yes. I am sure, very sure. But what will people think if we marry that quickly?'

'Who cares what others think?'

She reached up to touch his cheek. 'I do. Besides, we can't get married straight away, love. There will be all sorts of practical things to sort out, like where we'll live and buying furniture. I think Walter would let us stay on with him for a while because I help out a lot at the farm, but I'd rather have a house of our own eventually, one no one can tell us to leave. I've never had that in my whole life, you see.'

'Then I'll make sure you have one with me. And I have to confess that I'm as bad as Edward and haven't thought out the details. I didn't plan to ask you yet, only I love you so much and enjoy being with you, so there really doesn't seem to be any reason to wait and the words just jumped out.' He gave her a wry look. 'I shall be glad to find a house to live in for another reason. I wasn't looking forward to living at the back of that workshop once I'd finished install-ing Edward's bathrooms. Apart from my own comfort, it'd look strange for a modern plumber to live somewhere without a proper bathroom, don't you think? Like a tailor not dressing smartly.'

'Yes, it would. We can ask Walter if he knows of any houses to rent. He may even have one that's suitable.'

Riley couldn't resist kissing her again. 'Good. We're agreed then. We'll marry as soon as it can be arranged. And just to set your mind at rest, I have money put by, enough to start my business as well as furnish our home. We'll not need to skimp and scrape, though we'll be careful, I'm sure. I never get into debt if I can help it.'

'I have some money saved too. And I'm always, always careful with money. That's not going to change, I promise you.'

He squeezed her hand. 'Keep your money for emergencies.'

She gave him a firm look. 'I'll use some of it to buy our household linen. That's a woman's job. Some girls start collecting things for their hope chests even before they meet the right man and I've certainly thought what I'd like to buy if I had my own home.'

He knew when a battle was worth fighting so he didn't protest any longer. 'Very well. You take care of that side of things. I'd not know what sheets and towels to choose anyway.' He probably had more money saved than she'd expect because he'd recently inherited what seemed a big sum to him from a bachelor uncle. He still wasn't used to the idea of that himself.

'Don't say anything to the others yet about getting married, not even Walter,' she warned him. 'Give me a few days to grow used to the idea first, love. At my age I hadn't expected to meet someone, you see. I still feel I'm dreaming.'

'You're exactly the right age for me and you're not dreaming.' He planted a kiss on her cheek then they heard voices coming closer to the house, so she picked up the basket and backed away from him hastily. 'I'll see you again later.'

'You'll see me sooner than that. I'm invited to discuss the house design as well. I'll just put my tools away before I join you.'

Lewis stopped abruptly at one side of an open space before they got close to the lodge and looked across at Edward.

'The ground seems to dip a little here, don't you think? I wonder why.'

He moved back a few steps, walked slowly forward again over the same patch, then beckoned to the other man to do the same thing.

Edward stared at him in surprise. 'You're right. I wonder why I didn't notice it before. Let's check exactly where it dips. We can stamp the grass and weeds down to mark it out.'

They did that and then at the back corner of the space Lewis found he couldn't stamp down the next patch of weeds, whose top fronds were leaning across something that felt solid when he stamped on it. 'Hang on! There's something in the ground here.'

He bent and pushed aside the weeds, uncovering part of a plank, then another attached to it.

Edward came to join him and uncovered two other planks. They were put together very roughly. 'This looks as if it was done in a hurry. Is it possible that there's another cellar hatch here?' He knelt to push some earth aside with his bare hands and Lewis joined him.

Once they'd cleared away the earth they leaned back on their heels and exchanged excited glances.

'It is another one!' Lewis said.

'Why? It doesn't make sense to put another hatch here,' Edward said.

'I agree. And it looks as if it's been deliberately hidden. Why, indeed?' Lewis looked round. 'Where exactly is that metal hatch? Can you go and stand by it?'

Edward walked down the slope, stopping next to it. 'It's here.' He found a chunk of rock and set it on top of the hatch, then walked back to the wooden hatch. 'Do you think this also leads to the cellar?' He frowned. 'I may be wrong but I think this would lead to beyond where the roof caved in.'

'I can't think why they'd want another hatch anyway.'

Edward bent down, studying the hatch. 'It can't have been opened for a good many years.' He tugged a corner, failed to move it, then stamped on it a few times before trying again to pull it up. 'Ouch! I've got a splinter in my thumb.'

'Let me have a go.' Lewis fumbled with the same corner. 'It feels as if it's coming loose.' The wooden hatch moved again, then suddenly he managed to lift it a couple of inches. 'Let's both pull it at once, now there's an edge free.'

They took a corner each and pulled upwards, then the whole panel lifted at that side. 'Let go!' Edward yelled and as they did so it continued its trajectory, flying all the way open till it lay flat on the ground, attached only by two rusty hinges and leaving a dark hole below it surrounded by a roughly made wooden frame.

Edward studied it. 'This one isn't as large as the other hole.'

'Just big enough for a man to slip into. And there are a few planks running down the sides of the hole, to hold the walls in place, I suppose.'

Edward knelt down and leaned over carefully to study it. 'I can see the bottom, which is only about three yards down, but after that it looks as if there's a tunnel leading to one side. You'd have to bend low to go along it, though. You couldn't stand up. It'd only take a small ladder to get down into that.'

'I doubt it was part of the original house. And it looks, well, amateur, as if it was made in a hurry. I'm surprised the interior has stayed open if it's as old as I think.'

'How old would you say it is?'

'Hand-sawn planks, old-fashioned hinges made in the seventeenth century, I should think, but moved and reused here later. Goodness knows why when there's another hatch not far away.'

'This estate is full of surprises,' Edward murmured.

'We could come back with a ladder and a lantern and find out where it leads.'

'We could, but I'd rather do it when there's no intruder sneaking around nearby. The only person we should mention its existence to until we know more would be Walter. I'm definitely not going down till I've got someone strong standing by in case the walls collapse, preferably someone who knows about tunnels.'

'I agree. You can't be too careful with unknown terrain. It may not be safe. I think people are usually more careful about building cellars these days than they were then.'

Edward pulled out his pocket watch and glanced at it. 'We're going to be late for our meeting. Let's drop the hatch down again and cover it up, then come back another time.'

Once they'd hidden the opening again, he grinned at the architect. 'Oh, and you've definitely got the first stage of the job if you're still interested, working out a basic design for a house and that will include using your architectural background to investigate the cellars with me. And if you want to stay on at the lodge while you do it, that's all right too.'

'I'd like that.'

He offered his hand and they shook, smiling at one another.

'I'll design you a beautiful home,' Lewis promised.

'Good. A home, not merely a fancy house. That's one of the reasons you got the job – the way you talk about homes made me realise that's exactly what I want.'

They kicked earth around the hatch, making sure there were no footprints showing in it, and pulled the remaining tall weeds back to lean across the edge of the hatch. Then they brushed as much of the dirt as they could off their clothes, doing each other's backs, before setting off for the lodge again.

23

Lillian decided to cut across from her back garden to the lodge for the meeting with Edward and the others. That would be much quicker than going round by the road. She was so looking forward to discussing the house he was going to have built. How interesting her life had become lately!

And she was looking forward to seeing him again. She envied Maude the easy, open way she and Riley had fallen for one another. It wasn't just Edward who was wary of following their example. She was equally afraid of giving in to her emotions, though she couldn't stop her heart giving a happy little twitch whenever she saw him.

Just after she'd climbed over the wall and moved a few paces up the slope towards the lodge, the man who had dug out the trench stepped out from behind some bushes and barred her path, glaring at her. She didn't have time to hide and he was so big and rough-looking that she felt instantly afraid of him.

'Get out of these grounds, woman. Don't you know this is Ollerton land?'

She took a hasty step backwards. She didn't try to refuse and started moving quickly away, saying meekly, 'Sorry. I was just looking for a few stones to edge my garden.'

'Then look somewhere else. The owner doesn't want trespassers. He's asked me to keep a look out for anyone coming onto his land and to send them packing, so don't you dare come back again. I'll see you if you do and make you regret it.'

His eyes lingered on her breasts in a way that made her feel extremely uncomfortable, then he studied her face.

'Who the hell are you anyway? I've not seen you in Ollerth-waite before and I'd remember you.'

She hurried towards the houses. When she glanced back and saw him still watching her, she guessed he probably hadn't seen which house she'd come out of because she'd been part way up the slope when he'd come out from behind the bushes, so on a sudden impulse she went past her own house and clambered over the wall into her neighbour's back garden, which had several fruit trees and bushes that partly hid her.

She didn't know what she'd do if he followed her because Gladys and Bill were both out at work. Run out round to the road and scream for help, perhaps, only there might not be anyone near enough to hear. This wasn't a busy road.

She felt a bit guilty about drawing attention to this garden, but Bill was a strong chap and would surely be capable of protecting his wife against the intruder if he came back here. She hoped that wouldn't happen.

As she got close to the bottom of the garden she glanced back again and saw that the bullying man was still watching her, but at least he hadn't made any attempt to follow her. She reached up as if to pick a fruit off a tree and saw him turn and walk away up the hill. Relief shuddered through her.

Knowing that no one was home she ran along the path at the side of their house next to hers and through their front garden to her own. The fence between them was too high to climb over easily so she had to go all the way round.

Unfortunately her front door was locked and bolted, so she couldn't get in that way. She went quietly along the fence at the other side of her own house and peeped round the corner. There was no sign of him near her top garden wall so she slipped in by her back door. She bolted it then ran up to the back bedroom to see if he was still hanging around and if so, keep watch on what he did next.

She could see him appearing and disappearing as he walked in and out of the trees and bushes further up the hill, going towards the lodge. He vanished for a few moments then came back again, scowling as he headed away from the lodge again, presumably avoiding the people meeting there.

She'd better warn Edward about the prowler but she didn't dare take the shortcut through his grounds again in case the intruder was still nearby. She'd have to go up the road to get to the lodge safely, so she checked it from the front-bedroom window first.

Seeing a small cart coming slowly up the hill towards her house, she rushed downstairs to try to go up the hill at the same time as it did. Should she use her bicycle? No, she wasn't good enough at riding it yet to get away quickly if that horrible man chased her, but she must warn Edward about him.

After hastily locking the front door she ran out onto the road and started walking along at the far side of the cart. It wasn't going very fast, thank goodness. She might be able to get to the crossroads without the intruder seeing her if she stayed near it.

The driver greeted her cheerfully with, 'You seem in a hurry, love. Are you going up to Crossways Farm?'

'No, the other way, to the lodge.'

'I'm going there too, delivering some food to Mr Ollerton. Why don't you climb up and ride the rest of the way with me? Can you manage to get up on your own if I slow down?'

'Yes. And thank you so much.' She had no trouble getting up on the driving bench and felt much safer sitting next to him.

'I'm Sid Petby.'

'Lillian Hesketh.'

'Nice to meet you. They said someone new had moved into that house. Are you all right? You look a bit upset.'

'There's a trespasser in the grounds of the estate, a big man with a bald head and a scar near his mouth.' She touched the corner of her own upper lip to show him where.

'Sounds like Terry Catlow to me. What's he doing there?'

'He said he'd been hired to keep people out.'

'*Him!* I don't think so. I usually hear the latest news first because I'm out and about delivering stuff and I hadn't heard anything like that. Besides, no one would employ him to do that sort of thing.'

'I knew he was lying because I've been invited to go to a meeting between Edward Ollerton and his architect about the new house they're going to build, so he'd hardly tell someone to keep me away, would he?'

'Do they want you to make their tea and serve refreshments?'

'No. They want to get a woman's ideas about what makes a house good to live and work in. After all, it's women who usually do the cooking and cleaning, isn't it?'

He laughed heartily. 'Aye, that's true. Eh, my wife would love to talk to people about that. She's got very definite ideas about anything and everything, and she shares them with me all the time. She's a good lass, though, a clever cook and a caring mother.'

He didn't try to chat after that because they were nearly there.

Edward and Lewis returned just as Maude came back round to the front of the lodge. They waved a greeting and she smiled back, gesturing to her basket.

'I brought you some scones.'

'That's kind. Thank you. Do come in. There's no sign of Lillian yet but I expect she'll be here soon. I hope Lewis and

I haven't kept you waiting.' Edward glanced at Lewis. 'We've just been, um, checking how steeply the land slopes beyond the shrubbery.'

Maude set her basket on the table and took out the plate of scones, before sitting where Edward had indicated. 'I was chatting to Riley, so it didn't matter you being late. He's putting his tools away and will join us in a minute. I—'

Before she could say anything else they heard the front door open and bang back against the wall. They all turned round in surprise as Lillian burst into the kitchen without knocking or waiting for anyone to answer the door.

She looked so anxious Edward stepped quickly forward. 'What's wrong?'

'That man's prowling round your grounds again, the one who dug the trench. When I started to climb over my wall to take the shortcut here, he warned me to stay out of the grounds, said you were employing him to stop people going there.'

'What? I did no such thing. I've never spoken to him, don't even know what he looks like. You shouldn't have taken the risk of coming up here after that, Lillian.'

'I came up by the road and got a lift on a cart with a man who's delivering something here, so I was quite safe.'

There was a knock on the door even though she'd left it open in her haste.

Edward went to answer it and found Sid standing there with a basket of provisions he'd ordered from the village shop.

'Is that lass all right, Mr Ollerton? She jumped down off the cart and ran inside as if the devil himself was after her.'

'She's fine now. She needed to tell me something urgently.'

'Ah. Right. Is it true?' the man asked.

'Is what true?'

'That Terry Catlow is now your gamekeeper. She described the man who warned her off an' it can only be him. He told her you'd asked him to stop people going on to your land. Is that true?'

'No. Definitely not. I've never even met the chap.'

'Ah. I didn't think it would be.'

'Actually, I'd be grateful if you'd spread the word about his lies.' He slipped a coin into the man's hand and it vanished rapidly into a nearby pocket.

'Happy to oblige, sir. I'll make sure folk know.' Sid quickly unpacked the food he'd brought, setting the various packets and tins on the table. He reached out to pick up the empty basket, then hesitated.

'Is there something else?' Edward asked.

'You might not know, you being a newcomer, but Catlow hates your family. He's made no secret of that for as long as I can remember.'

'Oh. Do you know why?'

Sid nodded. 'His father was arrested and imprisoned for theft by your grandfather years ago and he died in prison. All the Catlows have hated Ollertons ever since. And that Terry can be violent if he's angry, so you'd better watch out for him.'

'That's a long time to hold a grudge. And what my ancestors did has nothing to do with me.'

'Ah, well, he's known for taking against people he thinks have harmed him and his family and trying to get back at them. Nasty devil, he is.'

'I'll keep my eyes open. Thank you for the warning.'

'You're welcome, sir. He won't be on your land for any good reason, that's for sure. He's probably looking for something to pinch.' Sid pulled out a watch and flicked it open. 'Eh, I'd better get on with my day. My customers will be waiting for their groceries.'

He left after a curious glance at Lewis, as if wondering why he hadn't been introduced to the stranger.

Edward realised that he'd been so interested in finding out about his intruder that he'd forgotten to do that. Well, the news would get around soon enough that he'd brought an architect here to design a house for him.

The door had hardly closed behind Petby than there was a tap and Riley came in to join them.

Edward nodded a greeting then turned back to Lillian, still concerned about how worried she was looking. 'You'd better not come across my grounds again to get here, Lillian. It'll be too risky until we can stop that fellow lurking there.'

'I'll be careful now I know about him.'

'Be sure you do.'

Maude had been whispering to Riley, telling him what had happened.

'Is there a police constable in Ollerthwaite?' Edward asked. 'I'd probably better report Catlow for trespassing.'

'Cliff Nolan is the constable but he's old and even Walter says he's not much use these days,' Maude said. 'My cousin told me the council has arranged to appoint a younger chap and pension Cliff off. Only they're taking their time about getting it all sorted out.'

'In that case, if I find Catlow on my land again I'll warn him myself to stay away.' Edward took a deep breath and added in a calmer voice, 'Now, let's get on with pleasanter things. I've asked Lewis to see what he can come up with as a design for my new home.'

Lewis smiled at Lillian. 'Edward has already told me you've suggested building the new house on the site of the older one, not the one that burned down. I'm inclined to agree with you. He thought you and Maude might have ideas about what the house will need to be like inside as well, what amenities you feel might be necessary so that the servants can do their job more efficiently.'

Edward saw both women nod, so took over again. 'We'll enjoy an interesting discussion about it today, I'm sure, but let's all go and study what might be the site for the new house before we get down to details of the interior. See if anything else occurs to us.'

But though they studied the site carefully and the views over the valley that it might give, not to mention the view of the lake with its water glinting in the distance, he didn't mention the discovery he and Lewis had made today. He didn't want word about it to get round in case the village lads came up to explore it. If they messed about with the remains of the strange older cellars they might get trapped down there.

He'd ask Walter if he knew of a strong chap who might be able to help them get down into that tunnel. One person must always be on standby outside when anyone went down, and no one should go down alone. Only then would he take the risk of investigating this discovery.

He suddenly remembered the loose flagstone in the other cellar and wondered if there was anything underneath it. It had rocked about when he'd stood on it, as if something solid was there. He'd make sure that was checked too and this time he'd take a spade down with him to help lift the nearby flagstones.

It was his land now and he already loved it, wanted to get to know every inch of it, even these strange old cellars.

And he was determined to end up with a home to be proud of . . . and a wife and family as well if possible.

He liked Lillian, liked her very much, but he couldn't quite shake off the thought that if she'd been married for several years without having children, perhaps there was a reason that she couldn't conceive. He hoped not, because she was just the kind of woman he would love to raise a family with.

The older he got the more eager he was to have children of his own before it was too late. And besides, he owed it to his family to continue their line.

24

Walter read the words printed on the back of the envelope that the postman had just delivered. It said *Queen Victoria's Jubilee Institute for Nurses*. A reply to his letter asking for their advice and help!

He'd left it to those he thought of as 'the youngsters' to discuss the plans for Edward's new house, because who knew whether he'd still be alive even by the time it was finished?

He was glad he was on his own to open this letter because the older he got, the less he liked to rush headlong into new ventures, especially big changes like this might turn out to be. He preferred to take time to think them through. And finding one of the new breed of better trained nurses to help his valley folk was a new thing for him and for a lot of people in Britain these days. It seemed to him as if it could only be a good thing, though, and that lives might be saved by such a person being there. He would be proud to be part of helping that to happen.

The letter itself was quite brief. Mrs Browne, a lady on the committee of the organisation, was in the north visiting a cousin in Preston and would be happy to come and visit Ollindale while she was nearby. She would discuss what their needs were and give him some idea of whether help could be arranged. She'd checked the train timetables and she was happy to spend a long day travelling to and fro from Preston.

She would also like to meet some of the local ladies who would no doubt be involved in appointing and then working with a nurse experienced in helping the poor of his town. It might be useful to schedule a meeting with the local doctor, too, because he mustn't be alienated by being left out of any planning or preparations.

A groan escaped Walter at this. Twilling was more likely to tell the visitor that the services of such a nurse were not needed, as he could perfectly well continue to cope with the medical needs of the town. And as the visitor was a woman, he'd no doubt be his usual patronising self when he spoke to her.

How could they get round this? Walter had several times wished there were another doctor here because he didn't get on with Dr Twilling at a personal level and had been relieved never to need his services. Sadly, he was certain that a man who was so old-fashioned in his ways would object to the mere idea of appointing a Queen's Nurse to help look after the health of the poorer people.

As for a lady doctor coming to work here, he'd heard Twilling rage in public several times about females who thought their inferior brains could cope with the complexities of being a doctor. Twilling would try to find a way to prevent one coming to the valley, whatever it cost him, that was sure. And sadly, there were other men in the valley who'd back the doctor up about that.

In the end Walter decided he couldn't solve this problem on his own. He'd speak to his family and friends after they'd finished their evening meal and see whether any of them could suggest a way of getting round these problems. If the Queen herself took an interest in the appointment and training of such nurses, then there must surely be some ladies in Ollerthwaite who'd be happy to follow Her Majesty's example. And he'd speak to some of the other people on the town council as well.

That evening as they chatted over their dessert, he raised the matter of bringing both a female doctor and a Queen's Nurse to the valley. He saw Edward look thoughtful, open his mouth, then frown and snap it closed again as if uncertain whether to speak, so he prompted, 'Do you know something about finding a female doctor, Edward, lad? If so, please tell us. I feel it's more than time we had one here. And it's rather urgent that we make a start on doing it before Twilling finds out and interferes.'

'Well, I have a cousin in London who has trained as a doctor and she's having difficulty finding a position because she's a woman. Della can't set up a practice of her own, because though she has inherited a little money from her family it's not enough for her to cover the expenses that would involve. In fact, she has barely enough to live on and she's too proud to let me help her.'

'You hesitated to tell us about her. May I ask why?'

'Because she's only just finished her training and is inexperienced, which she would be the first to acknowledge. She's told me very firmly that she would benefit at this stage from working with a more experienced doctor for a year or two before setting up on her own. She's been looking for a way to do that, but hasn't had any success so far.'

'If she hasn't found anything, perhaps she could come here and discuss her situation with us? I'll pay her rail fare and put her up for a few nights. What do you think? It seems a pity to leave a doctor unable to practise her trade when there are sick people needing help everywhere. And there are doctors in nearby towns to whom she could speak if she needed help.'

'I can ask her but she's fairly determined to do everything her way.'

'Let's hope this Mrs Browne can help us get a start by finding an experienced nurse willing to work here, then. That at least seems as if it can be achieved.'

Cam didn't often join in their conversations, though he listened with every appearance of interest. He was frowning now. 'Don't get your hopes up too high, Grandad.'

'I shan't. But I can't stand by and do nothing.'

Riley said, 'Don't hesitate to call on me for help if there's anything I can do. I have no objections to lady doctors. As a neighbour of ours used to say – we'll all have to keep our fingers, toes, eyes and knees crossed that this can be worked out.'

That lightened the atmosphere a little and won smiles from most of them because who hadn't heard that silly old saying?

'There's something else we need to sort out,' Elinor reminded Walter. 'You said this Mrs Browne wants to meet the local ladies involved.'

'I don't think there's much I can do about that. There isn't a group of ladies involved in this sort of thing yet. In fact, I haven't got round to finding even one lady who'd help me!'

'I volunteer to be your first, then. It's in my own interest, after all, to get a better doctor to settle here.' Elinor patted her stomach, then cocked her head, as if considering something. 'I'm sure I can find one or two other ladies for you as well. I'm getting quite friendly with the new minister's wife for a start and I'm sure she'll approve of this idea. She may know someone else as well. That'd make four or five of us to meet Mrs Browne if we include you, Maude.'

'You can definitely include me. And how about Miss Gorton who lives near the church in Ollerthwaite?'

Walter looked surprised. 'Twilling told me she was very ill and not expected to recover.'

Maude hesitated, then said, 'She told me in confidence that when she stopped taking the medicine he'd prescribed she started to feel better. She said she'd taken a long time to recover from a bad bout of influenza but he told her she was in a final decline and should take to her bed. The medicine he'd prescribed would calm her and see her through her final days.'

There was dead silence in the room as the implications of this sank in and people shared shocked glances.

'He really said that?' Cam asked sharply. 'He gave up trying to help her?'

Maude said it aloud. 'If she'd done as he said, he would have done worse: he'd have killed her.'

'That's . . . unbelievable.'

'Well, luckily she refused to take the medicine. I called in to see her the other day and she was looking well again. She was furiously angry with Twilling but didn't dare accuse him openly.'

'I thought last time I saw him that he didn't look to be in the best of health,' Walter said slowly. 'He's got to be about eighty, though he won't tell anyone his actual age. Surely he can't be losing his wits? He's a doctor, for heaven's sake.'

There was another silence till Cam said, 'I've not heard any good about him from the other farmers I meet. They're finding him hard to deal with lately.'

'I've seen him haranguing people in the street,' Elinor said. 'And I know one lady from the church group who will do anything to avoid running into him.'

'Well, that convinces me that we have to do something about finding more medical help, and quickly. After hearing that, I'd not like any of you consulting him, especially you in your delicate condition, Elinor, lass.'

Cam's eyes went to his wife. 'In your condition . . .' He shook his head and didn't finish what he'd intended to say.

She finished it for him. 'The mere thought of Twilling helping me birth a baby is enough to give me a week of nightmares, love. I'm not risking our child's life.'

'We have a few months yet before it becomes urgent.' Cam took hold of her hand. 'And if we haven't found someone else round here to help you by the time you're close to term, I shall take you to stay somewhere else for a while. There must be doctors in nearby towns who're not only kinder but whose skills can be trusted.'

'I'd rather have a woman doctor than a man,' Elinor said wistfully.

'This only makes me more certain that my cousin shouldn't come here till there is some doctor other than Twilling whom she can work with,' Edward said.

Walter hadn't expected the medical situation to be revealed as so urgent. He'd always been fortunate to have robust good health. But he'd lost beloved family members last year and didn't intend to lose any more because of Twilling's increasingly strange behaviour, or to allow other people to lose their loved ones, either.

Before Edward and Lewis left to go back to the lodge, Edward had a quiet word with Walter about their discovery of the hidden tunnel.

'I'd like to see that myself,' Walter said at once.

'Do you know someone strong and reliable we can trust to help us explore it?'

Walter frowned, stared into space for a moment then his face brightened and he exclaimed, 'Ah, yes, I do, actually. His name is Shorrocks and he's a good man. I think his given name is Ronald but I'm not sure because he's been nicknamed Rufus ever since he was a little lad on account of the colour of his hair. He went away from the valley as a young man to work in the mines for the extra money, then his father died last year and he had to come home to support his mother and help her raise his younger sister.' He hesitated, then said, 'His mother isn't good with money, which sometimes makes matters difficult for him.'

He paused again, then added, 'I know Rufus is fretting about not having a proper job even though he's earning enough to put food on the table and pay the rent. He's a hard worker and is well respected so he gets more casual work than most, but there isn't a permanent job in either Upperfold or Ollerthwaite that suits him. I keep my eyes open because he has a fine brain and it's sad to see it being wasted.'

'He sounds like a good chap.'

'He is. And his mining experience might come in very useful from what you say about this other cellar you found. I'm sure we can trust him to keep quiet about it.'

'Can you tell me where he lives? I'll go and find him while I'm in town tomorrow.'

'Better let me call him in for a day's work, Edward, lad. I use his services every now and then so it won't cause comment, which you going to see him would.'

'Tell him to come tomorrow about nine and wait at the lodge for us to get back. I'll pay him a full day's wages even if I'm wasting his time with this tunnel.'

'Fair enough.'

Edward and Lewis walked back to the lodge, agreeing to go into Ollerthwaite early the following morning to pick up some more fresh food and send a telegram to Mrs Browne for Walter.

'For a small valley there's a lot going on, isn't there?' Lewis said.

'Maybe we can just see more of what's going on here than you would in a city. I found that the details of life seemed to get lost in the hustle and bustle of urban surroundings.'

'You could be right. We can ride into Ollerthwaite together by bicycle, if you like, and you can show me where the post office is. I want to buy some postage stamps anyway. And perhaps we could come back via that lake and take a proper look at it. I keep seeing it in the distance and I'd love to go closer. There's something about a stretch of water sparkling with reflected light, isn't there?'

'Rufus will be waiting for us.'

'It'll only extend our journey by a few minutes.'

'Oh, all right. Jubilee Lake is one of Walter's pet projects. He wants to get the path round it finished so that people are able to walk round in comfort and use it more easily for recreation. He wants to finish off a proper path and put benches at the top so that they can have a sit down.'

'Sounds like that's another excellent idea. Walter's amazing, the way he cares about Ollindale. The valley's lucky to have him.'

Edward nodded. 'He is amazing but he's only one man and no one can sort out everything a town needs. But the medical problem has to be the most important thing to deal with at the moment if this Dr Twilling is starting to behave strangely. I can perhaps be of more help with medical matters once the house plans are sorted out and the building has begun. By then perhaps my cousin Della will have gained some useful experience and can come and live here. She's a really nice person, cares so much about her patients.'

The following morning the two men cycled into Ollerthwaite, sent the telegram and made their other purchases. After that they cycled home the long way round, which would take them along one side of the lake Edward had already seen. They stopped briefly at the lower end to stare across the stretch of water.

'It's rather a nice little lake at this part,' Lewis said. 'Whoever planned the retaining walls and the water outlet into the river did a good job.'

When they got near the top end, they met some very uneven ground and Lewis stopped. 'My tricycle won't cope at all well with this sort of terrain, I'm afraid.'

'My legs aren't coping all that well with it, either.' Edward looked down at himself ruefully. 'I've worked in offices and sat at desks for so many years that I'm out of practice at prolonged physical activity. Anyway, we'd better get back now because Rufus will be waiting. He should know about going underground safely if he's worked in mines. I hope he'll agree to help us go down and explore what's there properly. We can take it in turns to keep watch at the top.'

'I'll stand guard at the top all the time, if you like. I'm not fond of going into rough, underground spaces.'

'You didn't say.'

Lewis shrugged. 'I can push myself to do it if I have to for my job, but I'd never do it by choice.'

'You can stay at the top then.'

'Thanks.'

They were both more at ease with one another now and Edward was hoping that Lewis would be able to design a home he liked the looks of, a place where he could raise a family and live for the rest of his life.

Only time would tell.

25

That same day, Riley arrived in the morning, telling Lillian he'd be finishing things off today in her new bathroom and would be working on his own today.

When he knocked on the inner door of the kitchen a couple of hours later, he flourished a mock bow at her. 'I've finished your bathroom now, milady. Come and see.' He wasn't managing to hide his pride in what he'd done.

She could hardly breathe for excitement as she followed him to the short corridor at the back of the house to stand in the doorway of the new bathroom. The walls had been distempered a clean, bright white and though you could still smell the paint, it had dried overnight as he'd told her it would. The window was high up and of frosted glass but let in plenty of light. The bath and handbasin were clear of debris now and gleaming white, and the floor was neatly covered with the patterned linoleum.

Walter had said she was the one who'd have to live with it, so he'd sent her to choose the linoleum from the little shop in Ollerthwaite, telling her not to go above a certain price. That amount had been more than adequate. She'd found lino with a pattern of lozenges about the size of her hand in subtle shades of red and black. It looked very smart and modern. The curtains had been supplied by Walter from his stocks and he'd chosen them after looking at the sample of lino. Very daringly for a bathroom they were a bright red.

Riley gestured to the door that led to the lavatory, which had the same floor covering. The small window high up in the wall now opened properly and had a neat wooden window sill beneath it. There were even some torn-up pieces of newspaper hanging from a hook on the wall for necessary purposes. She'd been saving newspapers for that herself.

Every detail had been attended to really well. She turned to beam at Riley. 'It's wonderful! Absolutely perfect.'

He gave a satisfied nod. 'If you have any problems, don't hesitate to get back to me and I'll come rushing to fix them.'

'I doubt there will be.' She looked round, picturing herself having a leisurely bath in a bright, clean room with hot water provided by the gas heater on the wall at the tap end of the bath. 'The new linen cupboard is going to be very helpful too. How clever of you to think of using the extra space that way.'

She couldn't help thinking it was ironic that she didn't own enough items to fill more than two shelves of that cupboard but she didn't say that.

'Walter will want to see it to check everything. Will you be at home this afternoon?'

'Yes. I'll be here.' She hadn't got used to going out whenever and wherever she pleased yet. She'd spent too many years shut up in a house, avoiding Stanley and his parents, reading or simply watching passers-by from her bedroom window once the housework had been finished. If the weather had been fine, she'd gone for walks on the excuse of buying something for her husband's tea or supper. But if the weather had been inclement, she'd had to stay in and only go to the library, which had made her feel like a prisoner.

She walked to the back door with Riley, watching him pick up his bag of tools and get on his bicycle.

He was about to set off when he suddenly turned round. 'I nearly forgot to mention that Walter will take away the bigger things I've left here when he comes to check everything this afternoon. I can't carry those on my bicycle.'

His cheerful expression faded as he added, 'I really need to find some way of carrying my tools and materials around. If I buy a cart, I'll have to buy a pony to pull it and find somewhere to stable it where people can look after it for me when I'm not using it, which would be an added expense. What I'd really like is a motor car with a platform at the back to carry luggage and bigger things. I've been reading about what Mr Daimler is doing in Germany, designing smaller vehicles meant to carry goods. Only, sadly, I know any sort of motor car would upset Walter.'

'I'm afraid it would. I'd hate to do that when he's been so kind to us.'

'He's going to be upset eventually and there's nothing I can do about it. I'm not the only person in the valley thinking of buying a motor car. Don't tell them yet but a friend will be coming to join me here, probably next year if things go well. We've been planning for a while to start a business making and repairing motor cars.'

'Oh dear. That will really upset Walter.'

'I know. I've discussed it with Maude and she's worried about upsetting him as well, but you can't hold back the tide of progress. If I don't do it, someone else will. People want ways of getting around without having to tend animals, which are hard to look after properly in towns. Besides, cars can not only go further and faster, but they can carry heavier loads.' He gave her a wry glance as he added, 'Well, they can go faster if you break the law about speed limits, that is.'

'And I'm sure you would never do that,' she said teasingly.

'Not when any policeman can see me.'

'For years I read in the newspapers about the big changes in daily life but my own life never changed much. I tried to keep up with what was going on in the world, though. The railways opened up the world to people travelling around in groups but tied you to using their metal tracks. Now, motor cars are enabling individuals to travel along any road they choose, especially as cars are starting to be made more cheaply and reliably.'

'That's a good summary, Lillian.'

'I did a lot of reading. Thank heavens for libraries. I must get round to joining the one in Ollerthwaite.'

'There's just one other thing – if someone is thinking of hiring me to put a bathroom into their house, would you mind me showing them yours to prove I can do it properly?'

'I wouldn't mind at all. I can never do enough for you after the way you rescued me from the Thurstens.'

'I was happy to help. I don't like to see people being bullied and picked on. And now, well, you feel like a cousin to me.'

'You feel the same to me.'

'I'd, um, better get on with my day now.'

He'd flushed a little at her compliment, she noticed. She smiled as she watched him ride away. He felt more and more like a relative and she was getting to know Maude better now. She got on really well with both the women who lived at Walter's house. That group of people were probably as close as she would ever come to family now.

She still worried about the Thurstens and what they might do, though. Surely they'd not come after her again? It was too late for them to pretend that she was carrying their son's child, but Lemuel Thursten was very spiteful if he felt someone had got the better of him.

At least she had people to turn to here if she needed help.

26

Rufus was waiting for them at the lodge. He was a sturdy fellow with an intelligent expression and dark red hair.

'Sorry to keep you waiting,' Edward said.

He grinned. 'I don't often get paid for doing nothing, Mr Ollerton.'

'We need to keep this job a secret, so let's go inside to discuss the details. I don't want anyone to overhear our discussion. Sounds can carry a long way sometimes in the open air, especially on a still day like today.'

'Mr Crossley has already told me of the need for secrecy. You can trust me to keep quiet about it, sir.'

'I'm sure I can. He speaks highly of you.'

'He's a very fair man to work for.'

Edward explained to Rufus about the two hatches that had been found fairly close to one another. 'We don't know where the second tunnel leads, so want to be sure whether it's safe to explore further, and we're wondering what caused the cave-in at one end of the first cellar. Walter thought your experience in mines might come in useful in dealing with both those concerns safely.'

Rufus looked thoughtful. 'It might. If you can show them to me I'll see what they look like and suggest the best way of investigating the second place safely. Though I won't lie to you: nothing is ever completely safe once you're working underground.'

'I suspected that and I don't expect miracles of anyone,' Edward said. 'Lewis will stay outside in case something goes wrong and we need help.'

'That's good planning.'

'I've got a ladder here that Walter gave me of roughly the right length. We can use it to climb down the shaft underneath the wooden hatch. I've got a spade, too, for levering up that paving stone in the other cellar if we have time. We'll take every precaution we can as we move about.' He paused for a moment to wait because Rufus was frowning.

'I wonder if we could go down into the other cellar first, sir, the one that's easier to get into? I might be able to gain some idea why parts of the ground thereabouts have caved in before I look at the unknown area.'

'That sounds like a good precaution. We left an oil lamp and matches down there but we'll take another with us to use in the second set of tunnels afterwards.'

Once in the cellar, Rufus asked to be left to check its perimeter walls on his own, so Edward stood near the ladder and watched him walk all the way round the edge of the big chamber, holding up the lamp and studying the walls and ceiling.

When Rufus went into the passage that led out of the cellar, Edward picked up the second oil lamp and followed him, watching him study the piles of earth that blocked the far end but staying back.

Rufus took the same slow care in the side cellar that opened off the passage and where there was also evidence of the cave-in.

'I've seen enough for the moment,' he said after a while. 'Perhaps I should tell you and Mr Brody what I think about it at the same time. And it'd be nice to get a breath of fresh air before we go underground again.'

When they got to the ladder, he gestured to Edward to go up first and extinguished the lantern that had been left in the cellar. Since there was daylight shining down through the open hatch he extinguished the other lantern and passed it up to his employer before climbing nimbly up himself.

Once he was back outside he said quietly, 'I don't think this cave-in happened naturally, Mr Ollerton. In fact, I'm certain someone caused it on purpose.'

That surprised the other two.

'Are you sure? How can you tell?' Edward asked.

'I worked in mines for several years, saw both natural and deliberately caused falls of earth regularly. There's something that's different about them.'

'That's another strange discovery I shall have to bear in mind, then,' Edward said thoughtfully.

'I may be able to tell you more about these cave-ins after I've seen what's in the other place, sir.'

This time when they went up the slope to the wooden hatch, Edward didn't hesitate to let Rufus take charge. He watched the man take a lot of trouble to fix the ladder Walter had lent them securely before he picked up the lamp and went down into the hole. He went slowly, pausing every couple of steps to examine the walls.

'Whoever created this passage knew how to shore it up safely,' Rufus said at last. 'I reckon the last bit was done in a hurry because the planks are only roughly finished off, but it's still safe.'

Edward had been kneeling by the hole, watching him go down, eager to find out where this led. 'So you think it's safe for me to join you?'

'I'd rather explore further by myself first, if you don't mind, sir. It's easier for one person to get out in a hurry than two if there's a problem.'

Edward shuddered at the thought of having to do that. 'Ah. I suppose that makes sense. I really appreciate how careful you're being.'

Rufus gave a slight nod, surprised at this compliment because employers didn't usually bother with things like that, not in his experience, anyway. He stepped off the ladder into the slightly wider bottom part of the shaft, from which the side tunnel started, crouching to hold the lamp in the opening as he once again studied the walls.

After that he placed the lamp down further ahead of him and started to crawl into the passage. He only went a short distance before stopping, leaving his feet sticking out.

His voice echoed up to them. 'The walls here have been carefully shored up too so I'll risk going to the other end, which is only about four yards away. If it looks safe, I won't call out again till I've seen what it's like at the other end.'

Rufus took a deep breath then crawled along the passage. He'd never told anyone how much he hated being underground, but he'd been determined to earn the extra money by working in the mines after he'd left the valley and now Mr Ollerton was paying well, too.

He wasn't going to do anything that was obviously risky, though, however much they offered to pay him. But Mr Ollerton clearly cared about safety and listened to more expert advice. And there was no stupid foreman here forcing the miners to take unnecessary risks under threat of losing their jobs, thank goodness, so he could move around slowly and carefully, and would make suggestions about what to do next if necessary.

After holding the lamp carefully outside the far end of the tunnel to see what sort of space it had led into, he felt a little better about crawling right out. He was waiting to call back to the others because he didn't really know anything about this area yet. He moved slowly forward, holding up the lamp, ready at any moment to abandon it and scramble rapidly back if things looked unsafe.

He still disliked being underground, but Mr Crossley had hinted that this might lead to a steady job. Like many other breadwinners he put up with what he needed to in order to earn a living.

This time the underground chamber he was in seemed partly formed by natural rock walls at one side and part of the roof too was natural rock. It looked as if this had once been part of a cave. He hoped this would make it more stable than a fully man-made underground space.

He held up the lamp and turned slowly round on the spot. It felt much older than the first cellar he'd inspected; he couldn't work out why.

He moved gradually round the edge and at the opposite side he was surprised to find a door set deeply into the wall just before the natural rock began at that side. It wasn't a rough door, either, but an old and beautifully made one, which reminded him of the front door of one employer's house, to which he'd taken messages in his early days at the mines.

He tried the door slowly and carefully and found that it still opened smoothly. His senses were on high alert and he was ready to flee at the slightest sign of a problem or the dreaded sound of earth starting to move. He looked down at the floor, which was dusty and saw no recent signs of people moving around. And yet, the door had opened as easily as if it were inside a house and used every day.

It opened into a proper cellar this time, one which must once have been under a large house, he'd guess, because its walls were formed of big square stones mortared together and there was a plastered ceiling.

To one side were several large lumps covered in dusty tarpaulins, some of them waist-high, some shoulder-high. He tried to take off the covering but found he had to fiddle with two layers, the inner one of waxed canvas guarding the contents under the outer layer of coarse material. He was surprised to find a piece of furniture underneath, one whose quality showed clearly in spite of its dustiness.

He stroked it gently, a little puzzled. This chest of drawers was old, but after a closer study of it he didn't think it was nearly as old as the door, several decades younger at least than some of the furniture he'd caught glimpses of while doing odd jobs in richer people's houses.

When he uncovered more lumps they also proved to contain well-wrapped pieces of furniture and again seemed newer than the door. The odd-shaped lumps at the far end proved to be several matching dining chairs with carved backs. Who could have put all these pieces here and why?

Then he saw another door at the far corner of this cellar and went to examine that and try to open it. Only he couldn't. It was locked and very solidly built of some hard wood. He'd need a key to open it or tools to break the lock open. Which would be a pity because it was a lovely old door and an ornate lock.

He walked round the cellar but found nothing else, so decided it was more than time to go back and tell the two gentlemen what he'd found. As he got into the tunnel he heard someone call out his name and yelled, 'Coming back now, sir.'

He was very glad to get out of the stuffy innermost space and even happier to get up into the fresh air. He took several big gulps of it before he described to the two men what he'd found.

When he'd finished they both looked as puzzled as he'd felt about the furniture.

After a while, Mr Ollerton said, 'I need to think about this. I won't go down till tomorrow when we have more time. But what we can do now is to go back into the first cellar and dig up the space where a couple of paving stones are loose. I'd like to find out what's caused one to sink markedly at the side, in case it's a sign of danger.'

He turned to their helper. 'That'll be our final job for today but if you can come again tomorrow, Rufus, we'd be glad of your help. I'd like to go down into the second cellar with you, so maybe we'll bring another lantern as well. It's a good thing I brought that spade today.'

Glad of your help, Rufus thought, not letting himself smile at the words. *It's the money I shall be glad of most, though it's good to work with such polite gentlemen for a change.*

Once he and Mr Ollerton were down in the first cellar again with the two oil lamps casting pools of light round them, Rufus took over. 'I'll try levering the flagstones up, if you don't mind, sir, but if anything shifts unexpectedly around us, I'll yell and you should rush back up the ladder. We don't want to risk anything.'

'No, definitely not.'

They were looking at him and speaking with respect, just as Mr Crossley did with people who knew more about some situation than he did. Rufus started working slowly and carefully. He wished he could always work for people like this.

What he uncovered when he took away the first flagstone was a space that felt damp to him, not soaking as if water were welling up, but damp as if moisture was occasionally dripping down into it, maybe when it rained. He levered up the next flagstone and found that part of the ground under this one had sunk as well. It would have taken many years he'd guess, leaving a hole all the way along underneath this side.

He managed to pull the flagstone gently out of the way, revealing a long thin object covered in canvas. He didn't attempt to pick up the object yet but showed Mr Ollerton what he'd found.

'I don't think this object was put in carefully but fell down then rolled into the gap at the far side. If someone trod carelessly on the flagstone, they'd have pushed it in so tightly it would have been impossible to get it out without tools.' He pointed upwards, adding, 'Good thing it's only been a small leak or it could have caused much more trouble. Shall I take that object out of the hollow now you've seen where I found it?'

'Yes, please.'

Rufus knelt down and pulled out a slender roll of canvas, not quite as long as his forearm. He could both feel and see smaller lumps here and there in its uneven surface. He stood up and held it out. 'I think it's safe for you to open it.'

'We'll take it up into the daylight to do that so that Lewis can also see what we found.' Mr Ollerton stuffed it out of sight down the front of his jacket. 'Will it be safe to leave that hole open down here, Rufus?'

'I'll put the two flagstones in loosely. I can bring some fine soil down another time in a sack to pack them more tightly. I reckon it'd be best to do that then we can level the floor and no one will trip up. And you should get the hatch above it fixed so that it doesn't leak.'

'Can you do that for me?'

'Yes, happy to. I'm pretty handy with small jobs of all sorts.'

This employer had been nothing but civil all through this exploration, so he dared say, 'And . . . I'm as curious as the next person and I'd like to see what exactly we found, if that's all right with you, sir.'

'It's not only fine by me, I'd expected you to join us. After all, you're the one who uncovered it and if the three of us are working together we'll need you to see not only what was hidden there but perhaps even help us to figure out why.' He raised his voice a little. 'Come on, you two. I'm dying for a cup of tea.'

Rufus closed the hatch, still feeling surprised by how courteously he'd been treated. As Mr Ollerton led the way back to the lodge he heard him say to Mr Brody in a low voice, 'I've got something hidden in my jacket to show you, Lewis, but I shall wait till we're back inside the lodge. I've been wondering if someone is watching us.'

'I've been getting that sort of feeling too.'

Mr Ollerton turned to smile at Rufus. 'Don't hesitate to give us your opinion of anything we see. We shall also need you to tell us in more detail about what you saw in the other cellar or cave or whatever it was. If you'd kindly go over the details again for us once we've got our cups of tea, we'll discuss it and think about it in comfort.' He added with a grin, 'I don't make the best pots of tea in the world, but they're drinkable.'

Since his companion was speaking in a low voice, Rufus did the same. 'Thank you, Mr Ollerton. A cup of tea would be lovely.'

They walked down the hill, but when Rufus would have fallen deliberately behind, because he knew his place with the gentry, Mr Ollerton beckoned him to join them. 'You're part of this, not the tail end, and you're far more skilled than we are about going underground, so I'm not going to pretend to be superior or stand on my dignity.'

Which surprised Rufus yet again, but in a nice way.

At the lodge, Mr Ollerton unlocked the door and led the way inside. Mr Brody gestured to Rufus to go next and followed them, locking the front door behind him.

It surprised Rufus that they would do this and when they noticed his reaction, Mr Brody said, 'There has been a prowler round here more than once, so we're being careful until he's been caught.'

'I see. I'll keep my eyes open too, then, while I'm working here.'

In the kitchen, Mr Ollerton was already opening the damper to get the fire burning up again in the range. He pushed the kettle onto what would soon become the hottest part and said, 'By hell, I shall be glad when we get a gas stove fitted here. It's like going back to the Dark Ages. Do sit down, Rufus. I'll make us all a cup of tea when the kettle boils, but while we're waiting let's look at what we found.'

When they were all seated round the table he set the narrow canvas bundle on it and unrolled it slowly. A narrow package wrapped in a crumpled, dirty piece of paper was revealed at one end and another one wrapped in a rag occupied the rest of the narrow roll. There was a clinking sound as he took off the paper and gasps of surprise when several sovereign coins fell out and Mr Brody had to grab a couple to prevent them rolling off the table.

The inner layer of the paper that had been wrapped round them proved to be a bundle of white five-pound banknotes. Rufus couldn't help staring because he'd never seen so much money all at once in his whole life.

The second package proved to be a soft canvas bag, rolled up tightly. When its contents were tipped out, more carefully this time, what looked like small pieces of jewellery were revealed.

Rufus stared at them, then at the two men, commenting in wonder that they weren't tarnished or anything.

'This is gold, Rufus. It doesn't tarnish. This package is full of valuables. I didn't expect to find a hoard like this. Who put it there, do you think?'

Rufus waited for one of them to point out something else that he'd noticed and when they didn't, he reached out to touch the crumpled paper and draw their attention to it. 'Isn't this an old envelope, sir? Look. It's got part of a stamp in the top right corner, and a name and address in the middle.'

He spread it out, smoothing it gently. This was just the front part of an envelope. The paper was dirty but the writing was still legible enough to make out the address, so he read it aloud. 'A.J. Hatton, Agent's House, Ollerton Estate, Upperfold.'

Mr Ollerton took the paper from him and stared at it. 'That was the name of the former agent, the one who was thought to have stolen quite a lot of things from the Kenyons. It looks as if this is some of his loot, only what was it doing down in the cellar?'

'Perhaps he'd hidden it to fetch later?' Mr Brody suggested.

Rufus shook his head. 'I don't think anyone put it there on purpose, sir. I think it fell down from the hatch above.'

Mr Brody didn't look convinced. 'Why didn't he retrieve it, then?'

'He wouldn't have been able to without a spade to lift up the edge of the first paving stone. Maybe he thought one hiding place was as good as another so planned to fish it out another time. After all, no one was going to come along and steal it, were they? Only he might have been killed before he could do that.'

'That sounds more likely.' Mr Ollerton spread out the contents of the suede bag: several pairs of earrings, a couple of fine gold chains and two delicate little brooches. He suddenly pounced on one of the latter. 'Good heavens! I remember this brooch. It belonged to my mother. She said it must have been stolen and my father yelled at her for being stupid and told her she'd probably lost it, but she was right, wasn't she?' He stared at them both then said in a tight, angry voice, 'What was this Hatton like, Rufus? Did you know him?'

'I only saw him once or twice passing by. He didn't bother much with people from Ollerthwaite, especially those like me from the poorer end of town. The properties he managed for the estate owner were mostly in Upperfold. I do know that he was friendly with Terry Catlow who's another local villain. *He* is still alive.'

'I'll consult Walter. I'm not sure whether I should report our findings to the police or not. After all, Hatton is dead now, so he can't be brought to justice, and if that's my mother's brooch, the rest of the stuff was probably taken from my family as well. And the Kenyons cheated me about the condition of the cottages on the estate so if any of these pieces were theirs, they owe me money.'

'People round here guessed Hatton had been stealing from the estate,' Rufus said, 'but they couldn't do much about it.

I don't think anyone guessed he'd stolen things as valuable as gold jewellery, though. They thought it was just a few pence here and a few there from the rents he collected. They were too afraid of being thrown out of their homes to say anything and the Kenyons never came back here after the fire anyway.'

The kettle boiled just then and Mr Ollerton made a pot of tea, opened a cake tin and took out a chunk of parkin, cutting three big slices.

Rufus was astonished that they'd treat him like an equal, but he wasn't going to refuse good food and, to tell the truth, the good company was just as welcome. He'd met one or two men working in the mines with whom he'd become friendly, men who used their brains and thought about the wider world, but no one since he'd come back. It had been . . . lonely. And he'd been busy seeing that his sister was fed, dressed properly and educated, as well as keeping an eye on what his fool of a mother was doing.

After they'd finished their snack, Mr Ollerton asked Rufus if he would repair the leaking hatch and fill in the hole it'd made below it the following day.

'Happy to, sir.'

'You seem to have picked up a lot of skills.'

'When you do anything and everything just to put bread on the table, you can pick up various skills if you keep your eyes open. I like learning things.'

'I won't forget. I don't have many practical skills. I worked with figures mostly till I came back here, buying and selling things, then moving to investments and shares to make my money. And there are going to be all sorts of small practical tasks needing doing on the estate.'

He snapped his fingers as he realised something. 'I'd better pay you for today while I remember it or you won't trust me in future. How much do you usually get for a day's work?'

'I haven't done a whole day, sir.'

'No, but I stopped you accepting any other work today so it's only fair that I pay you for the entire day.'

Rufus told him the amount he usually earned from a day's labouring and was given the money on the spot with an extra five shillings.

'That seems a fairer amount because we really needed your special skills today. You weren't merely labouring.'

'Thank you, sir.'

'So you'll come back tomorrow as well?'

'Yes. What will I be doing so that I know whether to bring any tools?'

Mr Ollerton shrugged. 'Whatever we find that needs doing. Lots of small jobs at the agent's house and the lodge at this stage. It might be worth bringing a few basic tools.'

As he walked home, Rufus marvelled at what they'd found, marvelled too at how well he'd been treated and spoken to. He hoped the work with them would last for a while. He might be able to slip a bit more money into his savings.

He hadn't told anyone in Ollerthwaite that he had money in the bank, especially not his mother who'd have gone out and spent it straight away whether she needed something or not. At the moment he simply let everyone think he was like the other unskilled men, and since no one needed his mining skills he counted as unskilled here. Such men were glad of any money they could earn for a day's work and always struggling to survive and provide for their families.

Only, he wasn't like most men. His whole point in putting up with working in the mines had been to earn more money. He'd never wasted even a farthing, so that he could save as much as possible. One day he was going to start a business of his own. He wasn't sure what exactly, but not mining, which was a risky sort of job.

He was more a jack of all trades anyway, enjoyed a variety of tasks. Only, where did that fit in? He didn't know yet, but he'd find some way of making money. But he really wanted to stay in Ollindale; he loved the valley and had dreamed of it while he was working away.

He'd avoided marriage and courting because if you had hungry children and no immediate way to feed them, you couldn't leave your money in the bank and see them fall ill, could you? He'd watched one pal's wife fritter away anything her husband earned just as his mother wasted money when she had any. He'd gone hungry sometimes rather than take money out of his savings.

For once, Rufus was looking forward to coming to work the following day, not just to fill in the hole they'd found or do other odd jobs, but to see what else was to be found in the cellars.

Change was in the air on the Ollerton estate. A lot of people were wondering what would happen if its new owner really did have another big house built. That would bring more jobs to the valley, improving life for the people dependent on the workers.

Maybe, if he was lucky, Rufus would eventually find a way to fit into the new system and change his own life for the better. It wouldn't be his fault if he failed to do that. It most definitely wouldn't!

27

When Mrs Browne got off the train in Ollerthwaite, Walter was waiting for her on the platform and, of course, guessed this was her immediately. Well, she was the only elegantly dressed lady to get off it.

The rest of the passengers were more comfortably, sometimes shabbily, clad, and had come to the town mostly to visit relatives or to sell items they'd made or produced to local shops. The people from nearby farms sometimes came shopping to Ollerthwaite, too, because it was the nearest town. Easy enough to get there on the local train that stopped at every tiny station.

This lady looked to be in her fifties and Walter thought her very handsome, as well as looking very much in command of herself and sure of her place in the world. Money did that for some people. She waited calmly for him to approach her.

'Mrs Browne?'

'Yes. And you must be Mr Crossley.'

'I am. If you don't mind, we'll spend the day at my farm just outside Ollerthwaite. You and I will be able to discuss the general situation privately there first, then some other ladies will be coming out to chat to you.'

'And your local doctor?'

'I'm afraid Twilling has declined to talk to you at all. He says I've overstepped the mark bringing you here and he has no need of any extra help, especially from an unskilled female like a nurse. He insists he's been dealing perfectly well with any medical problems in the valley on his own for many years and intends to continue doing so.'

'You don't sound as if you agree with him.'

'I don't. He's very old-fashioned in his ways and considers women and poorer folk inferior creatures.'

'Hmm. Did he send me a note, even?'

'I'm afraid not.' He was afraid she'd take umbrage at that but she merely rolled her eyes, looking rather amused.

'Then I can guess what one of your problems is, Mr Crossley. I've met arrogant old medical men like him before.'

'He is indeed arrogant and I apologise for his bad manners. However, he would only have harangued you if he had come to meet you, so you are better off not wasting your time on him. I'm the one trying to organise the appointment of a nurse and there's nothing he can do to stop me taking action to improve people's access to medical help. But as I'm new to dealing with this sort of thing, I'm extremely grateful to you for coming to speak to us and give us some guidance. I'd like to do this as efficiently as possible.'

'We knew you'd need help. Yours is a situation we've encountered before, unfortunately.'

'Good. I'll welcome any help you can offer. Now, tell me which train you wish to catch back so that I can plan our day and I'll make sure you get back to the station in time.'

'I believe there's one leaves around teatime. That would suit me best.'

'It'll make a long day for you by the time you get home, Mrs Browne.'

She smiled cheerfully. 'Then it's a good thing I have plenty of energy, isn't it?'

When they got to the farm, she spoke briefly to Elinor and Maude, accepted a cup of tea and a scone, then said frankly that they had no time to spare, or she'd have enjoyed getting to know them better and asked to continue speaking to him privately.

He took her out across the yard to his office, the best place for them to be left undisturbed.

She took over immediately. 'Let's speak frankly, Mr Crossley, since we've no time to waste on chit-chat. First of all, please go through the specific reasons why you need a nurse so urgently. Don't leave any relevant fact out, however small or upsetting. And you'll need to tell me more about this doctor. I can sense that there is something about Twilling that's worrying you.'

'You're very perceptive. And yes, we not only need a good nurse but I've recently discovered that we're going to need a new doctor, preferably two, only how to persuade this one to stop practising is more than I can work out. Moreover, I think it desirable, essential even, that one of the new doctors should be female. Only, it isn't as easy to find such ladies when you live in an isolated valley.'

'Why the new doctors? Is this Twilling fellow retiring?'

He hesitated then told her about his latest worry, that the elderly doctor wasn't doing his job properly 'due to failing health'. He didn't specify what exactly this meant but after a moment, she said, 'I promise you that anything you tell me will be kept in absolute confidence between myself and the committee, Mr Crossley, only we do need to know the full truth if we are to do what we can to meet your needs.'

'Very well, but this is in the strictest confidence. I hadn't realised how urgent it had become until a few days ago.' He proceeded to share further details and she was as horrified as he had been at the thought of what Twilling might have done in the past or could do in the future if he wasn't prevented.

By the time Walter had finished his tale they were on comfortable terms, as sometimes happened when two people who respected one another exchanged full and frank views and information, and shared a similar moral code.

She studied his face. 'While we're being so open about the situation, I'd like to say that you seem to be doing far too much on your the own without proper support from the people of the valley, Mr Crossley, estimable as your efforts may be. We don't want a man of your value to the community dying of overwork. And I have seen that happen.'

He shrugged. 'Someone has to tackle these problems. I can't leave bad things continuing to happen.'

'Yes, but if I can lighten your load at all, I shall. It does sound as if you need help urgently. Hmm . . .' She frowned into space briefly and he waited patiently till she looked directly at him again.

'I'm wondering if Miss Vardy might suit you and the folk here, Mr Crossley. She's an amazing woman, has been a nurse for several decades and has dealt with some very difficult situations at times. She's particularly dedicated to helping poorer people and women struggling with babies and small children, and she's currently looking for somewhere she can use her skills more fully without being run ragged. Sadly, the doctor she used to work with closely died suddenly two months ago.'

'Did no one take over his practice?'

'Yes, a cousin of his, but after a few days she refused to work with such an old-fashioned doctor because, as she put it, she refuses to "kow-tow" to anyone except the Queen and she lives in the modern world not ancient Babylon.'

He couldn't help chuckling at that. 'What is this Miss Vardy doing at the moment, then?'

'Voluntary work at a centre for poorer women in Bradford run by a friend of hers. But she's nearly sixty now and wants to settle down somewhere quieter, preferably in the country, though her idea of quieter would probably be anyone else's idea of busy. She'd like to train a few other nurses to continue her sort of work, too, and I think it'd be wonderful if she could share her skills and knowledge. They're starting to call women who do that sort of work "Queen's Nurses" because Her Majesty has contributed money and support to training them.'

'Yes, I've read about it. An excellent thing for our Queen to do.'

'I think if Miss Vardy had been born a few decades later, she would have become a doctor, and a superb one too.'

'You clearly think very highly of her. I'm impressed.'

'Oh, yes. Very highly indeed. Mind you, she has some very strong views, especially about the treatment of women, and can be rather forceful at times in achieving her goals.'

'What do they say? You can't make an omelette without breaking a few eggs. She sounds to be exactly the sort of person we need here, someone who can stand up to Twilling, not to mention certain members of the town council. Might she be interested in coming to Ollindale, do you think?'

'I shall suggest it to her. I'd better warn you, though, that when I say she's outspoken, that's putting it mildly. Even this arrogant doctor of yours would find it impossible to browbeat her. But she's absolutely brilliant at looking after sick people, seems to have an instinct for knowing how best to help them.'

'An encounter between them would be interesting to see. He doesn't know any other way of dealing with those who are not his social equals than ordering them about in a loud voice, and now that I've realised how strangely he's started behaving, I have to find other medical help for the people here as quickly as I can. Would you ask Miss Vardy to come and visit us, see if she'd come to our aid?'

'Yes. I'd be happy to do that.'

'And if you'd bear in mind from now on that we're searching for a couple of other doctors, one of whom should preferably be a lady, I'd be grateful for help with that, too. Should you find anyone, please ask them to come and see me as well. I'll reimburse their train fare and provide a room for a night or two here at the farm whether they decide to settle here or not. We don't have a hotel in the valley, unfortunately, you see.'

Mrs Browne nodded and gave him another of her wry smiles. 'I'll keep my eyes open. Going back to Miss Vardy, I'd better warn you as well that she will want to take over the nursing project if she feels it worthwhile to come here, which I'm fairly sure she will. It sounds to me to be exactly the sort of work she's looking for. Do you wish to keep on running the daily details of the project?'

'Heavens, no, though I'll help if needed. I have enough on my plate with my other ventures. Only, there's been no one else to do it and once I realised about Dr Twilling's condition, I couldn't just ignore the situation.'

'No, of course you couldn't. Well, see what you think of Miss Vardy, then. I think you'll be impressed. She won't let this Twilling fellow bully her and I should think sparks will inevitably fly between them. I wish I could be here to see it.'

'You keep warning me of the possibility of her butting heads with people. Is she, um, contentious?'

'I'd call her forthright but she's not gratuitously argumentative, no. Well, she isn't as long as people respect her undoubted skills and medical experience. She won't put up with what she regards as a mistaken attitude, however. The doctor she used to work with thought the world of her and she admired him greatly professionally, too. He said she'd saved a lot of lives and she said the same about him.'

Mrs Browne chuckled suddenly and added, 'I should warn you that unfortunately for those she runs up against, she's usually proved right, even when people start off by being sure she can't possibly be. She won't give in to what she calls "wrong thinking and wrong treatment of patients". Sadly I've seen for myself that many male doctors don't recognise the skills of a mere nurse, nor do they always understand their female patients' needs. We women do, after all, have different bodies and therefore needs from you men in some ways.'

'Dr Twilling was that sort of arrogant person even before he began behaving oddly. I have always felt sorry for his poor wife.'

'So you'll risk Miss Vardy coming here?'

'Risk? I'd welcome her with open arms. She sounds to be exactly the sort of person we need.'

Only then did he realise they'd been sitting talking earnestly for well over an hour. 'We'd better go back to the house. I'm sure you're more than ready for a meal, which my lasses will have ready. And you'll no doubt welcome a rest from my litany of needs.'

'I am a bit hungry now. But let me say that I find it refreshing not tiring to speak to gentlemen or ladies like yourself who are open-minded about the modern world. It makes me feel there's hope for our species, which some sorry examples of humanity can make me doubt at times.'

That compliment pleased him greatly.

By the time they'd finished a quick meal, the group of ladies had arrived to meet the visitor. They left the farm two hours later with a strengthened desire to improve medical matters for the poorer folk in the valley and some practical plans for making a start on gathering support.

Since there wasn't going to be a meeting with Twilling, Walter was able to continue chatting to Mrs Browne and this time he brought Elinor and Maude into the discussion, especially Elinor who confessed to worrying about Dr Twilling interfering with the birth of her baby.

Like the others, Walter gained a lot of useful information from their visitor and managed to scribble down notes about some of the aspects of the situation for which she said she might be able to find further help. She seemed sure Miss Vardy would indeed take on the job in Ollindale because it was just the sort of situation that lady relished working to improve.

He was exhausted by the time he'd driven her back to the station and waved her goodbye.

But he smiled as he drove slowly back up the hill. He felt hopeful that they might be able to help some of the poorer valley people – in spite of Twilling. And best of all, Elinor would have expert help when the time came for the baby to be born.

He couldn't wait to meet this Miss Vardy.

28

When he arrived at the lodge at eight o'clock the following morning, Rufus found the two gentlemen up and looking forward to continuing their explorations.

'I want to go down into the second cellar with you today,' Mr Ollerton said at once. 'If what you found there remains as puzzling, we'll bring Walter in on it. However, Sid Petby told me when he delivered the bread this morning that Walter had an important visitor yesterday and today will be holding a meeting with some gentlemen who're interested in getting together to improve the medical services available in the valley.'

He grimaced. 'Sadly, I had to decline his invitation to join them but I shall be seeing him this evening when Lewis and I go there for our meal. I can tell him then about what we find today and ask his advice if necessary.'

'If we take some tools with us, we can try to open that locked door,' Rufus suggested.

'Have you had any experience of breaking into locks?'

'No, but I'm usually good at solving practical problems, and I'm happy to have a go at it.'

'The trouble is, I don't have many tools, hardly any in fact, just a screwdriver, a hammer and a small saw.'

Rufus frowned at that. 'I can't break a lock open without more than that.' He thought for a minute. 'If you'll lend me your bicycle, sir, I'll ride home and fetch some more of my own tools. I have some that might do the trick from what I saw of the lock but I'd have to charge you if any of them get broken.'

'I should think so too.'

He tried not to show his relief, just said, 'My going home again would be time well spent if you want to get that door open.'

His tools were locked in his trunk and even his mother didn't dare touch that, though her own possessions went into and out of pawn shop regularly. He refused point blank to redeem them for her, because he hadn't been able to stop her wasting the money she got for them immediately. It was as if she was frightened of it vanishing and nothing he said or did would persuade her that he was a good breadwinner and wouldn't let her and his little sister go hungry.

Mr Ollerton looked regretful but nodded. 'Please do that. We'll be grateful for the use of them. I presume you're used to riding bicycles?'

'Yes, quite used to them.'

'Then borrow mine.'

Rufus set off immediately, secretly delighted to be riding a bicycle in the fresh air and getting paid for it. When he arrived home, his mother thought at first that he'd been sacked and burst into tears, so he had to calm her down and reassure her. 'I've never been sacked in my life, Mum, and I don't intend to start now.'

He packed everything he thought might come in useful today in his special canvas tool bag, which had a long strap-like handle that he could shorten or lengthen to put across his shoulder and body according to weight. He locked the trunk in which he stored the rest of his things immediately after-wards and saw his mother looking at it regretfully.

'If you ever break into my trunk I'll move out immediately,' he reminded her.

She scowled but walked with him to the door. 'What do you want for tea?'

'I've already told you I'm not fussy. Anything will do.'

'The problem is I – I don't have any money left.'

He didn't ask what she'd spent it on this time. Could she not even save enough for one meal? 'Leave it to me, then. I'll buy some fish and chips on the way home once they've paid me.'

He gave her a quick hug because she was looking so shame-faced, and got on his borrowed bicycle, waving her a cheerful goodbye.

But his smile faded as he rode off. She was only fifty-four but looked at least ten years older and sometimes had a yellowish tinge to her skin and eyes. He worried about her health but she brushed his questions aside and refused point-blank to consult Dr Twilling.

Thank goodness his sister was still at school, which got her away from his mother's foolish ways of behaving. Nina was eleven and legally, she could have started working half time and attending school alternate weeks of mornings and afternoons. His mother had tried to arrange that the day after Nina's birthday, but he'd insisted his sister continue attending full time. She was a clever lass and the teacher had asked if there were any chance of her staying on. Nina could become a monitor and eventually go to college to become a teacher.

His mother had told the teacher that was for rich people and said she was in charge of the girl and she'd found a part-time job for Nina rolling cigars. She'd boasted about that to Rufus, expecting him to agree that with a real job in the offing his sister should start work immediately.

Instead, he'd taken Nina for a walk and asked her privately what she really wanted to do. She'd looked at him with tears in her eyes and said it didn't matter what she wanted because their mother was desperate for her to start bringing in money. He wasn't having that, so had told her he could afford to keep her at school if she wanted and he'd actually prefer it if she stayed on.

When she'd cried for joy, he'd given her a hug and told her he couldn't think of a better use for his money.

It had taken a big row with their mother and a repeat of his threat to go away and leave her to manage on her own. She'd not given in until he'd started packing.

Was she so uncaring or was she feeling too ill to cope on her own?

He'd been lost in thought and suddenly realised he was nearly back at the lodge, so set his personal worries aside. The two gentlemen were waiting eagerly, so he needed to concentrate on the matter in hand.

Mr Brody said he preferred to keep watch at the hatch again, so Rufus led the way down, relieved that Mr Ollerton was agile and didn't seem afraid of being underground. He walked round the cave-cum-cellar with Rufus, expressing amazement at how it had been built, then they went into the proper cellar.

Like Rufus, Mr Ollerton was astonished at the furniture hidden there. 'You're right. These are old pieces, probably from my grandfather's time, and they're of extremely good quality. I wonder why they were put down here.'

Rufus spoke without thinking how it'd affect his employer because Mr Ollerton had shown no signs of touchy pride. 'I reckon the furniture was hidden before they set the house alight.'

That won him a puzzled frown. 'You seem very sure the fire was deliberately lit.'

'I'm certain. A few people in the village knew about it and let the information slip over the years. One or two of the local villains had helped Hatton start it, you see, and couldn't resist boasting to their families and friends.'

'I'm amazed they got away with it. Why did the authorities never investigate?'

'Because the Kenyons wanted the insurance money and there was only one policeman in the valley, and he was afraid of the agent. Besides, Hatton not only paid his helpers well but also threatened to kill them if they told anyone in authority.' He waited a minute then added, 'I reckon you should keep the furniture for your new house, sir. Who else is there to cherish it now? It's so beautiful, it should be seen and used.' He couldn't resist stroking the top of one of the chests of drawers. Such lovely dark wood. Mahogany, probably.

When they reached the locked door, Rufus took out his tools. After some rather forceful fiddling with the lock he managed to break it open. He didn't open the door fully but set it slightly ajar and stepped back, gesturing to Mr Ollerton to go in first. If there was one thing you learned when working for rich people, it was to let them go first, even the nice ones.

Rufus followed him through and found they were in a much smaller space at the bottom of some stairs leading upwards. Even after all these years there was a faint smell of burning near the top, where they faced another locked door, and once again he had to force it. This time he could only get it to open a short distance.

He wrinkled his nose at the much stronger smell of burning now coming through. When he glanced down he could see sooty sand and tiny bits of charred debris on the floor beyond the opening. The space was barred by some big stones, the sort usually used to build houses. Luckily they weren't mortared in place, but he had to push hard to shove a couple away so that they could see what lay beyond.

'I reckon they were piled against the other side of the door to protect it from being burned.'

'You could be right.' Mr Ollerton looked through the gap he'd made. 'This must have been another cellar.'

It contained only piles of burned material. What was left of the ceiling now had charred beams in some areas and gaps open to the sky in others.

Rufus studied it. 'We must be right underneath the house that burned down.'

'I agree and I think you were right in your guess about the furniture.'

'Only the thieves never came back for it. I reckon Hatton paid them to leave it for him. Towards the end he used to get furiously angry with anyone who so much as set foot in the grounds without his permission. And he thumped any children he caught trying to sneak around. He said he had strict orders from the Kenyons to keep everyone away.'

Mr Ollerton was looking thoughtful so Rufus waited quietly for him to speak.

'Well, Hatton never managed to retrieve the furniture or his stash of valuables, did he?'

'Did you recognise any of the furniture, sir?'

'No. Furniture isn't the sort of thing that sticks in a child's mind. And since I bought the estate back to include everything on it and that was spelled out in the contract, I'm going to consider anything I find here as mine. When Lewis builds my new house, we'll bring the furniture out and polish it up beautifully again.'

'If you'll take my advice, sir, you'll not tell anyone except Mr Crossley about the furniture at this stage. There are still one or two villains in Ollerthwaite, especially Terry Catlow. I promise I'll say nothing.'

'I never thought you would.' He smiled and suddenly clapped Rufus on the shoulder. 'Could you start calling me Edward, do you think? All these 'sirs' and 'Mr Ollertons' don't feel like me.'

This was the last thing Rufus had expected to be told. 'Are you sure?'

'Yes. Very sure. I've met and made friends with people from all sorts of backgrounds during my years of living simply and concentrating on making money. And I most definitely don't like being called "sir" and "Mr Ollerton" by those I respect, whatever their backgrounds.'

'Well, all right. I'd be honoured.'

'Do you like being called Rufus or do you prefer your given name?'

'I don't like my given name.'

Edward grinned. 'What is it?'

He hesitated then admitted, 'Ronald, but I'm always Rufus in my own mind. Even my mother doesn't use my given name.' She didn't dare because he refused to answer to it.

'Well, there you are, then.' Edward held out his hand and they shook on the decision. 'Pleased to meet you, Rufus.'

'Pleased to meet you too . . . Edward.'

'Let's go back outside now. We'll pull the pieces of stone back to hide the door, then leave this collection of furniture to stay quietly hidden until my new house is finished.'

Edward paused before they went up the final shaft from the cellars to rejoin Lewis, setting one hand on his companion's shoulder to stop him moving on. 'Will you work for me full time from now on, Rufus? I'm talking about a permanent job.'

He couldn't help beaming. 'I'd be very happy to do that but what would I be doing?'

'I don't know. Anything and everything. I'll pay you more than the usual day rate because I'm sure you have a good variety of skills.' He named a sum slightly higher than Rufus had earned even in the mines.

'Thank you, sir – I mean, Edward.' He hoped he'd hidden his surprise at the amount. He wouldn't tell his mother how much it was, but continue to live frugally and save some of his money. And he'd only give her enough money each day to buy their food still. Weekly was no good. She'd spend it within two or three days.

Nothing would stop Nina becoming a teacher now, he thought with pleasure, and though he'd work for Edward for a year or two, Rufus was definitely going to look for a business where he could be his own master. He wasn't sure what, but he'd find something.

Very occasionally life could be kind to you. He just hoped that this time it would last longer. He was sure he'd learn a lot working with Edward Ollerton as well as earning better money. He enjoyed learning new things.

And he'd give good value for his wages, doing his very best.

29

Lillian was going out more often now, getting used to her new freedom of movement. She'd visited Walter's family on several occasions and each time they had other guests joining them as well as her for the evening meal. But she didn't feel it right to impose on their hospitality too often.

However, that afternoon she had been feeling lonely. She'd been lonely for years but now that she was spending time with people who liked one another and met regularly, the solitude seemed to bite harder.

Maude called in on her way back to the farm from Upperfold. After one glance at Lillian she said, 'You're looking very down in the dumps. What's wrong?'

'Nothing.'

'I don't believe you.'

'I was feeling a bit lonely, that's all.'

'No need for that. We'll cheer you up. You're coming to have tea at the farm tonight. In fact, we'll set off straight away. I'll wheel my bicycle and we'll walk briskly up the hill together, then someone can walk you home after tea.'

'I can't keep imposing on your family for meals or on other people to walk me home. I have to learn to stand on my own feet and not be a burden on people's generosity.' It was usually Edward who walked her home and she enjoyed his company too much, yet wasn't sure how he felt about her. She was starting to worry about that.

'Oh, pooh! No one wants to live all alone. It isn't natural. And you'll only be coming to tea when we invite you, so you'll know you're truly wanted. Put your coat on and lock your door.' She grinned and wagged her forefinger mockingly. 'Do as you're told.'

Lillian couldn't resist obeying.

As they started walking up the hill, Maude said, 'You shouldn't be afraid to join us, you know. Walter loves having company. And anyway, tonight he wants to tell everyone about the visitor who came to see him yesterday so it's particularly good that you're coming and will know what's going on.'

'Who was this visitor?'

'Mrs Browne, who is involved in the new Queen's Nurses arrangements to help poorer people. She's going to send a nurse here to see whether she likes the idea of living and working in our valley. And guess what? The woman she's spoken to hasn't waited a day even, but is coming to the valley tomorrow. That sounds hopeful, doesn't it?'

'Yes. I do hope she likes the looks of us. It'd be good to have a woman to talk to if we had any personal problems.'

'I agree. Apparently this woman is very experienced indeed. Mrs Browne said anyone should consider themselves fortunate to get her services. Walter won't tell us any more details, just smiles and says it'll be better if we form our own judgement about her.'

'That sounds wonderful.'

'There's another thing – Mrs Browne said this nurse would probably refuse point-blank to work with Twilling if he treated her scornfully. Ooh, I'd love to be a fly on the wall if that happened.'

'From what I've heard he treats all women as if they're stupid. Who wouldn't refuse to work with him or consult him as a patient if they could?'

'I agree. I can't stand the man.'

Lillian stopped walking. 'Do you know what he did two days ago? Gladys next door was telling me and she's furious about it. She has a niece who's expecting her first child and the poor thing has been sick all day long, not just throwing up in the mornings then feeling better but being sick every hour or so all day long. She apparently looked so ill and had lost so much weight that her mother insisted she went to see the doctor. And what do you think Twilling said? *Snap out of it, woman!* They're the exact words he used.'

'How cruel! And wrong.'

'Yes.'

They started walking again and Lillian went on, 'He told her she was only seeking attention and should get on with her housework and forget such fancies. But Gladys said her niece had started being sick before she had the faintest idea she was expecting, so how could she have been doing it to gain attention?'

'Women don't *choose* to be sick anyway!'

'Of course not. The young woman's mother was so outraged she told him he was a disgrace to the medical profession. He threatened to take her to court for slander if she said that to him or to anyone else about him ever again, and she told him to go ahead and do that. He got so furiously angry then, waving his arms around and going dark red in the face, that she was terrified he was going to thump her.'

'I've heard quite a few people say he's becoming more difficult to deal with. Not that he was ever easy. I'm glad I've never needed to see him.'

They arrived at the farm just then and Lillian couldn't help cheering up because she enjoyed not only a good meal but good company too. And she was sitting next to Edward.

When the meal was over he offered to escort her home and save Walter the job. He and Lewis had come together but Lewis said he was rather tired and would go straight back if they didn't mind.

Lillian didn't mind at all and she didn't think Edward was upset about it, either. He wheeled his bicycle and they walked down the hill, not hurrying but enjoying the balmy moonlit night and continuing to chat happily about a novel they'd both read.

She had never met anyone as interesting. They even liked reading the same sort of books. She doubted that her late husband had ever read any sort of book in his whole life, but Edward said public libraries had been a cheap form of entertainment while he was making his money so he'd used them a lot. They'd both enjoyed *Thelma* recently, a book most men would have despised because it was a romance and by Marie Corelli.

Edward only chuckled when she said that to him and told her you had to escape from real life sometimes. What's more, as the book had sold enough copies to need over forty editions printed, he couldn't be the only man to have enjoyed it.

At her house he said, 'I enjoyed our walk tonight. You can't always chat properly in a crowd. Um, I've been wondering – would you like to go for a walk to Jubilee Lake with me on Sunday?'

She stared at him in shock. 'Does that mean . . .' But she couldn't finish the question, was too embarrassed to put the rest of it into words, shouldn't even have said that much in case she was misreading the situation. Only, when younger people walked to the lake together at the weekends, it usually meant they were courting. Everyone in the valley knew that, even a newcomer like her.

'To be honest, I'm not quite sure what it means for you and me, Lillian. Not yet. That's what I want to find out. I know Riley and Maude dived headlong into their courtship, but I find it hard to leap into any new situation. I've spent too much of my life treading carefully, working hard to make money so that I'd be able to buy my family home back. All I'm certain about at the moment is that I'd like to get to know you better.'

He gave her one of his solemn stares, then added, 'Would that be all right as a reason for a walk?'

She could only nod and feel surprised at how delighted she felt. She had been telling herself she was never going to let another man court her. Only, this was Edward, and she'd been at ease with him from the start, and in a way she'd never experienced before, even with Riley. Was that how it started when two people were well matched romantically?

Why had she been fooling herself about her feelings for this man? Because she was afraid, that's why, and had vowed never to marry again.

But she couldn't imagine Edward alternately ignoring her or tossing insults at her, or at anyone else when he was in a bad mood, which Stanley had often done. Indeed, she couldn't imagine this man losing control of his temper at all.

'On Sunday morning we'll walk to the lake and back, then, shall we?' he prompted.

'That'd be lovely.'

'I'll look forward to it. I'll call for you at ten.'

He smiled, gave her hand a quick squeeze and stepped back, waiting as she unlocked her front door and walked into the hall. She turned and waved goodbye to him before quickly locking the door again and rushing to peep out of the front-room window. As she watched him get on his bicycle and ride slowly up the hill, she wondered what had made a man as lovely as him invite her out.

As Edward rode away, he was wondering why he enjoyed Lillian's company more than he did that of other women. She was quietly pretty, clearly intelligent and easy to be with. Nothing remarkable and yet, just the sort of woman you could live with happily.

Live with!

He wouldn't, couldn't let himself rush into marriage after so many years of being careful how he dealt with the world.

But he could tiptoe into it a little way, so to speak, get to know her better, see if she was always such a pleasure to be with, couldn't he?

Yes, he could definitely do that.

He'd find out whether love blossomed between people in real life as it did with the characters in novels. He'd always hoped it could really do that. It was such a lovely idea.

Hidden in the trees, Terry Catlow watched the two of them come slowly down the hill from the farm. He spat sourly on the ground to express his feelings and stayed where he was. It looked like that sod was courting her. That had happened quickly!

Well, Terry wasn't having it. He'd not *let* the last Ollerton breed more of that cursed family, not *let* them nest in this valley again. They were *not* going to raise more generations of arrogant devils to prey on poorer folk and make their lives even more miserable than need be.

People here had had two decades of peace without the Ollertons and the Kenyons. Life ticked along much more pleasantly without rich folk poking their noses into your affairs, thank you very much.

Mind you, that Crossley chap still needed pulling into line. He had far too much money for his own good, taken from poor folk as them sort always did.

No one here needed more people and jobs bringing into the valley or do-gooders like him interfering in people's lives.

He scowled at the figure walking slowly down the hill with that mouse of a woman. It was time to do something about this latest Ollerton, this *last* Ollerton, something that got rid of him permanently.

Terry strained his ears as the two of them came close enough to her house for their voices to carry up to him in the still night air. Going walking together on Sunday morning, were they? Starting courting, were they? Oh, no, they damned well weren't!

Sunday would be their first and last outing together. There was one way to make absolutely certain of that: wipe that sod off the face of the earth. The question was how best to do it.

He had a quick think as he watched them linger to chat in front of the house.

The Ollerton fellow wouldn't be on a bicycle then. He would probably cut across his own grounds to get to her back garden on Sunday, as he'd done before when he was out on foot. The time to catch him would be on the way back from the walk, when nobody would miss him.

No need to do anything about that architect chap who was staying at the lodge as well at the moment. With Ollerton dead that one's purpose in being here would be gone and he would leave.

As he watched Ollerton start back up the hill, this time on his bicycle, anger seared through Catlow at the memory of how happy he'd looked when chatting to that scrawny bitch. He didn't deserve to be happy.

They were not going to get together!

But Catlow didn't intend to get caught and hanged for the crime, so he'd have to plan this carefully to look like an accident.

When Edward got home he found Lewis sitting at the table, studying one of his preliminary sketches, so engrossed it took a couple of minutes for it to register that his host was there.

'Oh! You're back already. Did you have a nice walk with Lillian?'

'Delightful. I like her quiet ways. She's very easy to be with.'

'She has a pleasant manner with everyone, though she seems a bit shy.'

'She's gradually getting used to being with lively people, such as Walter's family and the others he invites to visit him.'

Edward went across to the kitchen range and got a pan down from one of the wall hooks nearby. 'Would you like a cup of cocoa?'

'Yes, please.'

When the milk had boiled and their drinks were made, Lewis pushed his big sheet of paper away, weighing it down and also mainly covering it with his pencil case. He didn't seem to realise for a moment that he was still holding his pencil and when he nearly used it to stir his cocoa, he smiled and put it down.

'I sometimes start to get into bed still holding a pencil.' He took a sip of cocoa then stared at Edward, his expression hard to read. 'You like Lillian a lot, don't you?'

'Yes. I'm wondering—' He broke off, wondering whether he should confide in anyone at this early stage.

'If you think I haven't noticed how well you two get on, how you never seem to lack for something to chat about, how often you smile at one another across a room, you must think I'm blind. I should think everyone at the farm has noticed that as well.'

Edward was surprised at his frankness. 'Oh. Is it so obvious?'

'Yes, it is. Very obvious. And nice to see.'

'I've never walked out with a young woman before.'

It was Lewis's turn to be surprised. 'Never?'

'I've always been focused on making money so that I could get my home back. I didn't dare start anything. But I do want a wife and family now, very much indeed.'

Lewis hesitated, but this time didn't say whatever he was thinking and it was a frown that accompanied the silence, not a smile.

Curious about what had made his companion suddenly stop chatting, Edward said, 'Go on. Tell me why you're looking rather concerned.'

'Well, Lillian is a lovely person but I was surprised that you called her a young woman. She's not exactly young, is she? She must be about thirty.'

'That's not old. I'm thirty-eight next birthday.'

'Thirty isn't old for a man, but age matters much more for a woman. And,' another hesitation, then Lewis said, 'she'd been married for a few years before her husband died and they hadn't had any children. Is there some problem about that, do you think? Sometimes women can't have children, however hard they try. I shouldn't say this, but I have a relative whose wife has failed to have any children and he tries to hide it but you can see he's upset when he sees other relatives with newborn babies.'

Edward stared at him in horror as this idea sank in, emphasising his own slight worries. 'I thought that since she and I get on so well, it'd be pleasant living with her and we might have children. I don't want to share the rest of my life with a woman who cares mainly about my bank account. Or one whose pedigree I've checked out as you do a horse you want to breed from.'

He wanted someone who could care about him and about his estate, a woman who wanted to share in creating a nice home, then have children. And one who was interesting to talk to. Oh, he needed that! He'd been without close family for so many years, he'd almost ached from loneliness at times.

He changed the subject, didn't want any more nasty ideas tossed at him like grenades in a war. 'How are things going with the house design?'

Lewis took the hint and dropped the subject of starting a family, thank goodness.

'I'm just going to put in another couple of hours' work and then I shall have something to show you in the morning. Not a completely finished plan of a house but what I think of as a detailed vision of what it might be like so that you can decide whether you need anything else adding to it before I really start work on the properly detailed plans.'

Edward was puzzled. 'What sort of thing might I want to add?'

'Well, um, let me think . . . a billiard room, for instance. They're very popular in some circles.'

Edward grimaced. 'I'm not good at games, have never had time to waste on them. No, I shall look forward to seeing the house plan you create with the usual rooms. I've already told you about wanting extra bathrooms and that's all I can think of. You've had quite a bit of experience but I've not lived in a big house since I was a child. My main desire is to have a *home*, not a place to show off.'

'Yes. I thought that was what you wanted and I've tried to achieve it but I needed to check that you hadn't thought of anything else to include.'

'I haven't.' Edward sipped his rapidly cooling cocoa, stared into the cup then drained the last few mouthfuls and said goodnight. He couldn't concentrate on houses when he was still thinking about Lillian.

He usually fell asleep straight away but tonight, Lewis's comments about her and whether she could have children or not kept him awake and seemed to magnify his own worries.

Why hadn't she had any? She'd been married for over five years, after all.

If she was definitely unable to bear children that would leave him with a very sad dilemma.

Edward wasn't the only one lying awake that night. Lillian couldn't get to sleep either.

Did she really dare think of marriage again? She'd had such a dreadful experience with Stanley Thursten and wasn't sure she was truly free of it yet because she was still worried about his family coming after her.

Of course, Edward wasn't like the Thurstens. She was utterly certain of that. He was a lovely man. But still, marriage was for the rest of your life, not something she would ever want to rush into, even with him.

She'd been astonished at how quickly and happily Maude had started courting Riley. And the two of them were already talking about getting married. It might have happened ridiculously quickly but they looked so happy, so right together that Lillian was envious.

How could you tell if a man would be good to live with for the rest of your life or not?

She'd known the opposite with Stanley, had disliked him intensely even before they'd got married. He hadn't seemed to like her, either. But her parents had made it impossible for her to refuse to marry him, had threatened to throw her out on the street with only the clothes she stood up in, literally, if she didn't because they wanted her off their hands financially. And Stanley had tossed it at her many a time that his parents had forced him into it as well by using similar tactics and he'd never have chosen to spend his life with an ugly lump of a stupid female like her.

The two of them might have shared a house after they married, but they had never really shared their lives. She'd felt like a frozen person but hadn't been able to work out any way of escaping from her situation because she wouldn't have had enough money to travel anywhere and hide, let alone to live on afterwards. She'd done her best to save but you couldn't keep much back from the mean amount of housekeeping he'd given her or she'd have gone hungry. He'd judged that amount to a nicety, or his parents had.

Thank goodness for her godmother and the wonderful bequest with its clever conditions. If only she'd received that earlier, she'd not have needed to marry him.

She'd been surprised how different it was spending time with Edward from spending time with anyone else she'd met in her whole life. She not only liked him but felt truly comfortable with him. And he was never anything but polite, to her or to anyone else.

But would that sort of behaviour last? Could they stay happy together for the rest of their lives?

Then she remembered how Elinor and Cam looked at one another and envy surged through her. It must be wonderful to feel like that, absolutely wonderful. She wanted the same thing, longed for a loving companion.

Well, she wouldn't find one without making some effort. She could *try* seeing more of Edward, couldn't she? And going out walking alone with him on Sunday would be a good start. She'd be a hopeless, cowardly fool if she didn't even *try*.

This time, however, she wouldn't need to tie herself down to marrying him unless she was certain she wanted to, because she now had enough money of her own to live on in modest comfort. So she wouldn't let anything permanent happen until she knew him far better.

She turned over again in bed, but, comfortable as it was, sleep still eluded her for a long time.

30

Miss Vardy arrived in Ollerthwaite sooner than anyone had expected. Mrs Browne sent a telegram saying the nurse would be arriving there later today. Maude immediately started airing one of the spare bedrooms, Elinor began to make a cake and Walter went down to the station in Ollerthwaite to meet her train.

He stood on the platform as the train chugged slowly to a halt and the carriage doors opened. When a tall, thin woman with silver hair tied back in a low bun and a rosy, healthy-looking face got out of a carriage carrying a small suitcase and some sort of Gladstone bag, he moved forward to greet her.

'I'm Walter Crossley. Are you Miss Vardy?'

She set down the suitcase and held her hand out like a man, giving his a firm shake. 'Yes, Flora Vardy. Pleased to meet you.'

'Let me take your suitcase.'

'I'd rather you got my trunks out of the luggage van and onto your cart. There are three of them, all clearly labelled, but it'll take two men to lift each of them because they're heavy. They contain all my worldly possessions, you see. You can leave me to carry my own suitcase and medical bag. I'm not one of these weak females.'

He gaped at her as this information sank in. 'You've brought everything you own with you?'

'Yes. Sybil Browne seemed very sure I'd like it here, and she's never been wrong before, so I took a chance and let a colleague take over my rented flat.'

He beamed at her. 'Well, that's very pleasing news, Miss Vardy, believe me. Did Mrs Browne also warn you about our . . . annoying problems?'

'Yes. All of them, including your doctor. The information will be quite safe with me, I assure you. Now, let's save our chatting for after you've retrieved my luggage.'

Flora looked around. The porter didn't seem to be there at the moment but as Walter Crossley stood near the luggage van, she watched a man who'd got off the train see him and stop, then walk across and ask if he needed help.

She gave a little nod of approval. The fact that someone would do that without needing to be asked for help spoke well for how the man who'd met her was regarded in the town. He must be near her own age but was still a fine-looking figure of a man, with vivid blue eyes alight with intelligence. She knew instinctively that she was going to enjoy working with him.

Walter called across to her and pointed out which cart was his and she went over to it, putting her two bags on the back before climbing up on the driving bench.

She continued to watch from that vantage point as Walter and his helper lugged all three trunks across and another man stopped what he was doing to come across and help heave them up on the back of the cart.

After he'd thanked the two men, Walter waved farewell to his helpers before joining her on the driving bench. He shook the reins and clicked to the pony, which set off at a gentle trot.

She began asking Walter questions about the town. If it was going to be her home, she wanted to learn everything she could about it as quickly as possible.

Once they were out of Ollerthwaite she said quietly, 'You're well liked, I see. That augurs well for this venture if folk come to help you so willingly.'

'People can be very kind.'

She kept turning to look from one side to another as they drove through Upperfold, studying the scenery and the people with great concentration.

Then, as the pony moved more slowly as it pulled them up a gentle hill, she relaxed, breathing in and out deeply. 'It's wonderfully bracing air here after the smoky haze you sometimes get in towns. I love breathing air like this. I wish some of the children I've nursed over the years could have come here and run around for a while. That'd have done them more good than any bottles of medicine.'

A short time later the pony slowed down even more and Walter pointed out his home ahead of them, not managing to hide his pride in it.

'Ah! Now that's what I call a pretty farmhouse, Mr Crossley.'

'I love it,' he said simply. 'My family have lived here for two hundred years, give or take.'

'You're fortunate.'

'I know. I do appreciate that and try to share my good fortune with those less blessed in life.'

The pony needed no guidance to trot round to the rear and come to a halt. Cam came out from one of the sheds and after a quick introduction said, 'I'll help you in with the trunks, Granddad, then I'll see to the cart.'

As Flora went into the house she met Maude about to come out.

'Miss Vardy?'

'Yes. And you must be Maude. I like to see a nice sturdy young woman, not one of these niminy-piminy creatures.'

'It's a good thing I am fairly strong. Excuse me, but I think the men need some extra help with those trunks.'

Another young woman greeted Flora inside. 'I'm Elinor and you must be Miss Vardy. Would you like a cup of tea?'

'I'd just about kill for one. I'm somewhat tired after my long journey today but from tomorrow onwards I'll take my share

of the housework and anything else that needs doing. I'm
going to enjoy living in Ollindale.'

Elinor was startled. 'You're already sure you'll be staying?'

'Yes. This is a grand situation for a home and I liked the
looks of your little town.'

As easily as that, Flora Vardy walked into their lives.

When Lewis produced his preliminary sketches and laid them
out on the table after breakfast for Edward to study, a thrill of
excitement ran through him. He did so hope they'd be what
he wanted, was so eager to make a start on building this home.

Rufus, who had just arrived, stepped away from the table.
'Shall I wait for you outside? I could be tidying the shrubbery.'

Edward shook his head. 'The more people who study the
ideas for the house the better as far as I'm concerned. We're
only going to build it once, after all, so I want to get it right.'

However, Rufus and Lewis still hesitated, trying to let him
look his fill without interruption until he suddenly realised
what they were doing and beckoned Rufus forward. 'Do you
understand house plans?'

'Yes, I do.'

'Take a good long look at these, then, and tell me what you
think of it.'

He studied the plans in silence for a minute or two, then
nodded. 'I like the look of it. Not too fussy. There are a few
houses in Ollerthwaite, in the better part, where the buildings
are so fussy you can't seem to see the door and window frames
properly because your eyes get torn every which way. They
belong to people with money so I've never understood why
they appear so . . . well, *wrong*.'

Lewis looked at him with interest. 'Are you talking about
those three red-brick houses just beyond the railway station?'

'Yes, sir.' He didn't know whether to call him sir or not but it
was always better to err on the side of being over-polite.

'If I'm Edward, he's Lewis.'

Rufus looked at the architect and got a grin, so relaxed and said, 'Thank you. Lewis it is.'

'Let's sit down and talk about the house, and please say exactly what you think, Rufus, or tell us why you've done something a certain way, Lewis.'

When they were seated, Edward began. 'I like the overall shape of it and the size it appears to be very much, but I wonder if it could be even more simple without those fiddly bits over the windows?'

'Of course.' Lewis scribbled a note on a piece of paper. 'In other words you want utterly classical Georgian architecture.'

'Is that what it's called? Yes, I do.'

They both looked at Rufus, clearly waiting for his opinion.

'I agree. And . . . well, it's a pretty house, but I'd have thought the entrance needed . . . something more.'

'Go on,' Edward urged.

'I probably don't have the correct words for it, but I'd want to see something to mark out the entrance better without it being overly fussy. Perhaps two or three wide steps leading up to the main door?'

The other two men stared at the front view.

'He's right,' Edward said after a couple of minutes. 'We do need to mark out the entrance better. I like the idea of steps and perhaps a simple portico as well.'

'Give me a minute.' Lewis pulled the piece of paper across, grabbed his rubber and scrubbed out the entrance, then sketched in two broad, shallow steps leading to a front door beneath a simple portico with one pillar at each front corner.

Edward studied it for a while longer, then nodded. 'Yes, that's much better. In fact, it all looks *right* now.' He turned to Rufus. 'You seem to have a gift for that sort of thing.'

'I've seen a lot of big houses in the past few years. Just from a distance, mind. I used to go for long walks in the country on my day off when I was a miner. I went out even on rainy days, because it seemed to help clear my head and set me to breathing better. Eh, I couldn't get enough fresh air. Those mines were not . . . nice places.'

He shook his head, clearly unhappy with the memories. 'I used to stop and stare at the big houses, watch the rich people coming and going, wonder what their homes must be like inside. I grew up in a two-up, two-down terraced house, you see, and lucky not to have to share that with another family. But we were always surrounded by a lot of people.'

They all turned to look back at the sketch again, then Edward nodded. 'Yes. That's much better. It's surprising what a difference a few small changes can make to a building. I hadn't realised how much.'

He nodded to Lewis. 'You've got the job of designing my new home, lad. Now, let's go out and decide exactly where we're going to put it. You too, Rufus.' Then he stopped and frowned. 'We should take Lillian with us for that and get her thoughts as well before we settle on anything. She's got an eye for houses too.

31

Two days after her arrival, Flora commented on how efficiently Walter and his family got around the valley with no bus services, and expressed a desire to buy a bicycle for herself.

'I've never owned one, though I did learn to ride my friend's and borrowed it sometimes. What fun it'll be having one of my own. Where do I go to buy a bicycle, Walter?'

'We usually buy them from Peter in Upperfold. I can take you to see him this morning if you like. He has a small workshop there and usually has one or two bicycles for sale, mostly second-hand but he does them up nicely. How quickly can you be ready?'

'Five minutes.'

She was true to her word, and two hours later had bought and started practising riding her very own bicycle, insisting on wobbling all the way up the hill back to her temporary home instead of sitting on the cart.

'I'd better go and meet this doctor,' she said after lunch. 'It'd be the normal courtesy.'

Walter gave her a worried glance. 'He'll only be rude to you. Is it worth it?'

She considered this, head on one side, then said, 'I think it would still be the thing to do so that I don't have anything to reproach myself with. Apart from anything else, I'd like to see how he behaves. If what you said is true, he could be gradually turning into a serious danger to the people of the valley.'

'I suppose so.' Walter had been dreading dealing with this if the problem became too acute.

'Had enough confrontations recently?' she asked gently.

'Unfortunately, yes. Especially with Twilling.'

When she laid her hand on his and gave him a little squeeze, he felt comforted and supported.

He really liked her. So far she'd been a cheering presence among them. She saw people's feelings too clearly sometimes, but as a nurse that could only be helpful, surely?

When they arrived at the doctor's home, they went round to the side, where the patients' entrance was, and found a group of people still standing in an untidy queue. At the sight of Walter, a few of them surged across, trying to talk at once.

'Hush, please! One person tell me what's wrong?' he said loudly.

'Dr Twilling holds a surgery in the mornings and it should have opened half an hour ago. He's usually punctual to the minute,' one woman said, cradling her left arm and leaning against another woman. 'I need help, but they won't open the door.'

Walter looked at the house in puzzlement. That was indeed strange. Twilling always made such a big parade of the need for punctuality in a civilised world. As he looked, a maid came rushing round from the back of the house and ran straight towards him.

'Oh, Mr Crossley, we're so glad you're here. Thank goodness Mrs Twilling saw you from the window. We don't know what to do about the master and that's a fact.'

'What's wrong?'

'He's not well.'

'I'll come in the back way.' He called to the group, 'Let me through, please. I'll try to sort this out.'

When Flora moved forward with him, the maid said, 'Mrs Twilling says only you, Mr Crossley.'

'This lady is a nurse, new to the valley. I think she should come too, especially if there's a medical problem.'

'He'll throw an extra fit at that,' she exclaimed, then lowered her voice to add, 'Eh, I can't be doing with him lately, Mr Crossley, and that's a fact. He didn't used to be this bad. I'm going to look for another position at quarter day. I've put up with enough rudeness from him.'

She opened the back door and locked it after them, then took them through to the front of the house to what he knew was the doctor's own entrance to the surgery. The patients' area was all at that side of the house, so he could still hear the people outside talking.

He tapped the maid on the arm before she could open the door and whispered, 'It might help if you can give us some idea of what's going on.'

'He's run mad, that's what's going on, and if he hits out at me again, I'll pack my bags and leave straight away, and hang my wages.'

'Hits you!'

She didn't elaborate but opened the door and gestured to him to go inside, then leaned against the door frame and folded her arms, not looking inside the room.

He'd been prepared for the doctor to be acting violently but he found Mrs Twilling kneeling beside her husband, who was lying motionless on the floor.

'He fell down a minute ago.' She began to sob. 'I don't know what to do. He won't answer me.'

Flora moved forward. 'I'm a nurse. Let me look at him.'

'Come and sit down.' Walter stepped forward to help Mrs Twilling up and guided her gently to one side.

'He won't like her looking at him,' she protested.

'My dear lady, Dr Twilling isn't conscious and needs any help he can get. Miss Vardy is a very experienced nurse. She'll know better than either of us what to do for your husband. Can you tell me how this happened? Go back to the beginning.'

'He looked dreadful when he got up this morning, really white and ill, and he seemed to be having trouble speaking. But he would insist on getting ready for surgery as usual. He never gives in to feeling bad. Only, when he came down for breakfast he suddenly leaned against his chair and couldn't seem to speak. My maid and I tried to help him but he pushed us away and then started making strange gurgling sounds.' She mopped her eyes with a handkerchief. 'He looked like he was about to collapse but he still hit out at us when we tried to help him. I didn't know what to do, then I saw you through the window, so I sent Brenda to fetch you.'

As she paused to mop her eyes again, he looked beyond her at what Flora was doing and to his amazement, she was closing the doctor's eyes in the way people did when someone had died. It wasn't possible – surely Twilling couldn't have just dropped dead as unexpectedly as that?

Flora stood up and came across to them. 'Mrs Twilling, I'm so sorry. There's nothing anyone can do to help your husband.'

'He's not dead?' Mrs Twilling suddenly began to weep. 'No! He can't be dead?'

'What do you think happened?' Walter asked Flora in a low voice.

'From the looks of him and what his wife says, I think he must have had a minor seizure earlier followed by a major one a short time ago. Is there another doctor in the valley?'

'No, I'm afraid there isn't. Twilling always resisted any other doctor coming to work here and the council backed him up, unfortunately.'

'Oh dear. I think I'd better stay here then, Walter. If there's any sort of emergency among his patients I may be able to help them better than most, though I'd rather have had a doctor available.'

'Anything you can do would be a big help, I'm sure.'

'How can we get a doctor to come here?'

'I don't know of any nearby. We're so isolated.'

'Then I think you should send a telegram to Mrs Browne. Don't stint on words, tell her what's happened. I'm sure if anyone can find you a temporary doctor in a hurry, it'll be her or a member of her committee, and she's still in the north. You'd better send for a magistrate to oversee the situation.'

'I can do that.'

'And can you please find me someone with practical experience of caring for people to help me here, preferably someone able to lay out a body?'

'Yes. I'll send for Mrs Yardley. She helps with the practical side of birthing, though Twilling has always kept an eye on things after the event, and she also lays people out.'

'Excellent. And an undertaker?'

'Phippen's. I'll send for them too.'

'Good man.' Flora turned to the sobbing widow and put an arm round her shoulders. 'I think you should come and lean back on the sofa, Mrs Twilling.' She looked across at the maid. 'Brenda, is it? Can you make a cup of strong, sweet tea for your mistress?'

'Yes, ma'am.'

She turned to Walter. 'We'd better leave the body where it is till a magistrate has seen it.'

'I agree.'

'If anyone waiting outside is desperate, Walter, I'll try to help them but if they can manage for the time being, they should go home. I'm sure Mrs Browne will find us another doctor to take over here as soon as possible. Will you tell that to the people waiting outside?'

'Yes, Miss Vardy.'

The maid bustled to and fro then returned for further orders.

'You're a good help, Brenda,' Flora said. 'Let's get your mistress up to her room to lie down now.'

As the maid drew herself up, trying to hide her pleasure at this compliment, Flora led the weeping widow out with one arm round her shoulders and could be heard speaking gently to her as they walked towards the sitting room.

Walter was shocked and amazed at how suddenly this had happened, but hurried off to do Flora's bidding. He was impressed by the way she had taken charge. Everyone had listened to her and done as she asked without a quibble, though she'd only spoken calmly and gently.

He asked the group if someone could find Mrs Yardley, tell her what had happened and request her help here. One young woman volunteered to do that and hurried off down the street.

He then repeated his instructions for anyone who could to go home again because clearly there was no doctor on duty now.

Most of the remaining people went quietly away, looking shocked. The woman holding her arm stayed.

He brought the three people still standing there into the waiting area for Flora to deal with once she'd settled Mrs Twilling, then hurried off to the post office to send a telegram to Mrs Browne. He told the man who took the details that if a reply arrived within the next hour, they might catch him most easily at Dr Twilling's house.

'Someone told me he'd dropped dead. Is that really true?' the man whispered.

'Yes. I'm afraid so.'

'He was over eighty, you know.'

'Yes. In fact, he told me so himself only recently.'

To Walter's relief, a telegram was brought to the doctor's house by a lad on a bicycle only forty minutes after he'd sent his message.

It said simply:

> *Will find someone and try to get them to Ollerthwaite tomorrow. It may have to be a female doctor but if anyone complains refer them to Flora. Don't bother to reply if this all right.*

He let out a sigh of relief and showed the telegram to Flora.

'She'll find someone if anyone can,' she said. 'What a relief that she was at home.'

To the horror of many people in the valley, it was a woman doctor who turned up the following day, a middle-aged woman whom Flora had worked with before. She whispered to Walter that Dr Coxton was good at her job and they could leave the medical side of things in her hands.

Flora then studied his face. 'You look weary, Walter. I'll stay here with Dr Coxton. You go home now and get a good rest. We don't want you dropping dead on us as well and we've got us a doctor to look after things here now.'

'I doubt I shall drop dead on you but I am tired, I must admit. Send someone to fetch me if I'm needed.'

She flapped one hand at him. 'You won't be. I'll make sure of that.'

32

The fact that Twilling had dropped dead didn't stop life continuing in the rest of the valley. Lillian still got ready to go for the walk with Edward on Sunday, feeling a bit nervous.

She waited in the front room, ready to leave as soon as he turned up, which he did almost exactly on ten o'clock.

She felt shy as she went out of the front door and turned to lock it, but didn't allow herself to be cowardly and walked towards him, trying to smile and hoping she'd succeeded.

He gave her a quick bob of his head. 'It's lovely to see you, Lillian. I hoped the fuss about Dr Twilling wouldn't stop you coming for our walk.'

'I heard about it. Who hasn't? But I've never even seen him let alone consulted him, so I don't feel very involved. Though it'll be hard for the valley not to have a doctor at all.'

'A lady doctor arrived yesterday but she's staying with Mrs Twilling and is only dealing with emergencies at the moment.' He rolled his eyes. 'Walter says it'll upset some people to have to consult a female, but they have no choice.'

'It ought not to make a difference whether it's a woman or a man.'

'I agree. It's whether the doctor is good at the job and properly trained, surely?'

'I agree.'

By the time they reached the lake they were chatting as comfortably as usual and she had forgotten her nervousness.

They were both wearing sturdy shoes, so managed to walk all the way round, detouring round the unfinished part of the lake edge at the top end.

They never seemed short of something to say or discuss, she thought in wonder, and when they got back to her house, she felt comfortable enough to say, 'Would you like a cup of tea?'

'I'd love one.'

'I hope you don't mind but for the sake of my reputation, could we sit outside on the bottom wall at the back to drink it? I often sit there when it's fine.' She was sure the neighbours would notice that.

'I don't mind at all.'

So she took out a tray with tea and scones and they continued their chatting for another half hour, then he said, 'I'd better go home now. We've got a busy day planned tomorrow, what with the house and sorting out a cellar we've found that didn't get burned when the house was destroyed.'

He didn't tell her the details and somehow he couldn't bear to spoil the lovely day by asking bluntly about her ability to bear children. How did you broach something as personal as that with a woman you'd not known for long?

Would it stop him courting her if she said she and her husband had tried in vain?

He didn't know, couldn't work that out. All he knew was he loved being with her, loved the little gurgle of laughter that sometimes escaped her.

He climbed onto the wall and turned to wave her goodbye as he sat astride the top.

When he got down he walked slowly away along the usual path, still thinking about her. Then a slight rustle in the bushes behind him made him turn his head. But the path was empty.

He paused for a moment, wishing he'd brought his walking stick, then started striding purposely down the path towards home.

'I'll kill you, Ollerton!'

He only had a second to recognise Catlow's voice before a rock hit his head and he was falling, and then everything turned black.

Lillian couldn't help standing watching Edward till he'd climbed over the wall and walked away, then she bent to pick up the tray. She put it down hastily again as she saw Edward's wallet lying on the ground behind the wall. It must have dropped out of his pocket as he'd sat there.

Picking it up she looked up the garden to see his upper body vanish from sight so ran up the steps, not wasting her breath calling out to him because she could easily catch him up and return his wallet.

Only he wasn't in sight at all from the top and he should have been. She'd watched him leave a few times and knew exactly the place where he disappeared completely because that was when she turned away and went back to the house.

Had he fallen over? The ground was uneven and dipped a bit in places. It was the only explanation she could think of. But why hadn't he got up again? He must have fallen awkwardly. Had he knocked himself out?

She started running towards him, not calling out, saving her breath to move as fast as she could.

To her horror, that horrible Catlow man was standing near to where Edward must be. He wasn't looking in her direction but was sideways to her and staring downwards. He had a vicious look on his face and was holding a big rock in his hand, which he began to raise as if he planned to hit something with it.

He was going to attack Edward!

She scooped up one of the many rocks lying on the ground near the wall and hurled it at Catlow with all her might, catching him on the shoulder and making him yell out in shock and drop his chunk of rock. By that time she'd picked up another missile and hurled that at him too, hitting him again.

He turned swiftly to scan his surroundings and the look he gave when he caught sight of her terrified her, it was so utterly ferocious. Instinctively she screamed for help at the top of her voice and scrabbled for another rock to throw. As she bent to pick one up, something whizzed past her head. He must have thrown a rock at her.

Why was Edward not helping in the struggle? Had Catlow killed him?

What could she do? Catlow was a big man.

Screaming as loudly as she could, she picked up another rock and threw it, but he started running towards her, so she ran for her life, heading towards her home.

His footsteps thumped along the ground behind her, seeming to get closer and closer. She was sure he'd catch her and what could she do against such a large and violent adversary?

Just as she'd given up hope of escaping, her neighbour Bill Hicks looked over the back wall next door, saw her and her pursuer and leapt over it.

Catlow cursed and veered off in the other direction, so she turned and started moving back towards where she'd last seen Edward.

Bill followed her. 'What was that sod doing to make you scream like that, lass?'

'He's attacked Mr Ollerton.' She ran back into the hollow, saw Edward trying to stand up, looking dazed. Relief shuddered through her as she went to support him.

Just then Lewis ran to join them from the direction of the lodge.

'I was in the garden and heard you screaming. What's wrong?' He broke off as he saw Edward and came to help her support him.

The poor man was looking as if he wasn't fully aware of what was going on. He had a huge bump and a gash on the back of his head, with blood trickling down the side of his face.

'I'll try to see where that filthy oik has gone. If I catch him, he won't know what day it is!' Bill said and hurried off in the direction Catlow had taken.

'We need to get a doctor to stitch this wound,' Lewis said. 'Do you know what happened? How did he get injured?'

'He was walking away from my garden when he suddenly vanished, as if he'd fallen. I suppose that horrible man must have attacked him. Why would he do that?'

There was the sound of footsteps and Bill came back, this time followed by his wife.

'Catlow's run off up the moors. I'll never catch him there. He knows them moors like the back of his hand.'

'Let's get Edward home before we do anything else,' Lillian said.

'We'll have to carry him,' Bill said.

'No. I can walk if I lean on one of you,' Edward said.

His voice was blurred and he still didn't look fully aware of his surroundings, but the two men stepped to either side of him and he managed to walk along slowly with their help. Lillian and Gladys ran ahead to the lodge.

By the time the three men got there, Lillian had found a stool and when Bill helped set Edward down in the bigger of the two armchairs, she put it under his feet and he leaned his head back with a low groan of relief.

Gladys had already poured warm water from the kettle into a bowl and she dipped one end of a clean tea towel in it. She handed it to Lillian, who patted the wound gently till it was clear of dirt.

'I'm fairly sure it needs stitching,' she said. 'Otherwise you'll have a bad scar.'

'I'll go and fetch that new lady doctor,' Lewis said. 'I heard she was having a meal up at Mr Crossley's today. I'll take your bike, Edward. It's quicker than mine.'

Edward said, 'He took me by surprise, shouting he was going to kill me and hurling a rock from behind. It hit me really hard. I don't remember anything else till you helped me up.'

Lewis had waited to listen.

'It was Mrs Hesketh who saved you, Mr Ollerton,' Bill said.

They all turned to look at her then.

'All I did was throw stones at Catlow,' she said, feeling embarrassed. 'Luckily I hit him.'

'And that probably, no definitely, saved this gentleman's life,' Bill insisted.

Edward looked across at her, seeming more aware of what was going on now. 'Then I can't thank you enough, Lillian.'

Lewis opened the door. 'I'll fetch the doctor as quick as I can. I hope she's still at Walter's. Let's hope she can stop you having a bad scar.'

'Perhaps a cup of sweet tea might make you feel a bit better,' Lillian said. 'That's what they give people who've had a shock, isn't it?'

'Yes. Please make tea for everyone.' Edward turned his head towards Bill, moving it slowly and carefully, but wincing even so. 'Why would Catlow want to kill me? I know he hates my family but what have I ever done to him?'

'Because he's a vicious sod with a twisted mind, begging your pardon, ladies. He was at school with my uncle, who always said never to cross him because he was a devil for getting his own back on folk, however long it took him.'

'Some people are like that,' Lillian said. 'But they don't usually try to *kill* people, especially people who weren't involved. That's a ludicrous reason for him to attack you.'

'What was the problem that upset him?' Edward asked.

'I'm afraid I don't know exactly what it was about. It was all a long time ago.'

Lillian didn't like the sound of this. 'You'll have to take care how you go from now on, Edward. If he'll hang on to a grudge this long, he could bide his time and try to get at you again. Perhaps the new policeman will be able to catch him when he arrives.'

Bill sighed. 'Eh, he's a bad 'un, Catlow is, and strange with it, he is. Always has been. But Mrs Hesketh is right. You'll need to take care from now on till they catch him.'

There was the sound of voices outside and Lewis came back in, accompanied by the lady doctor, who was younger than they'd expected.

She nodded to them all but went straight across to Edward.

Lillian took the teacup from his hand and stepped back.

'Mr Brody has told me what happened. I wonder if someone could get me a bowl of boiled water and a clean cloth.'

She went to examine Edward's forehead, clicking her tongue in disapproval. 'Were you in a fight?'

'No. A man I didn't know threw a rock at me, knocked me out. I think if Mrs Hesketh hadn't been nearby and thrown something at him, he'd have killed me.'

She stared at him in shock. 'Whoever did this must be insane. It has to be reported to the police. A man who'd do that needs locking away.'

'I doubt they'll catch him,' Bill said. 'He knows the valley and the moors round it better than anyone. And our policeman is old and weary, past doing much.'

She stepped back and looked round. 'I'd be grateful if you kind people would leave me with my patient, though perhaps Mrs Hesketh could stay and assist me. I'd like to concentrate on the sewing. We don't want to leave a bad scar. If I did such a thing sloppily my former tutor would throw a fit.' She turned back to Edward. 'You've probably got a concussion too,

Mr Ollerton. You will need someone to stay with you tonight and make sure you're all right.'

Edward instinctively nodded his head, which made him wince. 'The gentleman who fetched you is living with me at the moment. I'm sure he'll do whatever you suggest.'

'Good. Now, lean your head back. This is going to hurt I'm afraid but I need you to lie still. No heavy meals tonight, by the way. Better just to have a light snack or two.'

When she'd finished, she nodded in approval. 'If I say so myself, I've done a nice, neat job.'

When she'd left him alone with Lillian, he stayed where he was. 'Thank you again.'

He knew now that though he still felt he needed to find out about her having children, it wouldn't make any difference to him wanting her. She was brave and caring as well as having other good qualities – and she was his Lillian.

'Will you ask the others to leave us alone for a while. There's something I want to ask you.'

She went out and spoke to Lewis, who nodded. 'I'll walk across to Walter's with the doctor.'

She turned to her neighbours. 'Thank you so much for your help, Bill and Gladys. I'll keep an eye on him for a while.'

When she went back inside she'd half expected to find Edward asleep, but he wasn't. Indeed, he looked wider awake than before.

'Come and sit down, Lillian. I need to talk to you. Pull one of those chairs over here, would you, so that I don't have to stare up at you?'

When she had done that and was sitting next to him, he reached out and took her hand.

'You're an amazing woman.'

She could feel herself flushing and tried to pull her hand away but he wouldn't let go. 'I don't need any more thanks, Edward. Anyone would have done the same.'

'That's not what I want to talk to you about. And I'd rather hold your hand as I say this. Lillian, I've never met a woman whose company I enjoy as much as I do yours.'

Her hand twitched in his and she stared at him in surprise. He smiled as he raised that soft hand to his lips. 'Do you think you could marry me? I know you had a bad experience with your late husband, but I promise faithfully to love and cherish you all the days of my life.'

She stared at him, solemn as an owl and then surprised him in turn. 'I never expected to say this, but yes, Edward, I would love to marry you. Seeing you in danger has made me realise how very much I love you.'

'Then perhaps you'd lean closer and let me seal the bargain in the usual way. Only it'll have to be a gentle kiss, because my head is so sore I don't want to bump it.'

His kiss was so gentle and seemed so full of love, she didn't want it to end. But he moved his head back with a reluctant sigh.

'This has to be the most unromantic time and manner in which to propose to anyone.' He chuckled softly. 'I hope you don't mind, only I suddenly couldn't wait to make sure of your feelings. And anyway, don't they say that if you save someone's life, that someone belongs to you?'

Feeling very daring, she raised his hand to her lips and kissed it. 'Good. I want us to belong together.'

'This time, you'll be happy. I promise you that.'

'I want to forget the time with Stanley. It was . . . horrible. But I need to tell you something first. My name wasn't Lillian when I was married. I changed it to help me hide from the Thurstens.'

'Good heavens! What was your name?'

'Mary.'

He pulled a face. 'You don't seem remotely like a Mary.'

'I don't feel like one, either, now.'

'We'll get my lawyer to sort that out.' He smiled at her. 'Any other secrets to tell me?'

'No. And I feel quite sure I'll be happy with you. It's just – wonderful.'

A few quiet, peaceful minutes later she realised he was asleep and was able to study his features, watch him, and realise with utter certainty that she wasn't afraid of this man and never would be.

33

Lillian and Edward didn't try to hide their happiness and made plans to marry as soon as possible, so Walter and his family helped in every way they could.

A wedding was a pleasant prospect to everyone they knew, especially after the terrible events.

Riley took Maude aside and made a suggestion that had her beaming at him. 'Yes! Oh, yes!'

So first they spoke to Lillian and Edward about making it a double church wedding, and they agreed to delay their impatience a little.

After that everyone joined in making preparations and happiness seemed to fill the farm.

That didn't stop the family and other people too keeping an eye out for Catlow returning. But there weren't even any reports of people seeing him.

His family refused to comment and his wife went around scowling at the world, speaking as if others had done something wrong and her husband was the victim.

Edward bought a special licence and the wedding was planned for ten days after the attack on him. By then, the agent's house would be fully ready for occupation and by combining their bits and pieces of furniture and sending for the pieces both of them had in storage, the two newly-weds would be supplied with enough furniture to manage for a while.

Lewis asked if he could rent the lodge, but Edward told him it wasn't necessary to pay rent as long as anyone needing to be lodged could use the other bedroom.

But Lillian still worried, muttering a number of times when she was alone: 'It's all going too well. Oh, please, don't let anything stop us marrying.'

The day before the wedding, three people got off the train in Ollerthwaite – two men and a woman. The woman was carrying a baby and one of the men was wearing a police uniform. All of them looked grim and determined.

The policeman asked the way to the local police station and they trudged along the main street, following directions.

What they had to say shocked old Cliff Nolan, the constable in charge, and for a minute or two he could only say, 'Nay. Nay, then. I can't believe it.'

'Can you direct us to where this woman is living?' the man asked. 'We heard she was getting married again and she has to be stopped.'

'Nay, then. How can we stop her? She's a widow.'

'We have a doctor's report that she is unhinged and needs to be looked after carefully.' He pulled a folded paper out of his inner pocket and showed it briefly to the old constable.

'I'm Constable Hurley. I have a warrant to take her to a hospital. See.' The visiting policeman held out another piece of paper.

'Eh, I suppose I'll have to help you, then. We'll need to get hold of a vehicle to take you up the hill. There aren't no buses or taxis here.' Cliff sighed, not liking this and only half believing what they said, but he knew his duty. 'I'll get hold of Tom Tetherton. He'll hire his cart and pony to you but you'll have to drive it yourself. I can't get on with that pony of his.'

'Hurry up, then. We don't want to give her time to get away and upset someone else's life.'

'Nay, then. Who'd have thought?' Cliff muttered. 'Such a nice lady.'

'She seems nice, but she isn't,' the older man said in a harsh voice.

The baby was asleep, had hardly stirred. The woman was holding it close, as if afraid for its safety and she hadn't said a word.

He sent a lad running to ask Tom for the hire of his cart and within half an hour the trio were on their way up the hill, with the visiting constable driving them and Cliff giving directions.

When there was no one at Lillian's house, Cliff snapped his fingers. 'Eh, if I hadn't forgot. She'll be at Walter Crossley's. The ladies there are helping her get ready for the big double wedding tomorrow. Eh, the poor lass.'

At the farm Cliff waited for the constable to get down from the cart and knock on the door, before reluctantly joining him.

A lady he'd only seen a couple of times opened the door: the new nurse.

When they said they were there to see Mrs Hesketh, she frowned and asked, 'May I ask why? She's rather busy.'

Laughter echoed from inside the house and Cliff could have wept for the poor thing.

Constable Hurley held out his paper and said he was here to apprehend the Hesketh woman.

The nurse stared at them, then said, 'Come in, then, and tell us why.'

By that time the older man and woman had got down from the cart and joined them.

'She's not in full possession of her wits and is to be given into my care,' he said.

'Rubbish. She's as sane as the next person,' the nurse said. 'Someone fetch Walter from his office quickly,' she called out, before showing them into the big kitchen.

Lillian let out an involuntary cry of shock at the sight of Lemuel Thursten.

'You know this man, then?' Flora asked.

'He was my father-in-law.'

Thursten snatched the baby from his wife and held it out dramatically, 'And this is her child, the one she abandoned at birth. Which shows how deranged she is.'

Constable Hurley moved forward as if to take hold of Lillian's arm, but she stepped quickly back and Maude stood protectively in front of her.

'I've never even had a baby!' Lillian declared. 'And I'm not going with them. That man wants to use me, has tried to act the husband to me before, and him my father-in-law.'

There was a gasp of shock from the group round her.

Flora studied her, watching both her and the Thurstens carefully.

'As if I'd do anything like that. I'm a happily married man. See how deranged she is,' Lemuel said loudly. 'Don't let her get away, Constable. We've made arrangements to care for her and the child properly once she's been treated in a proper mental asylum. She must be stopped from throwing herself at other men, as she did to me.'

Walter had come into the kitchen through the back door in time to hear all this and he also came to stand beside Lillian.

'Fetch Edward,' he said to Maude. 'Quick as you can. I won't let them take her away.'

'You can't stop us. We have the law on our side,' Lemuel said, still speaking far more loudly than necessary.

The glance he threw at Lillian was triumphant.

'If she's gone to fetch the poor deceived chap who thinks he's going to marry her, it'll make no difference,' Lemuel added.

'We have all the legal papers necessary to take her away,' Constable Hurley said, but he looked extremely uncomfortable.

'But they're lying!' Lillian cried loudly. 'I have never had a child.'

'We'll wait for her fiancé to get here.' Walter's quiet, calm tones were a big contrast to Thursten's harsh and over-loud voice. He put one arm round Lillian's shoulders. 'Do you know why they are claiming this to be your child?'

'They always wanted an heir, wanted one desperately, and he was prepared to do anything to get one, including—' She had to pause to take a breath and gather her courage before she could put it into words. 'Including fathering a child on me himself. I don't know where this poor little infant comes from but it's not mine.'

She couldn't help shuddering at the thought of that man getting power over her.

While they waited, Lemuel tried twice to persuade the constable to handcuff her, but he looked at Walter and the women standing protectively around the woman who was supposed to be mad and refused.

When Edward arrived he went straight across to Lillian and took over from Walter, putting his arm round her.

She spoke only to him. 'They're telling lies about me, Edward. I have never had a child.'

Flora came across to her and looked back at Constable Hurley. 'There is an easy way to resolve this question of the child.'

He frowned at her. 'What?'

'I'm an experienced nurse and I will be able to tell from signs on her body if she's recently had a child. If I gave you my word faithfully to tell the truth would you let me check that? I'm a nurse with over thirty years' experience. I would know, believe me.' She turned to Lillian. 'Would you trust me?'

'Yes.'

The constable nodded at Flora. 'Go on, then.'

Thursten cried out, 'No! She's lying. She must be taken away.'

The constable gave him a dirty look. 'Let the nurse check her.'

'My bedroom is upstairs. Is it all right if we go there?' Lillian asked.

'I'll come and stand outside the door,' the constable said.

'Well, it's not all right with me!' Thursten's voice was almost a howl. 'We have the law on our side. She could fool this woman. How do we even know she's a nurse?'

It was Cliff who spoke up. 'Since she's been in the valley, Miss Vardy has been looking after people, and looking after them brilliantly. She's not only a nurse, she's a good nurse. I can vouch for that. And our new doctor will say the same if you ask her.'

Flora ignored the Thurstens and walked across to the hall, taking care to stay between Lillian and them. She was particularly concerned about the man, worried about him getting violent. Mrs Thursten was not doing anything but cuddling the baby, which had still hardly made a sound, hardly moved at all, even though its eyes were open as if it was awake. Flora was beginning to worry about it as well.

In the bedroom Flora said, 'You'll have to undress, I'm afraid.'

'I trust you,' Lillian said simply. 'And I'll do anything I need to avoid that horrible man. But can we lock the door first, please?'

'Yes, of course.'

The examination didn't take more than a couple of minutes, then Flora looked at Lillian in puzzlement. 'You can put your clothes on. You not only haven't borne a child; you show every sign of being still a virgin.'

Lillian flushed. 'I am. Stanley tried to bed me a few times but never managed it.' She shuddered at the memory of that. 'And thank goodness for that. I hated him even to come near me, let alone touch me. And in case you're wondering, my parents forced me to marry him and his parents forced him. We loathed one another.'

After another hesitation, she said, 'I think Stanley loved men, from the letters I found after his death. I've read about love like that.'

'Ah. That explains it. You poor thing.'

'I was intending to tell Edward about myself before we got married, but I haven't been able to bring myself to do that.'

'I'm afraid I shall have to tell everyone now that you are untouched.'

'It might be embarrassing but it's worth doing anything to stay out of Thursten's clutches.'

When she'd finished putting her clothes to rights, she followed Flora and the constable down the stairs and back into the kitchen where everyone was standing round looking uncomfortable and embarrassed. Lillian was sure she felt far worse than they did.

'Mrs Hesketh has not had a child. In fact her so-called marriage to your son has never been consummated, Mr Thursten.'

'I don't believe you.'

And suddenly anger at their lies boiled over in Lillian. 'He was never able to consummate our marriage, if you must know. And maybe that was because he was in love with a man. I found their letters.'

There was dead silence, then various muttered exclamations.

'It's not true!' Lemuel yelled.

'It is, I'm afraid. I wasn't going to tell you but you kept on telling lies about me.'

The very quietness of the way she spoke was more convincing than any loud yelling would have been.

Lemuel stared at her, open-mouthed and then suddenly he erupted into shouting and attempted to get to Lillian, his fist clenched ready to hit her.

'She's lying. I'll beat the truth out of her. My son was a proper man. Let me get to her. Let me go!'

When the police constables tried to haul him away, he went berserk, and it took them both and Edward to hold him. In the end Constable Hurley got out his handcuffs.

'I think he's lost his senses,' Flora said.

Thursten yelled a stream of curses and insults at her and something about the way he looked made Constable Hurley say, 'He looks mad to me, too. Is there a doctor in the valley?'

It was Walter who'd replied. 'Yes. She's living in our former doctor's house. Constable Nolan can show you where it is.'

They'd expected Thursten to gradually stop his yelling and cursing and struggling, but he didn't. He stayed violent, kept on yelling at them.

Mrs Thursten said suddenly. 'Lemuel was like this once before. They put him in the asylum but it was weeks before he calmed down. I've been terrified of getting him angry ever since.'

'Can you manage if they lock him away again?' Flora asked.

'Oh, yes.' She lowered her voice, one eye on her husband. 'I'd prefer it.'

'What about the baby?'

'I'm going to keep it. He made me drug the poor little creature to bring him here but I shan't do that again. I didn't love my own son, who did nothing but cry and fret as a baby, but little Lionel is delightful when I have him on my own.'

Flora nodded. 'I could tell something was wrong with that child. I'm glad it's only temporary. I think you should stay at the police station in town until they've dealt with your husband, then maybe Constable Hurley can escort you home? Or perhaps Mrs Twilling will be happy to let you and the baby wait in her house. She's been really kind to the new doctor.'

When they'd left, Edward said, 'I'd like to talk to Lillian on her own, please. May I use your front room, Walter?'

He waved one hand permissively.

In the front room, Edward held his arms wide open and she walked into them, nestling against him and struggling not to cry in sheer relief.

'You've been carrying the burden of that knowledge all on your own, my darling.'

'I couldn't seem to tell anyone, I was so ashamed.'

'What did you have to be ashamed of?'

'My husband never stopped telling me all the ways in which I was lacking, including not being attractive enough to rouse a man.'

'I find you very attractive and if he truly was that sort of man, I doubt you could have roused him. I feel sorry for him. They put the poet Oscar Wilde in prison for that sort of thing. Your husband must have lived in terror of being discovered.'

After a pause he added thoughtfully, 'If you needed to, you could get the marriage annulled.'

'It doesn't matter now, as long as you still want me.'

The smile he gave her was wonderfully tender. 'I want you very much, my love. And in every way possible. I can't wait for us to get married.' He looked at her. 'What is there to cry for?'

She fumbled for a handkerchief and couldn't find one so he took his out and wiped her eyes for her, looking at her anxiously. 'Have I upset you?'

'No, darling. It's the utter relief. As if a heavy burden I've carried for years has been lifted from me.'

When she'd stopped weeping, they went to rejoin the others and by the time everyone had hugged her, one after the other, Lillian was looking visibly happier and after a while was even persuaded to help finalise the catering preparations for the next day, though they refused point-blank to let her see the wedding cake.

As Edward walked home, he felt gladness glowing warmly inside him. He'd committed to marrying Lillian before he'd found out the truth, but it was a relief to discover why she'd never conceived in her last marriage.

Now, he was like any other bridegroom, hoping for children, happiness and a long life with the woman he loved.

Epilogue

Lillian woke early on the day of her wedding, lying there for a moment wondering why she felt so carefree. And then it all came back to her.

She was truly free of the Thurstens, free of what she felt had been the taint of being married to a man she didn't love, free to be truly happy. It was the first time in her adult life she had felt so carefree.

At the thought of marrying Edward she felt like getting up and dancing round the house. She was going to be Lillian Ollerton from now on. How wonderful!

There was a knock on the door and Maude poked her head in. 'There! I was right. You are awake.'

'I couldn't sleep.'

'Well, get that down you.' Maude produced a cup of tea and set it on the bedside chest of drawers, then moved down the bath that was balanced against the wall, ready.

'Do you want your breakfast first or your wedding bath first? I had one last night so that you could have a long one this morning.'

'Thank you. I'm not hungry.'

'Bath it is, then. I'll start bringing up the water.'

But in fact everyone in the house brought up a bucket of water and then Lillian enjoyed the deepest, must luxuriant bath she had ever had in her life, dipping the back of her head into the water and washing her hair, then going down to sit drying it by the kitchen fire.

'Nervous?' Maude asked.

'No. Not at all. I can't wait to marry Edward and help him design and furnish a house.'

'I wonder if you'll ever find out about those cellars?'

'Who knows? Whatever, we'll have a rich and interesting life, and I don't mean rich in the sense of having a lot of money.'

'I know that. I feel the same about Riley.' Maude let out a blissful sigh. 'I think he's the nicest man I've ever met.'

'Apart from Edward, of course.'

They both laughed.

When the two brides went outside to get on the cart, the sun was shining even though it was quite a chilly day.

Lillian stopped to stare at the cart, which was decked with ribbons and even a few flowers.

'Won't it look . . . a bit silly for a woman my age?'

'I was wondering that too,' Maude admitted.

'Well, it won't. It'll look like the happiest group of people in the valley are attending the marriages of two of their own,' Elinor said firmly.

From the driving seat, Walter called, 'Come on, ladies. Let's get our Lillian and our Maude married, then we can enjoy all that good food.'

The two ladies in question beamed at one another.

Lillian clutched Maude's hand. Walter had called her 'our Lillian', she thought and joy hummed through her veins. She had a family now, friends, and within the hour she'd have a husband.

She waved to Rufus and his friend, who were going to keep an eye on the farm and the houses while they were gone. The need for that was the only blot on the day. But then nothing was perfect and this was as close as it had ever got in her life.

The church ceremony passed in a near blur, with a large audience of people from the village sneaking in and sitting in the back pews. Everyone enjoyed a wedding.

And then, it was over. Maude and Riley walked out rapidly, beaming at the world.

Lillian walked more slowly, leaving the church on her husband's arm.

'I love you,' he whispered again.

He'd said it twelve times so far today. She'd been counting.

'I love you too, Edward Ollerton.' She'd said it back twelve times too now, had loved saying it, intended to do so every day from now on.

The cart made slow progress up the hill to the farm, because so many people stopped them to wish both pairs of newly-weds well.

Once there, the meal seemed to go on for ever. Even though the food was superb, Lillian and Edward could hardly eat. What they were longing for now was to spend their wedding evening together in the former agent's house, sitting quietly and happily in their first home together.

Riley and Maude had borrowed Lillian's old house and had slipped out earlier without telling anyone, walking down the hill hand in hand. Walter didn't tell anyone they'd gone until they'd 'got away' as he thought of it.

Not long afterwards the other newly-weds were able to leave, driven by Walter.

'No need to linger and be polite,' he said as he waited for them to get off the cart. 'Be happy together.'

She'd forgotten about the bride being carried over the threshold, and squeaked in shock as Edward picked her up, then she clutched him tightly and rained kisses on any part of him that was close enough for her lips to reach.

After which they shut the door and locked the world out while they created their own happy life and love for the very first time.

Notes about the story

Writers often use incidents from their own lives or experiences in their novels. You may be interested in some that I've used in this story.

1. *My grandma left school half time like Rufus's mother wanted his sister Nina to do. My grandma then attended school mornings one week, afternoons the next – and yes, she worked rolling cigars by hand. My husband's grandmother had the same job at roughly the same age in another part of England. My grandma always referred to her teacher during that final year till she left school for ever at twelve as 'the mester'.*

2. *When I was a child even in the 1940s we lived in a house without a bathroom and with a lavatory across at the far end of the back yard. We had a narrow cellar under the house with a hatch through which the coalman emptied the sacks when he delivered them. We went back to a lavatory outside at the back when my parents bought their first house, but that one was enclosed in a small shed-cum-conservatory, so although it was cold to get to the lavatory in winter, you didn't have to face the weather.*

   Our tin bath hung on the wall out there, to be hauled in and filled by hand each week. That doesn't mean we were dirty! Like many people we all had an all-over wash with a facecloth every single day and woe betide any child who skimped on that!

3. *Like my character Elinor, I was very sick when I was pregnant, starting before I'd even missed a monthly or suspected I could be pregnant. And when I went to see the doctor, his exact words were, like those of my doctor in this story, 'Snap out of it, woman!' I didn't go back to see him. I continued to be sick until two days after giving birth. I was a teacher then, and we needed the money so I had to continue working. I had to leave nearly every lesson to go and be sick, that's how bad it was. But the students were wonderful. No naughtiness while I nipped to the ladies' next door.*

I hope you'll enjoy the next story in the Jubilee Lake series. You've already met one of the heroes – Rufus.

If you loved *Golden Dreams*, read on for an exclusive sneak peek of the final gripping novel in the Jubilee Lake series, *Diamond Promises* . . .

I

Early 1895 – Lancashire

Abigail Dawson hurried round the house, making sure everything was tidy and in the places her father insisted were 'right'. She did this every day just before he came home from his office because she didn't want him in a bad mood all evening. He didn't seem to realise that it was mainly he who left things lying around.

When she heard the key turn in the front door she lit the gas under the kettle at a low flame and turned to greet him as he came into the kitchen.

To her relief, he was smiling and didn't even wait for her to greet him before speaking.

'Wonderful news, Abigail. We're moving house on Monday.'

She stared at him in shock, her hand still outstretched towards the teapot. 'Moving house? Where to?' And why had he not told her before now so that she could prepare for it?

'I'll tell you all about it after I've had a quick wash and changed out of my shop clothes.' He ran up the stairs to their tiny bathroom.

She had done the same too when she'd worked in the shop for a couple of years after she left school. She'd hated the place and its sleazy customers, not to mention the dusty and sometimes smelly items they had to deal with.

Her mother had trained her as a small child not to defy her father or even protest once he decided on something. The trouble was, he never hesitated to make important decisions like this without consulting either of them, and sometimes there would have been better alternatives.

As she waited for her father, Abigail's thoughts went back eight years to when he'd also made a similarly important decision without consulting her. She'd been courting, looking forward to getting married and having a home of her own. Oh, the dreams she'd had about her future!

Sadly, after a few weeks her father had decided he didn't want her to marry Harold after all. He said the fellow was more stupid than he'd seemed at first and though he might have provided good-looking grandchildren, he'd not have given them good brains, which was a far more important attribute.

She'd found out the hard way. She had gone out on to the landing when there was a knock at the front door, but her father always answered it if he was at home. She'd been shocked and horrified when she heard her father tell Harold that he couldn't marry her or even speak to her again, and had started to cry.

Her mother had dragged her back into her bedroom and told her to stop weeping this minute – unless she wanted her father to go into one of his rages. It had been one of the hardest things she'd ever had to do.

Three months later, Abigail had wept again in the privacy of her bedroom when she found out that Harold had married someone else.

Shortly after that her father acquired an old piano in payment of a debt and put it in the back room of the shop. She'd fiddled around with it a few times when he was out and quickly learned to pick out tunes.

She'd told her mother how much she loved playing the instrument, and sighed at the thought of him selling it.

An unexpected look of determination had crossed her mother's face. 'Leave it to me, love.'

Her mother had chosen her moment carefully and suggested to her husband that he let their daughter have the piano at home, and even pay for her to take music lessons for a while. Abigail clearly took after him and was showing musical promise.

He must have been in a good mood because he had the piano delivered to their home the next day and found a man who played in a pub to teach her what he knew, which didn't include reading music, just putting the chords and popular music hall tunes together.

Fortunately, Abigail found out that, like her teacher, with a bit of practice she could play any tune she knew, picking out the notes by ear and then figuring out which chords to add.

After that she was allowed time to practise and became proficient enough to entertain her parents occasionally in the evenings. Her father even favoured them with a song or two then and to her surprise he had a sonorous baritone voice.

She saw Harold and his wife in the street about eighteen months after his marriage and was shocked at how scruffy and down-at-heel he looked. And he didn't look at all happy, either. He was scowling as he walked along beside a pregnant, weary-looking woman pushing a pram containing a pinch-faced baby, which was wailing loudly. He'd made no attempt to help the poor woman with the pram at any time.

Abigail realised then that her father had been right about the sort of person Harold was. But oh, how she wished she'd been allowed to find another young man. A piano was no substitute for having a family and home of her own, and escaping her father's control.

Then, during the following winter, her mother died suddenly of pneumonia, gasping her way out of life in just three days. Abigail didn't need telling that there was no chance whatsoever of her ever being allowed to marry from then on.

As soon as her mother died, her father told her to take over running the house. That weekend he said they would stop wasting their time at church on Sundays now that her mother wasn't there to be upset about it. And that was that.

Not going to church meant she had little chance to meet or chat to people. Her main consolation was that she much preferred looking after the house to working in the shop, even though it was hard work physically and she was lonely.

Music gave her another consolation. Her father bought her a better piano and still asked her to play to him occasionally in the evenings. He even let her hire a part-time scrubbing woman so that her hands wouldn't be spoiled for playing.

She jerked suddenly out of her memories of the past when her father came back downstairs. She poured his cup of tea, put in the usual three teaspoonfuls of sugar and handed him the cup and saucer. He was still smiling, so clearly he was extremely pleased about this coming move.

He took a big mouthful of tea, then gestured with one hand. 'Sit down and I'll tell you all about it.'

She did that, trying to look pleased at the idea of a change to their lives.

'A few weeks ago I had a chance to buy that big house at the corner near the top of Railway Road at a bargain price, the house we've stopped to look at and admire sometimes on our Sunday walks. I always did love the look of it.'

Another pause to slurp down some more tea, then he continued. 'I bargained them down a bit so it took a while to come to an agreement, but we signed the final papers at the lawyer's office today. I've sold this house to pay for the improvements we'll need to make at the new place. The sale will be finalised the day after we move out.'

Her heart sank. The new house was huge, far grander than this one, but the outside was shabby and she guessed the interior would be sorely in need of updating and renovating.

Her father was the one who'd always stopped to admire it. She'd certainly never done so and didn't feel happy about the move. A house that size would be much harder for her to clean and look after. Would she even have time to play her piano from now on?

She'd definitely need to do something about getting more help with the housework, which meant persuading him it was necessary. She'd have to work out how best to do that.

Her father sat sipping a second cup of tea, continuing to issue information and instructions between slurps. 'I've arranged for some tea chests to be sent here this evening plus some old newspapers for packing our crockery. More chests will arrive tomorrow morning. You'll be able to start packing after tea and get on with it again immediately after breakfast. I'll pack my own things on Sunday when I don't have to go into the office.'

He always called it 'the office' and spoke as if it were an important business, but the place was actually avoided by respectable people. Many of his customers couldn't borrow money from banks and her father arranged loans for them at a higher rate of interest. He had a pawnshop, too, with a second-hand shop next door where unredeemed pledges were sold. He also bought and sold other items from members of 'the trade' as he called it.

The business must be bringing in a lot more money than she'd thought if he could afford to buy the house in Railway Road, because he never got into debt personally; he said borrowing and paying interest was a mug's game. That didn't stop him making money by arranging loans for the mugs he spoke about so scornfully.

'Could we go round to the new house this evening, Father, so that I can see what it's like inside? That way I'll have a better idea of how to pack our things efficiently. I've only ever seen the outside so have no idea what the interior is like.'

CONTACT ANNA

Anna is always delighted to hear from readers and can be contacted via the Internet.

Anna has her own web page, with details of her books, some behind-the-scenes information that is available nowhere else and the first chapters of her books to try out, as well as a picture gallery.

Anna can be contacted by email at
anna@annajacobs.com

You can also find Anna on Facebook at
www.facebook.com/AnnaJacobsBooks

If you'd like to receive an email newsletter about Anna and her books every month or two, you are cordially invited to join her announcements list. Just email her and ask to be added to the list, or follow the link from her web page.

www.annajacobs.com

The best books live on in your head long after they are finished. As you read, you are turning the pages faster and faster to find out what happens next, only to feel bereft when you reach the end.

If that is how you feel now, you might like to join us at www.hodder.co.uk, or follow us on Twitter @hodderbooks, and be part of our community of people who love the very best of books and reading.

Whether you want to find out more about this book, or a particular author, watch trailers and interviews, have the chance to win early limited editions, or simply browse our expert readers' selection of the very best books, we think you'll find what you're looking for.

And if you don't, that's the place to tell us what's missing.

We love what we do, and we'd love you to be part of it.

www.hodder.co.uk

@hodderbooks

HodderBooks

HodderBooks